UNBROKEN MONTANA

VOL. I

THE SAGA OF BIG MIKE AND ROY

BARRY BENNETT

BARRY BENNETT

For and because of Sheila.

PREFACE

As a small boy, I was up at 6 A.M. on Saturday mornings to watch Gene Autry ride and sing on a black and white TV. Raised on a row crop and cattle farm in Southwest Minnesota, I was a lucky kid and had a handsome, but miserable Shetland pony named Jeff. I would fasten clothes pins to a bath towels and attempt to gallop and reach cape-fluttering speed. I now realize that cowboys had no capes.

The cowboy as a hero has never left me and I'm too ancient to learn new truths or fresh lies. My hero's have always been...

Even when I didn't reside in Montana, it was always my home. I first stepped off a Greyhound bus in Missoula in May of 1981 and the smell of the air is still in memory. My small young family lived in Fergus County in the early 1990's and the place and kind people never left me. And now Jefferson County is our home, surrounded by Douglas Fir trees and cradled by rocky mountains. All Montana is touched by magic. If you crave pure Montana, find your way to Lewistown. Buy some chokecherry syrup.

Montana is still the best dream I'll ever have.

ACKNOWLEDGMENTS

I begin by thanking my long-suffering wife, Sheila. Her loving, constant jabs for me to stop talking and start writing, finally worked. She would listen to me read the first draft in the evenings, listen to endless story ideas while driving together while proving to be a surprisingly clever editor. All I have is because of her.

Thanks to my old friend John Boggs for his positive wisdom and for talking me through a long Montana winter of writing while he smoked cigars on his sailboat in Florida.

Whitney O'Daniel has been like a little brother to me for nearly 20 years. His encouragement, patience and wide-world-of-smarts have propped me up during spells of great doubt. He is a rare friend that is always searching for a way to help with no return on investment.

Bowen Greenwood, www.bowengreenwood.com , patiently answered 1.2 million questions about writing and how to be a self-published author. His unselfishness and calm demeanor mask a savagely skilled and creative writer. All who call him friend, consider themselves lucky.

Thanks to my editor, Sherrie Dolby who provided the expertise and sensible corrections to a rookie author, and took this from reading like a phone book (pre-21st Century reference) to a readable and nearly Award-winning book, (the award being that my wife loves the book). Disclaimer; she did not edit this page.

My old friend Francis Till was an early guru and encouraged me to write. He was my first critic and editor, heavy on the critic side. He told me I was no Faulkner and that I wrote as I spoke. I still remember his advise 30+ years later. He was a brilliant man who fought his own soul and emerged to create a winning life, raised children in New

Zealand and rebuilt his life before passing in 2024. It sounds very literary old school to share this, but Frank and I volunteered to close many bars down together in Ocean Shores Washington, play chess and drink scotch until sunrise. In retrospect, this was my Hemingway esque period, but no foreign wars were fought.

Finally, I want to recognize and honor Janelle Cater. She is an old friend of my daughter-in-law Brandie Bennett, and I also consider her a friend of the past 9 years. Janelle has battled Metastatic Breast Cancer for over 8 years and during that time, she has shared her fight with hundreds on social media. She maintained her incredible physical fitness while dealing with cancer treatments and has showed me how to be a better and stronger person. Janelle will appear as a heroic character in a future book of mine. I hope Janell, her daughter Katrin and her husband Jeff will all take pride in knowing that her life and strength will live on in a story that will outlast us all. You are a powerhouse of a human, full of beauty and love.

Without the kindness, intellect and patience of these friends , this book would have been completed two years later and probably would have stunk up the place way more than it current does.

I offer genuine thanks to all.

INTRODUCTION

Montana in the 1890's was booming. Thirty years earlier, mining had provided the territory with the wealth and jobs needed to begin settling a wild, harsh land. The Grant family began running cattle in the Deer Lodge area in the 1860's and this operation evolved into the famous Grant-Kohrs Ranch and showed that livestock would become a huge part of early Montana.

Sheep were first brought to Montana to help feed miners and the vast lands supported large flocks. Unlike other places in the West, sheep and cattle operations mostly got along, with many ranches raising both with few issues.

Montana was full of opportunity and thousands of immigrants were drawn to the land. Hard work, luck and more hard work gave the dream of freedom and success to men and women not born to privilege.

These people would be the core of modern Montana.

The Hanson Ranch was born of simple struggles and had developed into a going concern in Fergus County, near the beautiful town of Lewistown. Big Mike Hanson had built a thriving sheep operation and was a widower with a young daughter. His foreman was a brooding, troubled soul named Elmer and Mike relied on him heavily.

Mike wanted to improve his flock and create a championship herd.
His ideas was to travel to Scotland to buy breeding stock and start a
new era for the Hanson ranch.

And this is where the story of Unbroken Montana begins.

A chance meeting with a young, smart but impoverished 18 year
old boy named Roy Douglas would alter the future for both.

Unbroken Montana is like a stew of stories, with histories and tales
of how settlers lived and often died, struggling for a new future.

CHAPTER 1

M ike Hanson was traveling through the Scottish Highlands looking for breeding stock to take back to the United States. An American sheepman known as Big Mike back in Fergus County, Montana, he had an idea to come to the United Kingdom and find a way to distinguish his herd back in Montana from other herds in America. It was late spring in 1892. He had come to the Isle of Skye for a local gathering of sheep, cattle, and a few horses.

The well-dressed, handsome, bearded American was talking to a local farmer who motioned for a lad walking by to come over. He told the American that this powerful young man was an expert sheepman and honest as well. The young farm worker was pleased to hear the farmer share his opinion on his abilities and refer to him as a man. At 18 years old, Roy Douglas was six feet tall, over two hundred pounds and looked and behaved older than his years.

Roy Douglas was born near Kyle of Lochalsh, at the mouth of Loch Alsh, across the sound from The Isle of Skye. He loved the countryside where the only real work available was farming or fishing. Fishing required working with other men while farming was mostly solo work, so he had chosen farming. He found he had a knack for tending animals and was a respected hand in the area. He worked with mostly sheep, but he was good with cattle and horses as well.

"Whatcha think of these here Hebridean sheep, young fella? I'm from America. We need some hardy breeds that can take snow and cold." The man stepped back to size up the sheep and also Roy.

Roy answered with confidence. "They are a fine handsome sheep and easy to manage. The rams are strong and randy when required, and the ewes are lovely little ladies. Queens of the field they be."

Big Mike shook his head and grinned. "I love the way you fellas over here talk about your animals! It's like they're family."

They all laughed at a polite level, and an old man chimed in. "Roy there is as big as a bull, and his lady friend has a real horse face, so he do know about livestock!" The locals roared and slapped young Roy on the back. Roy grinned and hoped to set the record straight that he had no girlfriend but the mood was loud and grand, and there was no profit in killing the fun. Roy had questions for the American, and he wasn't going to miss the opportunity.

Roy tapped the American on the shoulder. He slid in front of the man boldly and quickly to get his attention. "Can I ask you where bouts in America would you be from, sir?"

"I'm from Montana, right in the middle, the county of Fergus. Near Lewistown. Prettiest spot in the state. Good grass, lots of water. Cold at times, but it's a good place to be." The man smiled and added, "You should come over and visit. Could use a good young man like you on the ranch."

Roy grinned and said he could never leave Scotland, and it would be too expensive to travel all that way. He shook the man's hand and told him thanks for the kind words and that one day he'd like to visit.

The man said, "If you get to America, come to Lewistown and ask for Big Mike Hanson. Good luck to ya, young fella."

As Roy walked away, the fantasy of going to America started to bounce around in his head. There was a local lad, Jimmy Burns, that had taken off for New York a year ago and hadn't been heard from since. Roy and Jimmy had been mates. Roy had no idea if he had fallen of the boat, was robbed, stabbed by ruffians, or had run away with intentions to disappear. A frightful mystery. *If I would ever go,* Roy thought, *I'd become an American millionaire and buy a big boat*. Roy had no idea how to do it, but from what he read, America was full of rich men, and fortunes were made there every day.

———

An hour passed. On the way home, Roy walked by a pen full of sheep and stopped to admire the fine flock. Just then, he heard a loud voice, an American voice, holler out his name.

"Roy! Hey, Roy! Hold up there, boy!" Roy turned and saw the American striding towards him.

Big Mike reached him and in a loud whisper asked, "How would you like to come to Montana, young fella?"

Roy was confused and a little shocked at the question. America was a honey-sweet word, and nearly every man, young or old, talked about going to The New World at some point, but he had no money saved up for boat passage nor any prospects of securing the necessary funds.

Mike Hanson walked quickly but listed to his left due to years in the saddle and a life of physical work. The 'Big' in his name was more for his voice and personality than his stature. He wasn't a large man, but he looked ornery and tough; a man you may best, but you'd pay a heavy toll for the effort.

"I bought more sheep than I had planned on, and I need a man to bring them to Montana for me. Got two rams and four ewes to haul back. Can't do it by myself. Interested?" Big Mike stopped and waited to get a response before laying out any additional details. He stood there, tilted his head, and shrugged his shoulders.

Roy tried to digest what he had heard, but the only words he could recall were, "Come to Montana." He went deaf after hearing that. He didn't want to misspeak or let this trout off the line. His dull life could be changed by his answer.

Roy blurted out, "Aye, I'm yer man, Mr. Mike!" He quickly realized he might have destroyed any opportunity to bargain or negotiate, so he followed with, "As long as it be a bonny arrangement fer da boat of us, sir."

Big Mike laid out the job rapidly and with no sugar. "I'll pay you twenty dollars American a month and that includes room and board. That's a good deal, boy." Big Mike paused for a reaction from Roy, but none was available as Roy felt as if he were underwater and couldn't breathe. He added, "I reckon it should take close to two months to get you and them sheep from here to Montana. I'll keep you on for two or three months after you get them and get you settled in at my ranch. After that, if you want to stay, I'll keep you on as a hand, but the pay after that will be $16 dollars a month, but you'd have a bed in the bunkhouse with the other boys and all the good food you can choke down. Got us a good German girl cook."

Roy had felt like this one time before in his life, the time Sara Faulkner kissed him after a ceilidh this past spring. He had been a wee bit shaken but well knowing he liked it for certain. Over Big Mike's shoulder, he saw two lads walking towards him. One was Hew Fraser, a good hand with livestock and a taste for knuckles. The sight of Hew boiled up an immediate response in Roy.

"Deal, Mr. Mike! It be a deal!"

Roy spit in his hand and jammed it toward Big Mike. Big Mike looked down and saw the gooey glob in Roy's palm, laughed, and grabbed his shoulder with his left hand. "Boy, I ain't slidin' my paw into that, but I'm glad to have you join the outfit! Meet me tomorrow morning. Need to gather up these six sheep and get them ready to ship. Do you know where Angus Muir's farm is?" Roy nodded. "Have your bag packed and be ready to go at 7:00. Can ya do that, son?"

"Aye, Mr. Mike, but what about the papers to get me to America? I know nothin' of that, and I don't have but three pounds to me name." Roy looked down, embarrassed by his lack of fortune.

"Don't fret none, son. I'll send a telegram to my pain in the rump lawyer in Lewistown, and he'll have the legal bull crap squared up by the time we reach Glasgow and get on the ship. That should take us two or three days. We'll travel on the ship together and the train in America. I'll sleep in a stateroom, and you'll bed down with the sheep to keep an eye on them. I'll get you a good bedroll, and I'll make sure you get three meals each day. There's good food on those big boats, ya know."

Roy had slept in a hay loft every night of his life. That would be no hardship. Three meals a day sounded like heaven. The only Scotsman that ate that well were soldiers in the Black Watch Regiment. A cousin in the army had told Roy it was the best way out of the Highlands and tenant farming.

"Sounds grand, Mr. Mike."

"Here's ten American dollars so you have some money. Get yourself some new boots and a new coat when we get to Glasgow. Gotta get you ready for America, son. And about that, Mr. Mike,' just call me Mike. I'm good with that, Roy."

Roy paused. "With respect, I was raised to call me betters sir or mister. I don't know no different. Not sure if I'll remember to call you by just one name. And it doesn't sound respectful ta me ear... sir."

Big Mike grinned. He had liked Roy from the get-go, and he was growing on him faster than expected. "If you need to call me that, I reckon I can learn to accept. See you in the morning, son." He privately enjoyed the name and saw no need to discard the respect.

Roy liked that Big Mike called him son. He had never known his father or mother. He had been orphaned at age two and had been raised by his mother's sister. Aunt Helen had reluctantly taken him in and had been a passable substitute mother. She had been widowed a year before Roy's parents had died from smallpox. Nearly a quarter of the village had been taken as well. Helen never re-married and carried the hurt and resentment with her daily. She was a joyless woman, and she chose to remain that way.

Roy had been a handsome boy and would grow to be a sturdy and powerful young man, but Helen had taken no joy in his raising or relation. People would mention and comment on how polite he was and how he was bigger than most his age, but she would barely acknowledge the kind words. Her only response was, "I suppose that happens to boys."

Roy had given up trying for any affection from her years ago. He was grateful for a roof over his head and meals. He learned that was more than some had. He knew no different, and the lack of kindness and love he was shown from Helen taught him to expect little in life. That contributed to his affection and caring for animals. He gave what untaught love he possessed to the sheep, cattle, horses, and dogs in his life.

He gave no thought to how the news of his departure would impact Aunt Helen. He honestly didn't care if she were hurt or disappointed, but he knew she would mostly be relieved. His concern was for the animals he would leave behind. Fortunately, Helen held a patience and affection for animals, and he had few worries that she would not see to their tending.

He felt relief that his dog Ned had died six months past, and that eliminated the biggest obstacle to his departure. If Ned had still been alive, he doubted he would leave. Ned was a border collie and worked the animals with Roy. They learned stock handling together, and there was no question that Ned had been Roy's best chum. He reminded himself to gather up the horsehair braided collar that he had made for Ned. He had no other belongings of any value. None. No photographs of his parents, no watch or coin from his father, or handkerchief that belonged to his mother. He always believed there were remembrances from his mother and father but sensed that whatever belongings were his, Helen had sold to offset his encumbrance.

Roy walked into the wee humble cottage of his aunt. "Auntie, I'll be leavin' fer America tomorrow. I asked cousin Myles to look in on the stock until you can sort it."

Helen made no movement or offered any reaction. "And just how do you expect to do that? Have ye been hoarding shillings or holden' on to stolen goods?" Her response was full of disbelief and mockery.

"Met an American at the festival today, and he needs a hand to handle sheep he purchased from Muir. He be payin' me way."

"Sounds like a dream or tales from a drunkard to me. I'll be expecting ye for supper tomorrow evening once ya find out it's a false tale. Now sit while it's fit to eat."

The only hunger Roy felt at that moment was to rid himself of Helen. He stood up, walked to the door, and told her he'd write once he was settled in Montana.

"Do that, lad. And let me know when you have dinner with the Queen President." She made herself laugh a bit with the rebuff.

Any affection he held for Helen slipped through his hands and was lost.

———

Roy was ready at daybreak and stood on the road to the Muir farm. An hour later, Big Mike showed up with two wagons hired to haul the sheep to the train station four miles away.

Big Mike took his large, tan, cowboy hat off and waved at Roy. "How long you been standing there, son? You look cold as hail!"

"Been here since sunrise, sir." Roy's hot breath fogged the damp morning air. He was excited and nervous, not sure if this was reality. He would remain slightly nervous until the sheep were on the ship.

Roy proved his worth immediately as he and Muir separated the sheep to be shipped. Four ewes and two rams. The rams were champion rams. It was common knowledge that Muir had the finest breeding rams in all of Scotland. Big Mike had plans to raise the finest flock in Montana.

The sheep were put into individual wooden crates with straw on the floor. They were calm and docile. Roy's job would be to keep the straw clean and feed and water the animals while ensuring they were kept safe and as stress-free as possible.

The two wagons backed up to the train depot, and four men grabbed each crate and slid the sheep inside a boxcar. Roy and another man grabbed the crates and pushed them against the walls of the boxcar, tying each crate to the wall to prevent them from tipping over or shifting.

"You all set, Roy? The train gets to Glasgow by tonight." Big Mike checked his pocket watch. "I'll come check on you at the stops and bring you some food. Let me know if you need anything. See you in an hour or so."

Roy settled in. He finally felt as if this were real, and he would actually be heading to America.

CHAPTER 2

G lasgow was more than Roy had imagined it to be. Inverness in the north was the largest city he had visited, but Inverness was not Glasgow. It was a thrill to see tall buildings, trolley cars, and the harbor; however, the thousands of people soon overwhelmed him. Within an hour, he craved quietness and to be around his animals.

The locals were curious about the American in the big hat and fancy boots. He was loud, laughing, and seemed to enjoy being in the eye of the storm. The years of ranching in Central Montana and isolation made the journey to Scotland an adventure that Big Mike Hanson would remember and utilize for colorful stories and tall tales for years.

"Montana!" Big Mike's voice boomed over the roar. "Do you fellas know where that is?"

A voice shouted, "America!"

"Yes, sir, but what part of America do ya reckon it's in?"

"Is it close to Boston? I have a cousin in Boston. He married an Irish lass, and now he's a firefighter in Boston. His name is Clyde Murdoch. Would you happen to know him, Mr. Cowboy?"

Big Mike laughed and answered, "Well, fellas, Montana ain't nowhere near Boston. It's about an 8-day train ride from there. Never been to Boston or met your pal." Big Mike got a kick out of the men thinking that America was a neighborhood. They had no idea that America was a huge country with enormous potential.

Roy walked up the ramp with the sheep. Each was on a large rolling table with noisy steel wheels being pushed by one man per sheep. Big Mike patted him on the back and said, "I knew I picked the right man for this job. Them sheep look to be in dandy shape, Roy." Roy felt a small wave of confidence and tipped his cap to Big Mike with a grin.

"Your papers to get into America will be ready in New York. My lawyer got it ready for ya. You still have to go through the government people when we get to New York. I'll stay with the sheep while you get that done. The lawyer fella, Will, said he'll have a man to help you go through the line. Don't want to lose any more time to a stupid paper pusher."

Roy felt better that assistance had been arranged. Big Mike kept surprising him with how generous and caring he was. They had only known each other for two days, but Big Mike behaved like a father to him. He'd never tell him that. Maybe someday, but not now. He wanted to find the right words to tell him thank you...thanks for changing his life.

Big Mike added, "Now here's a bag with some bread, apples, cheese, and a little bottle of something to keep you warm, boy. This sack has two blankets in it. Get yourself settled in with these critters, and I'll come down to check on you in a few hours after we get under-way. I talked to one of them fellas in the white coats. I paid him to bring you food three times a day. I'll come for a visit each day. It should take seven, maybe ten, days to get to New York. The weather will set that schedule. There's a couple of books for ya in that bag. *Tom Sawyer* and a book about Abraham Lincoln. You can read, can't you?"

Roy confidently nodded that he could. The little schooling he'd had proved out to at least have given him the power of words and their understanding. Arithmetic was an evil master, and he could do the basics but no more. However, Roy could read, and he used that skill to teach himself a variety of issues.

"Mr. Mike, I be wantin' to tell ya thanks fer..."

Big Mike cut him off, threw his head back, and raised his hand with his palm towards Roy. "Don't thank me yet, son. Lots of hard work ahead." He paused, and his voice lowered. "You're welcome, son." Big Mike liked most people he met and was a genuine man of principle. He saw promise in Roy.

"I'll head up the gang plank now and see you later tonight. Heard they have a big poker game at night, so I'll be down before that starts." Big Mike strode up the walkway with a porter hauling his trunk up to the deck where another porter showed him to his stateroom.

Roy busied himself with water buckets and feed bags, organizing and cleaning. He would be down in the hold with the sheep, a few cattle, two fine racehorses, and an Irish groom, all headed to America and a world of dreams, danger, and promise.

CHAPTER 3

The Irishman tapped Roy on the shoulder. He had dozed off for a short nap against a pile of hay.

"Ya may want to go up and take a look. We're close to New York, and you'll want to see The Lady."

"The Lady?" Roy asked.

"Aye, The Lady. The big statue on a tiny island. Everyone goes daft to see it. Me, I seen it the first trip over, and that's good for me. I don't even get off the bloody boat. Just hand the horse over and grab the beast they bring to me to take back. I'll keep an eye on your sheep for a few minutes, lad."

Roy and the groom had talked a few times, but neither felt like chatting much. He didn't even know his name. No point in finding out now.

Roy headed for the stairway. He could go up two decks and find an outside walkway around the ship. The aisle was already getting crowded as the Statue of Liberty was just ahead.

A woman yelled out, "There it is! My god, she's a beauty!"

Roy stood behind a young mother and her son. The boy looked up at Roy and grinned. Roy smiled back. The excitement of the moment continued to grow. Roy didn't think he would be interested in seeing

The Lady, but as she came into view, he felt an unexpected rush of emotion and pleasure.

For the first time, he felt as if he saw a future. Someone believed in him and saw that he was a hard worker and smart. Roy had never felt that back in Scotland. If he didn't like America, Big Mike would pay his way back home. He already knew that there was zero chance of him returning to Scotland. He hadn't touched American soil yet, but he realized this was his home.

The ship docked, and Roy had no idea what was ahead. He didn't need to worry as he felt Big Mike had everything under control.

The chaos was immediate. The noise from the city and the dock blanketed any engine noises, creaking, and mammal sounds on the ship. The animals were getting jumpy. Roy was wondering how smoothly this leg of the journey would proceed.

A cargo handler came down and opened the large steel door to begin unloading cargo and the animals. The cargo boss told Roy and the Irish groom to get their animals off first as there would be twenty or more men unloading barrels and crates. Roy and a dock worker pushed the first crate with a ram down to the dock. He was concerned about leaving the animal unattended while he returned to get the other sheep.

As he scanned the dock for any sign of Mike, a New York police officer stepped forward.

"Are you Roy?"

Surprised to hear his name and especially from a police officer, he answered by saying, "Yes, sir."

The police officer told him, "Well, this cowboy in a big hat told me to find you and watch the sheep for you. Must be pretty valuable sheep. He gave me three dollars to watch you and them."

"Yes, sir, they are, all the way from Scotland."

"You're a Scotsman, ain't ya?"

Roy nodded.

"Bet the sheep are worth more than you kid!" The copper laughed and sat on a crate.

Roy knew he was kidding around, but the comment had a little bite to it. He figured he'd better get used to it in America. He had heard people were louder and acted tougher in America, and this was his first taste.

Roy spent the next 20 minutes directing the dock workers while the other sheep were collected on the dock. Once all six sheep were in a group and Roy had his bag, the police officer gave a wave, and Roy leaned on a barrel and waited.

Big Mike finally showed up, followed by a black porter with his trunk. Mike gave a holler, and Roy jumped up, relieved to have the boss back in control.

"I got a wagon coming to take us to the train station and get loaded up for Chicago. The train don't leave for about four hours, but we need to move. Roy, walk over to that big, brown, brick building right there and get your papers. You got everything I gave you? This fella here is a friend of my lawyer William. He's going to walk you over and make sure you get through paperwork just fine."

Mike could tell Roy was unsure. He sensed that Roy felt out of place in a city that was a wild new place. To speed up the process and get Roy the proper papers, Mike had 'donated' two dollars to a police officer to usher Roy through the shortest line.

"You'll be fine, son. Get in there, and we'll be waiting in the wagon for you." Mike knew the small bribe would be worth the cost.

Roy walked to the building with the assistant and the police officer. A sign above the door said, 'US Immigration to be a Legal Visitor to the USA' . Big Mike pulled a bottle of Aberlour Scotch Whisky from his trunk, took a swig, and offered the bottle to the porter who laughed and politely declined.

There were just a few foreign passengers on the ship from Glasgow as most were returning Americans who went through the Customs window. Roy was one of twenty-five foreigners in line to get their papers approved. After a 15-minute wait in line, Roy walked up to the window, escorted by his own New York copper. A man with a dark uniform, mustache, and a flat top hat with a shiny gold badge looked at the police officer, spoke with the man assigned to help, looked at Roy, and gave a nod. Roy stepped up and answered the man's questions. The paperwork was in order and after one minute, the man slammed down a big rubber stamp on the yellow paper. He was now welcomed to stay in America. 1891 was the last year it was a straight-forward process to immigrate as new laws would be passed to control immigration more tightly.

Roy came out feeling relief and alive. He spotted Big Mike and the wagon a few hundred feet away and ran to them. Mike was surprised that it hadn't taken longer but was pleased this phase of the trip was over. They both shook hands with the police officer and the assistant and climbed aboard the wagon.

Mike told the teamster to get them to the railway depot. This odd parade of a Montana cowboy, a Scotsman, and six sheep was finally rolling through the streets of New York City.

Roy was dazed by the whole scene: tall buildings stacked up like books on a bookshelf, trolleys running on rails laid in the street, and more people than he knew existed in the rest of the world was over-powering. He enjoyed seeing it firsthand, but he felt no attraction or longing to stay in the city; too much noise, too many odd smells, just too much of everything.

The wagon pulled up to a loading dock, and more men came walking out to grab the sheep. Big Mike yelled out, "Whoa, boys! Before you start pulling my sheep off this wagon, how much are you charging me to get them on the train?" Big Mike may live in the coun-try, but this wasn't his first trip to a city. He knew the scams and was bargaining with the men before any problems arose.

"Five dollars a head to get them loaded and safely handled," said a small balding man. It was obvious he was a lead hand but not a boss.

Big Mike laughed loudly and said, "You boys must think I'm an idiot from Texas! I ain't payin' five dollars a head! I'll pay a dollar per head, or I'll load them myself." He made his statement and then sat still waiting for a response.

"One dollar fifty," the bald man barked back.

"One dollar and one bit. Take it or get out of my way." Mike was firm in his counteroffer.

"Done. What train you catching, Mr. Cowboy?"

"The 3:05 to Chicago. The boy here will show you how he wants them handled."

CHAPTER 4

The journey would take at least seven days and was a little more than 24 hours to Chicago. Roy rode in the boxcar with the sheep and made a comfortable bed in the middle of the crates. He set the sheep crates two on the sides and one each at his head and feet. He climbed onto the middle, and this arrangement made it possible for him to be close to all the sheep. It also made a cozy and warm bed. He was not bothered by the familiar smells. He'd spent his entire life sleeping in a barn, and this was an improvement. He slept well and in short bits. He would doze for an hour or two and then get up, feed, water, and put down clean straw for the sheep. He would slide the boxcar door open a foot and peek out to see America. He was unimpressed with New York City and felt no pull to ever revisit. It stunk, people were everywhere, and there was endless noise.

The countryside was beautiful on the other side of the river as they left New York City. It was green, peaceful, and familiar. The pastures were full of cattle, horses, and Jersey Brown milk cows. It felt a bit like Scotland but bigger. The pastures and fields had wooden posts and wire fencing instead of rock walls, and they were three times larger. He was shocked at the size of the farms they passed and wondered how large Big Mike's ranch was.

Shutting the door and grabbing a book, he sat against the wall of the car and read *Tom Sawyer*. He'd heard of the book but doubted he'd ever have the time to read or the money to buy a real book. Things just keep getting better for this 18-year-old farm boy.

Events like these rarely happened in life and certainly not to a Scottish orphan. His life back home was basic, dull, routine, and void of variety. No one talked about things like ambition or dreams. Scotland was a beautiful and dramatic place, full of characters and old men with long stories and short fuses. Men that had seen the ambitions of local lads rise and fade for decades. It was a place of few improvements or advancements. The same after same. Farmers remained farmers. Millers' sons, grandsons, and great-grandsons all ground flour and meal without options for change. To outsiders, the life of a rural villager and farm family may sound confining and dull; however, the basics of food, shelter, and clothing were being met, and happiness was not scarce.

Roy's past life was all he knew, and it suited him. Tradition would have Roy one day meet a pleasant farmer's daughter, marry, and become a part of her family. He would raise sheep and a few draft horses and watch their children repeat the saga. The only other solid option available to young men was to join the army, see the world, and possibly die in a foreign land. Roy had considered the army option. Scarce prospects would prove this to be the best doorway to the world.

When you are raised up and live in a world with nearly no opportunities, you do as a hungry man would do. You eat what's put on your plate without asking if the meat be mutton, rabbit, or horse.

Fortunately, a loud, bearded man under a big hat, had come to be his salvation and alter his life that no imagination could concoct.

Roy was on a running horse, and his best choice was to hold tight and stay in the saddle until he got bucked off or the mount ran out of steam. He was young and if this move wound up being a mistake, he had time and energy to start again. Each hour on the train increased his confidence and his cheekiness grew. He'd make it in America. Maybe he'd become a millionaire and show the world to never stand in his road. A man can dream bigger dreams with American folding money in his pocket.

The train squealed and shook as it started to slow. It was coming into a station for water and coal. The stop would take 30 minutes at least and would give Roy a chance to get some food and see more of America.

Big Mike came walking alongside the train with a bag and handed it to Roy. "How're the critters taking to the train?" Mike asked. "Little rougher than the ship, eh son?"

Roy nodded and opened the cloth sack. It had apples, bread, cheese, and ham wrapped in paper and was more food than Roy would normally see in a week.

He grabbed a mysterious round object, held it up to Big Mike, and asked, "Now what be this?"

Big Mike let out a typical laugh and replied, "Hell, son! Ain't you seen an orange before? It's sweet, juicy, and hard to get. We don't get them in Montana except when I go to Helena. They have oranges and other silly food at The Montana Club there. Enjoy it. May be a while before ya get another'n."

Roy rolled it in his hands, and the citrus oils smelled clean. He looked at Big Mike, grinned, held it like an apple, and took a bite. The bitter rind stuck in his teeth, and he spit it out while digging into his mouth.

Big Mike shook his head and laughed. He winked, gave Roy another pat on the shoulder, and delivered him another lesson in America. "I gots lot to learn you, don't I son? Ya gotta rip that orange part off first and get rid of as much white stuff too. Then start busting that thing open. That's the part ya eat. The orange colored inside part. Save the peel for the sheep. They may like it."

Once peeled, Roy pulled a section away and cautiously put it in his mouth. The explosion of sweet juice surprised him, and he allowed the flavor to coat his mouth.

"Never have I tasted anathin' like this afor. Sweet Jasus, this is somethin'."

Big Mike was talking with a conductor for a minute and then returned. "That fella told me we get to Chicago in about four hours and then we have about six hours until the next train leaves. Maybe we can find a pen or corral close by and let these sheep out and run a bit there. They've been boxed up for days and need some freedom."

Roy nodded in agreement, took the sack of food, and headed back to the boxcar. He stuffed the rest of the orange in his mouth and let the juice coat it like paint. He chewed and paused then chewed and paused again. Who knew such a thing as an orange existed? This was now his favorite food, and he doubted that anything would ever best this experience.

————

Rolling into Chicago was a severe letdown for Roy. The train ran through the stockyards. All he could see was flat land and ugly buildings stuck up in the air. Roy thought, *This is it? This is the famous Chicago?*

The stench from the stockyard was gagging, even for a boy that slept in a barn. There was cattle as far as could be seen. There were hundreds of wooden pens and thousands of cattle.

The train stopped just on the edge of the stockyards. The boxcar Roy and the sheep where in hung out in a bare spot away from the platform and the passengers. They were the last car in the train with only the caboose behind. Roy slid the door open enough to jump out and get a look. It was early May, damp from melting snow, and the air carried a wet chill.

Mike came striding towards him.

Roy admired the way he walked. With arms swinging and closed fists sawing across his belly, Mike was funny and intimidating at the same time. He walked with his chest out and shoulders spread like wings. He took big steps, covering the same ground in two paces that most men would travel in three. He wasn't a tall man, but he had long legs for his size, and Roy reckoned that gave him an edge in walking. Roy would attempt to imitate his walk, his style, and his confidence. He'd never had a role model. Big Mike was a worthy idol.

"We got no place to let them out, Roy. That son-a-bitch in New York lied to me. What ya expect from an east coast city boy?"

Roy said, "We can let them out of their crates and roam around the boxcar a bit."

"All we can do I reckon. Let the rams out first and then the ewes. Don't want them ewes getting knocked around. They should be goin' into heat soon, and I don't want those rams nosin' them and gettin' them riled up." Big Mike looked at Roy to ensure his instructions were understood and then pointed to the car. "Let's get up in there."

"I can do this, sir, no need fer ya ta soil yer suit."

Mike gave a huff. "I care more about them sheep than I do this suit of clothes! I miss those noisy stinkers. I've had enough talk with old women from Baltimore anyway. This old girl was chewin' my ear off telling me about going to the Iron Range up in Minnesota to see her son. He's a big wig with a mine company, and she's going for a visit to help her daughter-in-law." Big Mike shook his head and spit. "I'll venture a thought her boy's wife ain't lookin' forward to that old nag nesting down!"

Roy pulled the end gates off the crates of the two rams. They bounced out and shook while looking for something to fight or avoid. The extra room to frolic changed the moods of both men and animal. Tending animals is caring for them. When they're fed and playful, it always made Roy feel calm. This moment made Roy think of his old dog Ned.

It took them both to get the rams back into their crates. They may not be as big as a cow or horse, but they can be stubborn and will run you over with no regrets. When possible, avoid turning your back to those devils as well. Many a sheepman went home with a bruised backside, mild whiplash, and/or a muddy chest from a forward fall. It does no good to rise to anger. It's well accepted that in the animal world, sheep are not the shiniest penny in the pocket.

The ewes were given their short parole and went into their crates with half the effort the rams had taken. The men used the time to pull all the straw out and replace it with fresh bedding. Mike was pushing the sheep, kicking straw, and lifting bales all while wearing an expensive gray suit. Roy took note. The animals were the priority, not the clothes.

Mike sat on a metal pail and tilted back. This was the world he knew and loved, not the suit and cities. Roy could see that he was relaxed and seemed pleased to be heading home.

Big Mike turned to Roy and said, "Here, take this money and run up to the station and get yourself a sit-down hot meal, anything you want. I'll stay with my babies while you're gone. They have a little restaurant there. But before ya do, find the washroom and scrub your face and hands. You smell like an old horse blanket!"

Big Mike laughed and handed Roy a dollar. Roy knew he could eat like a king with that.

"Grab yourself some chocolate bars or hard candy too. May as well live it up on the road, boy, because once we get to the ranch, it'll be a spell before we see town again. We only get into Lewistown once every two months if we're lucky." Mike looked at his pocket watch. "Best get movin', son. We got 80 minutes before we roll."

"I'll not be late, Mr. Mike. I'll be fast as a trout."

"Don't rush it, son. Keep an eye on the time, and you'll be fine."

After a good scrubbing in the white tiled washroom, Roy walked out and scanned the train station. It was not as big or fancy as the New York station, but it was still a busy, noisy place. He stopped and saw a man cooking.

There were eight round stools with red seats at the counter. He sat down at the end thinking he didn't want to upset the order of the seating. The man behind the counter wore a white shirt and white dirty apron and motioned to Roy to come to him.

"Too far for me to walk, kid. What ya want?" He pointed to the wall in back of him and above the cooking area.

"What do you eat here, sir?"

The man smirked and said, "Anything that ain't spoilt. Where you from, kid? Ireland? Got lots of Irish around here."

"Scotland, sir."

"Well, that's good. Got too many damn Irish here now. You'll have better luck getting work with ya not being an Irish. They don't bother me none, but lots of folk don't care much for 'em. Ever have a hamburger?"

"No, sir. I been eating ham on the train for five days straight, so I'd prefer to not ha' ham." Roy strained to read the blackboard.

"Boy, it ain't ham; it's beef. Just called hamburger for a reason I can't figure. It's good. I'll make you one and a bowl of cooked cabbage and some beets."

Roy nodded, and the man turn around to commence the cooking. The meat sizzled and smelled grand. After five minutes, the man set the plate in from of him: two slices of white bread with a flat cooked piece of beef, a bowl of cooked hot cabbage, and a small bowl of beets. Roy looked at the beets knowing he'd never eat them. He'd rather eat sheep dung. The worst tasting thing he'd ever had in his life was beets. He had talked with a man who was once in a British prison, and he told Roy they served the prisoners beets three meals a day. Beets. Prison food. No thank ye.

Roy grabbed a knife and fork, but the man stopped him. "Pick it up with your hands and take a bite. Use the fork with the cabbage."

What a taste. The juice dripped onto his hands, and he licked the back of his hand not wanting to miss anything. He kept biting and chewing and in one minute the hamburger was gone. He then turned to the cabbage and inhaled that as well.

The man stepped up and asked, "Well?"

"That was grand, it was. Can you cook me two more so I can take them with me on the train?"

"Glad you like it, boy. How about them beets?" the man asked, looking at the untouched red turds.

"I'm full up; can't touch 'em, sir," he said to be polite.

The hamburgers cost a nickel each, so he slid the paper dollar across the counter. The cabbage and beets were an additional five cents, and the man gave Roy 80 cents in change. Roy grabbed the hamburgers wrapped up in old newspaper, headed to the newsstand next to the door and bought five cents worth of hard candy.

Roy was in a hurry to get back. The last thing he wanted was to be late or be the cause of any trouble for Mike. The truth was he didn't want to disappoint Mike. Ever.

Fast walking back to the boxcar, he slid open the door. The rumbling door startled a napping Big Mike.

Mike pulled out his watch, pursed his lips, and asked, "Well, that was a short shift, son. Did you eat? Did you chew your food, or did you swallow it like one of them pelican birds?"

"I ate a ham...ham burger he called it. Something new. Good. I bought two more. Would ye care ta try one?"

"Well, you only took 25 minutes, so you must have run up there and back too. No need to be in that much of a rush. Enjoy things." Mike spoke as a man regretful of past enjoyments avoided.

"I got done what needed done. Maybe I'm faster at things than your American fellas!" Finally, a boast and hint of confidence from Roy.

Again, the laugh from Mike. "Well, maybe you are, son! Remember, it's always bad to be late but not always good to be early."

Puzzled, Roy hesitated, looked at Mike, and said, "I dunno what that is supposed ta mean, sir. Being honest wi ya."

Mike stood up, grabbed Roy by both shoulders and looked at him straight on. "Guess I don't know either, son. Sounds like bullshit to me too!"

They both laughed, but no one could ever top that laugh of Big Mike's. That laugh is how most men want to feel inside and how many want the outside world to see them.

Roy pulled the $.75 in change and handed it back to Mike. Big Mike looked down at the money and pushed his hand away.

"Keep it, Roy."

"But I no did anathin to earn it, sir."

"You earned it by being an honest man. It wasn't meant to be a test, but most fellas would have pocketed that money and never said a thing. Hell, ya even offered me one of them hamburgers! You're a good man, Roy Douglas. Keep it that way."

Mike jumped out and walked back towards the pullman car. As he put a foot on the step of the Pullman, he smelled something and sniffed the air. Backing away from the car, he walked into the station and straight to the lunch counter and the man in a dirty white apron.

"Give me one of them hamburgers. No...give me two."

CHAPTER 5

hicago to St. Paul was a more scenic journey. St. Paul had a different feel than Chicago: more trees, rivers, and farms. It was a city but cleaner than most he's seen in the U.S. Unfortunately, it was still a city full of people and unwelcomed sounds.

He had heard that Minnesota, Montana, and other new western states were filling up with Germans, Swedes, Norwegians, and additional hardy cold weather peoples. The Scots were closer in history and temperament to these nationalities than to the Italians, Greeks, and Russians that were part of the controlling numbers in those eastern cities. This whole country was filling up with people walking away from limits and running towards riches and the chance to be like new royalty. No Earls and Barons. No repeating the work and the lives of hundreds of years of fathers. New starts. Scary starts. Fear of the present isn't acceptable to a certain percentage of people, regardless of country or creed. Men that sleep soundly will never understand dreamers and the joy in sleepless nights. It's not an acquired taste. You're born with it or you aren't.

Ambitious men look at the quiet men of the world and wonder, *Why don't you want more? Why not want better than you have?* That would be like a tall fellow asking a short man, *Don't you want to be taller?* It simply is who they are.

This America thing wasn't for everyone, but Roy could already tell he was born to it. It would be worth any and all efforts. What would he become? Who would he be?

Another stop in St. Paul allowed time for another uncrating of the sheep similar to the one in Chicago, and Mike appeared before the train stopped rolling. He was eager to get out of the train and back around his familiars.

"Morning, Roy! How's my little flock tolerating the ride?"

"All is well this morning, sir. One of the rams got a little randy last night and thought he'd break out, but I got him settled all right." Roy was impressed that Mike showed up in the car so quickly. "Did ya jump off the train and roll back here?" It was Roy's first gentle poke at Mike and a quick flash of humor.

"That's a good one, son!" Mike was pleased to finally hear some banter from Roy. "Naw, I was sittin' having breakfast with this woman from Mobile Alabama, and she, well, she wouldn't shut her pie hole. Once she found out I was a widower, she lit on me like a mare in heat."

Here was a detail about Mike Hanson that Roy didn't know. He got to thinking…*I don't know much at all about Big Mike, except he raises sheep in Montana, and that he likes whisky.*

"She kep' on askin' me about how big my ranch was and how many sheep I had." Big Mike turned and looked at Roy. "Here's a lesson for you, son: NEVER ask a man how much land or number of livestock he has. I've seen men get a beatin' for talking like that. It's no different than asking a city fella how much money he has in the bank. Nobody wants to be sized up like that, especially to a stranger. They may be fixin' to rob ya thinking you're a Vanderbilt."

Roy absorbed the lecture. He knew there'd be many more and that all he had to do was listen.

Big Mike continued. "She told me she was from Bay Minette, a little town in Alabama near Mobile. Her husband was a cotton buyer and was killed when a stack of cotton bales fell on him. She told me he was a good man, had a blue eye and a brown one and was not very handsome. And I'm sittin' there nodding my head like a duck, thinking, 'she's trying to sink her meat hooks into me!' Well, sir, I ain't getting' saddle up with some woman who never worked a day in her life. She had one eye that wasn't right, like she could see around the corner before she got there, so I got up and ran back here. She was MY cotton bale if ya know what I'm sayin'."

Mike sent Roy into the station for another chance to buy some food and to use the running water in the WC. There were no hamburgers, but a man was selling sausages and sauerkraut, so he grabbed one. He never had sauerkraut and wanted to try it. The smell was a little off, but he took a bite of meat and then the kraut. Again, it was a flavor he had never tasted before and now he wanted more. That was a good thing because he was heading into the land of sausage and kraut lovers. He'd blend right in.

After he had purchased another refill of hard candy, a loaf of bread, a small block of white cheese, and two apples, Roy walked back to the boxcar and his little family. The train rolled out of St. Paul headed northwest on The Great Northern Railway into North Dakota and then northern Montana. They called it 'The Hi-Line' as it was close to Canada in spots and was as far north as a train in America would travel.

Once they crossed the Red River, he could see rich farmland fed by the flooding of the river for hundreds of years. It had the blackest ground he'd ever seen. There was still snow on most of the ground, and even though it was good land, he thought it was boring to look at. He hoped Big Mike's ranch was in prettier and mountainous country. He scolded himself for getting picky about where he would land. It was all Americas.

Fargo, North Dakota lay ahead; a town built around the Red River. Again, it was just another stop on the way and nothing special except a place of opportunity for farmers from Europe to start a new life. Roy could see the potential of a place like this, but it held no mastery on his desires. It might be a good place for others, but not for him.

The train stops were becoming routine and tiresome now. The only change was the length of the stops and the size of the train depots. The further west they got, the longer the stops and the smaller the depots. The layovers became longer as fewer lines were available and the number of trains traveling decreased. This offered travelers more time to connect to their desired destinations, but it slowed things down. In addition, the train depots went from big and shiny places with white tiles everywhere to wood floors and basic construction. Suitable and practical for the environment but not as elegant or clean.

Minot, North Dakota was next, but it was hours down the line. It was another flat, nondescript place full of more Germans, Swedes, and other blonde Europeans. Roy thought that the women were more attractive out here than in the big city and wondered if that may be due to his isolation in the boxcar for days on end. However, there was no denying the fact that some of these girls were beautiful, and he hoped to find a similar collection of potential wives in Montana. His luck so far had been strong, and he didn't see why his winning ways shouldn't continue.

Leaving Minot there was nothing but small depots and desolation ahead. Havre, Montana would be the next town of any size, and Havre was at least two days away. In Minot, he told a man they would be passing though "HAV ree," and he was quickly corrected that it was pronounced "HAV ur." He was a little overwhelmed with all these new places to learn how pronounce and not sound stupid. He was constantly asking Big Mike and others how to pronounce the town or river's name correctly. If it wasn't some French sounding word, it was an Indian name. He was learning a whole new language.

The land continued to get larger, longer, and flatter. Roy thought he had gotten used to everything being bigger and then bigger yet, but this country was huge and had no edge. It seemed like an ocean of brown dirt and round green balls of a short tree they called sagebrush. *If a fella could farm this sagebrush, he'd be a millionaire in a month*, he thought. There was just enough space in between each plant to walk or ride a horse through, and it filled the air with a smell that wasn't sweet but wasn't bitter either. It wasn't a bad odor, but it was definitely not one he'd choose to spend time with. He would find out later that the smell of sage would be a constant in his life, and he'd grow to ignore it.

Minot was a busy place, with more people and activity than Roy had expected. It was still flat and not exciting, but it was not a complete disappointment. Again, the stop, release, clean, eat, and recrating of the sheep was repeated. By now, Roy and Mike had a process and routine. It was a shame that so much learning, energy and success would soon be obsolete. There wouldn't be another trip or adventure like this in his lifetime.

Mike came to the boxcar, grabbed the hand bar next to the door and pulled himself up and into the car. Letting out a big puff of air, he said, "Gotta tell ya, Roy, I'm gonna miss this."

"Miss what, sir?"

"THIS! The travel, the new country, the handburgers! I've been to California, but I have never been to places like this trip took me. Now, I've been to the other side of the world." Big Mike's usual pounding voice slowed and got quieter. "It took me to Scotland and meetin' you, son."

Roy stopped kicking straw out of a crate. He was surprised to hear Mike, or any man, express a kind thought to him. He'd never heard admiration from anyone.

Before Roy could answer, Mike grabbed the awkwardness out of mid-air. "I mean, I don't think I could ah brought a good hand all the way with me to Scotland now could I?"

Roy answered, "Aye that would not be good or cheap."

Mike laughed, grabbed a bag of oats, and got busy. Roy knew what he had heard from Mike, and he'd hear it in his head for a long time. When you survive with zero to almost nothing, a little can be stretched a mile.

———

Endless repeating sounds. The metal on metal, like an out-of-time grandfather clock. It sounds the same at 3:00 a.m. or 8:00 p.m. One beat down, one beat up. But every so often, the beat skips for half a second, and it throws a small lump into your throat until the rhythm returns. You count on that rhythm to keep you moving, keep you alive.

Roy would love trains forever. Boats and ships can travel roughly 70 percent of the earth, which is water. But a train, now that can take you to dry and high places. Green places and brown places. Maybe not to the exact spot, but it can get you close. It can get you to your new adventure or a new home.

This stretch of the journey seemed to equal the New York to Fargo leg. This was a long rather than exciting trip now, and Roy was ready for the travel to end if this were how it would continue. On the other hand, he'd rather see the ground change than the expedition end. Sweet lord let's see some change.

Havre was still hours away, and there was one stop for water in an hour. It only took 10 to 20 minutes to take on the necessary water, but the engineers needed to check the oil and do a walk around the engine. It was a good time for any of the passengers to walk on a still surface after hours of shaking and balancing while walking up the narrow aisle between seats. Some of the men would walk briskly to get the stiffness out of feet and legs and others would take a few steps and then stare across the enormous prairie, with a mixture of wonderment seasoned with a fear of what may lay ahead.

There was one woman in a long, dark, blue dress wearing a colorful wide brimmed hat with feathers and a long red scarf that wrapped around the hat then fell off the back and swept at her shoulders with the breeze. She walked fifty feet or so away from the train and stood on a little mound of dirt that elevated her view. She looked like a statue, an elegant western sculpture. Roy watched her and wondered, *Is she heading to a new beginning like I am or is she running from a bitter past? If she were on the run, what danger could have been so severe as to force a woman to travel to and through THIS country? Maybe she wasn't alone. Was she escaping from an evil man or was she a temptress that held stolen goods in her carpetbag?*

She held her stare for a few minutes and then suddenly spun around as if she knew she was being watched. She caught Roy staring directly at her. As she turned, he saw a small smile and eyes filled with pleasure. She met Roy's glimpse with a sweet smile of kindness as if to say, *I am very well, young man. Thank you for your concern.* Roy then knew she was headed to a happy genesis, a new place and time for hope. He returned the glance with a small smile of his own, tipped his cap to the woman, and headed back to boxcar. He wanted to call out to her, let her know that he, too, was headed to a place of anticipation and faith. He knew how she felt. However, the hat tip would be all the chatting up he would or could muster.

It was at that moment that Roy knew his shell had cracked and fallen off. No longer would he be the quiet boy trying to hide and not be seen. He realized that he no longer would avoid people or events. His natural curiosity would be rewarded in Montana. He wanted to know the stories, the truths, and the lies. A life with potential and a healthy future needs to be used and lived. Bust open that jug, boy, and take a long, hard tug.

He would think of the woman often in the future he supposed. Not in a manner of lust or longing, but in a curious way. Did her dreams bloom or did they die on the vine? Was HER America as pleasurable as HIS America? He hoped a good life would welcome her in this new land. He believed that she would have similar thoughts towards him as well. A silly notion, but a healthy and happy idea.

Roy liked the idea of believing in good things now. It felt unusual to have happy dreams and to think that hard work and being smart would offer a genuine pay day.

There were few dreamers in the Highlands, small numbers of big thinkers with grand ideas. Centuries of dominance and hard-handed rule had created a ceiling for ambition in most Scots. Nevertheless, the spirit of William Wallace and Robert the Bruce lived inside most lads and would never be extinguished no matter how hard the bloody Brits tried.

The sudden jolt of the train beginning to move was the one thing he didn't enjoy. If you weren't prepared or braced, you could easily find yourself on the floor or tossed against an unforgiving hard surface. Roy had collected two good sized bruises on his legs so far on the trip, and he was adamant to gain no more.

Back to the hay and *Tom Sawyer*. He enjoyed the book, but his head was jammed full of new ideas, old fears, and endless questions about the future that left little room for additional information or fables. *I'll read this when I have some time to myself and Twain's words ain't in a fist-fight with me own thinking.*

He fell back asleep with a pillow of hay. An ewe sniffing his hair through the wood slates of the crates tickled a little, but Roy grinned, enjoyed the affection, and dozed off.

Remember, Roy: it's HAV ur, not Hav-ray.

Havre. Havre.

The next stop was Havre. Then, they moved to another train and went south to Great Falls. *Nice name for a town. Must be a good story behind that name,* Roy thought. He would have to ask Mike. He'd know, of course.

As the train slowed, he peeked out the door to see if this part of Montana was any different.

Nope. More grass and rolling hills. Endlessly amazing.

An hour long stop in Havre allowed the train to add water fire-wood and a few passengers. Two railcars full of cattle were on a side-track, ready to be connected for the ride to Great Falls.

Roy had seen a painting of Niagara Falls and wondered if the falls he would soon see would be similar. The town IS named Great Falls after all.

A few more hours and then they would spend the night in a hotel and enjoy being motionless and still.

CHAPTER 6

Endless rolling hills with infinite grass. More flat top hills (which he soon learns are called buttes) are visible, and he thinks he can see the Missouri River in the distance. There was also a state named Missouri, and he wondered if this was the usual practice of naming a state and a river the same. But why was the Missouri all the way up in Montana? Maybe it went through Missouri too. He didn't honestly care; he was simply curious. He'd spend his time learning about Montana. He did learn that the state of Montana alone is much bigger than Scotland; it was even bigger than England and all the British Isles.

Roy slid the door open to a welcome breeze of fresh air, as many days spent with a carload of animals, especially sheep, can create memories in the nose not easily blown out or slyly removed by a skillful pick. Sheep smelled like granny's dirty boots. A horse had a richer aroma. A sweaty horse smelled better than whisky, at least to Roy. And he had no quarrel with a glass of Scots Whisky at all. Girls will break your heart, and whisky will fix it or make you believe repairs have been made and will numb the memory until the next tart appears.

He sat for nearly 20 minutes before the biggest wagon he'd ever seen drove up, pulled by two fine matched sorrel-colored Belgian draft horses. Sorrels were always his favorite colored horse. The rusty light reddish coat was very common, but it was pleasing to his eyes.

A large part of his Montana dream was to work with and be around horses of any size and kind. He only knew draft horses like the Belgians and had ridden them bareback with a rope harness. It was a joy to ride instead of walk, and the power of these magnificent beasts was pleasing and puzzling, but they were huge creatures and not easy to throw a leg over. It was much like sitting on top of a whisky barrel laid on its side. It required constant readjustment and defense of the parts most prized if fatherhood was a future consideration.

As the huge wagon backed up to the door, Roy imagined being astride a sleek and fast American Cowboy horse. That would come soon.

Three men stood in the wagon with Big Mike as it bumped into the side of the boxcar, and the man quietly, in a near whisper, gave the command to 'whoa boys.' This man was a teamster, and it was obvious he was a master of both beast and cart. He pulled back on the long brake handle to lock the wagon down still. The men crawled up and into the car while Roy reached an arm out to Big Mike and half pulled him in.

Big Mike leaned back against the wall, pointed to the sheep, and gave the men a thumbs up to confirm they were his as they moved the sheep on the wagon.

Big Mike was quiet and not his normal brassy self this morning. Roy looked him in the eye, wondering how he would tolerate the next few hours. Big Mike caught the silent question and answered promptly. "Too much fun and whisky last night. Found a couple of boys from around Bannock and Virginia City and played poker 'til sunrise. Them boys from that part of the country are pretty rough and tough ya know."

Roy nodded as if he understood but of course he carried no knowledge of Big Mike's declaration. He doubted Big Mike would quiz him on lack of information due to his current diminished brain power.

Even in this moment of physical persecution, Big Mike bravely continued his tale. "Ya see, son, that area was the first Capital when Montana was still a territory." Roy would read up on what a territory was later. "And they were some tough old sons-a-bitches. Things got out a hand with a lot of thieving', killing, and handlin' the women way too rough, even with being whores and all, so they started a gang of their own. Called themselves Vigilantes, or Virgil's, or some damn word sounding like that. Hell's fire, I can't remember. My head feels like I been mule kicked."

"So, them Virginia City boys grew up watching fellas get drug down the road with a rope around their ankles behind a running horse. Watched men swing from ropes kickin' and cryin' fer their mommies, while piss runned down their pants and out their boots until they ran out of air. They grew up learning how to fight and kill. That don't mean they're all killers and bad men supporting evil ways. They see that being violent, if backed into a corner, comes in handy."

Gotta learn where Virginia City is and avoid it like a flooded river. Roy had a head full of fresh information, but this latest news jumped to the top of his list.

The sheep were loaded, and it seemed that Big Mike was carrying a poke of pain under his hat as well.

Roy grabbed his bag of clothes, books, and food then jumped down into the wagon for the ride. Big Mike was slumped down against a crate with his chin dropped, possibly sleeping or passed out. Hard to tell. Just then, a ram stuck his nose through the crate and attempted to make a breakfast out of Big Mike's hat. That provoked a response out of Big Mike and a fresh order to the driver.

"I got a corral over by that big cottonwood tree. They'll be a fella over there waiting for us."

Big Mike slid to the outside wall of the wagon to a sheep-safe-zone, and an uncommon quiet fell over the formerly lively man.

Roy had seen his share of drunkards before, sloppy men full of bottled courage, so seeing Big Mike in this condition was no shock.

He was surprised that Big Mike was stable enough to remember the tasks at hand and to do so without sounding stupid or angry.

Big Mike motioned for Roy to come closer. Roy dropped down and sat next to him as if to hear a military secret regarding a morning attack against an ill-prepared foe. He leaned in for the news from his General.

"So, Roy, we gotta put them sheep in a corral for the night 'cause the train to Stanford don't leave until tomorrow afternoon, so we got some time to kill. Me, I need some sleep to pay for my sinnin' ways." He winked at Roy a rascal's wink. "Let's get them out and let them loose in the corrals for the night. Rams in one, ewes in another. We'll come back and feed and water them on our way to supper tonight." Before Roy could ask, Big Mike put his hand on Roy's shoulder and continued. "And don't worry, son, you ain't sleeping outside with them sheep tonight. You'll get you own room in the hotel. First, we'll feed these critters then go to the bathhouse and then to a nice supper. Sound good?"

"But you gotta do all the work right now 'cause I feel like my saddle slipped and I been ridden with my head hittin' the ground." Another pat on the shoulder told Roy that was the end of the instructions and of Big Mike being conscious. His head rolled to his left like a piece of bacon sliding down a greasy frying pan.

Roy thought of patting him on the head but then realized he was being watched, so he assumed the role of bossman, grabbed a commanding tone, and gave the orders to the men as if he was an artillery Captain.

The sheep were sorted. They enjoyed their short freedom and bounced around both pens like spring lambs, happy for the chance to move. In addition, there was a cowboy patrolling the pens and corrals to keep them safe.

The cowhand was the first real cowboy that Roy had seen up close. The rider had a revolver in a big leather belt wrapped around his waist. It was full of bullets, ready for Indian raiders, rustlers, or gunfights in the street. He wore a simple flat top hat with a short brim. Roy thought that all American cowboys wore giant wide brimmed hats, but he would learn that those hats were not popular in a country with heavy and constant winds. And Great Falls appeared to fit that description well. The cowboy wore a heavy brown wool coat, he had a large cloth wrapped around his neck, and he had on well-worn gloves. However, it was his leggings that caught Roy's fancy. Wooly covered legs that looked as if the man was half sheep. They looked warm and important. He would attempt to duplicate this man's appearance in the future.

CHAPTER 7

B ack in the wagon, Roy was forced to shake Mike to gain information about the hotel.

Mike muttered, "Hotel Arvon" and fell back half-awake but not functional.

Roy told the teamster The Hotel Arvon. The driver answered that it was about the only hotel in town, and he figured that it was the stop.

Great Falls was a new town of about 1,200 residents and was quickly becoming a crossroads for immigrants, homesteaders, and livestock growers like Mike. He could see the growth, and the odor of fresh milled wood was in the air like blooming flowers. It smelled like the future.

They pulled up to an impressive three-story red brick building standing alone full of pride and progress. Roy didn't expect to find a building like this out here. Mike had the teamster haul his large trunk inside while Roy provided Mike with a human safety net in case of a stumble. Big Mike thanked the driver and reminded him to pick the sheep up tomorrow afternoon at 2:00 p.m. to catch the Stanford train at 3:00 p.m. He handed the man two silver dollars and then headed to the hotel desk.

This was quite a place. There was a livery stable and freight office, and they sold vegetables and green food all in the same block as the hotel. Maybe they had some of those oranges that Mike had introduced him to.

Mike slowly ambled up to the desk clerk as if he had nails in his boots. The man was feeling lowly for certain. "We need us two rooms for the night. One for me, and one for my boy here."

"Yes, sir," answered the clerk. "Is the young man responsible for himself?"

"What the hell ya mean by that? He's a grown man! He's my top hand, and he's like a son to me. Why would THIS man right here be a problem?"

"Sorry, sir, we have to ask. There are some hoodlums and wild cowhands that ride through, and we don't oblige those men. This is a new hotel. You understand, sir." The clerk repeated this practiced line, and it was clear he repeated it daily.

"I reckon, but it's best not to insult a man as he's standing there with no ill-intent or evidence of such. Now you best give my top-hand here the nicest room you got to make up for the insult, and we'll leave the matter at rest."

Roy wondered if his own father would have defended and cared for him more than Big Mike did. Feeling respect at any level was a new sensation for Roy, but it was easier to absorb than he expected.

"Yes, sir. Of course, sir. You have the Governor's room, and the lad will be next to you in the Missouri room."

"The Governor's room sound better. Why did ya give it ta me?"

"Well, sir, you are his senior and are the one paying. I assumed..."

"Listen here, Willie. I told you I wanted my man to have the best room. Is that a problem?" Mike's voice got quiet, and he trailed off as to not alarm the clerk but to deliver the message firmly.

"Absolutely, sir. And the boy's name is?" The clerk had pen in hand, ready to nervously dictate the next sound.

"His name is Roy. Roy Douglas. Remember that name 'cause he's gonna be a big man in this state someday. And he ain't no boy. Please refer to him as a man. Just asking for the courtesies offered to any man." Mike was weary of this exchange and slapped five dollars down on the desk as a sign to the clerk to wrap this up.

"Top of the stairs. Both rooms are to the left, and the room names are on the doors. Can the young man rea…?"

Before the clerk could finish, Big Mike looked at him and said, "Yes, he can read! He's a man of letters. Want him to read to ya something? Roy, grab your book and read something to this…gent."

Roy reached into his sack, but the clerk again quickly apologized and said there was no need.

"Where you from, sir? Ain't none of us here *from* here. Hell, even the Indians that are here now came from someplace else and chased off the previous squatters." Mike dropped an elbow on the counter and rested his jaw in his hand, as if waiting for a schoolboy to answer.

"Connecticut, sir," the clerk answered firmly and nervously.

"Well now, that untangles the situation. Did you like living back there with all the dandies and dudes? All the silk hat horseshit and fainting women in bustles?" Mike made no movement, his chin still resting in his palm.

"No, sir, I did not care for Connecticut. That's why I made my way out here. There's promise and opportunity here. None back there unless you are born into it." The clerk felt the strength of truth come over him, and he stood his ground.

Mike slapped the counter. "Ha! Now that's a good answer, boy! First thing you said that was from your own gut, wasn't it?" The clerk gave a quick and firm nod. "Now that style of thinkin' right there will serve you well. We ain't dudes out here. We're the men that laugh at the dudes and don't want anything to do with dandy men. You'll learn our ways, sonny. You'll be fine. I expect to hear about you in the future as well and to not be surprised by your advancement and future success."

The clerk was visibly a changed man, no longer feeling defensive but accepting the advice and praise. He relaxed. You could hear a deep breath filled with relief escape from the young clerk as he gave a gentle tug at his collar, and his chin jutted out an inch.

What just happened here? Roy was replaying this encounter in his mind and trying to quickly glean some understanding. Two minutes ago, this had been a tense encounter and could have gotten bitter very quickly. Roy's first impression was that Mike was a wise man and had learned how to succeed. He was a builder of men, not a destroyer of dreams and potential. Just that quickly did the clerk become a friend to and advocate for Mike Hanson.

"Now, is there a...I never did gather your name, young man."

"The name is Lowell. Lowell Perkins, sir." He reached across the desk to offer his hand to Mike.

Mike grabbed it, grinned, and gave one hardy tug on the boy's hand. Again, Roy was impressed by this instant diplomacy from Mike.

"Well, Mr. Lowell, inspiring to meet you. Now, can you direct us to a bathhouse? We both have thousands of miles of stink on us that we need to leave behind here in Great Falls."

"My pleasure, sir. We have our own bathing facilities here in the hotel. I will be pleased to have the chamber maid draw a bath for you. We also offer a new and exciting feature: a shower of water. Some prefer that. Which would you like?"

Mike's eyes opened wide in a false shocked reaction in order to make Lowell feel accomplished. "Well, damn me to Tuesday. Never expected that. Roy, do you want to try that shower machine and I'll soak in the bath? Need the soak as much as the cleaning!" Roy gave a nod to Mike, and the order was placed.

"Allow us 30 minutes to prepare the bath for you both. The tub is separate from the shower but within the same room so you can commence your ablutions then." Lowell turned to the wall, picked an earpiece from the phone, and turned the crank to ring a bell. "Betsy, please prepare the washroom with a bath and a shower for Mr. Hanson and son."

Mike did not correct the clerk when he misspoke about Roy being his son, and Roy did not as well. Why would he?

"The girl will knock on your doors when the baths are ready for you. Anything else for you, Mr. Hanson?"

"Young man, I've been halfway around the world on this journey, and you have offered me the finest attention I could expect. I reckon we're all sorted for a bit now. Think about where you can send us to have a fine supper, and we will be well pleased." Mike tipped his hat to Lowell and began his way up the stairs with key in hand. As he took the first step up, he heard the clerk declare, "And not to worry about your trunk, sir. I'll have it hauled to your room straight away."

Mike thrust his right arm into the air as he walked in a signal of triumph and job well done to Lowell.

They settled into their rooms; they would go to get scrubbed up in half an hour. Mike realized Roy only had one change of clothes, so he told him to come to his room, and he'd loan him a fresh change of clothes. Roy threw his dirty bag on the floor of the handsomest room he'd ever seen and stared at it for a minute to soak it in. He'd never stayed in a hotel before and could not imagine a finer place, short of Buckingham Palace.

————

A tap on Mike's door was greeted by a muffled, "Yep," and Roy took that to be the secret word to allow passage. Mike's trunk was on the floor, opened and full of clothing, some clean, some not so fresh.

"Let me see. I got a shirt that the laundry on the ship shrunk up, and it feels like a hug from your granny now. Here, try this." Mike tossed the shirt to Roy.

It was as fine a material as he'd ever touched, pale blue with fancy buttons and a collar sewn right in. He held it and thought, Lord, I does hope this fits. He slipped it on over his dirty undershirt. It was a little big, but that was better than too small.

"Take that off so you don't get any old stink on. Now try these britches. You're taller than me, so they might be a little short for ya." Mike was digging for more clothes he either couldn't wear or didn't like.

The pants were indeed short by about two inches, but that was not a disqualifying feature for Roy. They were bigger around the waist, but he could draw that up with ease. They were fine looking pants with thin white strips going all through the fabric against medium gray material.

"Fix yer fly there, son."

"My what?" Roy asked.

"That flap in front of your dinger there."

Roy had never seen such a contraption. His pants all had a big flap with two buttons to hold it up, but these pants had a slice of metal right in the middle. Why would a man want that there?

"Sorry, sir, but just how does all this work?"

Mike snorted, still too tired for his signature laugh. "There's a little tab or ear down at the bottom. Grab that then pull up, and it closes the barn door. But try it slowly first. You'll get used to it. They call it a zipper. Stupid name."

Bravely, Roy began the operation. He found the metal tab and gave a pull. Nothing. He then realized he needed to hold down the cloth underneath and tried again. The zipper started to move and with each fraction of an inch, Roy felt a small victory was at hand. He stopped at the top and, with the biggest grin he's shown in weeks, he stared at Mike and yelled, "By God, I did it!"

Mike shook his head and said, "Easy there, son. Make sure you have all your gear tucked inside those pants because if not, that machine there will bite you like a bulldog. You'll find out for yerself soon enough."

Roy nodded with understanding and stood at attention to look at the mirror with his new duds. He expected an improvement, but he felt he looked quite grand.

"Just keep that stuff, Roy. Here's another shirt and some socks. The socks are dirty, so get them rinsed out with our other clothes. You need more duds. Tomorrow, we'll get you some working clothes. I'll pay for them. You can owe it to me against your wages."

Wages? He forgot he was going to get cash money for working as well as a bed and food. Felt like a Prince he did.

"You look good in that gear, boy. We'll get you all outfitted, and the next time we go to Lewistown them town girls will be trying to rope you. You tickle me, son. Everything new is good to you, like you were just hatched out of an egg and born in a barn." Mike was teasing, but it was good natured banter.

"I was, sir."

"What's that?"

"I was, sir. I was born in a barn. And the only bed I've know me whole life has been straw on a barn floor."

Mike stopped and dropped his head. "So, you never slept a night in a real bed?"

"Not one night, Mr. Mike."

Mike stood up and walked toward Roy. He put both hands on Roy's shoulders and quietly said, "No wonder you act green boy... you ARE green. Green as spring pasture grass. I need to remember that."

The tap on the door was followed by a small voice announcing the bath was ready and they could both follow her to the room. Mike called out for her to come in, and the door pushed open, but she stayed in the hall.

"Come on in, girl," Mike told the round-faced young woman. She had braids and dark yellow hair. Probably a German girl.

"No, sir, hotel rules say I stay in the hall when there's men in the room."

"Sure, sure, that's fine. Give us a minute, and you can lead us there. Can we give you dirty clothes and have you get them laundered and back to us by morning?"

"Yes, sir. That is not a problem. Just leave them on the floor, and I'll collect them. There is a Chinese laundry out the back, and they could have them for you by this evening. The town is quiet now, and they need the business." The maid clasped both hands at her waist and looked down to the floor submissively.

"Lead the way, girly." Mike walked out, and Roy followed not knowing what to expect. He had never had a real bath or a shower before. A splash from the water trough and a swim with his mates was the best he'd had. And all cold water, very cold water. Warm water may be a pleasant shock.

Roy marveled at the hotel's beauty and how clean and new everything was at that. The maid opened the big six-paneled Douglas Fir door to a large room with short walls between areas. They were just short enough to see the top of a tall man's head and short enough for conversation.

"The bath is over here, sir, and the shower is in this corner. There is soap in each and a fresh towel. This chain here will ring the bell to let me know when you're finished or you need assistance." Again, the glance to the floor finished the instructions. "And I shall go collect your clothes for the laundry straight away."

"Well done, girl. This is a dandy set up, just polished up and dandy!"

Mike started to undress. The maid took the hint and quickly backed up and closed the door behind her.

"Livin' like a King we are! Enjoy it, son."

Roy stepped over to the corner with a hole in the floor, undressed, and hung his new duds on some fancy brass hooks he figured were there for that purpose. He stepped into the shower behind the wall and looked it over, unsure of what came next.

After a minute, Roy called out, "Mr. Mike, what happens now?"

"What ya talkin' about, Roy?"

"Well, I be standin' here and nothing is happenin'. Ain't there some water involved?"

The giant laugh was back, and Mike was genuinely amused. "Son, look for a rope or chain hangin' and give it a pull."

Roy turned to his left to find a shiny brass chain hanging down. He gave it a hard pull, and the thrill of a sudden burst hit him full on with cool, then warm water out of a dozen small holes drilled into a silver dish above his head. He gasped and then coughed as he took in some of the unexpected flood from above. He let loose the chain as quickly as he had pulled it.

"Sounds like you got it figured out, Roy!"

"Aye, I did, sir. Quite a devilment this thing it is."

Roy gave a shorter softer tug on the chain, and the water returned as soft as a spring rain. He could hear a groan of relief from Mike as he heard the slow splashes from the tub and the quiet joy of a grown man returning to boyhood.

The soap had the smell of flowers and not the nose-sting of the lye soap he had used in the past. He stood there naked and wet, with flower soap sliding down his front and back, and thought, *It was worth the journey just for this.*

He held the chain down and allowed the water to rinse him even after the last bubble had long escaped down the dark hole in the floor.

"Mr. Mike, have ye got a shower back to the ranch?"

Mike shot back, "Hell no, son. I ain't poor, but I ain't that rich neither. We have a water pump in the kitchen, but we have a tub that the boys all use on Saturday nights. They draw cards to pick the order. If you are the last one, the water can get a little muddy."

Fair enough, Roy thought. He considered volunteering to be last to get things off on the right foot with his new work family. *Yea, they'll appreciate that and may refuse my offer as a gesture of kindness. Any man should respect that.*

Roy reluctantly let loose of the chain and stood still for a minute to let this new feeling sink in. He grabbed the white fluffy towel from the chair and dried off. He sat with the towel over his head and leaned back with his eyes closed.

Roy dressed, but he quickly found the new pants were wool, and he had no underwear on. It was not a joyful sensation.

Mike was also out and dried and had the towel wrapped around his waist. "They got some hair tonic and a brush over here. Try to get that pelt of yours under control, son. Just a little tonic though, not too much. Just a spot, then brush."

Roy had a head full of unruly Scottish hair; it was wavy, had some curls and, like a spring colt, was generally uncontrollable. He normally shook it out and let it fall to its natural destination. It was getting long as few men cut their hair in the winter. It wasn't quite to his shoulders, but it was getting close. He shook a dime sized spot of oil onto his hand and tapped his head a few times.

"Damn, son! You gotta rub that goo in there! All over and down to the skin. Don't leave any spot, you hear?"

"Aye, sir."

Roy got with the program and rubbed deeply and vigorously. Even that felt good. Then he grabbed a big brush, a little smaller than a horse brush, and tried to pull the hair into order. But the hair refused. The oil did little and offered no control, just shine.

"Just take that towel and dry it the best ya can, Roy, then shake it like a saddle blanket. That's the best you can do with that mess. We take the shears out once a month in the spring after the baths and give haircuts. Better hope you can find a wife that likes that curly tangled hair you got!" Mike chuckled softly. He doubted Roy would have any difficulty finding a girl, but he didn't want Roy to think the Fergus County girls weren't worth putting forth an effort.

On the walk back to the rooms, the maid spotted them.

"Your clothes will be returned to you within an hour. I'll knock and set them at your door."

"That is splendid news, girl. Come here for a second if you would."

Mike dug around in his pant pocket and pulled out a silver dollar. He grabbed her right hand, turned it palm up, and placed the dollar in her hand. He then wrapped his big hand over her tiny, rough hand and closed her fingers over the money.

"Please, sir, no need for that."

"You will offend me if you refuse. You don't want to offend me now, do ya?" Mike tilted his head and smiled.

"No, sir, never."

"Good. We'll await the delivery before we leave. I think my friend over there may need a few items from the batch of wash."

Mike winked at Roy. He could see that Roy was walking as if he had just jumped over a campfire and the flames got too close.

Roy smirked, realizing that Mike didn't miss anything and saw all. Roy walked into his room and closed the door. His own room! He'd never had a room to himself, even for one night. And that bed was a marvel, a masterpiece. He stripped naked to avoid further wool bites. He walked to the bed, turned, fell back, and allowed the bed to embrace him.

———

Roy heard a tap at the door that woke him. He had fallen asleep unexpectedly, and it startled him. He sprang out of bed and rushed to the door. He quickly opened it, and the maid was standing there with a bundle wrapped in brown paper and tied up with string. Her eyes quickly widened, a look down as quick as a hiccup and then back with a straight look of shock in Roy's eyes.

"Ah, your clothes, sir." She shot the bundle straight armed out towards Roy.

He took the package and mumbled, "Thanks to ye."

The maid immediately turned and nearly ran down the hall as if to escape a sizzling stick of dynamite. Roy glanced down the hall watching her and was confused by her rapid retreat. He stepped back into the room and tossed the bundle onto the bed. He then slowly backed up to see himself in the mirror.

Sweet Lord, I'm naked as an egg!

How was he going to tell Mike he'd have to stay in his room and then sneak out the back in the dead of night so as not to be seen again. Will the local police come to arrest him for his vagrancy? Will women on the streets point and scream at him and yell, "That's him! That's the man! The vile creature with not a drop of decency!" He feared jail was his future now.

He dug out his union suit underwear and put it on and then his new donated clothes. This felt much better, and he felt sharp.

He walked over to Mike's door and knocked. His knock was answered with a soft, "Yep." Roy entered, as Mike was pulling on his boots.

"Tomorrow, we got a lot a gear to get you, son. Some decent boots, work pants, socks, shirts, and a hat. I may not be giving you more than a dollar at the end of the month after it's all tallied, but you can't work on a ranch without proper clothes. Oh, and some gloves. Gotta have good gloves. I like goat skin myself."

Roy thought this must be what Christmas Eve felt like, thinking about a present that would appear the next day. Even more, this was a Christmas to make up for never having a Christmas before. Sure, different villagers always invited him to have Christmas dinner with them as they knew his Aunt Helen never bothered but getting a gift that had meaning had never happened. He was getting weary from receiving so much so fast that it triggered thoughts of how little he had before.

They started down the stairs to ask the clerk about a spot for supper; however, near the bottom, Roy spotted the maid turning to climb the staircase. His entire body puckered as he passed her. He looked at her. She looked back, and he mouthed a silent, "I'm sorry." She glanced up and a quick smile gave him instant salvation. *Reckon I'll not spend the rest of my days in a dark dungeon.*

"Young man, tell me about this grand new hotel. How does something like this come to be? It's quite a place, especially for Montana," Mike said to the clerk.

"The owner and builder is Mr. Robert Vaughn. He built this entire block with the livery and shops. He's quite a successful and brilliant man. If he were around, I'd introduce you to him." The clerk welcomed the opportunity to brag about the hotel.

"How long has Mr. Vaughn been in Montana? Where is he from?"

"His country of birth is Wales, and he is the first European to settle in this area. Some refer to him, respectfully, as The Celtic Cowboy, due to his being a Welshman. He owns a large and successful cattle business near the Sun River Valley to the west of here. He saw the need, and Great Falls is a growing concern."

"Well, I gotta say, I'm impresses with all this. Damn impressed, and you can tell Mr. Vaughn that Mike Hanson from Fergus County is hard to impress."

Mike paid the clerk a dollar for the laundry, raised his arm in the air in thanks and walked to the street. Great Falls was not a big town, but it was bigger than Lewistown. Great Falls held two huge advantages over Lewistown and many other locations. It was on the river, and Mr. James Hill brought the Manitoba Line railroad in 1887. Both areas were filling up quickly with pilgrims and sodbusters from all over the world, a lot of northern Europeans with a few Italians and Slavic stoneworkers.

There were only a few basic shops and stores in Lewistown, so the extras would be purchased here in Great Falls.

"That clerk fella said Mildred's Café has good steaks and pie. Let's try that out after we go check on the sheep." Mike gave a back slap and pointed down the small hill to the stockyards.

After a quick inspection, feed, water, and a chat with the watchman, the men walked back up looking for Mildred's.

"I am sure hungry, Roy. Hit me like a mule kick about 30 minutes ago. Hope I don't fall to hunger, and you have to carry me over your shoulder to rescue."

Roy paused, but an elbow in his ribs let him know that Mike was joking.

In they walked to a nearly full room and grabbed a round table against the wall. A tall, lanky, balding man walked up. "We got mutton chops and potatoes or beefsteak and potatoes. Lemonade or water. What suits ya, gents?"

Mike answered quickly. "Two beefsteaks, lemonades, and pie after. Are you Mildred?" A wide grin followed.

The man answered, "Never heard that one," while rolling his eyes. "I'm Mr. Mildred." He spun around and shuffled back to the kitchen.

"Nice fella. It seemed that everyone to some degree was a good person to Mike. Roy hoped to adopt this outlook, but he knew it was a tall hill to climb. Mike was the most confident man he knew.

The steaks were good, the potatoes hot and swimming in butter, and the apple pie was a first-time treat as well. Mike had his with a big slice of yellow cheese, and he enjoyed every bite as if he were swallowing gold bars.

Mike mumble between bites, "Apple pie without cheese is like a kiss without a squeeze."

The cheese was an interesting choice, and someday Roy would try it, but tonight it was about the sweetness of the hot apples and the crust.

Roy thought how this was the best day of his life so far.

The bill was paid, hats were tipped, and the men walked outside.

"Time for a little perambulation, my boy."

Roy had to ask, "What are we doin'? No notion of what ye just said, Mr. Mike."

"Perambulation. Fancy two-dollar word for walking about." Mike nodded, grabbed his lapels, and took a step.

"Aye, I can do that as well as the next man," said Roy.

The two walked slowly for a change and enjoyed the five blocks walk back to the hotel. They both would sleep well tonight. And in a real bed. This had been a splendid day for both.

The next day began with a knock and a muffled voice saying, "It's 6:00

a.m., Mr. Douglas. Mr. Hanson will meet you downstairs in thirty minutes."

Roy woke up wondering, in all the commotion, if he had thanked Mike at all or enough. Roy realized that he had not moved in this bed all night. Not an inch. It swallowed him, and he did not want to be spit back out.

He unenthusiastically pulled away from the bed as if leaving his first love behind. Dad gum, he loved this bed. There will be other beds, but none like your first.

Roy dressed, gathered his things, but hesitated at putting anything into his old, smelly cloth bag. It was one of his few possessions, and he was fond of this silly old bag, but it had traveled the world with him, and it was his. It was a constant reminder of how little he had when he started on this trek. He wanted more now, not because of want, but because he now knew he would need more. The people he would eventually live life with, a wife and children, would need his help and leadership. And that meant he must learn how to get things. Mike learned how. He would learn from Big Mike.

"Let's grab some breakfast, Roy. I'm hungry as a spring lamb this morning. How'd ya sleep in the bed son?" Mike was back to full steam and busting to start the day.

"I have to say that yesterday was the best day of me life, sir, and I thank ye fer that. Have not told ya, sir, but thank ye much for all a dis. It's a miracle and a dream."

Mike's left hand landed on Roy's right shoulder. "I know you're grateful, and I thank ya for saying so. I know you're glad to be here just from watching you. You're a good man, Roy. You'll be fine. You'll love being in America. Not every day is good, most are hard, but Montana is a good place for bad days."

Montana is a good place for bad days. Roy doubted he would ever forget that.

Another café around the corner provided the men with strong coffee, eggs, ham, and fresh bread. Roy watched as Big Mike ate faster than a pony eating oats out of a bucket. When it came to eating, Mike was a top hand. He must need it because he wasn't fat, just very muscular and solid as a stump. This American food was good, and there was a lot of it at every meal. Besides the beets in Chicago, every-thing Roy had tasted was first-rate.

Leaving the café, Mike pointed to the Southeastern sky and said, "Looks like a little rain down toward Fergus County. Good thing we'll be in the train and not in a wagon."

This was the first time that Roy got his bearings and had a look, a very distant look, at his new home. Now, he was getting a little nervous. How many men would he be working with? What type of men? Fine Christian men or mean pub crawlers looking for blood and battle?

And what about women? The local girls. The sassy one of ill-repute! Hoots mon! Never heard nothin' about women or girls. Only thing he'd heard was when Mike ran from the woman on the train, but that was all. He'd save that information gathering for the final leg of the journey.

CHAPTER 8

"We got a lot to do in a short amount of time, son. I have some feed and animal medicine to pick up. We can grab that before we get on the Stanford train. First, we need to load you up with the clothes you'll need to get through the summer."

Time for Roy's first Christmas.

"We'll get you some good heavy clothes for winter, but that can wait. We'll get you all outfitted. Now, I'll pay, and you get whatever you want 'cause I'm takin' it out of yer pay but not all of it at one time. Reckon you can live with that, son?"

"That is a bonny plan, Mr. Mike. Can't thank ye too much for certain. I'd be open if you could tell me what I be needin'; that would be grand. I dunno what a cowboy wears." Roy had been thinking about how nice it would be to look and dress like Mike and not like a poor Scottish farm boy.

"I'll help ya, son, no worries. There's a store called The Hub in a building called Ulm House, a few blocks from here. Let's go."

The wide dirt streets were already busy with horse riders, wagons, walkers, and a stagecoach with a four-horse team moving slowly up the street. Roy watched the stage pull over in front of a three-story brick building that was next to a cut stone two-story building. He looked up and saw a sign that said ULM HOUSE. The Hub clothing store was on the corner.

The two men walked across the street, stepped up on the wooded sidewalk, and went into the store that had just opened. They were greeted by a small man with a slight foreign accent.

"Good day, men! My name is Thisted, and that is my partner Mr. Brosnan. I'm sure we have all that you need and at a fair price, dats for sure."

"He's a Swede or Norway man; I can tell by his talk," Mike leaned towards Roy and whispered.

Roy was so overrun with new sounds, places, and people that he failed to notice any accent. Everything these past few weeks was new to him except for the sheep.

"I am Hanson from Fergus County. This young fella needs a whole riggin' for working and just livin'. Let's start at his head and work down."

Mr. Thisted became even more energetic as the day would begin with a strong sale just minutes after opening.

"This way please, mister, and veel see to find you a hat that the cows and the girls vill find pleasing!"

Mike let out a small sigh as he knew this man understand the art of selling, which Mike felt would lead to selling large and expensive. Fortunately, Thisted seemed honest. Mike wasn't worried, but he would stay alert.

Roy's eye went straight to a tan-colored, big, round-topped hat that looked like a hat any cowboy would wear with pride. After all, he *was* about to be a cowboy, a real American cowboy. Well, really a sheep-herder, but he'd think of himself as a cowboy.

The clerk handed him the hat. Roy slowly turned it around, then looked inside to the white silk cloth. *What a thing this is*, he thought.

He carefully lifted and placed the hat on his head in a manner similar to a Bishop crowning a King. It was a little snug, but it fit. Even better, it made him feel like a millionaire.

Thisted took the hat from Roy. "I can get a steam to that and give it a stretch. Then a fit that is perfect."

Mike gave a thumbs up and then pointed to the shirt counter. He didn't want to dampen the boy's experience, but they needed to keep the process moving forward.

Next came the shirts. Roy saw one that had small blue dots on white cloth and another that had red strips that ran straight up and down the arms and body. The clerk looked at Mike, who held up two fingers to indicate Roy needed both.

Roy tried one on for size and was delivered two fine new shirts properly and professionally sized.

The britches came next, following Mike's instructions of top to bottom, a suggestion of order and gravity.

Again, Mike held up two fingers. Thisted walked around the counter with a roll of yellow cloth marked with numbers and lines. Without announcement, he reached around Roy's waist to measure. Roy recoiled like an unbroke colt hearing a rattlesnake, not accustomed to being wrestled in such an intimate manner, and by a man no less.

"Forgiven, sir, but ve need to get the numbers right so da pants they fit good."

Thisted reached around from the back and said, "Thirty-four, a big fella ya." Roy didn't think of himself as big, but he was strong and carried no fat. However, compared to the clerk, he supposed he did seem fairly strapping. Another measurement down the outside of his leg delivered the needed arithmetic for the clerk.

Mike had been occupied looking at a bin full of socks and thankfully missed this little episode. Roy's luck was holding up in matters tiny and giant.

The pant choices were basic dark grey with very thin white stripes or black with thin white stripes. One of each were piled next to the shirts.

Next came the underwear. Roy pointed to a red union suit that covered upper and lower in one piece with the convenience of a flap on the backside with two sturdy buttons. However, summertime was coming, and Thisted suggested two pairs of drawers for lower comfort with no top. Roy nodded approval. After all, he was, in reality, paying for it.

Boots.

Next to the hat, Roy knew that boots finished the painting of how a man should appear to the world, and he could only fantasize about how they would feel.

"Sit here, and ve look at how big the foot is." Thisted pulled out a wooden stick with a shorter piece crossing the stick. More numbers and lines, but they made sense to the clerk, so Roy was not concerned.

"Try these, please" The clerk handed him a smooth black boot that smelled like earth and air combined. "Grab the holes and pull. It may be tight."

As Roy was taking off his old, ankle-high thin shoes, Thisted dropped a pair of new socks on his lap. "Please take those old socks off and put them here." He pushed a wooden box at Roy that was full of cloth, paper, and other rubbish. He surmised that this was farewell to the barely recognizable hose.

With new brown socks on, Roy grabbed the holes at the top of the boot and gave a tug. He had to work at it and use a little geometry to get the angle of entry corrected, but the boot covered his foot with what felt like tiny angels rubbing his leg. It felt a little tight, but nothing hurt. A repeat of the next foot equalized his heavenly ascent to American manhood. He stood up and was pitched forward a bit. It was a little awkward, but he reckoned that's how it was done.

"Lean back a little, please. The boot has a heel to catch the stirrup on de saddle better ya?"

A slight tilt back, and the posture problem was corrected. Still, there would be some time needed to break the boots in, but they felt impeccable.

"Don't forget a good wool coat, Roy." Roy was so taken with the boots, he doubted he'd need a coat.

A medium brown wool coat with five buttons and a large collar fit well and was tossed on the pile. It was not a heavy winter coat but a solid coat for most of the times above freezing.

The addition of three pairs of new socks completed the outfitting. It was time to wrap and tally the purchases.

Mike walked up next to Roy and set a fine-looking leather satchel on the counter. "Time to throw your old filthy bag away and carry your gear in this. My treat."

Mike could beat him with a broom stick later, and it would do nothing to diminish Roy's respect and affection for this man.

This is what it feels like to have a father.

"What do I owe you, friend?" Mike asked as he set both hands on the counter.

The clerk slipped a small bill toward Mike and was met with a gold coin pushed back to settle the debt.

"Did ya get a decent belt, son? Damn! Forgot a belt." Big Mike huffed at the additional lost time and not the expense. "And gloves! Go grab some good gloves."

But the clerk was a mind reader and had a black leather belt laid on the counter before Mike could take his next breath. He reached under the counter and set a pair of nice leather gloves with a four-inch cuff. Done.

"This little fella sure knows his business," Mike said to Roy under his breath.

He was right. The entire shopping spree took under 30 minutes. Quality goods and service were delivered as promised.

"Now, take this satchel and your new duds and change into your new clothes. These clothes you got now are too good for working sheep later. Thems your good cloths now for when you go on a picnic with some girl. I'll pay, and we'll figure it all out back at the ranch in a day or two." Mike stepped closer to whisper in Roy's ear. "But them boots, you ain't paying for them. My present to you. Welcome to Montana, son."

As if the day couldn't get better, it did, and it became more memorable.

Roy walked behind a curtain in the back of the store and changed into his new armor. He placed his extras in the shiny leather bag, picked up his new hat, and put it on with his new coat slung over his right forearm.

Two steps out, and he saw himself in a large mirror. Head to toe, he saw an entirely new human. He really looked like a cowboy. This was the first time in his very young life that Roy felt pride. The man he was looking at in the mirror made him proud. He was from Scotland and would always take pride in being a Scotsman. However, he was now… an American.

All goods and livestock were smoothly loaded in Great Falls. The 2:00 p.m. train to Stanford was a 60-mile trip and would take two to three hours.

There would be no more boxcar rides with the sheep today. Roy sat in the train seat across from Big Mike, holding his new hat with both hands, slowly turning it as if it were a plate full of food. He had never possessed anything this fine. Two weeks ago, his entire life had fit in a small cloth bag. Now, he looked and felt like a man of means.

And the boots. The strong smell of clean, tanned leather with a touch of boot polish was, well…it was just bonny.

This was only the second time that Roy had been on a train, sitting in a seat. He was enjoying the views and the stability, but he missed the privacy of the boxcar. It felt slightly odd at being so visible.

He thought, *Now is the time to get more information from Big Mike about himself and the ranch.*

"Can I ask ye a question er two, Mr. Mike?"

"I bet you got more than two! What's puzzlin' ya, Roy?" Mike continued to look over the Great Falls newspaper.

"Does yer ranch have a name?"

"Just goes by The Hanson Ranch near Glengarry. The ranch is on Beaver Creek, so sometimes people call it Beaver Creek Ranch. Then I'll get a bill from town addressed to the Hanson Beaver Creek Ranch or Hanson Creek. Heard a drunk call it The Mike Beaver Ranch. Cripes. People know who I am."

After a short pause, Roy asked, "Are ye a married man?"

Mike stopped reading, but his gaze remained low.

"I was, Roy. Not now because she got sick two years ago, and she up and died."

Roy waited to see if Mike would say more.

"Her name was Clara, and I met her in Bismarck. She was pretty enough, but mostly she was funny, and that made her more beautiful to me. Damn, she was a smart, funny little gal. Got really sad when she died." Mike cleared his throat and looked to the sky. "But ya wake up the next day and get back to work." Mike got quiet, but his voice never broke. Roy felt that he had figured out how to handle the loss by now.

Roy had one more question.

"Do you have a son or daughter?" He was very curious to hear his answer as Mike had referred to him as 'Son' many times since they first met.

"Got the cutest little girl. Grace. She's eleven, almost twelve and she's more like me than her momma. Looks like her but acts like me, and that makes her a bucket full of ornery." Mike gave a small twist of his head and a short puff out of the side of his mouth.

Roy was happy to hear that he had no son. His reasons were honest and logical. He also liked a clean future with no girl his age giggling and fussing around him. He had no experience or idea how to operate girls or women. A lifetime around his Aunt Helen had instilled a reflex to avoid talking to girls or even entering a room with a female. Any female.

That was enough information for now. Roy knew how to stay quiet when need be. He was private by nature, possibly due to the fact that his life, pre-Mike, was boring and had little flavor.

"My man, Elmer, will meet us at the depot, and we'll load up and head home. Should be home by supper time. I been on the road for over a month, near two. It'll be good to be home. I sure miss my little Gracie pretty dang hard. Let's just enjoy the end of the ride, son." This was the first time Roy had seen Mike look alone and empty.

The countryside stayed flat and wide. The grass was a springtime light green ocean with no end in sight, just dips and holes that came back to level. There were mountains in the distance that seemed to be closer than their true distance. Off to the left and the east were the Judith Mountains and to the southeast the Big Snowy mountains. The closer they got to Stanford and to Lewistown, the better he liked the country. The hills began to remind him of The Highlands, and he was beginning to understand why the county was named after a Scotsman.

Strange how this all began in Scotland and would end in a place called Fergus.

CHAPTER 9

Stanford was a rail stop more than a town, with fewer than ten buildings and shacks and the same number of corrals and holding pens. A pair of ramps next to the tracks led down to a small maze of runs to the pens, and it looked like a map would be required to navigate it.

The depot and corrals were empty. It was a quiet, late afternoon and the slow time of year for moving most livestock to or from market. Roy had seen enough movement and newness. It was time to concentrate on the work ahead and to learn American sheep operations.

The big wagon had Hanson Ranch painted on the side, and the sheep were loaded, double stacked, and lashed down. The switch over was quick and flawless. Little time was wasted. Mike pulled on the ropes, climbed up, and told Elmer to roll.

Elmer Barney was driving the big wagon. He wore a large wool sweater and a small driving cap, not a brimmed hat. Roy sensed that there was no need to start any conversation or unload his life story at this point. He would wait and see if Elmer would crack the egg or see if the hen would go broody and sit on the nest. Ranch work allows for many hours of silence or curious palaver.

Elmer was Big Mike's top hand and had been with Mike and

Mike's father, Olie Hanson, since they were both boys. Much of the early story of Olie, Mike and Elmer remained untold. Elmer had come up from Missouri to Montana with Olie and Mike. Elmer was an important person to the success and survival of the ranch, nearly as much as Mike himself. Elmer knew everything that was required to keep things moving and safe. After Olie died in 1878, Elmer became a father-like figure for Big Mike, but he was only two years older. Mike had been born in 1851 in Boone County, Missouri near the river town of Rocheport. His mother had died when he was a baby, and he had no memory of her or any other family or parental symbol. Mike knew little of his own history and past and realized that even if he was curious, there was no one left who knew. This was an all-too-common condition among settlers and pioneer families.

Olie worked as a farmhand and would occasionally find work on the riverboats traveling up and down the Missouri River. When Mike was ten, the Civil War broke out, and Missouri became divided even though it was a slave state. Olie hated slavery and had tolerated the evil practice to earn a living, but he wanted nothing to do with the war. He had taken work on a northbound riverboat and landed in Fort Benton, Montana.

Mike's early instruction had come from Olie and then from Elmer. Small schools in various counties had given Mike enough education to read, write, and learn his numbers. Mike was a very intuitive and naturally smart boy, so a little learning stretched a long way. He was the classic 'self-taught' authority on many topics and issues. He was particularly fascinated with ancient Rome and would re-read *The History of the Decline and Fall of the Roman Empire* by Edward Gibbon with biblical repetition. He also greatly admired Sir Issac Newton and his brilliance, but Newton's work, in general, was much too complex to comprehend, a fact that irritated Mike and made him ache for advanced understanding. Still, he enjoyed the frustrations of intricate issues.

Elmer was a quiet, medium-sized man in his early forties. Age was seldom an exact figure amongst single, western working men or women.

Birthdays were for small children and adults needing to be noticed.

Roy rode on a bale next to the sheep and was attempting to ingest as much of the road and landscape as he could. When everything is new, information needs to be sorted out and graded for significance. He knew he would not need to remember directions or routes now, so he took notice of plants, hills, and sounds.

It was the smell that hit him first. The air held no distinctive aroma, but the lack of strong scent still made it memorable. Maybe it was the days of coal smoke from the ship and then the trains that had dominated his senses and were now being rinsed away. This was a unique clean, and he welcomed the bare air.

Roy watched as the two men sat on the bench seat staring ahead and not talking. He thought it was a little odd that very little conversation was exchanged between men who had been apart for many weeks and who shared the concerns of production and commerce. Yet, they sat, bouncing and rocking in all directions, much like a flag would fly in a soft breeze.

———

Just short of six hours in the wagon and riding on ridges and benches, the road to Lewistown branched off to the south and began to angle its way down to the tree-lined creek bottom. A mile away, Roy could see a group of small buildings, a barn, and a one-story house with chimney smoke.

The Hanson Ranch. Home.

Or Hanson-Beaver-Creek-Big-Mike-Beaver Hanson…ranch.

The wagon jerked as the horse's stutter stepped and locked their legs a bit going downhill. The occasional pull back on the large brake lever biting into the front wheels helped with safety but subtracted a fair amount of comfort from the ride.

The ranch was spread out but had a cozy attitude. The main house was near Beaver Creek with what looked to be a bunk house for the hired hands, fifty feet from the log home.

Cottonwood trees were thick in the creek bottom and created a shady oasis that was the reverse of the bare grasslands on the benches and endless pasture grasslands surrounding the entire area. The trees were just beginning to bud and throw off the cotton that floats though the air and could cover the bare ground as thick as snowfall. Nearly every body of water in Montana, whether flowing, pond, or lake, has cottonwood trees guarding the water's edge.

The wagon headed to the main house first. Mike jumped off and told Roy to grab one end of his trunk and help haul it to the front porch. He then told Roy to toss his leather bag there as well. Elmer drove the wagon to the large barn door to unload the bounty of this Scottish journey.

The sound of running feet was heard, and a young girl in a brown dress ran towards the wagon and directly at Mike. There were no loud yells or screams of joy; just the quiet emotion of seeing the person that means the most to you.

Gracie.

Mike reached down, swallowed her up in his arms, and she laid her head on his shoulder as tight as she could while whispering, "Papa."

Nothing more was spoken. These two needed each other and very little else. He had lost a wife and she a mother, and that singular event glued them together forever. Mike would not let go of her. He shifted her little body to a hip, pointing with his free hand to direct the action. Grace could have stayed like that all day.

Two more men appeared from the barn. They were smaller men with colorful shirts and unique hats that laid flat on their heads but slipping to the side. Two rust-colored, medium-sized dogs ran next to them, circling and watching. The men walked quickly to the wagon, lifted the back board, and waited for Elmer and Mike to come help. Roy knew to follow and stay close to Elmer. Mike walked up to the wagon, but Roy nudged him out of the way, standing next to one of the new men, assuming the boss would not involve himself with a dirty chore such as this. Mike still had his fine traveling suit on as well, but he ignored the dirt over the care for his prized animals.

No one barked out instructions or gave directions, not even Mike. It was clear what the job required . All men knew what to do. Roy watched while helping to learn how the task was attacked.

Each crate was slid to the back, with Elmer pushing in the wagon and then jumping down to lift a corner to the ground. The two men in the odd hats pushed the sheep into the barn, and the process was repeated five more times. Pens inside the barn were already prepared and ready for the new royal guests. Fresh water, oats, and a small scoop of barley were given to each animal.

They looked good: heads held high and no injured legs or visible marks. Roy had heard Mike say that it was nearly five thousand miles from Montana to Scotland, so he took some pride in a flawless delivery.

"Good work, son. They made it just fine." Mike's praise was said loud enough for all to hear but low enough as to not elevate the new man above the veteran hands. "Leave them in the barn for the night, and we'll turn them out in the morning for some fresh grass and running." Mike took a deep breath and released months of planning, travel, thinking, and moving.

A few locals had made it known that they believed that Mike's Scottish venture was foolish and would yield no benefits. Mike knew why he was going and what the gamble would possibly produce. The rams were as fine a sheep as anyone in Montana had seen: Bigger, thicker, and impressive breeding equipment. These two boys would produce an entirely new and stronger herd for Mike, and he had bet a great deal on this idea. The ewes were hardier and bigger than his current flock, and they were beautiful little gals. His Scottish princesses.

The men stacked the crates outside, and Roy found himself feeling sentimental. These crates were built with wood not far from his home, by men he knew, and they represented a good place, but one he knew he'd never see again. The crates were the last touch of Scotland for him.

Roy noticed a nail that had worked its way loose and was barely hanging on in the wood. He grabbed it and, with an easy tug, it came out. He put it in his pocket and imagined it to be his new charm. A nail. A bent old nail. That nail may outlast them all.

"Roy! Where you at, son?" Mike called out from inside the barn for Roy to gather up with the other men.

"Roy, these two men here are Anders and his brother Lon. They're Basco. They're from some place up in the mountains in Spain where none of them gets along, but they're about the best sheepherders in the world. Elmer here worked with some Bascos, and he trusts them. Good boys. Work hard, and they don't speak hardly any English, but we all get along. They stay to themselves, and their little brown sheep dogs are workin' fools."

Roy walked towards the men, took his new hat off, and extended a hand. Each man returned the gesture with one firm pump of the hand and then a release, while touching their foreheads with a tiny salute.

"The dogs are bonnie lads. Good stock." Roy offered the compliment but was met with a stare and no reply. He reached down to pet one of the dogs, but a short whistle quickly called the dog to his master's side.

"They don't know what ya said, Roy, but they know what to do and work hard. They be pickin' up a little language here and there. They repeat what Elmer says sometimes, but he don't say much either. However, he does spit out, 'Sona bitch' a few times a day."

"SOOONA BITCH!"

The younger Basco repeated the words and then smiled, proud to have spoken some English but having no clue as to its meaning or impact.

Mike glanced to the sky in hopeless effort and whispered to Roy, "Little bastard says that 20 times a day."

"So, the four of you stay in the bunkhouse. Elmer will show you. Get settled and then you boys come to the house for supper. Lon and Anders already ate 'cause we were running late. See you at the house in 30 minutes." Mike wheeled around and walked to the house while Anders and Lon returned to the barn to finish the day's last chores.

Roy walked behind Elmer who was heading to the bunkhouse. It was a short, small building, maybe twenty-five feet wide, with a short door. Roy thought he'd need to duck his head to get in.

"I'll grab my things, Mr. Elmer." Roy trotted over to the front porch of the main house to fetch his belongings and then caught up with Elmer.

"Don't call me mister. Just Elmer."

"Fine, sir, I will."

"And no sir either. There's only one boss, one sir, around here and that's Mike."

Roy picked up no anger or frustration from Elmer. He was just stating facts that he wanted understood.

Through the heavy wooden door was a square room, larger than the outside would suggest. There was a medium-sized square wooden table in the middle and five single beds arranged around the perimeter. Each bed had several large nails sticking out from the wall and random shelves of various sizes and materials. A kerosene lamp sat on the table, and small hurricane globe lamps were near each bed.

"The brothers stay in the corner, and I'm here." Elmer pointed to the bed closest to the door. It was tidy with few items displayed. "Pick one of them over there and settle. I'm hungry, so let's not linger."

Roy walked towards the more inviting bed in the corner. It offered more privacy and looked like a little home to him. This was a real bed. It had wooden corners, and a gray blanket was stretched out and waiting. A puffy bag was at the head of the bed filled with loose wool. An actual pillow. It was not as regal as the Hotel Arvon in Great Falls, but it contained all the necessities.

He placed his satchel on the bed and pulled out his few new belongings and his new clothes. Some he hung on the nails, and others he placed on the shelves. He then tossed his hat on the bed, which earned an immediate warning from Elmer.

"Don't do that."

Roy wasn't sure what the problem was or what infraction he had committed.

"Don't throw your hat on a bed," Elmer said without looking up. "It's one of them stupid things some folks think is bad luck. I think it's what idiots think, but don't do it no way. Never know how some fella may be looking for a fight."

Roy snatched the hat and motioned toward the corner post on his bed that stuck up about two feet above the mattress, waiting for Elmer to respond with approval or suggest another action. A quick nod from Elmer cleared the path for acceptable behavior, and a cultural blunder was avoided.

Roy was attempting to learn Elmer's ways. He was like most men

Roy knew. Quiet until provoked, plain on the outside and simply trying to get through each day without drama. Roy had one friend, Big Mike, and he saw no harm in growing his own flock.

Elmer walked to the door and waited. Roy took the hint and fell behind. He would learn from watching more than listening.

Elmer kicked his boots on a rock near the side to the kitchen, more out of habit than need, and walked inside with his new shadow in tow. The kitchen smelled like baked bread and cooked vegetables. Mike was already sitting and halfway through a glass of buttermilk and a slice of bread.

"Couldn't wait, fellas. Sit here, Roy." Mike grabbed the top of the chair to his left and pulled it out a few inches.

"Roy, I ain't gonna feed you, so your gonna need to reach out and take whatcha want, son." Mike appreciated how well-mannered Roy was but was tiring of giving him permission for every movement and action. Nevertheless, Mike understood and was patient.

"Anna, this is Roy. He come all the way from Scotland with me ta handle the sheep. He's a good hand, but he talks too much!" Mike poked an elbow towards Roy's ribs and gave a snort.

Anna Torkelson was a round, short woman of thirty-five. Her blonde hair was braided, wrapped around her head, and pinned high. She had dimples but was otherwise best described as plain and featureless except for her bright blue eyes. She wore a dress in a tent-like fashion with a blue apron around her neck and down past her knees. She had no straight lines about her and resembled a cloud rolling through the kitchen.

"If you vant mur, yust ast me, and I get."

No doubt Anna was a German girl. No nonsense, no real warmth, just work. But this was how strangers in a new land surrounded by uncertainty naturally behaved. The world is a hard place full of treasure and beauty but a hard place, nonetheless.

"Aye, ma'am. Thank ye." Roy looked at the plate full of steaming hot food. It was more food than he would have eaten in one day, maybe two, back home.

The plate was full of a potato, bread, some meat, and bright orange carrots. Carrots. He'd seen them a few times, and always in the summer, but not in the spring. Miraculous. The meat was mutton, of course, and there was butter for the bread. This couldn't possibly be how they ate every day?

"Good, huh?" Big Mike mumbled between bites. "Anna's a fine cook. She cooked up a feast for me tonight knowing I had been missing her cooking all these weeks away. Can't eat like this every meal."

Roy would learn that Anna was a childless widow who had come to America five years ago with her Swedish husband, when he promptly died from a fever, leaving her alone and far from her familiars. Mike had met her down in Billings at a sheep sale two weeks after her husband passed. She had been walking around selling meat pies and small cakes amongst the bidders trying to earn enough to survive. Mike had bought one, found it to be exceptional, and had asked her if she made it. Speaking very little English, they both struggled to be understood, but they managed to create a connection. She then followed Mike around for the rest of the day, ready to sell him more the instant he was ready. He found her persistence amusing, and she was also a fine cook and baker.

Near the end of the day, Anna reappeared with another young woman, who would act as an interpreter. Anna uttered some fast and hard German looking straight at Mike. He shrugged and the other girl spoke up.

"She needed you to be cook at your ranch of you," the girl said in understandable, but busted, English.

"I got a cook, lady."

That was technically correct but not accurate. A few months earlier, his cook, a Russian woman, had left without warning, and the cooking duties were being shared by Elmer and himself. He thought he could survive without a real cook, but no man on the ranch had had a tasty meal for months.

"Hold up now, how much you need for pay, girl?" Mike quickly reassessed his current eating dilemma and saw a quick fix staring right at him.

The friend whispered to her in German, and Anna turned and held up all ten fingers, flashing them twice.

Mike wondered if she meant twenty dollars a week or per month.

Twenty a week was too much and twenty per month wasn't a fair wage for anyone. Mike tapped the interpreter on the shoulder and said, "Tell her ten dollars a week, and she would have her own room."

The message was relayed and in less than 5 seconds, Anna was repeating, "JA! JA! JA!" until Mike held up his hand to quiet her. She smiled, grabbed his big hand, and shook until he was sure walnuts would fall from his head.

"Tell her to be at the hotel at 10:00 tomorrow morning with her things, and she can come back with me."

Again, a short delay, another bucket full of JA's, a curtsey from both women, and away they trotted.

The next day, they rode back to Lewistown on Mike's huge wagon. They would get about halfway home and stay the night at a friend's ranch near Roundup. She looked innocent, happy, and safe. Mike was a caretaker and attached himself to the needy, whether human or critter. Anna was in need of a kindness.

Anna picked up the empty plate in front of Mike. "I has the Chokecherry pie made for you, Mike. Special for coming home now."

Roy was about to taste the best thing he'd ever put in his mouth.

Chokecherries were a local favorite. They grow in other places but, for an unknown reason, they thrived in Fergus County and were a prized treat. Small, hard, and a dark red, the Chokecherry is about 90% hard pit and the size of an acorn. Women had been canning and preserving these sour little bullets for years, and the county fair tables were unusually covered with jams and pies, all competing for ribbons. A fair amount of sugar is needed to balance out the tartness, but when the balance is correct, it becomes a beautiful thing.

Mike loved two kinds of pie: chokecherry and rhubarb. He would take a horse kick to the head for either one, but rhubarb was a summertime treat, and the Chokecherries stayed better when canned.

"Der you have, Mester Mike."

A beautiful, golden pie was placed in front of Big Mike, and Anna waited for his reaction.

"Holy smokes! That looks mighty tasty, girl. But did you make two 'cause you and the boys may want a piece, and this one is all mine!"

Roy saw Elmer crack a small grin while looking at the pie. This must be something good.

"Oh, Mike, you are a big funny man. You get fat like me if you eat whole pie!" Anna wiped her hands and grabbed a knife to cut the pie.

Roy took a bite and let it sit in his mouth. The crust soaked in the dark purple juice, and he let it dissolve slowly. He chewed deliberately while Mike took small bites and moaned with satisfaction. His pleasure made Anna feel like a queen, and she loved how much he showed his enjoyment.

"Nobody will ever make a better pie than Anna. Nooooo body!" Mike winked at her, and she turned away in embarrassment.

When they had all sat down for supper, Roy could only see the food. He viewed The Hanson Ranch as a group of workers and immigrants in the first few hours.

Now he could see family.

CHAPTER 10

The first few months of life on the ranch for Roy were smooth and routine. It helped that he was familiar with farm work and that sheep are sheep whether in Scotland or Montana. Every day was filled with hours of work and that leaves little time for personal conflict or other distractions. This scenario could not have been better for a new man like Roy to learn and assimilate. Pressures were low, and life was quiet and routine.

Horses were quickly becoming Roy's new passion and curiosity. He had been around animals of all sorts in Scotland, and he was familiar with horses, mainly large draft horses. The Hanson Ranch had two very fine Belgian drafts, one Bay and one Gray dappled, the team that Elmer was driving when Roy first came to the ranch.

The real bonus for Roy were the other horses: the riding horses of assorted colors, sizes, and temperaments. The ranch had a decent string of working stock and a few mounts that stood out. Each hand had an unwritten list of favorites that included two or three ponies that were mostly exclusive to each hand. Roy enjoyed the process of discovering how each animal behaved and responded to the world and to being a work partner with a rider. Sheepmen need good horse stock too.

Cowboys need a strong and agile horse with great endurance. It was not unusual for a cowboy to change horses two or three times each day so as to not harm to his mount. His string of horses was critical to his ability to work, his comfort, and often his survival.

Working sheep is not as hard on a horse as dealing with cattle. The speed required is less, and the need to cut or separate sheep is slower. When roped, a sheep weighs a fraction of what a cow does, and the strain of dragging an animal is less.

However, sheepmen still need good stock to ride, and they can spend many hours in the saddle. A smooth gait and ride make the day better for certain.

A good dog can be a lifesaver for both man and horse.

And they all needed good dogs.

Working cattle is different than herding sheep. Both are greatly helped by having dogs. Cattle dogs work in a slightly louder and more aggressive style. A heifer with a calf can be nearly impossible to move at times and, when coupled with a mother's protective nature, are not manageable beasts. Cattle dogs bark more and will nip at the hooves and fetlocks to pester and irritate them until the animal moves. A good dog is a working cattle horse's best friend and will save the cowboy and horse from making runs into rough terrain, heavy brush, and hillsides that will wear a good horse out. The dogs can dart side to side and allow the horse and ride to stay on the level trail.

A good cow dog has a little wild dog in him. They are stocky, have great endurance, and are stubborn. They are unique and dependable animals.

Sheepdogs are different than cow dogs. The sheepherder needs his dog more, and the bond between dog and human is stronger and can be more affectionate. The average sheepdog is a fine, handsome animal. They have longer hair and a sleeker body. Overall, they are beautiful creatures.

Both cow and sheepdogs are smart, but sheepdogs tend to be clever and thoughtful. They run on instinct but can also be highly trained to respond to whistles and hand signals. Few shepherds would prefer to work without a dog or dogs. A sheepherder's life is more isolated and lonelier, and the companionship of a good dog is unequaled.

The dogs that Anders and Lon owned were spectacular little fellas. They were Basco dogs and were more brown and shorter coated than the Border Collies more common in the British Isles. Durable, smart, and very quick, they were fun to watch as the brothers worked with the dogs to sort into groups and pens. The brothers were immensely proud and highly protective of their dogs. They were not pets, and no one besides Anders or Lon interacted with them. They considered them tools, but when the work was done, the dogs were showered with affection and attention. Roy thought of his old dog, Ned, often while watching them work, and he knew the future would give him another barking brother soon enough.

The horses on the Hanson spread were not top stock but dependable animals, bought and sold often or when a 'deal' appeared. Springtime was a good time to refresh ranch stock. Most ranches kept their best stock near the ranch in the winter. Most animals had shoes removed and were turned out to roam free. The tough and strong would survive, and the weak would not. Keeping and feeding hay and grain to the twenty or more horses was an expense most ranches could not afford. Depending on the winter, it was common for a small number of horses to not find their way back. Cold, old age, predators, and lack of good feed all culled the herd and was a necessary process for the natural order.

Roy had quickly become a solid horseman and rider. He loved the horses, and they returned the affection by behaving slightly better for Roy than the others. He had a gentleness and soft touch when handling animals of any sort, and he was rewarded with responsive obedience from most of the stock.

He had his favorites, but he seemed to find the best in all and enjoyed the individual habits of each animal.

Mike could see that Roy was a fine sheep handler, but his affections and skills were growing quickly for horses. He was proud of how Roy had assimilated and melted into the fabric of Montana.

The spring lambing season was nearing the end, and all were glad to get past the 24-hour schedule and constant attention the ewes and lambs required. Roy had spent his entire life pulling, cleaning, and bottle-feeding lambs and required no instruction from Mike or Elmer.

In fact, Mike told him he had no idea how they had gotten through the past few springs without him, and even Elmer complimented him after helping to deliver a difficult pair of twin lambs.

Daily work, more horse riding, and training made the days speed by, and the evenings were always filled with fine suppers cooked by Anna and a sit down in the rocking chairs on the porch with Mike and Elmer. Some evenings were filled with words and conversation, while others were quiet and celebrated the sunsets. A quick good night and the short walk back to the bunkhouse ended yet another day of hard and honest work.

Roy often thought, *How could this be any better? This is the best way I can live.*

In a few weeks, he would experience his first American Independence Day, and he had no idea what to expect.

CHAPTER 11

Lewistown was prettier than Roy had expected. Coming from the western part of Fergus County into Lewistown felt like a pageant. The flat, wide prairies and benches led to the edge of town and the highest point of the surrounding area. The main road led to the edge of the bowl and below to the east lay Lewistown. He had imagined what it would look like the first time Mike told him about Fergus County, but it was wider, cleaner, and had more trees than he had invented in his head.

The road headed straight down the hill and into the low area where the town was built. Stone buildings on each side of the street gave it an older and more powerful presence than most of the other towns he had passed through. Stone and rubble lay on the ground all over as new construction was underway, and it was easy to see how the town would grow and prosper in the coming years.

"This town's gettin' a bunch of stone cutters from the old country. Some place called Crow something. Ain't Crow Indians, just Cro...I don't know." Mike trailed off. He wasn't interested in sounding uninformed.

Roy would later learn the stone cutters were from Croatia. It was across the sea from Italy. They spoke a new language and had taken to living and working in Fergus County. They were excellent craftsmen and were welcomed and fully employed.

Roy and Mike could see the red, white, and blue banners and bunting hung across Main Street and on nearly every building that had a bare spot. There was lots of color, and the warm morning breeze brought life to the scene.

As a Scotsman, Roy felt that he could share in the celebration of whipping the British and kicking them out of America. Most Scots, while not actively rebelling against the Brits, had a long history and distrust of the ruling class and the British government. All Scots knew and revered William Wallace and Robert The Bruce, and he carried extra rebellion in his heart today.

Wagons and bales were lined up and down Main Street waiting for the parade to start at noon. The Hanson Ranch wagon brought Mike, Grace, Elmer, Anna, and Roy into town for the celebration. Lon and Anders preferred to stay at the ranch. There would be too much noise for the dogs to handle. Anna was especially buoyant and perky today. Roy enjoyed seeing her in sunlight and happy. She was a simple woman, and the occasional flash of joy from Anna was fun and soothing. Days like these were important to ranch families and townsfolk alike. Repetition, drudgery, and bone-aching work were the standard. This day wasn't simply a holiday; it was a necessity.

Horses and riders carrying flags began nervously walking and stomping to lead the short spectacle. A wagon covered with flags followed, and a man in a fancy suit and big tan hat stood and waved to both sides of the street. Roy had no idea who the man was or why he was waving, but he clapped his hands along with everyone else and felt proud. A small band of musicians followed and played very loud and rousing music. The six men marched in unison. Despite having blue ill-fitting uniforms, they managed to project respect. A fire wagon covered with hoses and brass was next, and the Lewistown Volunteers marched together, six men on each side. Each man carried an axe, a bucket, or a long pike, and they all looked like giants. Roy could sense the pride these men displayed, and he absorbed it as they passed.

He thought, *America is full of real men.*

Finally, a wagon stacked with barrels marked Montana Brewing Co. Great Falls concluded the organized parade and kicked off the rowdy and loud portion of the day. Men quickly walked up to the wagon, and any empty container or cup was filled with foamy beer. Roy noticed protective mothers and a few clergy in tight collars shepherding small children from the area and covering their eyes as they walked. The decent folk of Lewistown would do their drinking at night and sin behind the barn privately.

Mike and Roy jumped down to the street. Grace jumped into her father's arms from the wagon, and Roy looked up to assist Anna. Elmer was already helping her. She put both hands on his shoulders, and he reached up to her waist to lift her off. There was something amusing in the way they reacted to being seen touching each other in public. They had just tipped their cards. Roy had no one to gossip with, so he laughed lightly to himself.

Food was everywhere on tables, and hundreds of people milled around piling tin plates with roasted pork, mutton, and beef. The tables covered in pies were a very popular spot, and women in aprons were handing out slices of pie on pieces of newspaper. Old men and toddlers alike enjoyed the sweetness and the pleasure of these local treats. Children gobbled the pie. They would occasionally drop some on the ground and would pick it up, blowing dirt and grass off the fragment. The older men and women took more care while eating, knowing that dirt and straw were not a desired ingredient to any pie. They chewed slowly, as if each mouthful were a kiss from a lost love, not wanting the memory of the flavor to disappear so soon.

Roy watched his new neighbors and thought how similar they all seemed to the people he knew in Scotland. Regardless of hair color or style of hat, they all smiled when happy and showed affection to their families and kindness to strangers as well. It was comforting to see and know that the differences between the people here in Montana and those in Scotland was small and often invisible.

A man walked by with a hand-painted board about three feet tall. It had an American flag with forty-four stars and writing below. Roy asked the man to stop and allow him to read the words. The man quietly stopped and stood at attention.

By signing the Declaration of Independence, the fifty-six Americans pledged their lives, their fortunes, and their sacred honor.

It was no idle pledge.

Nine signers died of wounds during the Revolutionary War. Five were captured or imprisoned. Wives and children were killed, jailed, mistreated, or left penniless.

Twelve signers' houses were burned to the ground.

Seventeen lost everything they owned.

No signer defected.

Their honor, like their nation, remained intact.

Roy reread the last line. The word honor jumped out at him. A minute ago, the gathering was about food and parades. He knew nothing about the history of the United States. He would read and discover all he could about this land that he now called home. He felt he owed it to the men named on the sign. He owed it to the man holding the sign.

"Me name is Roy Douglas, sir. Thank ye fer showing me this."

"I'm Walter Madsen. Fought in the war with the 2nd Minnesota Infantry Regiment. Took a mini ball in my leg at Chickamauga. Born in Norway, but I 100 percent American."

Roy put out his hand, and Madsen took it. They shook. Roy felt he had touched a part of history. He needed to learn about this place called America.

Two hours passed of handshakes, chatter, and food.

"Best be headed back home, Roy. Help me find Elmer. If you find Elmer, you'll rightly find Anna," said Mike as he walked with Grace trailing just behind him.

As usual, Mike was correct in his predictions, and Roy soon spotted Elmer and Anna walking together. He pointed to a walking Mike headed back to the wagon. Elmer nodded and instantly took a full step sideways away from Anna so as not to contribute to the budding love story more than needed.

"Papa, if we go home now, we won't see the fireworks! They said there was going to be some pretty fire up in the sky. Can we stay to see it?" Grace tilted her head with a combination of innocence and cunning as only a pampered daughter could manufacture for use on a father.

The others in the wagon wondered the same thing but did not speak. To do so would seem ungrateful for the gifts of the day, but all on board had hopes of seeing the arial treats.

"Don't fret, Lammy Girl, you'll see it. We'll watch from the top of the hill on the way home, best place to watch." Mike kissed Grace on the head and nodded for Elmer to start rolling.

Once again, Roy saw how Mike took care of everyone in his world and never missed large or small events and details. He wished many times that Mike was his father. Minus the legal paper and long history, he was. Mike was as much of a father as Roy would ever need.

The ride back to the ranch was a little less than two hours, and the long Montana summer nights made traveling in the evenings an easy, enjoyable event. The sun would hang color in the northwestern sky until nearly 10:00 p.m., and they would all be home before lighting a lantern would be necessary.

Elmer pulled back on the reins and set the big brakes on the wagon. They were on top of the hill to the west of Lewistown They could see all the people still gathered and could hear their loud and happy voices.

Mike took out his watch and said, "They should start making some noise and fire in a few minutes."

Elmer climbed down, dropped a lead rope from each halter of the Belgians and held the rope in case the sights and sounds caused a blow up. He had a pocket full of oats and would offer the treat to the mighty beasts if they startled.

"Look, papa! There's one!" Grace's sweet voice rose a full octave and was full of happiness.

The sky sparkled with color as the fireworks shot up one at a time. Fortunately, the noise was not alarming, and the animals didn't seem to notice. Thunder was louder, and they had heard that many times before.

Anna walked to the horses and stood about two feet away from

Elmer, just close enough. Roy spent more time watching his 'family' react to the sights and sounds than he did the fireworks.

These are all fine people, Roy thought. *What luck to be near so many kind and decent folks.*

Mike was the hub, and this was a wheel that was balanced and true.

CHAPTER 12

The months passed through summer and into fall. Roy watched, absorbed, and learned about American ranching, American culture, and Montana society. The amount of knowledge and experience presented to him since his departure from Scotland was staggering but manageable. It was also the most exciting time of his young life.

Each day contained lessons worthy of time spent at a college. Mike and Elmer were both excellent professors in the general education of land and animals. Both possessed practical knowledge and smaller doses of book-learned knowledge.

Elmer turned out to be a more patient man than Roy had first expected. He talked very little but shared knowledge through intentional moments of work stoppages meant to give Roy time to observe and then implement. The hands-on lessons from Elmer were efficient and effective. They also revealed a small dose of humanity from a man who had no son himself and understood the value of patriarchal presence. Elmer knew that Mike was the true father figure in Roy's life, but he felt he also could contribute to Roy's delayed upbringing. He showed little to no emotion, but his actions were an obvious display of tutoring and teaching.

Elmer was a fine horse handler, and Roy was keen on stealing every ounce of guile and magic he could from Elmer. Roy fell in love with the horses early, and his respect for these beasts was broad and genuine. He loved them all. He enjoyed the differences in size, temperament, and gait of each horse. The variety made them fun. While most men shied away from the rougher stock, Roy liked the challenge of taking a mount that most would avoid. He felt each animal had a reason for any ill behavior they displayed, and he was patient enough to learn and manage this conduct.

Roy was a natural horseman, which was a fortunate attribute for anyone whose job required long hours in a saddle. He was a natural, but he worked at it hard and took pride in his above-average stock handling abilities.

The Basco boys were also adequate riders but emphasized care for sheep much more than horses. They used the horses as it was easier to ride than to walk, but in hilly or rough terrain, most Shepards found it easier to walk. You would often see them unmounted, picking their way over rough ground.

Sheepmen spent long miles mounted as well, but it was a slower way to ride. The dogs do most of the running and gathering while moving sheep, and that allows the herder to be more watchful and aware of minor events and situations. Sheep move in much different ways and speeds than cattle and require patience. They generally stay close together and move as a group. They will dart off and disrupt this pattern, but the dogs are the perfect tools for any attempts at independence. Yearling sheep move more like a school of fish. They get nervous when they're not in direct contact with other sheep and will rotate as a giant ball with the sheep on the outer edges running while the interior of the ball will barely move. There are few straight lines while moving sheep, and this is one of many differences a sheepherder faces compared to a cowboy moving cattle.

————

The summer was spent moving sheep in the foothills of the mountains into the higher pastures where the grass was long and healthy. Anders and Lon spent the entire summer in the mountains with the main flock, living in a sheepherder's wagon. These wagons looked like pioneers' covered wagons but often had a metal or tin roof and a solid back end with a door. A bed and small cooking area gave them all they needed for long stays away from the ranch. They preferred the isolation, and it was easier for most Basque shepherds not to have contact with other nationalities. Language and culture were the main reasons, but generations of working alone and isolated created a loner mentality in the men as well. They needed nor wanted little.

Roy would accompany Elmer to resupply the Basco boys. Elmer drove the wagon, and Roy rode ahead to scout and locate the flock, which was in a new location nearly every day. Some trips took two or three days and, as the sheep moved deeper into the mountains, a four-day round trip was more common. Roy loved the rides and the time in the mountains. He never tired of the long hours on the trail.

He imagined someday riding behind a great cattle herd, pushing heifers and calves to fresh pastures, and the continuous sound of hundreds of cattle. He had been around sheep his whole life, but cattle seemed to be a step up and possessed more romance. Unfortunately, he didn't know how to rope cattle, but he was determined to learn soon.

———

As autumn neared, the roundup would begin. This was an event that every ranch, cattle or sheep, participated in with no exception. Animals spent the summer in high mountain pastures grazing and getting fat on rich grasses, and when the air snapped cold in September and October, it was time to come to the valleys and lower pastures for the winter.

The entire ranch would pack up and help with bringing the sheep home. It was not easy work, but it was a time for a ranch to feel like family and spend a few days together in the beautiful mountains. Grace was always thrilled to be included on the roundups. She had her own horse, a small little chestnut gelding that was almost 20 years old. His name was Apple. The horse had stolen a crab apple from Grace's hand when she was two years old. She yelled out, "APPLE!" and the name stuck, replacing his original name that no one seems to recalls. He was the perfect horse for a young child, and all on the ranch treated him like a prince. He did, after all, belong to the Princess.

The big wagon was covered with a heavy canvas cloth, and the belongings and provisions for the party were all inside. Food, water barrels, extra clothing, bedding, and two small tents were loaded, and Anna would come as the camp cook.

For ten days, the small band worked their way from the rocky high pastures down to the more open, large bowls and then to the flatter, open ranges. The sheep moved easier as they sensed the move to warmer conditions and safety. Each day would begin with a good breakfast, wrangling of the horses, and then breaking camp. Roy was raised on tea but quickly learned the taste of coffee in the morning was more helpful and was more American. Coffee was harder to make, but it was worth the effort. He doubted he could ever return to tea after the strong, bitter punch that cowboy coffee delivered.

The constant threat of predators in the mountains made the already nervous critters more skittish and noisier. They knew they were an unnatural part of the food chain, and the coyotes, wolves, and bears all feasted on the odd wandering sheep. The best that could be done was to limit the loss and hope that the number of lost animals was smaller than the previous year. The Bascos relied on loud shotguns and their dogs to deter the killers, and constant vigilance was the only effective prevention.

The wandering crew finally made its way to the pastures surrounding The Hanson Ranch by mid-afternoon on the tenth day. Gates were opened, and the dogs made quick work of routing the thousands of sheep into the controlled area. They would attempt to count the sheep, but the only accurate measure was during shearing time in the spring. The number of sheep was always surprising, as they were small animals and packed into any area tightly. The same pen that held one hundred cattle could hold five hundred sheep.

Their wool was getting heavier and would allow survival even in the harsh Montana winters. The ranch offered running water with

Beaver Creek flowing for miles throughout, regular hay feedings, and protection from the wind with many natural rock formations and a few wind walls that Mike had constructed. The extreme cold and occasional predator that would come down for an easy meal were the only real dangers to the flock.

The ranch was settling into the routine of winter. Now the sheep, horses, and the five milk cows would need daily manual feeding. Sunny weather or blizzard, the chores must and would be done. Roy had not experienced a true Montana winter and had only the memories of cold and damp Scottish winters. He would find this place to be an extreme environment. The 100-plus degree days of summer would be replaced by 30 to 50 below zero temperatures. The first snow fell on September 19th. It was early but not uncommon.

———

Mike had returned from one of his monthly trips into Lewistown late in the day. He would leave before sunrise and return late the next day. Sometimes, he would haul a few sheep to market and sell or barter for goods. There was a local slaughterhouse on the edge of town that would butcher and process the sheep and keep the ranch supplied with meat. He would exchange some mutton for beef, but the cost of the beef was much higher than the mutton, so beef was an occasional treat. Mike was as tough as leather, but he had no stomach for killing the animals that he shared the ranch with. It was necessary to do so in the winter at times, but he preferred to hire out the job when possible.

Mike rode one horse and packed another animal when a wagon was not needed. The horse with the sawbuck pack saddle had two large canvas bundles hanging from each side and another less uniform pack on the top. He rode up to the hitching rail near the front porch of the main house and was met by Anna and Elmer who helped untie and off load. One would lift while the other loosened the ropes, and the packs were laid on the porch. Most of the load was food stuffs, flour, sugar, coffee, etc. Some mail and older newspapers were tied up with string and set aside for Mike.

"Come over here, son." Mike held a package wrapped in paper about the size of large bag of flour. He tossed the package to Roy and said, "See if these work for ya."

Roy rolled the package over trying to assess the contents and value.

"It ain't gonna pop open by itself, fella!" Mike watched while hiding a small smile.

The string was untied, and the paper peeled away.

It was full of shaggy black wool. For a moment, Roy had no idea why he was gifted with a sack of wool. Then he saw a belt with a brass buckle. Then small straps that were sewn to the sides.

"That Finnish boy in town told me he'd make me a pair of chaps if I gave him some fleece, so I gave him six sheepskins, and he made me a pair of these wooly chaps. Well, the dang things is too small for me. Try 'em on. I bet they fit you."

Roy knew that Mike already had a new pair of beautiful shotgun-style wooly chaps. Roy had commented on how much he admired them and how he was saving up for a pair of his own. He gave them a shake and held them up for inspection. He swung the left legging around his back and buckled the belt. Then, reaching down the back of each leg, he buckled the four thin, smaller straps with the attacked buckles. He felt like a cattle baron.

"Lucky that they fit you 'cause they're too tight on my old fat ass!" Mike said this loud enough for all to hear and to confirm his story of mistaken construction versus a gift to Roy. "The Finn boy felt bad, but I told him I'd find a use for them." Mike continued the ruse for effect. "How about you buy them for five dollars, and we'll be done with it?"

Roy had purchased an old leather pair of shotgun chaps from Elmer in the spring for three dollars and had worn them all summer and fall. Elmer had also instructed him on the proper pronunciation of the item: SHAPS. Like sheep, not like cheap. It's how the Mexicans said it. A new pair would cost eight dollars, maybe ten, in Great Falls. And new wooly chaps would cost a working hand at least $12 dollars. Three dollars was a solid transaction, but it was as close to free as possible without causing a ruckus.

"That's a deal, and I'll be proud to wear these, sir." Roy shook

Mike's hand and gave a small extra squeeze to further relay his gratitude.

Mike looked him in the eye and gave him one of his signature winks. "Your helpin' me out, son, by taking them ugly things off my hands."

There was nothing ugly or worthless about these chaps. They were beautiful, and any man that saw them would believe the same.

Roy's new chaps became a necessity as the snow flew two days later, and this time, it stuck to the ground. Just two inches, but it was nature announcing its intentions to get ornery.

————

Elmer, Mike, and Roy all spent the next day pulling shoes off most of the horses as they would be turned loose for the winter into the pastures and would surely roam far from the ranch. They kept eight horses in the barn for winter riding stock as well as the two Belgians who rarely saw a day without work.

Elmer was a good farrier, and it was his job to keep the horses shod and healthy. He took extra care with the Belgians and babied them whenever he could. They worked hard, and Elmer always spent more time with them. They were the most valuable animals on the ranch and were worthy of special attention.

"I'm gonna show you how to shoe a horse, boy. It ain't easy. It's easy to hurt their feet, so watch close."

Roy was a bigger man than Elmer and, as he first bent over and raised a front hoof between his legs, he realized how skilled and strong Elmer was.

An hour of lifting, struggling, and pulling told Roy all he needed to know about farrier work.

Shoeing was not something Roy enjoyed, but he needed to learn how it was done.

"Is Mike good at shoeing horses?" Roy was curious and was sure Mike was an expert.

Elmer responded without looking up and continued sliding the file across the bottom of a hind hoof. "He's no good at all. Hates it. That's why you and me is stuck doing this."

Roy was surprised to learn of a skill that Mike did not possess. It also gave him reassurance that if a man became the boss, he could escape certain jobs, and the job that Roy would most like to avoid was shoeing a horse.

Elmer was done with the first Belgian before Roy hand cleaned up the front feet of the next horse. He would learn how to clean, nip, rasp, and file the hoof before he was trusted with fitting and nailing, but he was getting faster and understood the process better with each completed hoof.

The day was spent in the barn, and after a few hours, the winter riding stock and the Belgians were wearing new iron. The shod stock would stay in the fenced-in pasture and were allowed access to the barn for feeding and to escape bad weather.

December 1891 was milder than the previous winter, but it was still cold, and early snows had painted the ground with six inches of fresh powder. Roy felt the difference in the snow between Scotland and Montana. Here, it was light and fluffy and didn't stick to your boots as it did in the Highlands. He much preferred the Montana snow. It came in a colder package that he felt was worth the price.

This would be his first Christmas in America. It was his first Christmas ever. Grace was constantly talking about St. Nick's visit and how they would sing songs on Christmas eve, songs her mama sang to her when she was little. She didn't remember much about her mother, but Christmas time seemed to revive the few memories she held.

Roy wasn't familiar with gift giving, and it wasn't standard practice with many families, but Mike had mentioned that everyone would get a gift, and none would be expected in return. The notion of receiving anything more from Mike was unsettling, and he wanted to tell him he didn't want or deserve a present. He had already been given a lifetime of favors and more would be gluttonous, but the idea of sitting with a family, his new family, singing songs and eating goose and custard pie was exciting and new.

Mike had a trip planned to head into Lewistown a week before Christmas, and this time he took the wagon. He bundled extra fleece and an elk robe in the bag and brought along wood and a bottle of kerosene for a fire in case he met with harsh weather. He said he had some bank business to see to, but everyone knew he was bringing back gifts, so they all played along to not spoil the delight Mike felt in giving. He gave a wave as the wagon rolled through the snow and headed to town.

CHAPTER 13

The normal routine had Mike leaving at dawn one day and returning by sunset the next day. However, by 10:00 p.m. in the evening of the second day, Mike had not returned. Over the years, he had been known to be late only once. That was during the summer, and his horse had come up lame, and he was forced to walk himself and the horse back halfway from town. He spent a few hours resting and napped under a tree for a few hours and showed up at the ranch early the next morning. However, this current delay was unusual and had the entire household on edge.

Elmer told Roy to go to bed and that he would wait up for Mike. He would take a couple of extra lanterns down the lane to help Mike see if he returned that night. Roy walked into the bunkhouse, Anders and Lon were sitting at the table. They both looked at Roy, and he simply shook his head no. The brothers looked down and continued playing cards. Roy knew he would not sleep, so he grabbed one of his books, laid back in bed, and read. He found himself rereading pages as he was not retaining anything he had just read. He surrendered to the failing effort and decided to try to sleep. He had no religion or beliefs, but he quietly said a prayer for Mike's return.

Roy woke around 5:00 a.m., dressed, and walked into the kitchen. Anna was up and had coffee made as well as biscuits. She was about to fry some eggs as Roy poured himself some coffee. He walked into the living room and found Elmer in a chair near the fire, asleep with his boots and coat still on. Elmer opened an eye and saw Roy standing with his coffee.

"I'm gonna head into town after I eat something." Elmer sat up, rubbed his head, and stretched his legs out straight. He rose up out of the chair, and Anna met him within two steps with coffee. He took a sip and let the warmth wake him.

"Let me go. I should go. You need to stay here and run things. I can't do what you can do here, but I can ride." Roy was asking more than telling Elmer what to do.

"I should go. Mike would expect that." Elmer took another taste of coffee.

"I think he rather have you here taking care of things and to take care of Grace." Roy played the Grace card early, and he felt it was the winning move.

Elmer sipped on the coffee and sat back down. He wanted to do everything himself and not rely on Roy or anyone, but he knew it was best to have Roy find Mike.

"Eat some breakfast, take an extra biscuit, and I'll go saddle a horse for you. Wear anything warm that you have. Anna, cook the boy two eggs and fill him up. He's riding into town in 30 minutes."

Roy doubled his socks and put on an extra shirt, a wool vest, and the heavy wool coat he had bought in Great Falls. He wore a large wool scarf that he used to tie down his hat and cover his ears. He put his woolly chaps on over his wool pants and a leather holster that held a Colt revolver. When leaving sight of the ranch, a rifle or pistol was required.

Elmer brought the horse to the hitching rail at the house. The sun would be up soon, but it was still very dark. The shortest day of the year was near, and the sun would not appear until after 9:00 in the morning. The stars were still on full display, and the sky was clear and cold. Elmer had tied two heavy wool blankets on to the back of the saddle and had put matches, loose wool, and a little sawdust in one of the saddlebags for fire starting if needed. Anna brought out a canteen full of water in a fleece lined bag to keep the water from freezing and hung it on the saddle horn.

"Hurry but don't be hard on the horse. Their shoes will catch snow and ice, so check their hooves. Go." Elmer stood holding the halter.

Roy grabbed the horn, pulled up, and took one bounce while throwing a leg over. He adjusted his heavy clothes and put weight in the stirrups. A gentle heel kick and pull of the reins turned the horse towards town.

———

Normally, it took around two hours to get to Lewistown. The snow made footing tougher, and it was wise to go slower. It had been light for an hour, but the sun was still below the horizon. Roy was not cold and found it odd that his first solo expedition from the ranch was a rescue mission. His head was battling thoughts of new adventures against concerns for Mike. He was irritated that he couldn't enjoy a perfect December morning.

Once in Lewistown, he started at the boarding house where Mike usually stayed. He didn't see the wagon or horses out front as they would most likely be at the livery. Roy walked up and knocked at the door. An older man answered, opened the door, and motioned for Roy to come in. He quickly closed the door on the chilly morning.

"I'm Roy from The Hanson Ranch. Mr. Hanson didn't come home."

The man nodded and waved for Roy to follow, not saying a word. He pointed to the stairs and said, "Room number two."

Roy walked up and knocked on the door with a small painted two.

"Hello? Who is it?" It was Mike's voice. Roy took a big breath and slowly exhaled.

"It's Roy, Mr. Mike."

"Come on in, son."

"I reckon I shouldn't be surprised to see you, but I am just a little."

Mike was still in bed and looked pale. Roy wondered if he had gotten drunk and couldn't make it home.

"Bet you're thinking I got oiled up and couldn't get back, aren't ya?"

Roy shrugged but didn't say a word.

"I like a little whisky, but I don't get legless with liquor, and you'll never see me knocked out, son."

Roy grabbed a chair, took a seat, and waited for the story of the delay.

"I got a bad foot. Swelled up on me so badly I couldn't walk and barely got my boot off. Hurts like hell, so I got my foot up on a pillow, and it feels better. The doc here gave me some foul-tasting stuff from a bottle, and that knocked me flat."

Roy was relieved to hear a story that had a logical and hopefully happy conclusion.

"Doc told me to wait until tomorrow to go home, but since you're here, we can head back this afternoon. Why don't you go into town, look around, and buy some hard candy or whatever you can think of. Then go to the livery and bring the wagon back to pick me up around noon. After you get the wagon, stop by Central Feed and get what I bought; they'll have it ready. Then I need you to go to Snowy Mountain Mercantile and load up my order there. Got that, Roy?"

"Aye, I can do that with no worries. I'll be back at 12:00."

It was around 9:00 a.m., so Roy had plenty of time. His mood was lifted by finding Mike quickly and in one piece. He could now enjoy his free morning.

Roy rode down Main Street and located the mercantile he would visit later. He also found another general store near where Big Spring ran under the road. Big Spring was more like a river and was flowing freely in the cold of December. He had heard it was one of the largest springs in the world and supplied the town with all its water.

Walking in, he stared, taking in the amount of goods available. The town had nearly everything you could want and need. Roy did wander over to the candy jars and asked for ten cents worth of some hard candy. The woman handed him a bag full of candy, which he planned on sharing with everyone back at the ranch. He knew the

Basco boys like the red candies, and he made sure there was plenty for them.

He then walked towards the door but stopped at a table with a few books propped up. There was a Mark Twain book, *The Adventures of Huckleberry Finn*, which looked interesting. He had read *Tom Sawyer* and was moved by the story. He bought the book and hoped it would keep him entertained through the long winter nights.

Roy tucked the bag of candy and the book into his saddlebags, untied the lead rope, and walked the two blocks to the livery. Lewistown was as pretty a place as a town could be. Big Spring running through the town, mountains to the northeast and southwest, and the substantial number of new stone buildings gave the town a clean and welcoming sensation. The people were ambitious and quietly friendly. He wanted no part of being a town man, but if it were forced upon him, Lewistown would suit him.

At the livery, he paid the man with the giant mustache for the feed and care of the Belgians and the wagon. Roy tied his horse to the back of the wagon with the halter rope. He then took off the bridle, saddle, and saddle blanket and put them in the wagon. It was now time to drive to Central Feed where he was loaded with ten burlap bags of oats and two bags of other dry feed.

Then, he went to the mercantile. As he made his way through the tables piled high with cloth, canned goods, pots, and pans, he reached into his coat pocket for the note that he was to give the clerk.

"Good day, young man," said a fine-looking woman in her thirties dressed in a light blue dress and white apron as she came around a long counter on the right.

"Morning to ye, ma'am. I'm here on behalf of Mr. Mike Hanson. He has a hurtin' foot and can no come for his goods." Roy took off his hat and held it in front of his chest with one hand had while handing over the note to the woman with the other.

"Sorry to hear Mr. Hanson is poorly. I'm sure he'll be in fine fit soon enough." The woman read the note and smiled. She looked at Roy. "Please excuse me while I fetch the goods."

She and another younger woman came out of the back room pushing a wooden cart with noisy iron wheels. It was piled high with nearly ten bundles all wrapped in brown paper and tied tight with white string.

"We shall help you place these in your wagon, Mr. Hanson."

Roy balked when he heard her call him Mr. Hanson. He was going to correct her, but they were moving quickly and headed to the door. The cart was pushed to the wooden sidewalk and next to the wagon. The two women handed Roy each package carefully and he then placed them in the front section under the seat. After the last bundle was set in place, Roy jumped onto the walkway and tipped his hat to the first woman.

"Never knew that Mike had a son, but it's a delight to meet you. You must have spent many years in Scotland. It's Scot I hear, is it not?" The woman turned to go inside and escape the mid-morning chill.

Roy was perplexed, not knowing if he should correct her assumption of his relationship to Mike. "I be askin' ye if there was any further instructions in the note I handed ye?"

"No, it simply said, 'please see that my son doesn't rip open any of the packages.' That's all. Safe journey to you." The woman stepped quickly inside.

With all packages picked up, Roy headed to pick up Mike. Parked in front of the boarding house, Roy saw a fine buggy with side curtains and a front glass with a gold leaf 'DR' painted on the side. *Must be Doc Fullbright looking in on Mike.* As he climbed the stairs, he could hear a man's voice sounding stern and loud. As he came close to the door of Mike's room, the voice got louder.

"Damnation, Mike! You can't do that. You can't wait!"

Not wanting to be discovered loitering and attempting to discover secrets, Roy knocked lightly.

"Yep! Come on through," said Mike as he struggled to stand up. He was dressed and packed. "This here's Roy; he's a top hand. Good boy."

Roy dipped his glance to acknowledge the remark.

"Roy, you make sure he takes a spoonful of this four time a day until I get out there." The doctor handed a dark brown bottle nearly as big as a bottle of beer with no label or writing on it at all to Roy. "I'll ride out and see you the day after Christmas. Do nothing, Mike. I mean nothing except keep that foot up in the air. Put a pillow under your foot and don't move. I mean it goddammit! And Roy, see that he puts a bag of snow on that foot two or three times a day."

The doctor grabbed his leather bag, opened the door, said, "Day after Christmas," and walked out and down the stairway.

"Get my bag and that elk robe would ya, son, and hand me that stupid stick the doc brung me."

There was a white, wooden, carved, walking stick near the door, and Roy handed it over. Mike gave out a "damn" as he put pressure on his foot and began to slide to the door.

"How did it get injured?" Roy grabbed the bag and Mike's arm to assist.

"Let me try to do it myself, Roy," Mike barked and pulled his arm away. He stood still, taking a deep breath. "Sorry, son. Didn't mean to bull whip ya like that. Damn foot feels like it's gonna burst and break off." He walked to the top of the steps, paused, and answered Roy's question. "I think one of the team stepped on my foot last week. Doc said nothin' was broken, but I did bleed some. He said it was infected. I'd rather have it broke."

Roy set the bag and robe down and used both hands to help Mike painfully descend the stairs. Mike was as tough as any man, but each step brought out a small moan of pain. Roy helped Mike to the front door and down the three steps to the walk. Once on level ground, Mike told Roy to fetch the bag and that he'd be at the wagon when he got back. Roy trotted back inside and to the bag and robe. On his way down, he could hear the doctor using the phone in the parlor.

"Helena operator, I need Dr. Humphrey at Saint Peter's Hospital. Be prompt, please."

Mike was nearly to the wagon as Roy threw the elk robe and Mike's bag into the wagon. He had made a little bed of straw surrounded by the bags of oats in the front corner for Big Mike to lay in, hoping it would be comfortable. There was just enough room for a man to lay down.

"I'll jump up and slide my big ass onto the wagon, and you lift and push the best you can."

It was an easier task than expected, and Roy helped Mike slide up to the front and onto the straw. Roy grabbed the heavy elk robe and tossed it over Mike's legs. Mike pulled it up and let out a slow breath.

"This will be capital, Roy. Right cozy. Thank you, son." Mike laid back, closed his eyes, and said, "Let's go home."

Roy climbed up to the seat, grabbed the reins, and sat for a minute.

Something is wrong. Why would the doctor call Helena? What's really wrong with Mike?

The wagon reached the top of the hill west of Lewistown. Roy leaned back and glanced down to check on Mike. All he could see was warm breath puffing out just above the elk robe and under a big black hat. Mike was sleeping hard. Roy knew he was sick but just how sick?

Roy had no idea how to deal with this news of Mike's sickness or how to feel about how things might change. He'd never had a reason to feel strong emotions before. He had no emotional tools or past experiences to draw on to help him sort out these unsettling and lousy feelings. He'd felt compassion and sympathy for animals, but these confusing thoughts about Mike and his welfare put a sourness in his stomach.

————

After two hours, the men and the wagon full of goods pulled up to the front of the house where the entire household greeted them. Elmer stood by the hitching post, tied up the team, and then quickly walked to the back of the wagon. He looked up at Roy with a 'tell me what's going on later' look as he passed. Roy set the wagon's handbrake. Mike was loud and cheerful and was trying to act as if all was well. All but Grace knew that was not the case.

Mike raised himself up to see over the sideboards. "Gracie, go back in. It's too cold to be out, and the boys will have me situated in a short time. Go on now." He blew her a kiss and smiled. "Just slide me out and get me to the ground, lads."

Elmer and Lon took a position on one side and Roy and Anders on the other. Each team took a leg and then allowed Mike to slide his arms over a shoulder.

"Why don't we just haul you into the house, Mike?" Elmer was asking as much as pleading for Mike to allow them to help.

"Give me that stick. I'll walk but stand-by in case I founder, boys." The pain of the walk to the house would be less than the concern he may cause Grace if she saw him carted in like a bag of laundry.

The painful walk was slow and was interrupted by a good healthy pause for a break for nature next to the big cottonwood tree in the yard, but Mike made it in house.

Once inside, Mike let out a holler. "Fine to be home next to the fire and with my sweet Gracie."

Grace ran up, wrapped her arms around his good leg and refused to let loose.

"Let me get my hide off and get to the chair, little darlin', and then we can burrow together." Gracie released and stepped back while Anna and Elmer took his hat and coat.

Mike eased back into his big chair, and everyone felt the same sense of relief that the King was back on his throne and in his castle.

Anna moved to his feet. "Boots, Mr. Mike?"

"Just the one Anna. Doc wrapped up the other with some fleece and leather. Let that one alone. Have Elmer grab a good stump off the wood pile and put a sack of wool on top for me to settle my bad foot on. Thanks for fussing over me, girl."

Elmer brought in a cottonwood stump, and Lon returned from the barn with a small burlap bag stuffed with wool.

Once situated, Mike gave the crew an update. He didn't lie, but he omitted large sections of the truth. Roy assumed this was done to not cause worry and to not cloud the celebration of Christmas in two days. Elmer looked at Roy to watch his reaction to Mike's mini sermon. Roy knew he was being studied and attempted to remain stoic to aid in Mike's edited report.

"Tomorrow, I want Roy and one the other boys to go cut down a small tree so that Grace and Anna can put some things on it. Anna has a plan. Something the Germans do, I reckon. Put it up over in the corner there." Mike adjusted his foot on the soft bag and continued. "Go grab the packages out of the wagon, bring it all in here, and put it next to me. It ain't for nobody to be digging into until tomorrow night, and I'll watch over."

Roy and Elmer brought the Christmas bounty in and set it behind Mike's chair. Back outside, they walked the team to the barn to unhitch.

"What's the story, Roy?"

Roy had a choice: give no more detail than Mike had given or keep Elmer informed and hopefully face the coming problems together. He chose to tell Elmer what he knew. Elmer was clever, and Roy didn't want to shoulder the load alone.

Elmer stared at the ground. "Let's keep this story dry. More of them that knows don't do no good."

Roy agreed and instantly felt relief not carrying the burden alone.

"Ya did good fetchin' him back home." Roy knew that Elmer was frugal with praise. It was a small moment of joy on a stormy day.

Unhitched, curried, and grained, Elmer turned the team out to the corral. The Basco boys had unloaded the bags of grain and had rolled the wagon into the barn. Roy grabbed his bag from under the wagon seat and walked to the bunkhouse. Supper would be ready soon. It had been a long day.

It was a day that would change everything.

CHAPTER 14

I t was Christmas Eve, And it was the first real Christmas in Roy's life. He never knew how to celebrate the day or even what the traditions meant. The Bascos volunteered to go cut a small tree and fetch it back after they rode out to check the flock. Grace started clapping when she saw the brothers ride up while pulling a tree behind a horse as if pulling a calf to branding. Roy untied it and gave it a shake to dislodge the snow and dirt picked up by the dragging. He brought it to the porch and walked inside for instructions. Anna and Grace had built a small rock cairn on a canvas tarp to hold the tree. Roy brought the four-foot-tall tree in and held it in the middle of the rocks as the females crawled around the base and stacked rocks around the trunk until it held in place.

"Lift me up, Roy! I have the star for the top." Grace was reversing the order of decoration installation, but no one objected. She usually got her way, but her desires were rarely excessive, and the entire crew loved and adored her. Her kind nature and sweet disposition balanced out the quiet, stoic personalities of the others on the ranch.

Next, she put up small paper snowflakes and some Christmas drawings on stiff paper tied with yarn. There were just enough ornaments to make it a sweet and warm addition to the holiday house.

Grace turned, smiled, then ran to Mike's side and asked, "Papa, do you like it?"

"Love it, Lammy Girl. You are the best tree fixer I've ever seen."

Roy loved hearing Mike call her Lammy Girl. It was sweet, and it fit.

Soon after, it was time for supper. The big meal would be tomorrow with a goose and more but tonight was a little extra special as Anna had made schnitzel with pork recently brought back from town, boiled potatoes, and sauerkraut. Again, these were things Roy had never heard of let alone eaten, but he would eat nearly anything, except beets. To complete the meal, there was a cake with lemon icing.

Big Mike shuffled to the table, took his spot at the head of it, mumbled a short, required prayer, and let Anna dish up the German feast. It looked to be the first time that Anders and Lon had tasted sauerkraut as well, but once they overcame the unfamiliar and aggressive smell, they became admirers.

This table of seven would be with Roy forever. He felt respected, needed and, best of all, loved.

Mike pulled Grace onto his lap. "Best to get to bed soon so Santa will show up tonight."

Grace flopped her head down on Mike's chest, and he held her tight. She began to pull away, but Mike squeezed her tighter, so she fell back and hugged him back. The two held on to each other as if clinging to a floating log in a flooded river. Roy noticed a small tear sliding down Mike's face, and he looked away so as not to embarrass Mike or himself. He wondered if the tear was caused by joy or uncertainty. He wanted to believe it was the happiness of the holiday, but his logical side told him otherwise.

All wandered off to bed, half with calm wonder, and the rest filled with fearful thoughts.

———

A cold, clear Christmas morning with a sky full of stars hit Roy's body as he opened the bunkhouse door and headed to the privy. As he sat, he felt his bare skin hit and melt the frost on the seat and things began to tingle. This was a hazard of being first to the outhouse on a frozen morning.

Back at the bunkhouse, he shook Ander's shoulder to wake him and he, in turn, woke Lon. Everyone was up a little early as no one wanted to disappoint Grace. Elmer was already missing, and Roy presumed he was already in the house.

Roy walked in, washed up, and entered the kitchen for coffee. He was expecting noise and activity. Grace was not awake yet, so Elmer, Anna, and Roy quietly sat with coffee and enjoyed the stillness of the morning. Soon, Anders and Lon walked in, picked up on the peaceful morning and carefully pulled out chairs so as to not make any noise. The five sat exchanging glances and silent conversation. It was the perfect discussion for people who knew not what to say. All had the same questions, but none had the answers.

"Let's get through this day and deal with tomorrow, tomorrow." Elmer's words were all that needed to be said.

Anna whispered, "Ve have big breakfast for ven Mr. Mike and da girl vake ups."

Another 20 minutes passed in appreciated quiet. More coffee was poured and slurped. It was rare for any ranch to have this much time with no activity and a part of it was uncomfortable. It felt lazy to them, but they soaked it in knowing it was as rare as snow in July.

Mike could be heard sliding his foot across the floor, and the tap of his walking stick on the wood floor telegraphed his movement. He went straight to his chair in the big room, near the now active fire.

"Can't believe she's not awake. Guess she had too much whisky last night. Don't give her none tonight, Roy."

Roy picked up his coffee to toast the first joke of the day.

"And before anyone asks, the damn foot hurts, but it ain't gonna ruin this day, and that's all we're gonna talk about it."

Just then, Grace came sliding out still half asleep, jumped on Mike, and burrowed in.

"Pretty sure Santa showed up. There's some new stuff mixed in with this other stuff, so it must be for you." He kissed her head and gave Grace a rub on the back.

"Good," is all she said and stayed still as a fawn.

The crack and popping of the fire and the scene of a loving father with his baby girl snuggled in was a picture of love and affection here before unknown to Roy. He'd never thought about being a father until this moment, but now it had become real to him.

No one moved, and the silence was reassuring and treasured.

A dropped spoon hit the floor and woke Grace. She climbed down, realizing she was hungry and knowing the presents would follow the morning meal.

Breakfast was chewed and swallowed in record time. Mike was served a plate in his chair, with his left foot raised on the stump and bag of wool. Grace knew valuable time was escaping and became energized and impatient. It was time for gifts.

All gathered in the big room. Anders and Lon sat crossed legged on the floor near the tree, silent as usual, but pleased to be included in the family atmosphere. Anna was fussing in the kitchen while Elmer sat on the old couch with the spot next to him obviously saved for Anna. Roy brought a chair in from the kitchen and positioned himself to have the widest view of the goings-on. He felt himself smile and felt no need to suppress the joy.

First was Grace. Mike had the bundles piled next to him, and he would serve as the elf. He had the first gift for Grace at the ready in a small cloth sack.

"This is for Gracie from an old fat man in a red suit!" Mike reached forward, and Gracie accepted the gift carefully and gently.

"Thank you, Papa," Grace said in a quiet voice.

"No need, my darling. That came down the chimney from Mr. Santa."

She sat on the floor, reached into the bag, and pulled out a small cornhusk figure. She dug in the bag until all four figurines were laid on the floor in front of her.

"Looks like a ranchin' family to me. How about that!" Mike helped to identify the gifts.

Grace grabbed the largest doll. It was a cornhusk doll about eight inches tall. It was the father of the doll family with a painted black beard, a red shirt, and black britches. The mother was next with black hair painted on the corn husk. She had a long red apron that slung over her neck and off the way to where her feet should be. The two small figures were the children, but no painting or drawings distinguished the dolls.

"Oh, Papa! They're a handsome family, aren't they?" She turned each simple doll over and examined them with affection.

Mike replied with a wide grin and a wink.

Mike knew he had done well in giving Grace a small family that she would cherish. China dolls with beautiful painted faces and silk dresses were sometimes available, but the cornhusk dolls were common and beloved possessions for many pioneer girls.

Mike handed her another small sack. Grace extracted two pencils, a pad of writing paper, and a small book of paper dolls. Grace stood next to the chair and wrapped her arms around her father. She kissed his bearded cheek and hugged him again. Life for a child in 1891 was without frills and offered simple treasures. For one day, Mike wanted Grace to feel like a princess.

Gracie was instantly lost in the new family and was already preparing them for a fine supper.

It was the Basco boys' turn. Mike reached down with two small sacks in his hand. He motioned for one of the boys to take the bags. Lon stood up to accept the cloth-wrapped items and sat back down. Handing one bag to Anders, they opened the bags at the same time. Each man held up a new pair of leather gloves and a fine woolen scarf.

It was evident that neither man had ever been gifted such fine offerings, and they both smiled, looked to Mike, and managed a broken English "Sank You." Mike returned with a thumbs up and a wink.

"Anna, this here's for you."

"Mr. Mike, I don't need nuthin," she mumbled.

"Nonsense! Get over here, gal, and take this." It was a thick paper wrapped bundle. Anna attempted to hide her pleasure, but a giggle spilled out as she sat back next to Elmer.

"Oh, Mr. Mike! Dis is very gut! Very gut!"

Anna pulled a new blue and white checked apron up and showed it to the room. It was practical and handsome. Then she held up a thick pair of woolen mittens. She slid them on and patted them together with soft applause. She was delighted. She sprang up and over to Mike, reached down, kissed his cheek, and patted the back of his big hand. Mike enjoyed seeing her happy and showing some child-like joy.

"You are most welcome, girl." He smiled back at her, and he could see a tear in her eye. He locked eyes with her for ten seconds with a look that said, "I love you and appreciate you", and then looked down as he fought back unfamiliar emotions. Anna was a sunny young woman who was a fine house manager. More importantly, she loved and cared for Grace, and they each needed the other.

Anna sat down and leaned over to Elmer showing him her thick, warm mittens. He nodded in approval, and she motioned for him to feel the wool. He touched the mitten, then his hand wrapped around hers, and he gently squeezed. She looked down and allowed the contact to continue and then slowly pulled away so as to not make the affection noticeable. Mike and Roy both saw the exchange, and they felt amused and pleased for both Anna and Elmer.

"Elmer, Santa brought something for you too. Come fetch it." Mike reached back but couldn't quite reach the sack.

"Grab that one there," he told Elmer. It was a large burlap sack and had some heft. Elmer sat and placed the bag on the floor in front of him. He pulled out some long leather straps that seemed to have no end.

"Thems for you and the team. I noticed the ones you got were pretty knackered." Mike raised up in his chair to get a better look.

Dark reddish-brown reins lay before Elmer. Two sets of team reins for the Belgians were curled up and had a striking look of quality and a masculine aroma. As usual, Elmer used few or no words and was a man for minimal expressions.

"Dandy, just dandy these are." This was maximum praise from Elmer, and Mike grinned at the approval.

Elmer reached in again and pulled up a bright red union suit, button flap and all. He squirmed a bit as Mike laughed.

"I seen the ones you been wearing for the last five years, and they're holier than a wagon full of Bishops!" Mike laughed at his own joke, as was his custom, and said, "No need to try them on now." Another snort of laughter followed.

A thinly embarrassed Elmer shook his head in agreement, but he was no doubt grateful for the gift of new comfort and warmth.

Roy piped up. "Mr. Mike, I don't ha much, but I do ha sum candy from town I wanna give out to everyone."

"Well go right ahead, Roy! Dang nice of ya." Mike learned forward with his left hand open and cleared his throat, indicating he'd be first in line and take a piece or two.

Roy stood up, reached into his paper bag, and gave everyone four pieces of rock candy. However, he gave Grace five pieces. The candy was welcomed, and the act of giving was appreciated more than Roy realized. Small acts matter in a world where little is expected. He had never shared a gift with anyone before. He felt pure happiness.

Now, it was Roy's turn. He had no idea what favors awaited him. He had already bought or had been given anything a new ranch hand could need or want. All his kit was fine and new. He was loaded with goods, and he desired nothing.

Mike held a small bag in one hand which contained a small item wrapped in cloth. He reached into the bag. "Close your eyes, Roy."

Roy felt Grace's tiny hands touch his and then place something in his hand. It smelled great and familiar.

"Open your eyes, son!" Mike was already chuckling.

Roy looked at his hand.

It was a bright and shiny orange.

Roy laughed and shook the orange at Mike. The thought and effort to find an orange to give to Roy was a splendid maneuver. Most men would not have remembered the 'Orange Incident', but Mike had and took pains to recreate the encounter. The two looked at each other, and the memory of Roy's first battle with an orange gave them both a laugh.

"Gracie, pass these other oranges out would you, little darlin'?" Mike gave the bag to Grace, and she handed everyone an orange. Each person placed their orange aside for a future treat.

Mike then asked Grace to deliver the cloth wrapped item to Roy, which she did. Roy felt the solid block and knew it was a book. He folded the cloth back and saw the illustrated cover of a man with a huge mustache launched into the air above a bucking horse. Mark

Twain was printed at the top and just below on the next line, *Roughing It*. It was a beautiful new book and had the smell of wood and ink.

Roy smiled and looked at Mike. "Thank ye, Mr. Mike. I'll wager it a fine tale. Mr. Twain is a magician with words, he is." Mike nodded, winked back, and then turned away.

"Now, one more thing. I have a new pair of heavy wool socks for everyone. Had Mrs. Hagedorn in town knitted them for me. It's lookin' to be a long cold winter, so we need them."

Mike once again employed Grace to hand out the new socks. She walked to each person, handed them a pair, and curtsied, doing so simply to be playful. Even Anna got a new pair, and she was surprised by the additional gift. So much so that she put her head in her hands and tried not to cry, but she failed. Grace walked back to her, put her arms around Anna's neck and put her cheek on Anna's.

"I sorry, Mr. Mike. I never had so much before. So much of every ting."

Mike was tight-throated and had no reply. He managed to softly eke out a quiet, "Good," and that was all he could muster.

Grace continued around the room and handed Roy his socks.

Grace stepped toward Roy, gave him an unexpected kiss on the cheek, tilted her head, and smiled. He hoped he could find that same sweetness in a girl his age.

"Time for the chores, fellas. Shouldn't take us long. A quick lunch then back for a big supper."

Elmer stood up as Anders, Lon, and Roy all followed suit. They headed to the back door and to the bunkhouse to bundle up for a few hours of work. The two milk cows still needed to be milked, the sheep and horses needed hay, and the water trough needed to have the ice broken. There was no extra work today, just the basic but necessary tasks.

———

After a couple of hours, the work was done. Following a late lunch of barley soup and bread, all four men headed back to the bunkhouse, hoping to maybe sneak in a nap as supper was still four hours away.

Elmer went to the house. Roy guessed he went to help Anna. Roy stayed behind and looked at his new book. He had a collection entirely of Twain works, and he felt like an aristocrat with his own personal library now. He leaned back in his bunk and opened the book to browse. On the inside of the book, he found a handwritten message.

Roy, I trust that you will find enjoyment in this book. You have a lifetime ahead of you to read, learn, and prosper. I know that you will succeed, as you are as fine a man as I've come across. I never had a son, but had I, my hope would have been that he was as good a fella as you. Remember, there is no bravery in being cruel, but there is courage in kindness.

Mike H.

Roy's eyes swelled with tears for the first time since his dog Ned had died.

What have I done to have earned words like these? I'm a boy of no certain talents and no education. Why is Mike kind to me? Maybe he sees more in me?

———

Roy felt a hand on his shoulder, tapping him awake. He had dozed off.

"Supper."

Elmer made sure he was awake before heading back to the house. Anders and Lon were also sliding boots on and headed to the house.

Lon looked at Roy and grinned. "Beg supper!"

That was a much English as Roy had heard from either of the Basco brothers. Roy rubbed his eyes and face and let his feet hit the floor. He still had his boots on, so he grabbed his coat for the short walk. Anders had just closed the door. Roy was up but turned and walked back to his bunk and the shelf that held his books, a knife, and a cigar box that held his few personal knickknacks. He reached into the box, grabbed the single thing that held any emotional value to him and put it in the front pocket of his woolen britches.

He was the last one to sit down for the special Christmas Supper. For men of this era, a fine meal held as much importance and value as some possessions. He had never been part of any meal this meaningful or unique. The Basco boys had been at the ranch for over a year, just a few months after Anna arrived, and had been at the Christmas supper table last year. They knew what to expect. Roy picked up on their excitement and knew he would not be disappointed.

Mike was seated at the head of the table with Grace on his left, sitting on two thick Sears catalogs. Anders and Lon sat next to her. Anna's chair was at Mike's right hand with Elmer next to her. Roy sat at the opposite end from Mike.

Anna hurriedly put a big bowl of mashed potatoes down in front of Mike, followed by a plate of green beans. Then she put a plate full of sliced fresh baked bread and a mason jar filled with strawberry preserves onto the table. A small bowl of brown gravy was added just before the big golden-brown goose was set in front of Mike.

"I can't stand up to carve this bird, so you may have to help me a bit, Anna." Mike grabbed a large knife and a small fork. Before he began the ceremony, he said, "Boys, look at all this. Ain't it somethin'? Anna worked all day making this for us. Thank you, Anna. You're the best cookin' gal any ranch in Montana has."

Anna blushed a bit. She tapped Mike on the arm in an affectionate manner and felt proud to have such kind words spoken on her behalf. Anna was not a complex or needy woman, but she was a hard worker, did more than was expected of her, and was a kind person.

Mike began to carve and slice. Anna helped him place the meat on each plate as they were rotated around the table. While the carving was in progress, other fixings were handed around and by the time the last slice of goose was installed on a plate, Anders and Lon were ready to start. Mike gave them a nod, and the attack was launched. Roy followed and within 30 seconds the entire table and he joined the assault. Small moans of pleasure escaped from all the males at the table and were collected and acknowledged by Anna with delight. The bread plate was the first item to begin a second round, followed by the potatoes. Roy had never tasted goose, and it was surprisingly good. He was shocked that a single bird could feed this many people. He would occasionally step in fresh goose droppings all over the ranch but now realized that it was a small price to pay if this was the payoff.

Nearly empty plates covered the table. Anna rose up and returned with a tall round cake covered in white butter icing. It was a work of art.

"That is one dandy lookin' object, Anna. But what is it?" Mike would have eaten the entire cake himself blindfolded, but he was curious.

"Dis is a vite cakes vis butter icing. Is da best. German are good cooks, but ve are the best of the bakers in da VURLD!"

Mike clapped his hands with amusement and held up his empty plate hoping for a near religious experience. Anna had marked the cake evenly, so everyone got an equal slice, even Grace. Little Gracie could eat like a starved coyote, so there was little doubt she could help in the destruction of the confectionary.

Never had Roy tasted anything as good as that cake. He wanted to pick up the plate and lick it like a dog. He realized that the better option was to back way off and take small bites to extend the experience. Anders and Lon were already running their fingers across their plates hoping to find any remaining baked treasure before Roy had taken his third bite. Mike was right behind the Bascos, following up with the same finger technique. Anna finished in a happy last place, and it seemed her finest gift of the day was the complete disappearance of all food placed on the table.

Anders and Lon pushed back from the table and walked over to Mike. They each shook his hand in thanks and then tipped an invisible cap to the boss before heading to the bunkhouse for the night.

Grace was next as Anna told her it was time for bed. She slid down off the chair and grabbed the papa cornhusk doll she had set in the chair with her. She gave Mike a long hug and a kiss on the cheek. She walked over to Anna and wrapped her arms around one of her legs before releasing her leg and quietly walking back to her tiny room. Elmer helped Anna clear and clean as usual as it was his time to be as close to her as possible.

"Help me over to the chair would you, Roy?"

Roy reached under Mike's left arm and helped lift. The instant Mike's foot touched the floor, he felt his body go limp from pain, and the reality of his condition was back in view. Mike had done an amazing job of hiding and ignoring his condition for the entire day so as to not dampen spirits. Roy helped him fall back into the big chair. He lifted the bum foot back onto the wool-filled bag. Roy stood next to Mike and paused before reaching into his pant pocket to retrieve the tiny gift for Mike.

"What ya got there, son? Sit down for a bit with me."

Roy pulled a chair closer to Mike.

"I need to thank ye for everything you gave me and did for me this year, sir. You changed me life. You're the kindest man I ever known, and I thank ye a thousand times for what ye done fer me Mike." Roy's head dropped as he felt the emotion about to roll over him.

He felt Mike's large hand reach over and clutch his forearm. He heard a small sniff from Mike, and he knew not to look up.

"And I read the words you wrote in the book ya give me. I'll try me best to not cause you any suffering and be the man you see in me."

Mike cleared his throat and answered, "I meant ever word I wrote, Roy. Not sure what I saw in you when we first met, but I knew you were a good lad and, if given a chance, you'd prove out. It may have been good luck for us to meet up that day in Scotland, but it's up to you to use that luck. You're a finer man than I expected and for that I thank you, son."

Roy stood up knowing he would need to be done with the conversation or he might break and bawl out like a lamb.

"I never had much of anything, and all I have now is due to you, but I have one thing that's mine, and I want it to be yours now."

"No need to..." Mike stopped, realizing to refuse the gift would belittle Roy and dishonor the effort.

"I have a stone that I was told was given to me mother by me father. I ha no memories of them at all, but I do have this wee stone. They say it's an agate stone. I carried wi me every day of me life. I never knew what a father felt like 'til I met you. I need for you to ha this to remind yourself that you gave me a life just like a father." Roy held out the oval shaped stone with a brass band around the edge and small hole in the metal at the top.

Mike reached out and accepted the rock in his left hand and with his right, reached across to shake Roy's hand. The men grabbed hands firmly with no shake and held on for longer than normal. Mike couldn't talk. He simply squeezed Roy's hand and shook his head in agreement.

After a minute of honest emotion, Mike managed to utter a quiet reply, "I'll carry this every day until I die."

Neither man had any ability nor need to continue. Roy asked if he could help him to his room.

"I want to sit here for a bit longer. Merry Christmas, Roy. Merry Christmas...son."

Roy stood. On his way out, he thanked Anna for a fine feast. He opened the door and felt the frigid air hit him.

CHAPTER 15

Anna was leaving the barn with a bucket of freshly pulled milk when she heard bells. It was Dr. Fullbright's sleigh. He had left Lewistown before dawn. She was surprised to see a visitor this early in the morning as it had been light for barely an hour. She scurried back to the house to announce the call from a mysterious visitor.

She walked back to Mike's bedroom and tapped on the door. "Mr. Mike, der is a man in a fine buggy driving to da house. Vat you like me to do?"

Mike yelled through the door, "It's probably the doctor. I'm not ready yet, so just let him come back to my room. He's gonna take a quick look at this old foot of mine. Can you coffee him up, Anna?"

"OK, I do dat den."

The doctor's arrival got the entire ranch up and running. The horses in the corral snorted and trotted around as they smelled and heard the visiting horse. The sheepdogs began to bark. That got a few sheep that were up close to the barn worked up and running. Anders and Lon were already loading a hay sled for the morning feeding. They ran to the end of the hay loft in the barn and looked down to investigate. Elmer was already in the kitchen drinking coffee. Roy was putting on his coat and headed to the house for breakfast. He came in, hung his hat up, and looked at Elmer for some news. Elmer shrugged his shoulders and went to the door to meet the doctor.

"Morning, all. I trust you had a splendid Christmas?" the doctor asked as he took his long black coat off and hung it on a peg by the door. He quickly walked over to the fire and stood with his backside to the flames and his hands behind his back. "It's a bit brisk out this morning."

Anna came rushing in with a large tin mug of coffee for the doctor.

"Milk vith da coffee, Doctor?"

"Bless you, no. This is marvelous. Thank you, my dear." He wrapped both hands around the hot coffee for warmth before any was consumed.

"Now where is our Goliath of a man?" Dr. Fullbright grabbed his large black leather bag and waited to be directed.

"He in his bed yet, Doc. I'll show ya." Elmer put his coffee down and stood up.

They headed to Big Mike's bedroom. Elmer gave two knocks and opened the door. "Doc's here Mike."

The doctor walked in and closed the door. Grace was still asleep, and no one saw the need to disturb her.

Roy looked over at Elmer. The two men looked at each other. Nothing was said, and no expressions from either man was offered. All three in the kitchen knew that there was a problem. A doctor doesn't leave town at 5:00 a.m. and ride through below-zero temperatures for two hours for a cup of coffee. They stayed quiet, listening for any talk that might spill out of the room.

"Let me see that foot, Mike." The doctor moved to the foot of the bed and pulled back the colorful quilt.

"Hurts bad, Doc. Can't play the fool. Hurts like no pain I ever felt before." Mike winced in pain just from the doctor lifting the quilt off his foot.

"Have you taken that medicine I gave you?"

Dr. Fullbright saw that the foot was swollen and purple. The skin was stretched to the point of bursting and was irritated. There was no space between the toes. He lifted the quilt back over Mike's foot gently.

"God yes, I nipped on it all day yesterday. Don't think I would a made it without it."

"I brought you two more bottles. You'll certainly need more for the trip."

Mike lifted his head a bit off the pillow. "What trip, Doc?"

The doctor reached for a chair in the corner and sat down next to Mike.

"I'm going to be forthright with you, Mike. Straight to it."

Mike was not looking for, nor expecting, a honey-coated opinion.

"It's damn serious. That foot looks bad. And it is not improving. I didn't expect it to, but I was hoping. You need to get down to Helena and see the doctor down there. He's a friend and a fine surgeon. He will have a better notion of how to treat this, and St. Peter's is a new hospital. Best around. Not sure, you may lose that foot or..." The doctor trailed off, and Mike didn't seem to hear the 'or', possibly intentionally.

Mike lay still. This was not what he had hoped to hear. He had imagined that the doctor would have a magic poultice or elixir, and he would be returned to the world in fine fit.

"Well shit, Doc."

"If you don't get down there, it could get very bad. You have an infection, and it's not settling down. Could have gotten it from a scratch or a cut, big or small. No way to tell."

Mike thought back to when one of the Belgians had stepped on his foot, but that hadn't broken the skin or bled. He looked at his hands covered with bruises, marks, and small cuts.

Mike thought, *How's a man to do any work if a thing like this can knock you down?*

"I spoke with Dr. Humphrey in Helena, and he has a couple of treatments to try to help you, Mike. I have no facilities or specialty medicines here. You need to get there, and you need to leave today before this thing spreads. I can give you medicine to help the pain, but that's all I can do, Mike. Sorry there, fella."

Mike took a breath and closed his eyes.

"Best time of the year to travel, ain't it, Doc? I'll take the boy with me. He's the only one that could lift me if I fall anyhow."

The doctor placed two large, dark brown bottles on the table by the bed and opened one.

"Take a knock of this right now and then a short snort every hour. No more, or this stuff will kick like a mare in a shed. When I get back to town, I'll call Humphrey and tell him you're pointed his way." The doctor gathered his bag and shook Mike's hand. He shook it hard and held fast for a few seconds more. "I'll have a little more coffee before I go."

"Anna!" Mike yelled out and down the short hallway. She came walking in.

"Anna, dear, make up some breakfast for this good man before he returns to the elements. This gal here is the best cook in Fergus County, my friend."

Dr. Fullbright patted him on the shoulder and walked to the kitchen. He pulled out a chair as Anna poured him a cup of coffee. Roy was at the table eating breakfast with Anders and Lon. Grace was in the main room playing with her dolls and out of earshot.

Dr. Fullbright looked at Elmer and shook his head. "That man is sick, and you need to get him out of here within the hour. No delay, gentlemen."

Elmer cleared his throat and asked, "Into Lewistown?"

"No, sir. He needs to travel to Helena. There is a fine doctor there, and I have strong faith in his skills and abilities. I will make him realize that this is a serious matter, and he needs to proceed with no delay."

Anna placed a plate of eggs, ham, and a biscuit in front of the doctor. He grinned politely and widely at Anna.

"We need to get up to Sanford and then the train to Great Falls to get to Helena. Hope the tracks are open. Could take a bit to get him there." Elmer was getting things organized in his head.

"Let me be the one to take him. Please. The ranch needs you here to run things, Elmer." Roy spoke quietly but firmly.

Elmer always wanted to run the show, and he wanted to see the job through and get Mike delivered, but he knew he couldn't be away from the ranch for a week or more. Roy was right.

"I'll get the wagon. We'll put him in the back, just like he was a couple of days back. We'll get straw in there and grab that elk robe. I'll drive you both up to Sanford. Roy, get dressed warm and stuff some clothes in a bag. You and he might be there for a week or more." Elmer pushed back from the table and looked at Dr. Fullbright for approval.

"That is precisely the course I would follow, sir."

Dr. Fullbright finished his breakfast and took another long shot of coffee before standing up to head back for a final check on Mike.

Elmer looked at the Basco boys. He said, "Wagon, horses," and raised two fingers. The boys nodded as they pushed their chairs in, threw their coats on, and headed out. Roy followed them to the bunkhouse.

Dr. Fullbright knocked on Mike's door and walked in. He was almost dressed and was sitting on the edge of the bed.

"The boys are getting the wagon ready for you. Roy is going to travel with you and be your valet and nurse. They'll make you warm and comfortable." He walked up to Mike and put his hands on the big man's shoulders.

"Will I still have a foot in a week? Just tell me, Stanley. I ain't one for sugar and bullshit." Mike was quiet and serious.

"I do not know, my friend. I cannot make that determination. But that foot looks bad. It may have to come off. That's why Dr. Humphrey is your best chance to keep the foot. He can save it if anyone can."

"Ah, what the hell, Doc. Something will eat us all someday. I will get myself one of them fine walkin' sticks, like those Englishmen all had. Maybe a wooden peg leg that I can take off and use as a club to use in a fight next I'm in Butte? Some roughies down there." Mike's attempt to ease his friend's distress was brave but failed.

"Let's get you moving, my friend, and traveling," Dr. Fullbright said, ignoring the light humor.

"Get me to the table. Ain't had any food yet, and I want to see my girl before I go."

Anna had breakfast waiting. Mike sat with the doctor's assistance. Grace walked up and put her head in his lap. He stroked her blonde hair. She exposed every tender nerve he had each day, but this was a testing moment.

"Papa, are you going again?"

"Yes, little darlin', I have to go over to Helena and see a doctor that can fix this lousy foot. He'll mend me up fine and then I'll come back in a week or two."

"Is he a good doctor?" Grace got close to his ear and whispered, "Is he better than Dr. Fullbright?"

A small chortle escaped from Mike, and he softly answered her. "No not better, just different. Like sheepmen are different from cowboys, yeah?"

She jumped up and sat on his lap while he finished his meal, stealing chunks of his biscuit while Mike pretended to take a spoon and rap the back of her hand. She smiled knowing he was teasing and that she was his favorite thing in the world.

"Anna, can you pack his things quickly and find a blanket to wrap up his foot? No boot will go over that thing now." The doctor looked around and saw a fleece over the back of a chair and knew that it would keep the foot warm.

Mike pushed away from the table and let the doctor have his foot. Anna brought a small blanket. Dr. Fullbright grabbed the fleece and began to wrap the foot. It was the size of a newborn lamb, but it was protected and warm. They could hear the wagon and team pull up. At the same moment, Roy came in wrapped up in the warmest clothing he had, including his wooly chaps.

Elmer appeared soon after covered in woolen goods from head to toe, prepared for a cold day.

Anna handed Elmer a basket full of food that could last Mike and Roy for three days. "You not eat dat city food 'til you must. I know what men like to eat," she said patting the basket.

Mike stood, and Anna helped him on with his big red wool coat with the fleece collar. Gloves were next, a scarf, and then his black hat. They moved towards the front door, and he turned to see Grace. She was already moving toward him, and he scooped her up. She nearly vanished in the big man's coat. She kissed his cheek and he in turn kissed her cheek and then lips.

"I will be very pleased to see you when you return to me. I love you, Papa."

The emotion of the unknown was overwhelming, but Big Mike Hanson somehow managed to push out, "I love you, Gracie."

"Go," was all he could say after that. The pain of parting was greater than the ache in his foot. Complete pain consumed him for a moment.

Anders and Lon helped lift Big Mike into the wagon and back into his straw den. Mike shifted, settled, and pulled the elk robe up. The boys looked at Mike and tipped their caps with respect. He returned the gesture, touching the brim of his hat and smiling. It was a very cold, cloudy morning with snow in the air, but Mike was warm and anxious to get moving.

Roy climbed up next to Elmer. The reins gently slapped on the team, and the wagon rolled. Mike was positioned to allow him to look back at the ranch. He could see Grace waving in the window. He raised his arm and gave a mighty wave, then looked down to avoid seeing more. The big man quietly cried. He had cried when Grace's mother was lowered in her grave, but not since. He felt the warm tears fall, and he allowed himself the release. He felt weak and angry. He was concerned about his ranch family and what they might face without him being a whole man. Worry is a misuse of the imagination, or so he had been told.

But what else was he to feel?

CHAPTER 16

"Come on down here, Roy, and keep me company for a while. Ol' Elmer won't mind. He don't like talking anyway unless he's chattin' up Anna."

They'd been on the road for about an hour and had five more to go. It was cold, bumpy, and his foot was throbbing, but Mike still managed to throw a little dart Elmer's way. Elmer heard but offered no reaction. Roy threw both legs around to the back, lifted himself off the seat, and lowered himself down into the loose hay. He was grateful to be ordered to the back and out of the cold wind. His face was wind burned and pinkish. He burrowed into the hay next to Mike and instantly felt respite from the Montana December weather. He plunged his feet into a deep pile of hay, pulled his hat down tight, and jammed his gloved hands into the deep pockets of his wool coat.

Roy settled and looked up at Mike. "Are ye doin' okay, sir?"

"I'm fine, son. Foot feels like hell, but I'm warm and snug. You'll like it down here better than up in the wind. I'd suggest that you offer to spell Elmer from the driving in a bit, but he's an iron-ass and stubborn to boot, so he'll turn you down. But a gentleman would make the ask." Mike, as usual, was thinking of the safety and comfort of others and playing out the drama in his head.

"Aye, I'll ask him in bit fer sure, sir. Can I do anathin at all ta be helping ye?"

"You can dig me out that canteen buried under the straw there. Just need a sip to rinse that brown poison the Doc gave me. Awful tastin' stuff. Like old coffee, sheep dung and dog hair." Mike licked his lips out of impulse.

Roy poked around and found the water. Mike took one short sip and handed it back. Roy returned it to a warm pocket in the straw and sat back. It was much warmer down here, and he was glad he could use the excuse of attending to Mike.

"We have a lot of time to talk, Roy, but right now, I'd prefer to just lay back and listen. I'm hearing things, familiar things, but they sound better to me this morning. I got a lot of thoughts going in my head, and I need to sort and stack them. Let's get a little sleep while we can."

The suggestion was appreciated as Roy had no idea what to say to Mike and dreaded creating conversation about serious problems. What do you say to a man who knows he may lose a part of his body and change his life forever? He had no skill in comforting or in lifting spirits. He had things to ask and say but quiet thinking was the best route this morning.

He looked at Mike, and his eyes were closed. He decided to follow suit. He tucked his chin down and made an effort at a nap.

———

A "WHOA" was heard, the wagon slowed, and the sound of the hand brake scratching the wheel was heard. Elmer brought the team to a stop.

He leaned back and said, "Gotta leave some coffee here." He quickly jumped down to begin the off-loading.

"Can you help me, Roy? Now that I hear him drainin' out there like a bull hittin' a flat rock, I gotta pull the plug too."

Mike began to throw off the elk robe and started sliding toward the back. Roy jumped out and waited for Mike to get his legs hanging over the bed of the wagon.

"The doctor did a fine job wrappin' the foot fer ya, didn't he?" Roy was impressed as the foot was wrapped like a prized ham and showed no sign of unraveling. He wanted Mike to get the message that he saw his foot and would be cautious while assisting him.

"Yea, he did. My foot is almost too warm, and I'm sweating under all that covering. It doesn't hurt much when I'm laying down, but it stings like a son-a-biscuit eater when I push down on it. Just help me stand up, and I'll lean back and make water."

Roy got on Mike's left side and let him put his arm around his shoulder. Slowly, Mike slid down and let out a hiss as his foot touched earth.

Roy walked to the other side of the wagon and started to dig through the layers of wool to get to his...utensil. Coffee and cold tend to make the body produce more fluid than normal. He could have hummed "The National Anthem" to the end as long as he was draining.

"*Amazing Grace, how sweet the...*" he sang in his head. He was empty. Finally. Now, he'd be humming the tune for days or at least while taking a leak. A Vicar would scold him if he knew how the hymn had been appropriated for this task.

He tucked and zipped. He grabbed a hand full of snow, rubbed his hands together, and dried his hands on his pants. He quickly put his gloves back on and into his coat pockets.

"I thought there was a bull on the side of wagon by the sounds of it!" Mike was rearranging himself and trying to keep spirits up, trying to introduce thoughts other than the obvious. "Roy, come here."

Mike stood at the back and, with a look of mischief, nodded for Roy to look down near his feet. In pale yellow, as if written with a fountain pen, he saw R O Y spelled out in the bright fresh snow.

Mike snickered like an eight-year-old boy and said, "Not enough in me to spell Elmer!"

Roy was tickled by the effort but had no idea how to respond, so he gave him a soft punch to the arm, which Mike received with paternal regard.

"Would you like me to spell you driving the team, Mr. Elmer? I'd be eager to give you a wee bit of relief. With ye driving up and then back home, it will be long day fer ya," Roy offered, although he secretly hoped the offer would be rejected.

Mike spoke up quickly. "You ain't driving back to the ranch today. That's an order. I told Anna that you'd be back around noon tomorrow, so she's not expecting you. She suggested it in fact. Didn't want you out in the cold alone at night. You'll bed down with us tonight."

Elmer conjured up a mildly disappointing reaction to Mike's order, but any man could see the wisdom in the decision. "Well, if you make me stay tonight, I'll keep driving. I couldn't sleep with anyone else driving."

Roy also had to show enough disappointment to continue the game of masculine poker, but he was very relieved to be back in the hay and out of the December breeze.

Roy and Elmer lifted Mike back into the wagon and into the front corner to his bed of hay.

"Roy, come help me check the rigging on the team before we roll." Roy thought it an odd request, but he moved towards the Belgians.

Elmer pretended to adjust the headstall on one of the horses and spoke softly. "Is he ok? I can't tell sittin' up there." This was as much concern as he could muster, but it was genuine.

"Aye, he's warm and seems to no be in pain." Roy shrugged a little to suggest that his opinion was just a guess.

"Keep an eye on him. He's hurtin' more than he's showing."

Roy gave a quick "Aye" and walked back to the bed of the wagon. He put a foot on the back wheel and climbed over the sideboard back to his den of straw and warmth.

"Was Mother Elmer checking on me?" Mike asked Roy, knowing the tack on the team was not in need of repair. He slid back down, pulled the big robe back up, and tipped his hat down a bit.

"There was some snow packed in the shoes, and we knocked it out. It was a quick job." Roy was surprised he had been able to concoct a believable story in such short order.

"Uh huh," Mike muttered and shifted. "You need to work on your lyin' a bit, son, if you expect to ever marry."

Roy was disappointed his ruse was so quickly exposed. However, he wasn't surprised that Mike couldn't be fooled. He simply accepted this minor defeat and pushed further into his nest of hay.

————

Both men slept for nearly two hours before Roy felt a tap on his thigh.

"Hate to wake ya, son, but fetch that bottle of medicine out of my bag. I can't reach it. Can you do me a kindness?" Mike rarely made anything sound like an order.

Roy moved quickly. "Aye, I can do that."

Mike's bag was in reach. He found one of the bottles, shook it to find the one that wasn't full, and handed it to him. Mike took a measured slug and handed the bottle back. Roy had the canteen of water at the ready to chase the bitterness, and Mike eagerly accepted the rinse.

"That should get me through to Stanford." Mike took a breath, waiting for the chemicals to hit his system. "How far away are we ya' reckon, Elmer?"

"Less than an hour, I think. Skull Creek is up ahead, so we're close. Hope that bridge ain't all iced up and slick." Elmer knew this road well and had been back and forth from Stanford often.

Mike stayed quiet. Roy knew to leave him be as the medicine hadn't hit its mark yet.

————

Again, the familiar sounds and shakes of the wagon stopping woke the men.

"That wasn't a bad trip now was it?" Mike asked, trying to stay upbeat.

It was an easier journey than Roy had imagined it would be. He doubted that Elmer would agree, but you would seldom get an opinion in either direction from him.

"Stay there, Mike. Roy and me will see about the train and a place to bed down tonight." Elmer climbed down, and Roy followed Elmer into the Stanford depot.

"Afternoon, gents. How can assist you?" the clerk, a short man in his fifties, asked.

"When's the next train up to Great Falls?" Elmer was quick and direct as usual.

"You're in luck today. Being that it's Saturday, there wouldn't be a train down and back until Monday, but the Friday train got kicked back to today because of Christmas and all. Should be here around three p.m. and back to Great Falls around four or five. That be if nothing breaks or calamity strikes. That work for you boys?"

What a break. Mike was expecting to spend the night in Stanford and had no idea how long they would be waiting for a train north.

"We need two tickets, but we need to get Mike in here out of the cold. Him and the boy are needin' the tickets." Elmer put his hat back on and quickly headed out to fetch Mike.

"Good fortune. Theys a train coming in a couple of hours, and you'll be in Great Falls tonight. Christmas Day ruined the normal schedule. Only reason the train's coming today. Let's get you inside." Elmer pointed to Mike's and Roy's bags, indicating for him to reach over and collect them both.

"First bit a good news we've had lately, men." Mike's face showed a moment of relief after days of stress.

Mike grabbed his pine stick from the wagon and slowly moved to the depot steps. Roy grabbed under his arm as he raised up one step at a time.

"Leonard you old thief! How are ya, pal?" Of course, Mike would know the clerk.

"What's ailing you with that foot, Mike?" The clerk was shuffling papers while he asked.

"Not sure. Got stepped on a few days ago, and the Lewistown Doc said I need to get to Helena. There's a doctor over there can fix me up, or so he seems to think." Mike made his way to a nice chair with arms and sat down heavily.

"Need a favor from ya, Leonard. Need to find a place for my man Elmer to bed for the night. I don't want him headin' back home today. Any ideas? I'll pay of course, and we could use a little food if you can figure that out too. Sorry for throwing a loose load at ya', my friend."

Mike could make small requests sound monumental and big problems easy to solve.

"Well, he can sleep in the back room in the bed there. I only use it when I'm expecting a train early the next morning and that don't happen now in the winter. Got a stove back there too. And you can keep the team in one of the corrals. I think there's some hay out there that you can help yourself too." Leonard grinned and was pleased to offer a complete solution.

"That's capital, my friend, just capital! You just solved fifty pounds of trouble for us. I'll pay, of course, and even throw in an extra dollar if you can find some oats for the team. They need a little boost to get home." Mike reached into his coat pocket for his wallet and some cash.

"I know you'll shoot me if I don't take something, so let's say…two dollars for the cot, the hay, and I'll get you a bag of oats." The clerk knew Mike would refuse any charity.

"Couldn't be a better deal if you were my brother, Leonard! Deal. If we can scare up some food for the three of us now and something for Elmer for a breakfast tomorrow, that would earn another two dollars."

"I'll run home and have the missus put something together and bring it back. I'll have you watch the depot for me while I'm gone. Doubt they'll be a soul come in today." Leonard was writing up the tickets while he was talking. "That will be four dollars and four bits for two tickets to Great Falls. You'll need to get the tickets to Helena when you get there, but the schedule says there's a train headed south Monday morning at eleven so you should be all set."

"Give him this." Mike handed Roy a handful of bills for tickets and the extras, and Roy set it on the counter for the clerk to sort. He pushed back two-dollar bills, but Mike told him to keep it for the effort. Leonard shook his head and left it sitting there.

"Let me run and gather up some grub for you men. Be back in a bit." Leonard left out the back and walked towards the tiny town.

"I'll get the team unhitched. You good if Roy comes to help?" Elmer popped his hat back on and gloved up.

"I'm swell just sittin' here. Go ahead." Mike eased back, straightened his left foot out on a chair and closed his eyes. The minor amount of good news was welcomed, and Mike allowed himself a moment of relief. He tried not to think about the coming days.

"You'll not be stayin' will ya?" Roy asked Elmer, expecting him to tell him he was planning on returning to the ranch that night.

"No. I'll stay. Mike, well he'd get pretty cooked up if he found out I did that. He told Anna and the boys not to expect me, so I reckon I'll stay here tonight. That sky back to the southeast is pretty ugly. They don't call 'em the Snowy Mountains fer nothin'."

Elmer took the big leather collar off the second Belgian and laid it in the back of the wagon with the other tack. He threw a small canvas tarp over the bed to keep tack and hay dry in case of snow. He grabbed a large armful of hay from the back, and Roy did the same. They threw it in two piles on the ground for the team. There was a water pump nearby, and Elmer asked Roy to fetch a bucket.

"I'll water them tonight and in the morning. As soon they get some oats, they'll do fine. Be too hard on these boys to go home tonight anyway. I feel the cold moving in." Elmer threw that last bit of reason and truth in so Roy would believe he intended to stay in Sanford that night and not bring it up with Mike.

The two men walked back into the small depot and found Mike asleep and snoring in the chair. They walked as quietly as possible and sat down on a bench near the front door. Elmer raised his finger to his lips, and Roy agreed to make no noise. They looked at each other, each with a look that expressed the deep concern and worry about the future. Apprehension about Mike's future and the possible avalanche that would affect every person on the ranch was expressed in each man's eyes. Each knew the events in the coming days could have a positive conclusion and simply be an inconvenience or take a sour turn with no good finish. The fear of the unsure was unnerving.

———

Forty minutes later, the back door opened, and Leonard was carrying a wooden box with MONT DAIRY stenciled on the side. he sat it down on the counter. Mike woke when the door opened and was alert when Leonard set the food down.

"Sorry, boys, but the wife was doing wash and had to set that aside before she could cook, but we got some hot food for you. The train will be here in an hour or there abouts. And Elmer, I'll bring you up a plate for dinner around 5:00 and some cooked bacon and biscuits for the morning. You get the horses corralled?"

Roy and Elmer walked up to the counter, and Leonard handed them each a tin plate to dish up.

"Stay put, Mike. I'll haul you a plate." Leonard was already picking out food for Mike. "Got some goose left from Christmas, some cornbread, and the wife had some canned peas from the garden she whipped up. You like peas?"

"Love 'em. My wife hated 'em for some wicked reason. It was her only fault. Can you imagine hating peas?" Mike smiled, a moment thinking of Clara removed him from the world and the pain. "But let me tell ya, she was a good woman, fine as fresh cream."

The men all ate well and in short order. The food, along with the fire in the stove, finally erased the chill they all felt from the cold morning ride. The plates were collected and returned. Mike offered a genuine thanks to Leonard and a request to pass the same along to his wife.

"Roy, you'll want to leave them chaps with Elmer to take back. He can bring them back when he comes to fetch us. You won't be needing them now on the train and in town. I'd hate to see you lose them or leave them somewhere." Mike knew the importance of those fine, black, woolly chaps and what they meant to Roy.

"Aye, fine idea sir."

Roy unbuckled the chaps and reluctantly put them in the back room by the cot. He did not want to leave them, but it was the practical thing to do. Roy had brought the leather satchel that Mike had given him back in Great Falls this past spring. It seemed he had been at the ranch for years, but it had barely been six months.

Roy had brought the fancier shirt and britches Mike had given him for town clothes. He figured to change clothes in Helena before taking Mike to the hospital. It was then that the roles were going to be reversed. He would be the caretaker and would make sure that Mike was watched over and protected. He was proud that he could repay him in this small way.

"Leonard, can you send a telegram for me? Send a message to the Hotel Arvon in Great Falls and have them hold us two rooms for tonight for Mike and Roy Hanson." Mike knew that Leonard was also the Western Union man for the station and the entire area around Stanford.

Elmers's head perked up a bit when he heard "and Roy Hanson." Mike saw his small reaction and clarified.

"It was easier to tell the clerk there that Roy was my boy. He thought Roy was a roughneck rouser and didn't think he was good enough to stay in their fancy hotel, so I told him he was my son." Mike made the story sound believable, and Elmer gave a small nod that he understood. "That clerk was dollar-dandy, wasn't he Roy?"

Roy snorted and answered, "He was a tea drinker now," which drew a quick and small laugh from Mike.

Leonard was scribbling on a paper. "I'll send this now but don't expect a reply before you get on the train. They need to send a messenger boy to the hotel and then get back to me, unless you tell them to not answer."

"Send the message. We'll hope our luck holds, and they can fix us up. No reply is needed. Give Leonard some money for the wire." Mike was tired of all the thinking and arranging, and it was beginning to show. He leaned back and closed his eyes.

"Would ye need the medicine now, sir?" Roy could see he was hurting despite his rugged nature.

"Wait until we get on the train, Roy. I'll need some after all that loading up. Right now, I need to get outside to piss before the train gets here."

Elmer sprang up and took the lead to help. He assisted Mike out the front door on the platform. Mike looked around. He didn't see anyone around, so he moved to the edge of the boardwalk and let loose. He grabbed a handful of snow and rubbed his hands together. When he was done, Elmer helped Mike back into the station and to the chair to wait.

"Can't thank ya enough for the service and the kindness, Leonard.

I've known you a long while, and you're a good and fine man. Just needed to be said." Mike held out his hand for Leonard to shake.

"No need for that, Mike, but I'm obliged. You're an honest man, and no fella in four counties would say different." Leonard felt the extra squeeze of power in Mike's hand. He could see some emotion in his face as well. "Get that foot doctored up, and we'll see you back through in a week or so."

Mike patted the back of Leonard's hand as they shook and then broke off.

"There it is." Elmer was the first to spot the heavy smoke of the train a mile away.

"They'll be stopped for 20 minutes to take on water and off load, so no need to get moving yet." Leonard went behind the counter and picked up a board with papers on it. He then put on his official railroad hat and waited.

The train bell rang and rang as the sound of squeezed steam slowed until a giant final push of air signaled the engine was stopped.

CHAPTER 17

The train ride to Great Falls was quiet. Mike slept, propped up against a window and feeling the effects of the laudanum. Roy preferred to see him still and not thrashing around in pain. He hoped nothing would interrupt his peace.

Mike was careful not to take too much medicine and was disciplined patient, even when unattended.

Dr. Fullbright had told Mike before he had supplied him with the two bottles of relief, "Unobserved actions are the true compass as to the direction of a man."

Mike had replied to the doctor, "I suppose, Stanley," not appreciating the pop-up sermon regarding potential vice.

"I'm serious, Mike. This stuff is like a short man in a saloon scuffle. It gets ahold of a man and will not yield." The doctor had taken his last swing at delivering a punch of wisdom that would connect.

Mike had held up the bottle in acknowledgement to the doctor with a 'message received' before sliding it in his bag.

"I'll make it last, that's for damn sure." Mike added the element of limited resources to close the topic.

———

It was dark when the short, three-car train pulled into Great Falls. Roy was glad that he was a little familiar with this location and did not need Mike's involvement. He could run things.

"Feel like I got cow kicked," Mike said without raising his head or opening his closed eyes. "Great Falls?"

"Aye, sir. The conductor said he would help me get ye inside." Roy was already moving and putting his coat on. There was no need to rush as the train was done for the day, as Roy and Mike were the only cargo aboard.

The conductor and Roy managed to help Mike off the train.

"Give him two bits, Roy, for the extra help." Mike dug into his coat pocket and produced a coin.

"Not takin' a penny from you, Mr. Hanson. You always been good to all of us, and that's worth more than money to me. I'll get your valises." The conductor tipped his cap and returned to the train.

"We got no val…vala," Roy spoke up quietly.

"He means our bags, that's all." Mike winced while adjusting his position.

"Sir, we need to make our way to the Hotel Arvon. They should ha' rooms for us, and a wagon or buggy, too, would be grand." Roy was surprised at how he took command so easily.

"I got a buckboard out back that's mine. Would the gentleman be able to load? The ticket agent was eager to help," the conductor said as he returned with the bags.

"Slide me in the back. I'll be fine. Rode for five hours in the back of that wagon; I can sure as hell endure five blocks." Mike began to stand by himself.

"We'll pay ya for the delivering us to the hotel, sir." Again, Mike was more concerned about being fair and not taking advantage of anyone at any level of life. Another lesson from Mike to mold Roy.

"Kind of you, sir, but I pass by the hotel on my way home." The agent glanced at Roy and smiled in appreciation of the offer.

Roy then thought to ask about the train schedule down to Helena.

"Afraid the next train is Monday at 10:50 in the morning. Trains don't run on Sunday in the winter. I can get your tickets when you come back on Monday morning."

"Better to be laid up in a swanky hotel in Great Falls than layin' on the floor at the Stanford station I reckon." Mike threw a spin on this development to let Roy know the extra day was not a problem and that he might welcome the additional rest.

———

The Hotel Arvon was a familiar sight.

"Welcome back, Mr. Hanson. Fine to see you again. We received your telegram, and I'm pleased to be able to accommodate you both for this evening. Is your father outside?" It was Lowell Perkins. He was extremely helpful and seemed to want to start off this visit on a stronger foot than their first encounter.

"Aye, I'll fetch him in now." Roy turned back toward Perkins. "Me father's foot is ailing, and he can no walk up them steps. Can ye ha another man or two to hep?"

"I can do better than that, sir. We have an elevated box in the back. We use it for freight and the such, but it will lift a man with no difficulty." Perkins smiled again at being able to solve a major problem so quickly.

Roy went outside to tell Mike the good news.

"They got rooms and some way to lift ye up to the next floor wi out climbin'."

"Good." Mike was now offering one-word answers, and Roy knew he was nearly out of pepper.

The agent carried the bags into the lobby. "I can send a boy to get you Monday if that suit ya gents. Nine o'clock?"

Mike heard nothing. All of his effort was on getting to a bed.

"Aye, that be grand." Roy again found himself as the captain of this battle, but Mike was still the General of this campaign.

Perkins and Roy both guided Mike towards the back of the hotel where a small thin door was opened, exposing cables and a dim light.

"Please step inside, and this will have you on the above floor." After pushing Mike into the box, Perkins managed to find room and shut the door. Roy could hear machine noises and hoped the contraption wouldn't bring an end to the journey now.

Roy picked up both bags and quickly climbed the stairs, two steps at a time. He beat the lifting box and was standing waiting, slightly out of breath but at attention as a good soldier would be.

The door swung out, and the first thing Roy saw was Mike's face. For a man that had had a mountain lion jump him while on horseback and had walked home for four miles in a blizzard after his horse spooked and bolted, he looked as if he had ridden up with a sleeping grizzly bear. His eyes were wide. He looked at Roy and rapidly shook his head side to side.

"Let me out ah here, fella before this thing drops us down to Hades!" Mike threw his good foot out and then dragged his bad one out, without any evidence of pain or concern for additional damage. He just wanted to get out of that fancy moving jail cell.

"Sorry for the bumpy ride, sir. The elevator is meant to carry linen, towels, and lighter objects. Two men is a bit much for it." Perkins was correct; Nevertheless, after surviving the effort, Mike was grateful to have avoided the long staircase.

"Yes, young man, I reckon you're right, and I'm grateful. But if this foot don't kill me, another ride in that upright coffin will." Mike kept moving toward the hall.

"Not many travelers presently, so I was able to place you in the same rooms you and your son had on your previous visit: The Governor and the Missouri." Perkins pulled out the key to Mike's room and opened the door.

"Here is you key, Hanson the Junior. Our maid is gone, but we could ready the bath for you tomorrow?" Perkins stepped back to the door while speaking.

"That suits us, fella. Now, forgot to tell ya, we'll be here two nights cause the train don't leave for Helena until Monday morning. Maybe you could point Roy here to some place for a little food. Nothin' fancy. Don't care if it's hardboiled eggs and bread. Just need a little some-thing. This medicine is rougher than a cob on belly." Mike ran out of air and relaxed his frame.

"Allow me to ponder the dining issue for a tick, but I will be happy to have you as guests an additional night. We will process the registra-tion and fees tomorrow at your convenience. If your son will come back down and allow me a few minutes to gather my thoughts, I'll provide him with food suggestions." Perkins seemed as if he could dig up new words like an Irishman can dig potatoes and talk all day and night.

"Yep, he'll do that." Mike pulled out his wallet from his inside breast pocket and thrust two silver dollars Perkins' way. "Take this, Mr. Perkins. Please. And I may need a doctor to stop up tomorrow if you can help with that."

"Yes, Mr. Hanson. I'll be able to arrange that I'm sure. I'll locate Dr. Basinger in the morning. And many thanks for the generous gratuity sir." Perkins walked out, shutting the door behind him.

"The fella is good at this hotelin', but he uses twenty words when six would do the work. I'm no idiot, but he threw a couple a words in there that I ain't sure are real English!" Mike gave a small laugh, his first on this long day.

Roy let out a tiny snort himself and, for a second, it seemed things were back to normal. Unfortunately, Mike attempted to stand and let out a yelp that quickly slapped the normal out of the situation.

"Pull that boot off, would ya, and then, hate to ask, but then help me out of these britches." Mike knew there were no other options.

"Pull my medicine out of the bag would ya, son, and pour me a glass of water out of that pitcher if you can." Mike disliked asking anyone to do anything for him, and Roy sensed his discomfort in being reliant on another man. "Go get yourself in your room and then see if you can scratch us up a little grub. Don't care what it is, just do yer best."

"Aye, should not be a problem." Roy was tired, but he felt needed and useful. He reached for the doorknob.

"And...I hope that fella calling you my son don't bother you none."

"Not a wee bit." Roy looked back at Mike. "I like it fer sure."

"Me too, son, me too." Mike let his head lay flat on the pillow. The words spoken were powerful and overdue medicine for both men.

———

Roy headed down the stairs to ask Clerk Perkins about food. Perkins was behind the front desk and saw Roy descending.

"Mr. Hanson, I believe your options are very slim indeed as it's nearing the nine o'clock hour, it is a cold winter's night and, well, we have few choices even in the daylight."

Roy had expected this sort of answer and would settle for nearly anything.

"Might I suggest we step next door to the green grocery and see if we can't pilfer a few goods to get you and your father through the night? I have a key as Mr. Vaughn also owns that business."

Perkins walked outside in the cold and put a key in a lock two doors down. Painted letters on the door said "Derrig Fruit Co.," and Roy was hopeful to find anything for them to eat.

Perkins reached over, touched something on the wall, and two lights erupted to life. The building was cold, and Roy's fatigue did not offer any warmth.

They walked to a table in the middle of the room that had some cloth rags and linen tossed over it. Pulling back the cloth revealed a variety of fruits, glass jars with jelly, and a pie. An entire pear pie. Roy picked up two apples, two pears, and the pie.

"Please let me know what we be owin' ye." Roy was pleased to have found something to eat, as odd of a dinner as it was.

Back to the hotel and climbing the stairs, he threw a final thanks Perkins' way and tapped on Mike's door.

No answer.

Another knock.

Nothing.

Roy's imagination instantly flew into high gear. *Is he…?*

He opened the door to find a snoring Mike, exhausted and medicated. A sigh of relief let Roy relax. He set the scavenged food on a small table. He tapped Mike's shoulder, and by the third effort, he woke.

"It ain't much, but it's all I could find. Me and Mr. Perkins walked next door. This is what was there. Hope ye like pears." Roy handed him an apple, a pear, and filled his water glass.

"Thank ya, Roy. This is all I need. Is that a pie? Good job on that one, son." Mike caught a small second wind and took a bite of the pear. "When my foot is up in a bed, it don't throb so bad, and it's a little better, so I hope I get some sleep. The food will help too." A grin to Roy was a small sign of hope. Small but positive. "Let me have a handful of that pie. That will shut me down for the night."

Roy held out the pie, and as no plates or cutlery were available Mike took two fingers, plunged them down the outside of the crust and came back with a large chunk. Into his mouth and while licking his finger, he grunted to Roy to follow suit and dig from the other side. Roy was surprised how sweet the pie was, and the crust was good. One more handful for each man left half a pie for tomorrow.

Wiping his fingers on the sheet on the side of the bed, Mike had had enough. Enough travel, pain, cold, food, and drama. The day felt like a week.

"Let me sleep a bit in the morning but check on me to see if I can fog a mirror." A Hanson wink followed the instruction.

"Sorry, but I dunno what ye wan me ta do with a mirror?" Roy was too tired to play along.

"Check on me to see if I'm still breathing, son. Sorry for jokin' with ya. Get some sleep." Mike pulled up the quilt, lay back, closed his eyes, and was snoring in 20 seconds.

Roy shuffled over to his room, stripped down, and climbed into the bed that had been his first. You never forget your first they say.

CHAPTER 18

Roy sat straight up in bed, startled and confused. For an instant, he had no idea where he was. Ten seconds passed, and then it all came to him. He wished he could have stayed in the fog of forgetfulness for a little longer. The day before, all 24 hours of that day, felt like a mule kick, and the pain was still lingering.

He dressed and looked down the hall, remembering there was a clock at the top of the staircase.

8:12 a.m. And it was Sunday.

He walked over to Big Mike's room and pressed his ear on the door. He could hear Big Mike snoring with an uneven rhythm, the way a dog or horse who isn't right does. At least he was asleep and not waiting on Roy to fetch, fix, or feed.

There was an older man sitting at a small table behind the front desk. He looked up and said nothing. Roy stood at the desk and, after a minute of silence and no movement, he cleared his throat and asked, "Mornin' to ye, sir. Would Mr. Perkins be present?"

"Out," was all he said.

Roy, a Scotsman, was frugal with words as well as money, but he had met a man that was as stubborn and skilled as a pine stump.

"Will he be returned soon?" Again, no response. Roy saw no

conversation in the future with Mr. Stump and turned to the front door.

"Yep."

Roy kept walking. At least he got all the information he asked for and truly needed, all gathered with two words. *There may be a lesson in that*, he thought.

The wind was biting and made the freezing air worse than it needed to be. He remembered where the café was where he and Mike had eaten a thick and hefty breakfast but couldn't recall the name.

Snow flurries swirled around, but nothing that would measure. The café was in sight and was open on Sundays. He could hear his stomach back talking. He was going to eat until he had difficulty breathing.

Eggs, beans, and fried cakes they called flapjacks covered with molasses were all on the table. Roy started fast and stuffed in food like a chipmunk. He had learned to drink coffee all too well and was already on his second cup.

"My father is back at the hotel. He can't walk today, but he be needin' some food this morn and the next." Roy tried to explain to the waitress as best he could and hoped his needs where understood.

"Are you up at the new hotel, The Arvon?"

"Aye, ma'am. We are fer certain. The Mr. Perkins that's there is in charge." Roy tossed out anything he could think of to fortify his story.

"Yes, we all know Perkins. East coast fella with plenty of east coast ways. He's slowly fittin' in. He's an alright young man." The waitress wiped her hands on her apron. "I can fix you up something, you take it to him, and I'll pick up the pot tomorrow at the hotel. That suit ya?"

"Aye, that be bonnie."

"You Scot boys are awful charming," she said with a grin. "You finish, and I'll be back."

Roy stood at the pickle barrel with a cigar box as a cash coffer. The waitress brought out a black pot covered with a red and white checked cloth. "Don't stop along the way or the food will be frosty before he gets to it."

Roy paid, touched the front of his hat to the woman, and headed to the Arvon with the pot held close to his chest to keep the breakfast and himself warm.

"Good day, Mr. Hanson. I hope your father is feeling chipper this morning. I see that you've been feed and about to deliver the same to Mr. Hanson, am I right?"

Roy thought, *Why can't this lad just say normal words?*

"Yes, sir. I have not seen him this morning." Roy kept walking towards the steps so as not to be engaged in further complex Perkins conversation.

"I will send for Dr. Basinger shortly and send him up upon arrival. Perhaps you both would enjoy our bathing room later?" Perkins was full of spare words, but he was damn good at his job.

"That would be grand. My thanks, Mr. Perkins." Roy was attempting to match the elevated word exchange as well as trying to play the part of a successful rancher's son.

"Very well." Perkins stood at attention and clicked his heels.

Roy rolled his eyes, glad to have ended the banter. He liked Perkins well enough; it was that they operated at different speeds, and it was taxing for Roy to maintain.

His tapping on Mike's door was answered with a gravely reply. Roy poked an eye around the door, and Mike waved him in. "How'd ya sleep, son? That bed as good as you remember it to be?"

Roy was embarrassed to not fire the first volley. "Yes, sir, it was good sleep. Tired as I'm sure you was last night. I brung some hot foot from that café we ate before." He held out the pot full of food and lifted the cloth. Mike raised up in the bed and patted his lap.

"The pie was good, but I'm needing for hot grub. Thank you for getting this." There was a fork and knife with the food as Mike made quick work of the first few bites.

"Damn, I don't have any coffee for ya. Shite." The raw frustration leaked out of Roy. How could coffee be forgotten?

Mike's eyes opened wide, and he laughed. "Roy Douglas, I never heard that language out of you before! Cross the street for the next preacher ya see."

"Sorry, sir. Fell right out a me." Roy was glad that he had broken the ice on his near-military demeanor.

"Yer fine, Roy. You've been calling me 'sir' for months. How about we switch that to Mike, unless ol' Perkins is around. Good to keep him thinking I'm your paw."

Roy grinned and nodded, figuring he was using plenty of words at present.

"Perkins is sending for the doctor, and he asked about the bath later, but that be all." Roy's report was prompt and accurate.

"A bath would be good later. Maybe after the doc messes around with me." Mike grimaced and shifted his bad foot.

"Still hurting ya fierce…Mike?"

Mike gave a wink upon hearing Roy use his name and continued to chew.

"Yep. All purple and swelled up like a bloated goat. As long as I lay still, it's not too bad, but I'm gonna need some help to get to the outhouse. I mean the one they got down the hallway here." Mike grabbed a flapjack and mopped up some egg in the bottom of the pot.

"Aye, but you be on your own once yer in it." Roy paused waiting for a reaction.

"Well damnation, Roy! That's a good one. Get you off the ranch, and you're quite a character." Mike was enjoying this late bloom of Roy's personality.

"Take this bucket off me and help me get to the privy before I pop. And once I get back to this bed, I want you to do something for me." Mike rotated out and set both feet on the floor, ready for the jolt of pain.

After a short visit to the WC, Mike slumped back on the bed. He handed Roy a folded note and some folded money.

"Get Grace the fanciest doll you can find in town. Spend five dollars if needed. And take five dollars and buy something for you."

There was a ten-dollar bank note folded in the note. Nearly a week's pay. Mike wasn't wealthy, but he was successful and was the most generous man Roy had known.

"Today is Sunday so not any stores open today. Can I go tomorrow, before we load on the train?"

Mike let out a huff. "Dad gum, I don't know what day it is. You bet, son. Rest up, walk, read, do anything you want and then check on me a time or two. Gotta feed me too!"

Roy tried to walk around, but the wind was strong and took the pleasure out of the adventure. Instead, he returned to his room for more reading and resting. He would fetch food for Mike after they both had enjoyed the bathing room of the Hotel Arvon. A days rest lay ahead.

———

Roy met Monday morning early, rested and antsy. He did not care for the lack of activity and had no experience with slothful ways. It just didn't feel right to him to not work.

He repeated the routine of the previous day: he checked in the morning to hear Mike snoring. Then he went off to breakfast and returned with food. The rest of the day would be filled with chores for Mike and a train ride.

Great Falls was not a big city or even much of a town yet, but it was growing and expanding extremely fast. The train lines and depot were next to the Missouri River, and the commercial district was a little north of the depot and two bridges that spanned the Missouri. The Hotel Arvon and The Hub Clothing Store, where Roy was first outfitted with American clothing, were both on First Street and no more than two or three blocks from the river and trains.

It was a chilly morning, and as Roy had only brought one book along on the trip, he decided he would find another to help pass the next few days. He did like Mr. Twain's books, but they required to be re-read many times to understand some passages. He never thought of himself as thick-headed, but he knew his education was not equal to absorbing all the princely words of Twain. At least he could read and write, and those skills did set him apart from most.

The train was leaving in about three hours. He wandered a bit away from the river, walking north and back south until he came upon a short stone building with two signs above it: Great Falls National Bank and next to it in the same structure was Murphy, Maclay & Co. He walked to the bank's windows and saw iron cages, tall tables, and men in fine suits sitting at large desks. He had never been inside a bank.

He took a good long peek until a man inside gave him a stern glare, and then Roy quickly walked toward the other store. He felt that there was no reason for the unfriendly glance, and he would carry a feeling of irritation and judgement towards banks and bankers for life.

All because I was looking at you, ya wee bald gommy.

The adjacent store looked much more interesting and inviting, and it was. Murphy, Maclay and Co. had nearly anything a man could want. A tiny bell attached to the door rang as Roy walked in.

A small sign on the wall said, IF WE DON'T HAVE IT, YOU HAVE NO NEED OF IT. Reassuring words.

"Good day, young sir. We have a fine variety of goods to fill any desires and all needs," said a friendly but unsmiling man in a wool sweater as he walked towards Roy. Roy tipped his hat, as was his custom, and continued to scan the floor.

Shovels, cooking pots, rolls of fabric, and hammers first caught his eye. The practical working man in him was drawn to the shiny tools, and he drifted towards them as if the floor were slanted and resistance was not possible. A wall full of polished steel hammers made him pause and admire. "STANLEY - The Toolbox of the World" was printed on a sign in the middle and on the counter were boxes of screwdrivers with dark brown wooden handles.

He thought, *This Stanley fella must work day and night to make these many tools.*

Hand saws, long sticks with fine black marks up the length of the wood, and small steel bars with the same lines were all available. Roy was familiar with the function of hammers, but the other items were not required to work sheep or horses and held his curiosity.

He moved down the wall to some beautiful new axes, doubled-headed and ready for battle. Roy had never seen a new axe; he had seen only a brown, rust covered one with a sharp, shiny smile on the edge. He had no idea they started life this handsomely.

Shovels, pick axes, and wooden and metal buckets of all sizes were laid out on the floor. Window glass, imported teas, and even explosives for mining were there as well. Every head turn revealed the world of labor and physical toil. But that was how men lived and survived, and the stock of the store was impressive.

"You seem to be high centered near the hand tools, young fella. You need a certain tool?" The clerk was ready to direct Roy to any available device.

"No, sir, just standin' at wonder of the goods ye ha'. Never seen such a lot."

The clerk took the compliment and replied, "We carry the finest tools and gear a working rancher and farmer can find north of the Yellowstone." His attitude softened, and he walked toward Roy. "Please look at these quality stoves we have as well. Come from Cincinnati, Ohio they do. Best stoves in Montana." The clerk lifted a heavy round top off the stove with a small lid lifter and set it back down.

"That's a grand stove, sir, but I'm in need of a gift for my wee sister." Again, Roy assumed the role and title of a Hanson to save confusion and time.

"We have items over here that would please any child." The clerk stepped back and allowed Roy to choose.

A carved horse on small wheels and a string caught his attention first, and he admired the craftsmanship. A book titled *Paper Dolls from Around the World* lay there, and he remembered that Grace had just received a similar gift from Santa. Beautiful small glass marbles in a leather bag caught his eye. Roy instantly thought of buying and keep those for himself and would pretend that it was a gift for 'his sister.'

"She likes dolls."

"They all do, don't they? I think there is a book with some on the table." The clerk had his back turned to Roy as he took the top off a small keg of nails.

"Aye, seen that, sir. Have ye one that looks real?"

"Wait, I got something on the top shelf. Had to put it up after a waif nearly shattered it, but it is not cheap. Think it's from Germany. Yep, says so right here. Got real hair too." The clerk brought over a wooden ladder with hooks at the top and leaned it against a tall cabinet. He brought down a cloth sack with a string tied at the top. He pulled out a 12-inch-tall miniature human-like figure that even Roy thought was pretty.

"They can sure make 'em look real, can't they?" The clerk lifted it up and slowly turned it for Roy to see. "That there is probably the nicest dress in all of Great Falls."

The doll had blonde hair in pigtails down to her shoulders and a round face with soft pink cheeks against a nearly pure white complexion. He scanned down the doll. She had on a bright red polka dotted dress past her knees with white socks and tiny black shoes.

"This will do, sir. Yes," Roy said while reaching for it and holding it up like a priest holding up a communion cup.

"This doll here is aces-high. Cost as much as a pair of boots, but she's pretty as a spring lamb." The clerk walked to the counter with the cash register, pulled out a black notebook, and began to flip the pages. He saw what he needed to see, closed the book, and walked back. Making assumptions, he reached for the doll saying, "Sorry, son, but she costs four dollars."

Roy recoiled from his reach as if avoiding a striking snake. He pulled back and said, "I have enough. I'll be takin' this to me sister please. Would you have a box or somethin'? She'll have quite a journey ahead of her."

"I'll attend to that this minute." Reaching for the bag, Roy handed the doll to the clerk. He covered her and carefully set it down. The clerk bent down under a table and, after some rearranging, pulled out a suitable box. He put the doll inside, carried it to the front, pulled out lengths of string, and cinched the top down.

Roy picked up the bag of marbles and went to the front to pay. "Sister will like these I think, so better bring these along. Would ya be havin' any books from Mr. Twain?" Roy didn't know of any other authors.

"We only have a few books but got that *Treasure Island* over on that shelf. Heard it's good." The clerk was leaning on his elbows watching Roy roam.

Robert Louis Stevenson, *Treasure Island*. It had a slip of paper poking out of the top with a handwritten sign: $.50. There were only seven books available, and this looked to be a book to keep him company for in the coming days.

Pulling cash out, he approached the clerk. "If that is all, the cost is a total of five dollars, four bits." A ten-dollar bank note was used, and the correct change was handed back to Roy. He put the marbles in one pocket, put the book on top of the wrapped box, and tipped his hat on his way out.

———

A quick stop to pay Mr. Thisted a visit was next.

Three steps in the door of The Hub, he was greeted with an energetic call from the center of the store.

"Der iz a young yentleman dat I have know of before! And ver iz da father?" Mr. Thisted was a true wizard at selling, and most of that was paying attention to people.

"Good day ta yea, sir, and tanks fer the remember. Pa is back at the hotel with a sore foot and sends regrets." Roy noticed that he was speaking more like an American and even more like a city citizen. He was not sure if it was working, but he was learning.

"If he hast a bad foot, vill new socks bring him some happy?"

Roy was fascinated by Mr. Thisted and his knack at expressing concern while going in for a sale. Remarkable.

"Aye, that would be a grand idea." Roy thought a pair of new socks would be a quick end to the sales avalanche from the Norwegian marketing genius.

"The time we was here, my eye saw a fine piece of neckwear. Had some string and a silver medal. Do you have such a thing, sir?"

Thisted's eyes got wide. "Ja, Ja, I haz them over here. Deh call dem Bolo. Right here de are."

Roy walked to a glass case. Inside were five pocket watches, cufflinks like a New York dandy would wear, collar stays, and various metal bolo tie tips and fasteners. There were big ones with a polished stone, and a few made from silver dollars. Then Roy spotted his prize. He pointed it out to Mr. Thisted who pulled it out and let him look at it and touch it.

It was in the shape of a shield, had a polished black background, and had a large gold leaf M in the center.

"De M ist for deh Montana ja? I had made by a Moormon man in

Salt Lake City. But he only have de von vife." Thisted was proud and promoting.

When Roy saw it, he didn't connect it with his new state.

He saw the M was for…Mike.

"Do ya have another one like it?" Roy had a notion.

"Vell, der ist another dats close. Dis von." The clerk raised up a larger round black disk with a silver M in the middle.

Roy couldn't decide which one he preferred, but it didn't matter. Both would suit his plans. "Do ye offer a price for da both of 'em?"

"You must be de big sheepman back home! A big rancher need zeez, ja? I do tree dollars for both. Good price for you friend. And dat iz vit da shiny tips on both." Thisted leaned forward expecting a sale.

"I take them both." Roy had a small twinge of happiness. A plan had been hatched.

Mr. Thisted strung the ties together, installed the tips, bagged them up with the socks, and handed Roy back his change.

"Please return vif da father soon." Mr. Thisted bowed slightly as Roy tapped his hat. He headed back to Mike to show him the treasures.

Roy was eager to get to the hotel in the event that Mike was needing help. He also wanted to be present when the doctor visited.

———

Mr. Perkins was back on duty and greeted Roy. "Dr. Basinger is due to call on Mr. Hanson within the hour. I trust that will suit your father?"

"I will ask him now. Sure to be no problem. Thank ye, Mr. Perkins. If you could give us a tally on the cost of the room and the food from the night before, grateful we'd be. Roy was evolving into a foreman with surprising ease. Talking and dealing with more people seemed to be improving his communication skills.

Perkins pulled out a slip of paper and jotted down a few notes and numbers. "I will have that all compiled for you before you depart, and we can then settle the account. I'll direct the doctor up when he arrives."

Attempting to appear more cultivated than he was, Roy turned and tapped his hat to Perkins and waited until the salute was acknowledged before ascending the staircase.

Roy knocked and Big Mike grunted. Walking in, he saw Mike in obvious pain, so much so that Mike was not attempting to mask his condition at all.

"Hurtin' ye more it is?"

"Mmmmm."

"Can I fetch the tonic far ye?" Roy's mood went from neutral to crisis. He reached for the bottle on the nightstand to give to Mike, but it was empty. He rummaged around in the bag on the floor, found the second one, and handed it to Mike. Even in his current condition, Mike was disciplined enough to only take one swallow.

He sat up a bit, let the vile tasting sludge slide down his throat, took a breath, and exhaled. "Damnation, not feelin' proper today. Got a fever startin' up too."

Roy could see the sweat beads on Mike's face and neck. Not good.

"Perkins downstairs says the doctor should be here shortly. Maybe he has some strong potion fer ye to try." Roy attempted to offer any comfort he could.

"Yep, we'll see," Mike replied in a doubtful tone. "What ya got there, son?" He pointed to the box.

Roy changed gears and saw an opening to improve the mood. "Oh, you be likin' this here, Mike." He untied the box, removed the bag, and just before he revealed the doll, he added, "This is for wee Gracie. A gift from you to her."

Mike's face began with a tiny grin and worked up to a full-tooth smile. He reached for the doll and held it, surely thinking about Grace's reaction to the gift.

The smile faded and gave way to a quaking lower lip and gust of emotion. Mike's face was covered with sweat, but Roy noticed tears mixing in, so he quickly turned to reach for something, anything, to give Mike a moment.

"She's a little princess." Mike's words came out slowly and peacefully. "Grace I mean. She's my princess. Some days after her ma died, the only reason to get up for me was her. She'd hug me around the neck and all I could feel was her future. She fixed me she did."

Roy knew Mike was a tender man and loved Grace, but he had never heard a man talk about things in this way. It was unfamiliar but comforting all the same.

Mike held his stare on the doll. "Ya know she thinks you're a top-notch fella, what do you say…a bonny lad, huh? She loves ya. Never got her a brother. A fence post got more talk in it than Elmer does."

Mike took a long pause. Motionless and deep in thought, he finally whispered, "I need you to tend to her…if…"

Roy found himself falling into being a member of the Hanson family with little warning, but he was there. Did Mike Hanson just ask him to watch over his only wee daughter in case he…he was not able? That's a thing for family, and Mike must think of Roy as kin. Roy already did, so it wasn't a tall step. Even so, as he heard a man on the train say, 'Holy buckets.'

"I do whatever you need, Mike. Ye know that. Anyathin."

Mike handed the doll back to Roy to stow. "You did a fine, fine job. That little girl will spin like a lamb when she sees this doll." With a deep breath and side look to the window, Mike added, "Wish I could a been with ya, so it woulda hit me like it did you when you saw it. We got the same eye. You and I would a wrestled for it." A Hanson wink ended the thought.

There were two knocks on the door. Both knew it was the doctor. Roy answered and allowed him in. Introductions were made, and Roy slid out of the room to give Mike privacy. Besides, he had heard enough about Mike's difficulties. He found a chair in the hallway between the rooms. He needed to sit one minute without distress.

After 20 minutes of sitting in the chair, the door opened. Roy stood up, and the doctor walked over.

"Your father is sick son and getting worse by what he's telling me. I left him another bottle to get him to Helena. Glad you'll be on that morning train in an hour. That foot is infected, and his fever is going to get worse. See if you can wrap some snow in a cloth tomorrow and put it on his head when he calls for some relief."

Dr. Basinger tried not to show undue concern, but he couldn't hide his feelings or silent opinion. Mike needs to get to Helena soon.

CHAPTER 19

Mike was well medicated. The more the narcotics helped ease the pain, the more dependent he became on Roy and others. Roy preferred it this way. Seeing Mike in pain was cruel.

The depot clerk was at the front door of the Hotel Arvon at 10, ready to help with the loading into his two-seat covered buggy. Mr. Perkins had given a smoother ride down to the first floor this time. Possibly his skills had improved at the controls or more likely Mike was more relaxed and nearly comatose.

Roy took Mike under one arm and Perkins did the same, each carrying a bag as well.

"We all square, young man?" Mike mumbled to Perkins, surprising all in earshot.

"Yes, sir. Mr. Hanson Junior and I settled the account this very morning. All is satisfied and closed. And I wish to thank you again for your patronage." Perkins never seemed to run clean of new and decorative words.

"Good. Roy, you gave him money then?" Mike was showing signs of confusion.

"Aye, sir, I did."

"Good, good. You know where the money is right, son?" Mike patted the breast pocket of his big coat. "Right here. Hell's fire, you know that. Here, you take it and keep a hand on it for us. They may rob me in Helena. Full of politicians and high-grading miners. Both are thievin' bastards." Mike showed more awareness and strength than expected, but he soon ran out of fuel.

Roy tipped his cap to Perkins, hopefully expressing genuine thanks for the extra care and service. Perkins gave a concerning grin and bowed slightly. The message was understood and valued.

Roy had a flashback to his first visit with Mike and the sheep to Great Falls. He wondered if that wasn't an easier occasion. Maybe not, but he'd ship one hundred sheep each week in exchange for this ballyhoo.

The train south to Helena had two passenger railcars and four boxcars. The train depot was next to the Missouri River, and Roy could see large chunks of ice flowing down the river. The train was going south as the river flowed north coming into Great Falls, and it gave the appearance that the ice was speeding by.

The windows were frosted, but the car was warm. The conductor gave Mike and Roy the seats closest to the wood stove in the front corner. The station agent gave two wool blankets to Roy for comfort, and he wadded one up for Mike to use as a pillow. Mike was medicated and groggy, and that would make the next five hours manageable.

As the train was passing over vast prairie land, Roy could see a large flat-topped mountain off to the right. Further down the line, the terrain charged dramatically. Rock formations began to jut straight off the flat earth, and beautiful canyons appeared ahead. Roy could see the Missouri River on the left side of the train as they headed into some deep canyons. The walls raised up, and he had to strain to see the top of the rocks. Snow stuck to half of the rock faces, making the view more theatrical. He turned around to see if others were as fascinated by the view as he was. He saw a young mother with a small boy also peering out and smiling at each other. He thought how Grace would probably enjoy the view much like the boy.

The canyons seemed to spread out and move back as the river

curved more and widened. The tracks straightened for a few miles, and then the tight canyons returned. Slowing down as the curves returned, he heard a man in the back say that Wolf Creek was ahead, and the train would stop there.

"Wolf Creek Station. Wolf Creek ahead," the conductor said loud enough to be heard but not wake Mike. Roy noted this small act of humanity on Mike's behalf.

"Where did the river go, sir?" Roy asked the conductor.

"The river is on the other side of the mountain to the east. It's called the Gates of the Mountains, and Lewis and Clark traveled through there. Pretty country. This is called Prickly Pear Canyon. Lots of snow down in here." He enjoyed sharing his knowledge of this unique area.

Roy wondered who this man named Lewis Clark was. If the conductor mentioned him, he must be a man of some importance.

A short stop at Wolf Creek allowed a few people to enter the small depot and find the outhouse. Three men got on and headed to Helena with the others.

More deep canyon walls blocked in Prickly Pear Creek for another hour until the prairie rose up again and mountains appeared on all sides. The train came to the top of a huge bowl and giant valley. It was vast and beautiful.

It seemed that the train would never get to the valley floor as the land stretched out like a ball of string falling down a staircase. The tracks clung to the side of the mountains and allowed a more gradual rise and fall. It was late afternoon and the train finally reached the floor of the northern part of Helena Valley, and the tracks were straight as a string. Roy could see Mount Helena to the right with its distinctive double peaks, standing guard over Helena, tucked at its base, and deep into the area called Last Chance Gulch.

The Great Northern Railway depot was on the edge of town in an area north and east of Helena. Helena had been in existence since 1864 and was growing fast, due in part to the high concentration of wealth in the city. The highest percentage of millionaires to citizens in any city in America lived in Helena, Montana. Wealth and power were everywhere and talk of Helena becoming the new permanent State Capital was constant.

The conductor, another railroad man, and Roy all helped to get Mike up and out of the car and to the depot. Mike was alert but slow. As the men moved slowly into the building, the conductor told Roy that he could find a carriage driver near the large double doors. Roy went up to a tall man with a flat top black hat and secured a carriage. He asked the man to take them to St. Peter's Hospital. He also asked if he knew of a comfortable hotel close to the hospital. The Hotel Helena was recommended, as it was a short walk up to the hospital.

Mike was helped into the back of the black carriage, and Roy followed him. They then headed west and then south to Main Street and the business district. The hospital was back up the hill to the left and over to Logan Street and 11th Avenue. St. Peter's was the largest hospital for many miles around and because of Helena's status as the current Capital, the newer building had been at this site for four years and was a handsome dark brown brick structure. It was easy to spot as it sat on a hilltop and had no trees near it.

The ride was under 15 minutes, and the carriage stopped at a door with a painted red cross over the entrance. The driver went inside to ask for help while Roy sat with Mike.

"We're here, Mike. We made it. Things gonna be fine now." Roy used as much reassurance as he had in him.

Mike said nothing but reached over and squeezed Roy's hand as if to say a silent 'thank you.' Roy reached and covered Mike's big hand with his, pressed down, and waited.

A large man in a white coat and a woman in a long dark cape came out pushing a chair with large wheels on the side. The man reached in and helped to lift Mike out. Mike's body went limp, and he slumped into the big man's arms. The days of fighting and determination to survive were no longer required. He released the last of his strength and struggle in an instant. He had no vigor left nor the need to produce his own power.

The man pushed the chair and Mike into the hospital. The driver told Roy he would pass by the Hotel Helena and tell the desk clerk to expect him later. Roy thanked him. He paid the carriage driver a dollar and tipped him fifty cents. That's what Mike would have done.

Inside, the nurse was touching and inspecting Mike and asking him questions. He did his best to answer and after a minute, she grabbed Roy by the elbow and directed him to a sliding glass window. A woman behind the glass opened and waited for Roy to speak with the nurse.

Roy began the story. "Dr. Fullbright in Lewistown told doctor, ah... doctor, ah." His mind went dark. He pulled a piece of paper out of his front pocket with a name written on it and handed it to the nurse.

"Dr. Humphrey. He's here to see Dr. Humphrey. I will go call the doctor. The nurse motioned for the man to bring Mike over.

"Take this man up to the second floor and find a bed. Tell the nurse on duty that he is a patient of Dr. Humphrey."

Again, Roy found himself in a new world within a dark new universe. There was little excitement and scarce promise of a sunny future here.

Roy followed the nurse up the steps and was shown to an area with two windows and four chairs. This would be Roy's second home for the coming days. He felt alone. Roy hoped Mike didn't feel the same and that he knew he was nearby and ready to help him if needed.

Ten minutes later, a man in a dark suit walked up the stairs followed by a nurse. He asked the nurse in which room the new patient had been placed. Roy hoped it was Dr. Humphrey.

The nurse that was trailing the man walked out, looked around, and saw Roy.

"Are you the companion of Mr. Hanson?" She spoke quickly and softly.

"Ay...yes, I am." In an instant, Roy's instincts told him to sound as American as possible. It was time to adopt a few words that placed him in Montana and not Scotland. He was worried that he would be seen as an irrelevant immigrant, and he wanted to be reliable support for Mike if needed.

"Please come with me." She turned quickly and headed to the open door down the hallway. Inside were ten beds with three other men laying quietly. He could see Mike on one of the beds being attended to by the man he had just seen walk by.

"I am Dr. Humphrey. Who would you be, young man?" The doctor was busy unwrapping Mike's foot, so Roy walked to the other side of the bed near Mike's head. "Mr. Hanson, would you like to answer questions, or would this young man be better suited to the task?"

"This is Roy. He's my best hand, and he's been my babysitter for a few days now, but I can answer ya, Doc." Mike sounded alert and not in pain. It was yet another display of how strong and tough Mike was.

The doctor picked up Mike's foot and pressed the skin. His foot was swollen and purple. Dr. Humphrey showed no emotion or reaction. He walked to a wash basin in the room, washed his hands, and went to put a thermometer in Mike's mouth.

"Open your mouth and put this under your tongue. And please don't speak for a minute."

Neither Mike nor Roy had seen a small glass pencil like this before and wondered about its purpose.

The doctor slipped the glass stick out of Mike's mouth, stared at it, and wrote down a number on a piece of paper that was clipped to a board.

"Nurse, please get the foot raised and place ice upon it. Hopefully, that will offer some relief. No more than five minutes on and then off, please." Dr. Humphrey reached into his pocket and took out a bottle. "Take two of these right now, please. It is quinine and is effective against fevers. Are you in pain, Mr. Hanson?"

The nurse gave Mike a glass of water, and he swallowed the pills. He shook his head no to the question regarding the pain. He was comfortable now as well as relieved to be under medical care.

"Mr. Hanson, you have a strong fever, and we hope to control that. The ice and the medicines should help you. Have you been taking a pain treatment?"

Roy reached into Mike's bag and showed the doctor the bottle.

"Let's resist taking too much of this, but let's continue taking it in smaller doses as it will deliver respite from the pain. Nurse, I will put this in his orders. Have you eaten today, sir?"

"Can't remember for truth doctor." Mike was sinking into the bed and relaxing more each minute.

"We had a small meal this morning." Roy hadn't realized that neither of them had had a full meal all day. Now, he felt hungry.

"Let's get this man a nice supper as soon as possible please, nurse.

Now Mr. Hanson, let's give you a night's rest. The nurse will treat your foot with ice and clean it. Let's allow the extra medicine this evening to work, and I will visit with you in the morning. I'm reassured to have you with us after such a long sojourn. Please eat all you can and rest well, sir." Dr. Humphrey's calm and confident demeanor gave both men hope.

"Roy, may I speak with you?" The doctor walked out to the hall and waited.

"Go ahead, son. I got some gas, and it's best if you avoid me." Mike snorted at his own joke, but it was a serious warning.

Out in the hall, Dr. Humphrey looked sternly at Roy. "Your man in there is quite sick." After five minutes of positive news, this was a kick to the belly. Roy stayed still and stoic. "He has an extremely high fever, and I hope to reduce that over this night, but I do not know what he will face tomorrow. Have you a room in town?"

"The Hotel Helena."

"The paper here says you are Roy Douglas?"

"Yep." He'd answer with that word as Mike would from now on.

"Very well. If we need you, we will telephone there and message you." The doctor turned to walk away.

"Doctor, will he have a foot? keep it I mean?" It was awkwardly stated but understood. Roy met the physician's eyes and waited.

"Attend to some sleep for yourself. Come back in the morning and ask me then. Good night, sir."

Roy walked back to see Mike. The nurse and another man were changing his clothes and dressing him in a nightgown. Mike was loose and allowing them any privileges required.

"Get to the hotel, have a meal, and we'll visit in the morning." Mike's finger motioned for Roy to come near. "You got money, don't ya? Don't leave any here with me. Keep it all with you."

"Yes, sir, I have the money." Roy patted his chest, and Mike laid back and closed his eyes.

A worker brought a cloth-covered plate of food in and set it on a board across Mike's lap. The smell perked him up, and he wasted no time.

Taking a bite, Mike's said, "Go, son. I'm in fine hands here with these good folk." Not surprisingly, he was already winning the hearts of the staff.

"Good night...Mike." It was a split decision whether to stay and sleep on the floor or leave, but Roy left and headed out.

He stopped at the glass window and reminded the woman of his name, and that he was there with Mr. Mike Hanson. She nodded politely and slid the glass window shut. He tapped on the glass, and the woman took a deep breath while opening the barrier.

"Ma'am, can ye tell me where the Hotel Helena be?"

"Walk down the hill to town and go about four blocks. It is on Grand Street, I believe. Five floors and brick. You will be unable to avoid it." The glass closed.

———

Following the street down with his bag in hand, Roy could barely see Mount Helena directly in front of him. There was enough light left to outline the two-topped monument as she ruled over the city. He felt that this view would stay with him until the end of his days. He hoped his remembrance would be for happy reasons and not recalled due to tragic events.

He found the hotel, and it was impressive. A large lobby filled with leather chairs, tropical plants, and exotic carpets removed him from Montana and dropped him into luxurious London. He could only imagine, as he had never set foot in England.

The clerk was friendly. He offered him the American Plan for three dollars a day, which included three meals each day in the hotel's dining room. Roy requested someone to wake him at six a.m. He checked if he could eat before going to his room and, after paying for the accommodations, the clerk walked him to a corner table in the dining room.

Roy was wearing his better attire and had acquired more clothing suitable for town visits, but he felt underdressed with a room half full of finely dressed ladies and their gentlemen of means. These were people of wealth and had societal skills, but this *was* Montana, and the dudes and society belles would be the outcasts once they departed the sophisticated hotel and Last Chance Gulch.

This evening, his room would either give Roy rest or prove to be a dungeon. His first step was to lay back, close his eyes, and hope for the best.

CHAPTER 20

The wind caught the big door as Roy entered the hospital. The wind was up, the snow was blowing, and he thought how good it was that Mike didn't need to travel on a day like this. He kicked the snow off his boots, removed his hat, and walked to the second floor.

Roy hung his heavy coat and hat on a rack near the chairs by the windows. He saw no one. It was noticeably quiet, with the only sounds being echoing footsteps. Walking into the ward, he saw the back of a nurse tending to Mike. She wore a light blue blouse but was otherwise dressed in white. Her large apron fell to an inch or two of the floor as she stood motionless next to the foot of the bed.

"Morning, ma'am," Roy said softly and with as much American in his voice as possible.

The face that turned his way made him feel as if he had lost his balance. It disabled him for an instant.

A beautiful young woman of twenty looked over her shoulder and smiled at Roy with her entire face. The corners of her gray eyes crinkled, and her thin upper lip revealed a delicate smile. On top of that, she had a small dimple in her chin.

Roy had a weakness for girls with dimples. It didn't matter what size, height, loud or quiet a girl was; he loved dimples. This nurse had a perfect one. He lost all thought, reason, and memory as to why and where he was.

"Good day. Are you Mr. Hanson's man?" The voice that came out of the nurse had a scratchy quality, but strong.

"Yep, I'm Roy. Pleasure, ma'am." He extended his hand to shake, but she grinned and looked down at her hands, both in use wrapping a fresh bandage around Mike's foot.

"Sorry, ma'am," he said nervously. He held hands with girls before and had gone to festivals and ceilidhs, but he'd never been near a girl of this high quality. Jings!

"Roy here needs to get to town more; he's been stuck on the ranch and hasn't been around many pretty girls." Mike piped up while laying still with his eyes closed. Roy had forgotten that Mike was in the room.

"Me name is Roy," he said while moving up to Mike on the opposite side of the bed.

"Yes, so you've said. I am Nurse Vera." She offered a corner smile and a side-eyed flirtation back.

"He's a handsome fella, ain't he, nurse? Big, strong Scotsman. Got a head of hair like a shaggy ram. Besides that, he's a dandy fella." Mike was selling hard, and Vera was showing interest. She looked at Roy quickly but was careful not to appear unprofessional.

"She's a, whatya always say Roy...bonny? Yep, bonny, that's it." Mike's voice trailed off. He was quickly running low on energy but reserved a final salvo to assist Roy.

Roy said nothing but looked at Vera indirectly and felt flush.

Vera Daggett had recently completed nurses' training at the Women's Christian Association in Council Bluffs, Iowa. Her family were German settlers in northern Iowa, near Sibley, and had immigrated when Vera was two years old. She was among the first graduates of the nursing school and had been a bright and capable student.

A fellow student from Helena had told Vera about the new hospital in town that would need nurses. Inquiries were made, and Vera came to work at St. Peter's. Her nursing-student friend fell in love with a mining superintendent from Butte on the train ride from Iowa to

Helena, was married shortly after, moved to Butte, and never worked as a nurse. Vera was well received by her schoolmate's family, and they insisted that she stay with them in their daughter's room for free. Life moves fast in a land full of dreams, death, and opportunity.

"How are ye, Mike?" Roy's head had been clouded, and he reminded himself that he was here for assistance and help.

"Hurtin', son. Didn't sleep well. Sweatin' like a pig. Thirsty. Hand me a water would ya?" Roy was able to focus and saw a man in distress.

Roy looked over to Vera. Her expression told him that she could not or should not offer an opinion on his condition. "Dr. Humphrey will be here shortly," she said.

Mike stirred, attempting to find comfort in any new position. Nurse Vera was still in the midst of changing the bandages and held on loosely to Mike's foot as he squirmed. He settled, and she finished changing the bandages. She placed a small milk bottle wrapped in cloth and filled with snow and water near Mike's foot. She carefully repositioned the bottle every few minutes to provide minor relief.

No reprieve from pain was delivered, and this was making Roy uneasy. Vera could see his concern and emotions grow for Mike's circumstance. She was taken by the fact that Roy did nothing to mask his honest emotions.

"I will return with the doctor when he arrives. Would you like to go to the parlor area and wait?" Vera addressed Roy, standing with her hands clasped.

"No, I'll stay right here." He pulled a small wooden chair from the corner and held it, waiting for Vera to leave before he sat.

She nodded with approval and a kind smile.

Thirty minutes passed before Dr. Humphrey visited. It was still early in the day, 8:10 to be exact, but Roy felt as if hours of observing Mike had passed. He was tossing, sweating, and making sounds of pain that Roy hadn't heard before.

"Good morning, young man. Good day to you as well, Mr.

Hanson." The doctor's greeting was followed by placing the back of his hand on Mike's wet forehead. He then placed a thermometer back in Mike's mouth. "Again, sir, allow the tool to rest under your tongue and remain still."

Roy studied the doctor's face, attempting to steal more information than was being offered, but he could collect no additional knowledge.

Moving to the foot, the doctor asked Nurse Vera about the condition and appearance of the foot. She gave a report of little to no change from the previous evening. Vera moved to Mike's head and applied a cloth to his forehead and face, drying the increasing sweat from his skin. She then took and wrung out another cool damp cloth and applied it to his head and the side of his neck, offering minor relief.

The thermometer was removed; Dr. Humphrey stared, read the instrument, and recorded the numbers. Mike was experiencing swelling and swollen skin in his upper leg and now his hands were also displaying inflammation.

The doctor whispered to Vera, and she left the room. "Mr. Hanson, I am going to administer a dose of morphine to settle your pain. I will inject this so as to take effect more rapidly. I need you to swallow this as well to reduce your feverish condition. Will you do that, sir, once the nurse returns?"

"Ummhum." Mike's answer indicated he would do anything he was asked or told to do.

Vera returned with a white porcelain metal tray with a syringe, cotton, and bandages.

"Very well, sir. I will place the needle of the syringe inside of your arm at the elbow. The medicine will find purchase much faster this way and will deliver you much relief. The pain will be short but valuable to you. Nurse Daggett will assist and hold your arm steady." The doctor checked the amount of morphine to be used and slid the needle into Mike's vein.

Mike gave no response to the needle and welcomed the aid. His body released all of the tension and relaxed moments after the injection. Mike's head slowly rolled to his left, and he lost consciousness.

"He needed that. He was in more pain than he was expressing." Dr. Humphrey looked at Roy. "He should rest soundly for an hour or so.

The next dose I administer will be less, so he remains able to speak with us."

None of this was striking Roy as being a good development, and he wanted to ask questions. "Doctor, would you explain this to me, sir?"

"Let us be removed to the hallway. We can speak there." The doctor walked as Roy followed, leaving Vera to attend to Mike.

The doctor sat and patted the empty chair next to him. "Sit here, please."

Roy felt worried and cold at the same time. He did not want to hear what the doctor was about to say.

"Mr. Hanson is not improving; in fact, his fever is much worse. He is in more pain, but I can help ease that with morphine." The doctor looked directly at Roy to improve his understanding. "His foot has an infection that has now spread to other parts of his body. His blood is poisoned. We will try to limit the fever, but it is very difficult to do this. Let us pray that some improvement is imminent."

Roy was having trouble listening now. He was hearing but not understanding after he heard the word poison. His brain and heart were both shutting down.

No. This is wrong, Roy thought. He wanted the doctor to start again but this time, tell him only good news.

Dr. Humphrey could tell he was shocked and gave Roy a moment to breathe. "I will be able to offer more details in an hour, but you must know that your Mr. Hanson is in peril. Please stay close by this morning, young man."

The doctor rose up, placed his hand on Roy's shoulder for a moment, and then walked away, leaving Roy frozen in place.

Eventually, Roy went back into the ward and took a seat next to Mike, who was still sleeping soundly.

How? Why? Why Mike? Why MY Mike? His brain was flooded, and he hoped for reason in a world where logic had been destroyed.

Roy had never been stunned or surprised like this before. He lived in a simple world with minimal choices. He was now faced with decisions and consequences. He began 1891 as an 18-year-old farm boy in Scotland with nothing. Seven months later, the role of caretaker and decision maker had been thrown on his shoulders. He did not want this job, and he doubted that he was fit to handle it in a crisis. He wished that Elmer were here in his stead, and he could spend the day feeding lambs and brushing horses.

Roy dismissed these weak emotions and self-pity when Mike's hand moved towards Roy, reaching for contact and comfort. Mike needed him, and he knew Roy would be the man that he knew Roy to be.

Roy leaned closer to Mike's bed, feeling lost and dizzy.

"Roy?"

"Aye, sir?"

"I heard what the Doc said." Mike's voice was soft but strong. "I need you to buck up and do some things for me if I don't climb out of this hole. Been thinking about all this since I was laid up back in Lewistown, so this ain't the fever talking through me or any high spirit. It's all in my head, and I need ya to help me get things tidy. Can you do that for me, son? Do it for Grace, for you, for all my family."

'All my family.' Grace was Mike's only living relation, but Roy had heard Mike's request and statement. He would do anything to help or save Big Mike Hanson.

Roy began to answer, but Mike raised a hand. "Need ya to listen, son. Don't spit out words to give me hope. It either is or it ain't. Got things I need done."

"I will, Mike," Roy responded strongly, assuring Mike his requests would be obeyed.

"Need you to get a lawyer up here. Tell him he needs to add things to a will, extra parts, and I need it done today. Don't concern yerself with understanding this, just be strong and get a lawyer fella here." Mike took a breath and rested for a few seconds.

Roy had no understanding of what a will was or about, but he'd remember the word and deliver its significance with power.

"That's all for now. Leave me be to rest and go haul me a lawyer to see me. Tell him he need to be here by noon, and that I'll pay good money for his services." Mike's voice faded out as the effort to speak took a toll on him.

Roy stood and looked down at Mike. He lifted his coat off the chair and left to find an attorney. Now was not the time to be shy or polite. He would find one no matter the obstacles.

———

Roy quickly walked outside, full of purpose. He paused and looked at Mount Helena ahead in the distance. The Capital city would surely be full of men skilled with words and papers. He thought that the man at the hotel might know of some lawyers, so he walked back down to begin his quest there.

The lobby was always in motion regardless of the time of day. The desk clerk was involved with an older man in a bowler hat, so Roy waited behind him politely but impatiently.

"Yes, young Mr. Hanson?" The clerks' eyes told Roy to approach. Roy asked about a man of law and was answered promptly.

"The office of Mr. Jacob P. Swindell is two blocks away. He is a man of character and fine reputation. I would hope that he would assist you." The clerk wrote the name on a scrap of paper and handed it to Roy. A tap of the hat, and Roy moved quickly back to the street.

A short and brisk walk placed Roy under a sign that matched the words written on the paper. He opened the door to find two men, one tending a fire and the other behind a desk.

"Would you be..." Roy glanced at the paper, "Be Mr. Swindle?"

"I'm Swin-DELL," the man behind the desk replied.

"Sorry. Mr. Swindell." Roy took his hat off, took a breath, and began. "I need ye to come up to the hospital and see my boss. We come over from Fergus County. We left the day after Christmas, we did. His foot is all bad, and we came all this way. He's in a bad way, and he told me to find him a lawyer and fetch ye back to see him. He said make you come before noon today." Roy spoke fast and flustered.

"For what purpose?" Swindell stood up and put on his suit coat.

Roy paused and thought about what Mike had told him. "A will he said; that's what he told me. A Will. Can ye come? And he said bring paper for ye to write on. That's all he said." Roy was direct and well-mannered, but there was an element of urgency.

"And what is the gentleman's name?" Swindell took pencil in hand and prepared for the answer.

"Mr. Mike Hanson, of The Hanson Ranch on Beaver Creek southwest of Lewistown in Fergus County. Somes call him Big Mike. He's the finest man I know." Roy held his stare on the man.

"Are you a relation to Mr. Hanson? Is he any kin to you?"

"No, but he's like a pa to me," Roy said with no emotion, just a statement of fact. "I don't know anathin' else to tell ye, but he asked I find one of ye. I don't reckon to not see the job done."

"Alright, sir. I can visit him, but I have an appointment in 10 minutes that I must attend to, then I will follow you to the hospital. Can you return to this office in one hour? It is now just before 10:00. Please come back in one hour." Lawyer Swindell reached out and shook hands with Roy. "I will help Mr. Hanson, rest assured."

Roy was satisfied that he had completed the first stage of his assignment, but he knew he still needed to get Mr. Swindell to Mike in person.

———

Roy had time to waste but had no interest in enjoying his free time or exploring Helena this morning. He walked fast enough to stay warm and circled the block at least three times. He stopped and looked across the street. Letters painted in a window grabbed his attention.

'James P. Ball and Son. Photographers.' There were photographs hanging in the window as well as pictures in elegant frames sitting on a table. Roy crossed over to look.

There were large photos of cattle ranches with cowboys on horseback, a man standing proudly in front of a shoe store, and photos of beautiful new mansions in Helena. On the table were three photos about the size of a large Bible. They were of a family. One was in a fine-looking parlor with a man and woman seated while three boys and one girl stood behind. Another was of the man standing with his foot on a large rock with a pickaxe in his hand. Roy guessed he was a successful miner, and the man wanted to tell the world of his triumphs. It was the third picture behind the others that he found to be the most important.

It was a photograph of the man and a younger man. It appeared they were father and son. They both were standing. The father had one hand stuck in his vest and the other hand on the shoulder of his son. Both men looked proud and memorable.

Roy entered, and a woman in her forties came out from behind a curtain to greet him. "Hello, young man, and good morning. May I be of assistance?"

Roy slipped his hat off and walked to the front window display. He very directly asked her, "Would this be a father and son?" She looked and answered, "Indeed it is. That is Mr. Murphy and his son." She waited to discover Roy's reason for asking.

He stood thinking of how to ask, and if he should. Fear occasionally leads to bravery.

"I am in need for ye to take a photograph of me and my father. Will you do that?"

"Of course. My husband would be pleased to help you. Could you and your father come to this location in two days time? My husband is traveling and won't be back for two more days." The woman smiled and again waited.

'Oh no, ma'am. That won't be good, not at all. Me father, he be up in the hospital sick as a goat, and I not be sure he will live to see tomorrow. I want a picture of da both of us. I need somethin' to remember him by."

The woman was moved by his request and took his hand in hers. "I am very sorry to hear of this, I truly am, but my husband is away." She offered sympathy but no answers.

"Me pa is more like to die tonight, and I was hoping for a photo." Roy said aloud what he had been suppressing all morning. He knew the situation but chose to let it evaporate in his head and give it no home.

"Please. Please, ma'am." Roy offered a final appeal. He could feel his body slump in defeat.

Mrs. Ball sat on a stool, feeling she had lost the argument. She was now thinking of solutions.

"My son, who is at school presently, will be home at three this afternoon. He is sixteen, and I am not sure the hospital would allow him into your father's room. He could take the photograph. He has been trained and works with his father often. Which hospital, young man?"

"The one right up the hill, this way." Roy pointed up and east.

"St. Peter's. That may help us. The nuns at St. John's are very strict about everything. We're Methodists ourselves," Mrs. Ball coyly answered.

Roy realized he had spent more time walking and bargaining with Mrs. Ball over the photo than he had planned. He needed to close the deal and get back to the lawyer. "Well, ma'am?" The open-ended question needed a finish.

"Yes…what is your name?"

"Roy, ma'am. And me paw is Mr. Mike Hanson. I can speak with Dr. Humphrey to let us take the photo."

"Oh, Dr. Humphrey is a kind man and is well respected in Helena. Let us say a prayer that he will assist us. I will bring my son up as soon as I can, and we will get that photograph for you, Roy."

"Many thanks to ye, ma'am. Very kind indeed."

Roy went out the door and back to the lawyer. They both headed back to Mike.

CHAPTER 21

"Mike...Mike, wake up please." Roy shook the big man's shoulder.

"What? When? Huh? Oh, Roy." A long sigh escaped, and Mike began to get his bearings. He slowly woke up a bit and snapped to when he saw he had a visitor.

"Mike, this is the lawyer fella. His name is Mr. Swindell. He said he can do the job for ye." Roy stood back and gestured towards Swindell. The lawyer took off his overcoat and hat and moved to the chair next to Mike.

"Mr. Hanson, I understand that you..." Swindell was cut short as Mike raised his hand.

"Hold up, mister, please." Mike looked right at Roy. "Me and this gent need to talk alone. I have things I need to say to him that only a lawyer can hear. Best if you go out for a spell and wait. Okay, son?"

"I be just around the edge." Roy started to walk out of the room. At the doorway, he looked back and saw the two men already in conversation. He was curious as anyone would be, but he was fine being excluded. He didn't want to hear it, think of it, or deal with it. Any of it.

He sat near the window, kicked his feet out, and stretched. He looked up and saw Vera, pretty little Vera, push a cart past him and down the hall. He tried to catch her eye, but she did not seem to notice him. He wanted her to notice him.

Five minutes passed, and Vera walked straight to him. He sat up and smiled.

"I saw you, Roy. I saw you wave your finger." She smirked a little and crossed her arms.

Good lord! She is a beauty. That face. And she's smart as a bobcat.

Vera made him breathe funny. He hoped he did something to her.

"Did you have a good night's rest? You and Mr. Hanson have had quite an ordeal."

"Aye, we have at that, ma'am." Roy usually looked down while speaking, but he stayed locked on Vera's face.

"Firstly, no need to call me ma'am. I'm 20 years old, and you are...?" Vera raised a questioning eyebrow and waited.

"Nineteen, two months away from." *Great news*, he thought, *she's nearly my age.*

"We are almost the same age. Please, I'm not a ma'am. Call me Vera."

"Vera it is."

"And are you a Scotsman? I enjoy hearing you speak, even though I can't understand what you are saying at times." Her smile told Roy she was enjoying poking at him a bit.

"Aye...ma'am. I be pure Scot!" He laid on the accent think and threw out a final, playful ma'am.

"Maybe you can tell me about your home someday, but I need to return to the ward now." She spun and walked away slowly.

"Me home is America now. Fergus County. Born a Scot, but I'm bein' an American." The words sounded and felt powerful to him. An American.

"Yes, of course. Tell me about your old home, Scotland." Vera bit her bottom lip, turned down the hallway, and left Roy full of confusing emotions.

Soon after, Attorney Swindell walked out.

"Please take care of Mr. Hanson there. He is, well, quite a fellow. My pleasure to speak with the both of you, Roy." He shook Roy's hand and walked away.

"Wait, sir! What goes next? What do I?" Roy didn't need much, but a small amount of direction would be welcomed.

"You know where my office is. Visit me when you have questions regarding Mr. Hanson. I will contact his legal counsel in Lewistown, Mr. Fix. That's all I should say. Good day."

Roy felt a little anger, not at the lawyer, but at the day. His thoughts were about getting Mike back on the train and heading home to Beaver Creek. He went into the ward and walked over to Mike's bed.

"Sit, Roy. We've got stuff to talk over." Mike was pale and sweating, but he needed to talk. Roy took a chair. He didn't want to listen to anything Mike was about to say.

"The Doc told me that I am pretty damn sick. I got blood poisoned. He ain't sure how to stop it. It don't hurt 'cause he's got me doped." Mike looked at Roy. "Looks like I'm losin' this hand. Makes me mad as hell. I'm thinkin' bout all I'm gonna miss."

Roy could feel his throat get tight. He didn't want to say something to upset Mike, so he just sat there. He felt scared, sad, angry, and alone. And suddenly, he felt abandoned. That hurt the most.

"Stay with me, son. Don't need anything else. Don't want to be alone when I go. Never did anything so bad in my life to deserve to die like that."

"Not leavin' ye, Mike." That's all he could get out. Roy raised his left hand and grabbed Mike's arm. Mike reached across his chest and laid his hand on top of Roy's.

"You're a fine, son." Mike's voice finally gave way to emotion and cracked. "Waited my whole life to be a father to a son. At least I found ya. Hope I been a good paw to ya."

"Grand, just grand. You be the only pa I ever known." Roy was struggling to speak, but he had to say things or live with regret. "I thank ye with all the thanks a man can have. You gave me a new life. You be the finest man I'll ever know. I need ye to know that, Mike."

Mike's eyes never opened but tears worked down his cheeks and disappeared into his beard. He sniffed, cleared his throat, and simply said, "Yep." He squeezed Roy's arm.

They both needed time to breathe and think. They both had to say what had just been said.

Mike's face was swollen and ruddy. His breathing was quick and shallow. He was a man packing up to leave this earth. Roy had never seen a human die, and he wished to hell he could avoid the experience.

A tall, solemn man walked in holding a black Bible in his hands. He wore a long black coat that nearly touched the floor, and it had plain gold buttons from collar to waist.

"I'm Reverend Beaton. Dr. Humphrey told me of Mr. Hanson's state. I have come to pray with you. Could we do that, Mr. Hanson?"

"Yep, can use some grace from the Almighty. Don't waste much on me sir. Pray for this boy here and for my little girl. Pray away, Reverend." Mike was polite and would not reject any well-intended relief.

The minister stood next to the bed, recited a practiced prayer, and asked God to heal Mike. And if the holy plan requires death, please prepare a place for him when the time came for earthly departure. He put an "Amen" on it, assured Mike he and his wards would be in his constant prayers. He walked out of the ten-bed ward silently and as if he were floating.

Roy hadn't heard a man pray aloud before. He had never been in a church. He had heard others talk about it but never felt strongly to one side or the other.

"Did not know ye was a churchin' man, Mike." Seemed like a fair statement to Roy.

"Don't deny a man his comfort. If he wants to pray, let him. If he wants to cuss, cuss away. We all got different things in our heads. Each man is his own." Mike breathed deep and kept talking. "If he wants to drink, let him have a snort but ya need to take care dealin' with the jar. Prayin's a lot like drinkin'. A little goes a long way."

"No church for me. Say words over me and then lay me next to Clara." Mike was running through a list in his head and wanted to be heard.

"Roy, you gotta help care for Grace. She's heading to be a fine woman. Damnation, I wanted to see her grow. Now, I'll never see her again. Promise me you'll watch over her like you were her paw or brother, will ya, son? Please. Do that for me." Mike's strength was fading, and Roy wished he would rest for a bit, but there was a purpose to his testimony, and he wouldn't be stopped until it was delivered.

"I know you're a quiet kid, Roy, watchin' and pickin' up lessons since you got here, but I need you to be louder. Step up son. Be the boss. Smart boy you are; use that brain. Pick fights with men of poor character. Never understood that 'turning the other cheek' crap. When you ignore a bad man, you put hurt on the honest men that work for you." Mike was nearly out of breath and fighting to be heard. He was trying to give Roy life lessons, paternal instruction that would and should have had been delivered over decades. The fever was making it hard, but Mike fought to deliver a final dose of wisdom.

"People spend their lives workin' to be safe, be in the center of things. Look at who lives in the middle. When the wolves start circling buffalo, the babies all go to the center. It's the strong that face out against the danger. The middle is no place to be for strong men and women, it just ain't. Face it and be a protector son."

Mike's hand reached toward Roy and grabbed his forearm. He was drained. He was conscious but unable to speak anymore. He relaxed his grip from Roy's arm and pulled his hand back. Roy wondered if these were the final words of the mighty man. He quietly called to a nurse attending to another man in the ward to come over. She finished her task and came to Mike's bed.

"Is he still..?" Roy asked the question.

She put two fingers on Mike's neck. "He's still with you, boy. He's resting, but the fever is getting stronger." The nurse washed her hands in a basin and walked out. She returned and told Roy that he was needed in the hallway. He followed her out to discover Mrs. Ball and her son, who was holding a wooden box and three long sticks.

The nurse looked towards Roy and spoke first. "Mrs. Ball told us that you have requested her services?"

"I did. I need her. I need a photograph."

"This is not an appropriate thing to allow inside of this hospital.

There are other men in the room, and we must protect their health as well." The nurse felt unsure and challenged. She had no idea how to proceed but did not want to appear flustered.

Roy saw Dr. Humphrey walk up the stairs. A solution to this problem was now possible he thought.

The doctor was updated as to Roy's wishes. He looked at Roy and then the nurse. "Thank you, nurse, you were correct to question the propriety of this. I will assume all duties and responsibilities from this juncture." It was clear that Dr. Humphrey would be responsible if concerns were raised.

"Doctor, I need a photograph. For his little girl. We never expected this. When I go back and tell her about her pa, a picture would help her." Roy's simple plea was easy to feel.

"Please be very quiet and prompt." The doctor looked at Mrs. Ball. "How long will you need to complete this?"

"My son will set up the camera very quickly. The photograph will be taken, and we will depart quietly and respectfully, doctor." Mrs. Ball looked at Roy with reassurance that his wishes would be realized.

"Please proceed with haste. I want to visit Mr. Hanson for a moment before you proceed."

The doctor walked into the ward, as Roy and the Balls followed.

Another check of Mike's temperature was taken, and Roy leaned over to inform him of the happenings.

"Mike, these people are gonna take a photograph for ye to give to Grace. I know ye not at yer best, but it won't take no work." Roy was more telling than asking and didn't expect resistance.

Mike nodded and attempted to sit up in the bed a bit. The nurse put another pillow behind his head. The photographer was still getting ready when Roy made another request.

He dug in his pants pocket and removed the bolo ties he had bought in Great Falls. He had forgotten to give Mike the gift but now seemed to be a good time. "I got a present fer ye." The voice and the cadence of a Scotsman was back in Roy's voice. "Got one fer you, and I get me one."

Roy showed him the jewelry. Mike gave a small wink of approval.

Roy took the silver-lettered bolo, placed it over Mike's head and let it rest on his chest just under his chin.

"Bet I look like a dandy. One's gold and other is silver. That's Montana. Gold and Silver."

"Yep, you do. Like a dude from New York," Roy joked.

Roy took his gold-lettered bolo and put it on. "I got these so we would…" Roy's voice stumbled and stopped.

"Look like a son and father? Grand idea," Mike finished the obvious sentiment. He reached up, touched Roy's tie, and said, "Even has an M for Montana. I like that."

Roy nodded, pleased that Mike understood the meaning of the gift. But his M would quietly stand for 'Mike.'

Mrs. Ball touched Roy on the shoulder. They were ready.

"Mrs. Ball, can we have one of Mr. Hanson and one of the both of us. Yea?"

She smiled and said, "Of course."

The natural light was sufficient, so the young Mr. Ball covered his head with a black fabric and counted down. Mike braced and created a small grin. Three, two, one. A click was heard, and Mike was told the could relax.

Roy then put his left arm behind Mike's head and leaned down. Mrs. Ball came over and gently pushed Roy closer to Mike. The men were asked to look at the box and be still. The click was heard again, and the job was done. Mike laid back and closed his eyes.

Roy walked out with the Ball family. "Thank ye, Mrs. Ball. You done me a great kindness."

She grabbed his hand and pulled him in for a hug. She knew this boy, pushed to be a man, was hurting and needed support. He didn't fully return the embrace, but he gratefully accepted the gesture.

"Come by tomorrow, and we will have these ready for you." She dabbed at a tear, smiled, and directed her son to the exit.

Roy took the bedside chair, sat, and waited for movement from Mike. The only emotion not in him was relief. He thought that if Mike were to die, that he would please go quickly. He wanted to end the suffering of wondering and waiting. Then the guilt of this selfish hope filled him with embarrassment and disgust. He wanted to not think. About anything.

———

It was late afternoon, and Dr. Humphrey came in again. He checked Mike's pulse and the level of his fever. He stood and stared at his patient then at Roy. He gently pulled Roy by the arm to the foot of the bed.

"There is nothing I can do for Mr. Hanson. I am regretful to have suggested that he come to Helena. Perhaps if we could have taken his foot a few days ago, he would have improved. However, in most cases, that would have made no change. His body is filled with an infection, and his blood is poisoned. It's in God's hands now. Pray for a gracious result."

How much praying will it take?, Roy wondered. The man in the long black coat had already done that. Why should more praying make a difference? Will it improve the odds? Does a man with hundreds of friends and family praying for health on his behalf have a greater chance to live than a solitary man with no companions? Roy struggled to apply logic to a mystical issue with no success.

———

It was dark outside, nearly 6:00 p.m., and hunger hit. Roy realized he hadn't eaten since breakfast. He wanted to stay, but he needed to eat. The decision was made easier when the Head Nurse came in and told him that visitors' hours were over, and he needed to come back tomorrow. He walked to Mike's bed to see if he was alert enough to hear him. He was...barely.

"Mike, I be heading out, well they be kickin' me out. I'll be back in the morning to see ye. Promise." Roy doubted that Mike heard him and was certain there'd be no reply.

"Bring me a donut. I love them donuts. Maybe a handburger too." Mike's voice was weak; nevertheless, his spirit was stout and fighting. "See you in the morning, son."

Mike put out his hand. Roy reached back to shake his hand and clasped Mike's rough hand. Mike squeezed firmly and wouldn't release. He held tightly for 20 seconds or more and when he let go of Roy's hand, he lifted his hand to Roy's face and pressed his hand against his cheek.

Roy was a beaten man, and the emotions of a horrible week fell out of him. He made no sound, but tears flooded down his cheeks, and Mike could feel them. "I'll miss seein' the man you'll be. A fine unselfish man. Don't waste life with worry."

Roy knew he should leave and allow Mike some peace, but he did not want to go. He would have slept on the floor if they would let him.

"One more thing," Mike spoke softly, eyes closed and with the last strength leaving his body. "Dig in my pants' pocket. The right side."

Roy walked to the clothes hanging on the wall. He reached into the pocket.

It was a rock. The rock Roy had given to Mike a few days earlier.

"Keep that. I got that from my boy." Mike faded and closed his eyes.

Roy was struggling to breathe.

Mike patted Roy's cheek, then lowered his hand to his chest and patted the bolo with approval.

"Remember me when you feel like giving in. Stay as hard and tough as you can be Roy. Somebody's always wanting to break you, see you fall." Mike took a long, deep breath. Each word was like a final punch thrown by a falling prize fighter.

"Don't break Roy, stay...unbroken."

Mike's head rolled to the side on his pillow. "Go and leave me to rest, son."

Vera was just coming to work. She stopped and watched the tender exchange between the American father and his Scottish son. She was affected by the exchange and touched by how genuine the connection was between Mike and Roy. She wanted to take a moment to comfort Roy, but that was not allowed or encouraged. She always told herself to be strong and professional at all times, and so she would.

Roy met her in the hall, head hung low and red eyed. He looked up at her. She saw total, undeserved sadness in his face. She knew she didn't dare embrace him, but she put her hand on his arm to connect.

"He's dying. He's in that bed dying." Roy said.

"I'll be with him all night. He will not be alone; I promise you, Roy." Vera withdrew her hand. "Come back in the morning. We'll both be here waiting for you."

Roy looked back in the ward. He saw Mike covered with a gray blanket, sleeping. He mumbled, "Thanks" to Vera and moved to the stairs. He may sleep tonight, but there would be no rest.

CHAPTER 22

Roy woke feeling no hunger, and he wondered when the craving would return. He had woken up often through the night, each time producing more pity and anger in his head. He had no skills to deal with this much thinking. He was a follower. This new role was proving to be unbearable.

Realizing the day ahead would either be jubilant or tragic, he forced himself to eat a breakfast of eggs, ham steak, and grilled bread. Nothing tasted good, but he knew it was needed. He pocketed an apple and a small block of cheese for lunch.

Roy walked up the hill to the hospital. He took a deep breath and paused on the hospital steps. He looked at the front door.

I cannot go in there.

A sudden gust of cold wind blew snow in his face and shifted his hat. *Stand as a man. Face it,* he told himself.

Inside, at the top of the stairs, he saw Vera. That gave him a short shot of relief. She stood there with her hands clasped and no smile, as if she were waiting for Roy. He felt a small wave of joy as he climbed the stairs, getting closer to Vera.

Then, all happiness left him and his world.

"He's gone, Roy."

Roy was hit hard, but not knocked out. He was expecting to hear this. Instead of standing in silence, he accepted the news, walked to the doorway of the ward and looked at Vera.

She walked next to him as close as possible without touching him. They stopped at the door of the ward. He saw a white sheet covering the body that was Mike.

"I need to see him." He was more composed than he thought he'd be. He would save his grief for later and in private. Vera followed as he stood on the far side of the bed opposite of Vera. She reached and lifted the corners of the sheet. Roy reached down and touched Big Mike's forehead. "He still be warm. When did he…?"

"Thirty minutes before you arrived. I told them to wait to take him until you came by." Vera was a professional, but she was also young and felt an unexpected connection to these two men. She, too, struggled with the moment.

Roy reacted to the news that half an hour ago, Mike was still alive and he selfishly took time for a breakfast. Years would pass before he would offer himself forgiveness for this decision.

"Did you hear him say anything?"

"No, Roy. When people are as sick as Mike, they sleep and then they die. It's not the time for words. He tossed at times in the night, but that was all. Even if you were here, nothing would have…" Vera realized it was better to stop talking.

Roy stared at Mike's hair and face to store the memory. He thought of Grace as he scanned down to her father's beard and how she would stroke it, grab a handful of whiskers, and pretend to pull hard. Mike would act as if he were in great pain, and Grace would giggle. Every time.

Mike's right hand was still laying across his chest, slightly covered by his beard.

"I need to lay his arm down before he…" Again, Vera stopped and allowed the obvious to speak. The palm of his hand was open and flat, and she carefully began to place his arm at his side before permanent stillness arrived. As she pulled his hand up, a black string followed and then dropped back down to Mike's chest.

It was the bolo tie.

Mike had left this world with his hand covering the gift from Roy.

Roy couldn't fight the emotion of that final act. He let go with a short burst, then he quickly collected himself and breathed deep. He did not want Vera to see him as weak. The look on her face revealed her growing affection for him. She admired his honest feelings and the tenderness within.

"Can you take that off a him, so I don't lose it?"

Vera reached around Mike's neck, pulled the braided string over his head and handed it to Roy. This was now the most valuable thing in the world to him.

"I'll leave you for a minute or two, but they are due to take his body down any minute. It is not good for the other men in the ward to leave him here." Vera knew that a long bedside farewell was not healthy for Roy as well.

Roy touched Mike's chest and remembered the moment he had met this grand man, standing together looking at sheep. It was now his job to fill Mike's place in the world. He doubted he would ever be this man's equal, but he would not drop the rope.

He leaned down and pressed his forehead against Mike's and held there briefly before lifting. Without thinking, he reached down, grabbed an inch or two of Big Mike Hanson's beard, and gave it a slight pull.

"Farewell. pa."

CHAPTER 23

I t was Thursday, December 31, 1891.

Paperwork and choices were filled out and completed. Vera offered assistance and kindness that was freely given and gratefully accepted.

Vera took Roy into a small office on the first floor. "This is Mrs. Orr; she has papers for you to sign as you are next of kin to Mr. Hanson. She will answer all your questions."

Roy looked at Vera. "I ain't his kin."

Thinking on her feet and without hesitation, Vera answered, "It's fine Mrs. Orr; he's adopted. His last name is Douglas. You have a lawyer in town that can help with all of this, don't you, Roy?"

"Mr. SWINdle."

"You mean Mr. Swindell?" Mrs. Orr corrected without looking up.

"Yep. I mean, yes ma'am. That be the one." Roy was already weary of this process, and he'd only answered two questions.

"Please sign here. That will allow us to release the body to the mortician. Do you have a preferred funeral home?"

"No, ma'am. Don't know of one. We're from Fergus County, not here."

"I would suggest Dickerson and Son. They're located just off Main

Street downtown. You can speak with them about how you wish to handle Mr. Hanson." Mrs. Orr could sense that Roy was not fully involved and needed to move on. "Would it be agreeable to send the invoice for Mr. Hanson's stay to Mr. Swindell also?"

"Aye, ma'am." Roy wasn't sure what an invoice was, but anything that could be sent to and dealt with by Swindell sounded simpler.

He scribbled his name on a blank line, and the paperwork was completed. He had four stops to make, but first he needed time to be alone and quiet. It was too cold to go outside. He didn't want to go to the hotel either, so he headed up to the chairs by the window outside of the ward Mike had been in.

It was not even 10:00 a.m., but it felt as if an entire day had passed. Roy moved a chair so he could look outside. It began to snow, and he wanted to sit in silence and stare with no purpose.

He thought of Mike. How they had first met. The 'handburger' he ate. The train ride he had shared with the sheep for thousands of miles. The Arvon Hotel and the shower. The Fourth of July in Lewistown. Riding horses side by side. Of Christmas and then these terrible past few days.

He was too numb to cry, but he knew that time would come. He felt himself smile thinking about things Mike had said and about how much fun he had been to be around. The sense of loss was building in him. He needed Mike to teach and mold him. Now, he had no mentor.

He told his mind to quiet itself and be calm, but a song kept sneaking into his head, and it was impossible to block out.

It was an old Scottish tune about Bonnie Prince Charlie. Every Scot alive knew this song. He sang it very quietly while the snow fell. This was his hymn to Mike.

Will ye no come back again

Will ye no come back again

He couldn't finish the verse. Roy bent forward in the chair, grabbed his head, and allowed the tears to well up. He tried to sing again.

Better lo'ed ye...

He was broken.

He felt a small hand touch his shoulder and gently sing with him. It was Vera.

Better lo'ed ye can-na be
Will ye no come back again

She knew the song. She sang it with him.

She KNEW the song.

Roy turned and looked at Vera standing next to him. Words would have spoiled the sweetness. He smiled, and she smiled back. Her hand stayed on his shoulder and, as he stood, he reached out and held her hand. He had wanted to touch her the second he saw her, and he would not miss out on this moment. He felt her squeeze back as she looked at him. Her eyes were wet. She took a small handkerchief out of her uniform pocket and patted her eyes.

Roy had no experience what love for a woman felt like, but he knew he had to be near Vera. She was beautiful and delicate as a honeycomb, but it was how she behaved, how she spoke, that made her unique and lovely to Roy.

"I'm going to get to the lawyer's office now. Have a lot to do to take Mike home." Roy was running through the tasks ahead with no time to mourn.

"I'm off work now. I stayed to see you and help with Mike. I can accompany and help. I do not work again for two days. Please allow me help." Vera asked but left no room for a refusal.

"That would be grand. I know a few places here, and I'd welcome yer help Vera." He felt a twinge of guilt at feeling happy to be with Vera for a few hours. Thinking about how she wanted to be around him was the first warm emotion he had felt in days.

Vera told Roy to wait and that she would be back in five minutes. He sat and felt a small dose of relief.

Vera came back with Dr. Humphrey. The thought of talking with the doctor hadn't crossed Roy's mind in the fog of loss, and he felt foolish for missing a step. He stood as the doctor and Vera approached.

"I am indeed sorry, son. Mr. Hanson seemed to be a fine gentleman. Please tell your family that I am regretful for your loss." Dr. Humphrey motioned for Roy to sit. "Mr. Hanson came to us with a very advanced infection. At the very best, I had hoped that it would have been confined to his foot. If that had been the case, we could have removed the foot and possibly saved his life."

Roy was focused on remembering this information. He would surely be asked multiple times to retell the story.

Dr. Humphrey continued. "There is no way to tell how the infection got into his body or how long it was with him. His chances to recover from this fever were very small. I kept him comfortable and with little pain until the end, and he passed in peace. Please deliver this note to Dr. Fullbright in Lewistown. It explains the happenings of the past few days. I hope we meet again under healthier and happier conditions."

The doctor stood and extended his hand. Roy rose, grasped Dr. Humphrey's hand with a firm grip, and said, "I thank ye fer all ye did to help Mike. I wish ye could ha known him."

Dr. Humphrey nodded his head in agreement and walked away.

———

Roy and Vera walked down the hill to the business district.

"I need to remember all the doin's this morning. I'm happy for the help I am." Roy stopped walking and looked directly at Vera. "I also am lucky to be walking with ye Vera; very pleased."

Vera smiled. "I'm happy to be with you, Roy." She didn't need to say anything more. The attraction between the two was obvious and natural. If they could endure this miserable day together, the future may hold some promise.

"The lawyer, the photograph people, and the undertaker. And the train. I need a ticket for me and for Mike. But let's go to the hotel lobby and get warm for a wee bit first." Roy pointed up the street to the hotel.

"Have you thought about sending a telegram back home with the news?" Vera knew that Roy needed to move that task to the top of the list.

Roy closed his eyes. "Did not think to do that. What do I tell them? What do I say? I never wrote anathin' to anaone." This was a delicate and necessary job that he hadn't thought through.

"I'll help you, Roy. You need to let them know that Mr. Mike has passed on and that you will bring him home. Tell them when to meet you at the train and the like. That should be enough." Vera finished just as they reached the hotel, and she waited for Roy to open the door.

They walked inside and sat on a couch together to plan the next few hours.

"I know where the Western Union office is, and we should start there. Do you have any money with you to pay for these things?" Vera was organizing the day in a logical order that would prove to be valuable and comforting.

"I do. Mike gave me his wallet, and it be full of money. Over one hundred dollars, I think." Roy touched his coat where the wallet was held.

"That will be more than enough. He was always watching out for you." Vera had come to admire and like Big Mike Hanson in the brief time she was around him. "He cared a great deal for you, Roy. I think you know that. He talked of you as if you were his son." She stopped. "We can talk about this later. I know this is causing you pain. We should focus on the many things to do today. Shall we go to the telegraph office?"

Two blocks away, they entered the Western Union office where Vera wrote down the message as discussed and gave it to the clerk.

"We need this to go to Lewistown and then be delivered to The Hanson Ranch. Where is the ranch, Roy?" Vera was attempting to carry as much of the load for Roy as possible, and he welcomed the assistance.

"The Mike Hanson Ranch on Beaver Creek. They all know Mike there." He paused and added, "best to send word to the lawyer man there, Mr. Fix I reckon. Send it to him and he'll see it done to the ranch. I'll pay the extra to send word to the ranch anyhow."

The clerk wrote all the information down. "That will be one dollar for the wire and one dollar fifty for the delivery of the message to the ranch."

Roy paid the man. He and Vera wasted no time and left to attend to the next issue: the lawyer.

Nothing in the business district was more than 6 blocks from anything. The law office was just around the corner, and a short walk delivered them to Mr. Swindell.

As they walked in, Swindell and his assistant both stood up but said nothing.

"Good morning, sir. This is my...friend, Vera. She be Mike's nurse. I reckon ya know why I've come to see ye." Roy wasted no time nor words and got down to business.

"Yes, I do. And please allow me to offer our condolences to you both. I'm quite sorry that Mr. Hanson is no longer with us. In the few minutes I spent with him, I believed him to be a fine man of strong character." Swindell seemed to mean what he said.

"Yes, he was the finest. He gave me a new life. A great man he was." Roy looked at the floor and then raised his head. "Mike told me to see you if he...well if things turned sour. Not sure why."

"He directed me to update his Will. We updated his Will that expresses his wishes for his property, his processions, and additional attention to how these things should be disbursed. I filed with the Lewis and Clark County Court, and it is recorded here. We will send these papers on to Fergus County. I will send them through the post later today." The lawyer took a seat, reached for a large brown file and handed it to Roy.

"So, he told ye what he wanted done, so we don't be guessin' how things should go?" Roy was surprised and relieved that the difficult assignment of decision making had been made simple.

"All instructions and avenues of financial disbursement are outlined in his Will, and his personal wishes have been updated. He was very kind and generous in his directives. Very kind." Swindell stood and walked to the front of his desk, closer to Roy. "I will be sending this Will and all other papers to his attorney there in Lewistown, a Mr. William Fix. He will arrange a time to read this to all concerned, explain what steps will be needed, and ensure that Mr. Hanson's wishes are met and are legally executed."

"What is in this package?" Roy asked.

"A copy of the Will. It may not be understandable in parts to the layperson, but you may read it and gather information of what will occur."

Roy stood and helped Vera out of her chair. "Thank ye for the work and for coming up to see Mike as ye did. Very grateful I am." Roy offered his hand to Swindell. The lawyer returned with a solid shake and an approving nod. "Now, how much do I be owein' ye for all the work? Mike told me to pay when I come to see ye."

"That is very much appreciated indeed. Ten dollars will settle all charges. I have a receipt for you."

Roy handed over the money.

"Thank you sincerely. It's a great loss for you and your family. I will allow you to proceed with your day and continue with your obligations." Swindell walked them to the door.

Roy held up the brown folder. He was curious as to what the paper would say. "We can take a squint at these papers later, but I'm not sure I be understandin' all the lawyer words."

———

The photographer was next.

A short walk took them to the Ball Studio. Roy was nervous. He wasn't sure how he would react to seeing the photographs. He had never been in a photo and was curious if he would look like a man or a boy. He would watch Vera's reaction before he would look. He desperately wanted her to like the photo and to like him. There was little time for courting or flirting.

Mrs. Ball walked out from behind her small desk and grabbed Roy's hand with both of her hands and held still. She was a kind person, and Roy felt her sympathy.

"We were told of Mr. Hanson's passing and knew you would be stopping by. I am so very sorry. Losing a parent is a bitter tonic for anyone, especially when they pass when you are in your youth. I am so pleased to have had the chance to meet your father and to offer our services." Mrs. Ball's eyes looked as if she could cry with little effort.

"Thank ye, ma'am." Roy couldn't match her eloquence and believed the less he said, the better. "This is Vera Daggett. She was Mister, I mean me pa's nurse. She's helpin' me to get things done today."

"Yes, dear, you were on duty when we were with Mr. Hanson. You are a kind young woman to assist Roy in such a time of sorrow." Mrs.

Ball held Vera's hand and offered a comforting pat. "Now, allow me to retrieve the photos for you."

She came out with two good-sized, rigid, thick paper photos.

"First, this is of the dear Mr. Hanson." Mrs. Ball handed the picture to Roy.

Mike was sitting up in the bed, looking unwell at best, but still giving a strong effort to smile. Roy had wondered at the time if Mike were aware of the photographer and of what was happening, but he could see Mike's eyes looking at the camera, and that was reassuring. Roy looked for 10 seconds and then handed the photo to Vera. He dared not study Mike's face for long without producing a strong reaction. "That is bonny, it is."

Vera looked at Roy with a sweet and soft glance. She liked it as well, but she knew it would be something Roy would treasure for a lifetime.

"And here is you with your father."

Vera was standing next to Roy this time and reached for his arm as they both saw the photo. Roy had a sadness in his face that could be seen and understood. His eyes were focused, and his curly hair was brushed back.

But what caught everyone's attention was Mike. The same pose, nearly identical photo like the first, but one detail made a difference. Mike's eyes were looking directly at Roy. The look expressed much, and both women reacted the same.

"Oh, Roy! Look at how he's looking at you. Goodness." Vera sniffed back a quick tear, and Roy felt her hand squeeze his arm. "You can see that he loved you."

Mrs. Ball, unable to comment, saw the same and simply nodded.

Roy saw it, too, and was a bit stunned. The men had never said it, but it was obvious. Mike had loved Roy, and the photograph was stronger than any words. Roy looked at Vera, who was tearing up, and she smiled back at him. It was at that moment that he became aware that he was in love with Vera and that she had feelings for him as well. Instead of looking at the picture, Roy gazed at Vera's face. Her kindness and gentle heart made her the most beautiful thing he'd ever seen.

Roy had to get control of his emotions, or he would break down. "I should have asked for two copies of each photo. Would that be possible?"

"Dear boy, we printed copies of each. I felt as if you would want two as you mentioned a sister. Allow me to put these with the others in a strong envelope for you." Mrs. Ball reached behind the curtain and placed the four photos inside a large envelope.

The bill was $2.00 dollars, which Roy felt was a small price to pay for such a memory. Mrs. Ball surprised them by giving them both a gentle hug and wished them well as they made their way back into the thoroughfare.

———

As they walked, Roy had thoughts of holding hands or offering Vera his arm, but that would not have been proper, particularly in town where the townswomen would have surely created a stir.

A simple sign hung over the door of Dickerson and Son, Est.1881. The words Funerals-Shrouds-Coffins-Embalming were hand painted in the front window surrounded by lace curtains. As they walked in, a short, balding man greeted them.

"I'm RoyDouglas, and I think you have Mr. Hanson here?"

"I am H.W. Dickerson. Yes, indeed. Mr. Hanson is in our care. Our condolences to you and your family at this time of sorrow and loss."

"This is Nurse Vera Daggett who has been helpin' me with all that needs done." Roy put his hand on the small of Vera's back. His instincts of affection for her came out with no effort, and he quickly pulled his hand back so as not to embarrass Vera.

Dickerson nodded a polite greeting and offered them each a chair in front of his desk.

"Sir, I have a few things to care for. The first, how do I get Mike back to Lewistown? That's all I need. Just get him back home." Roy jumped past multiple questions and asked how to achieve the end result.

"Certainly. Of course we have provided embalming services. You signed papers at the hospital that authorized us to receive and care for

Mr. Hanson." Dickerson looked at Roy for his acknowledgement and agreement. Roy nodded yes.

Dickerson took a paper from a folder that listed all provided and needed amenities. "We also have selected a coffin suitable for shipping Mr. Hanson's remains. It is a plain and very affordable item. We assume that most families will select a more fitting final item when the need arises."

"Can ye deliver the... Mike to the train station tomorrow?" Roy was running down the list in his head. He looked to Vera to assist with any issues he may forget.

Dickerson spun in his chair to retrieve a large, printed card. "I have the train schedules right here." Less than a minute later, he had an answer. "The train from Helena to Great Falls leaves at 9:30 a.m. each day, except on Sundays during the winter. I assume you can make arrangements to connect once in Great Falls. We will be proud to have Mr. Hanson at the depot tomorrow morning at 8:30, in time for a proper and respectful journey home."

This was simpler than Roy had expected. Mr. Dickerson was very familiar with the desires and process of moving the deceased to all parts of the state and country.

"Thanks for helping, sir. Grand of ye to do this. I reckon I need to square up with ye. I be ready to pay ye now. And could I ride along to the train depot tomorrow morning? It be a long walk." Roy pulled Mike's black leather wallet out. He would keep this personal item of course.

"Of course, you may ride with my son as he delivers Mr. Hanson. Please be here before 8:00 a.m. Here is a list of the charges. Ask if you have a question. The preservation of remains charge is seven dollars. The simple but sturdy coffin is twelve dollars. We also must charge for picking up Mr. Hanson from St Peter's and then the travel down to the train depot. The fee for both is ten dollars. As you are not incurring any funeral expenses at this time, we have attempted to offer our services at a very reasonable and professional cost."

Roy was adding in his head, but Vera whispered, "Twenty-nine dollars, Roy." He smiled at her and nodded. He handed two twenty-dollar bank notes to Mr. Dickerson, who promptly handed him the difference.

"Can we see him?" Roy wanted to be sure that it was BigMike he would be escorting home.

"Of course. This way please." Dickerson opened a door to the back. Roy did not want to see anything except a box with Mike in it. Fortunately, they had a small room designated for such viewings; the unsavory side of the undertaker business was not seen. There was one simple wooden box on sawhorses in the room. There was no top on the box. Mike was there. Peaceful and still. Roy quickly gave approval but needed to leave. Vera allowed him to walk out first to avoid more reactions. He felt he was not following custom and waited for Vera to walk out first.

"We will be with Mr. Hanson and he is under our watch. Have no worries." Dickerson shook hands and held the door open for Vera and Roy.

"A very simple process, was it not?" Vera saw Roy was relieved to have all of this behind him and offered reassurance in a time of confusion.

"Aye, can't imagine it's all done. I am in yer debt for the help, Vera." He wanted to hold her hand or touch her shoulder. He held back, but they both could tell he was drawn to her and she to him. "Might ye have supper with me tonight at the hotel? I have the meal included, and I can buy your meal." This was an inelegant invitation, but he had marshaled enough courage to make the ask.

"I would enjoy that, Roy. May I please return home to take a short nap and to change from my working clothes into a more suitable evening dress?"

"Sure, sure." In his mind, he believed his odds for an acceptance from Vera were 50/50 at best. His gamble had paid off.

"Would six p.m. be acceptable? I will take a carriage back to the hotel and meet you in the lobby." She knew this would work but offered Roy the chance to accept out of politeness.

"That be bonny." Roy was working on sounding less Scottish and more Montanan, but nature overruled

Vera smiled. "I like to hear you talk, Roy. It is very endearing. I will return in a few short hours." With that, Vera walked a bit before catching the eye of a carriage driver.

Endearing? Need to find out what the word means. Hope it's good.

CHAPTER 24

Roy was in the lobby at 5:30. If Vera was early, he didn't want to miss a second of extra time with her. He took the opportunity to settle his hotel bill, pay for Vera's meal, and to inform them that he would be leaving in the morning. He told himself to be ready to walk to the undertaker's and hitch a ride. He would feel better seeing Mike's coffin loaded and to know it was him inside the box.

Vera was ten minutes early, looking different and elegant. Roy had only seen Vera in nurse's garb. Roy quickly walked to greet her. She wore a dark blue dress that fell to the top of her shoes. A small white collar framed her delicate face. She handed Roy her long, dark coat as if to unveil a Greek sculpture She was a fine and handsome young woman. They would allow the sorrows of the day to be suspended for the evening and would concentrate on enjoying each other's company.

Roy pulled out the chair, and Vera sat. He saw a man do that yesterday in the dining room, and the woman seemed pleased by the gesture. Roy would give it a shot. They read the menu before saying anything, as neither knew how to break the ice.

Vera spoke first. "The lamb sounds delicious, with turnips and potatoes."

"I get all the lamb and mutton a man could want, so I'll have a beefsteak."

Vera giggled softly. "I forgot you live on a sheep ranch."

"Aye, but Anna is a fine cook. She's a German girl, and Elmer is fond of her." Roy cut himself short, thinking it was impolite to talk too much at this point in the evening. "Before I talk you into tears, would you tell me about you?"

Roy had a sharp memory, and he would remember each detail of Vera's life that she revealed.

"Oh...I am not much of a talker, so forgive me if I bore you with my chatter."

Roy smiled. Vera? Boring? Don't be daft.

"My family came from Germany when I was two. My father and one of his brothers farm near Sibley, Iowa, but they are moving up to Minnesota. Another of his brothers, my uncle John Daggett, moved to farm near Windom, Minnesota, Cottonwood County. They have very rich soil there and are raising corn and soybeans as well as flax. Flax is what you make linen with. I have two younger brothers who are in the home and farm with my father. My father and mother are very fine Christian people. German Lutherans. Uncle John is Baptist." Vera finished with the tale of how she had come to Helena. "That is my life and who I am."

Roy was listening for any mention of a beau or farm boy back in Iowa that was left behind but heard nothing regarding past affections. Relieved, he was fine-tuning the master plan in his head, scheming to win Vera's heart.

The waitress came over, took their orders for supper, and brought them both hot teas.

"Now you. Tell me about yourself, Roy." Vera sat back a bit and tilted her head, which Roy found to be magical. He found her to be hypnotizing. Her walk, the way she spoke, the way she scratched her nose...she was elegant and gentle.

He told her about being an orphan, raised by a sour aunt, and sleeping in a barn his entire life in Scotland. He moved past 18 years in an instant so as to get to the day his life really began when he met Big Mike Hanson.

Vera watched Roy's expressions and how he relaxed as he spoke as his story took on more color and humor. He was not performing to impress her. His affection and admiration for Mike was obvious and true. Roy wasn't aware of how open and honest his story was, and Vera was increasingly charmed by this country boy.

How could she avoid falling for him? He was a handsome young man. Green eyes, over six feet tall, muscular, and a head of hair that lived life on its own terms. Combined with his genuine nature and kind soul, she was falling for him nearly as fast as he was for her. Their love story would soon begin.

She asked him to repeat the part about the bathhouse in the Hotel Arvon as she found it to be funny and cute. He filled in more blanks to the tale on the second telling, and his true Scottish heritage of story-telling was blooming. He was shedding his youth and accepting manhood.

The meals were delivered. Roy carefully observed how Vera handled the dining procedures and parroted her actions. He was smart enough to know that he didn't know the nuances of etiquette. He wanted to appear to have a little culture but would stay true to himself and not turn into an East Coast Dude. The food looked fine, and Vera commented as to its high quality. Roy was too roped up by Vera to have any memory of taste or smell but remembered later that the beef was memorable.

Roy made sure to finish chewing before he continued. "So, we rode down from Great Falls on Monday, and that is when Mike got the hospital. You know the rest." His voice disappeared at the end of this sentence.

"Would you like to have some cake? They have pies, but ye don't get many cakes on the ranch." Roy found a way to redirect and not spoil the pleasantness of their supper together.

"I would." Vera agreed with his maneuver and wanted to keep the dialogue on the future.

Roy asked for lemon cake with butter icing, and Vera chose pound cake with lemon icing. They also ordered coffee because that's what civilized people do: drink coffee in swanky tiny porcelain cups while eating cake.

Small talk about Helena and St. Peter's Hospital filled the short gap between ordering and the delivery of the desserts. The sweet cakes were an indulgence, as sugar was still a precious commodity in 1890's Montana.

Roy took the moment to connect the dots with some farming information. "Did ye know that they grow sugar beets down near Billings? Good crop, and it may make this cake thriftier come next year!"

Vera was amused with Roy's ability to pull up worthwhile knowledge and weave in humor at the same time. In this rare case, the more Roy talked, the better he sounded. She thought, *he's not a simple man at all*. And, in her mind, never boring.

Roy tried to get a reading on how Vera was feeling about him, about them, about all of...this...whatever this all was. She did smile often and never in a manufactured way. When she didn't have a grin, her eyes seemed to smile. Her face was made for small expressions. In the few times she looked serious, it was due to being deep in thought and intense concentration.

"What are smiling about, Roy?" There was no answer, so Vera asked again. "Roy?"

"Sorry, did ye ask me somethin'?"

"Yeeess," Vera let the word stretch. "I was curious as to why you were smiling. It's been a difficult day, and I'm pleased to see you smile."

The question caught him unprepared because she was the source of his smile, causing his happiness.

"Reckon it's your fault it is," he said with a mouth corner smile. "Just listening and lookin' at you. What a pretty girl ye are, Vera. Got ta say it. And you be loaded with kindness." He stopped himself as he had a toe up to the line of embarrassment. Even so, he was glad he said what he said.

It was much too early to declare Vera and Roy a duo, but they had quickly become important to each other. Any relationship is tipped to one side or the other, never perfectly balanced. The balance may change each day or hour, but one side will always have a surplus of affection and love. Happy couples don't need 50/50, just something close.

Roy felt as if he had his hand on the scale, and his longing and admiration for Vera outweighed hers for him. That didn't surprise him. She was a treasure. Any man could and would find happiness and contentment with Vera. He would have competition. He felt that she must have a long line of suitors. He had to take his shot.

"I should head home shortly before it gets too cold." Vera dabbed at her mouth and laid the cloth napkin on the table. "May we go sit in the lobby for a bit before I depart?"

"That be grand. I settled the bill earlier, so we can leave." Roy stood and walked behind Vera's chair. It appeared to be a sign of a gentleman.

As Vera rose, she turned back to Roy, gently put her arm around his arm and let him lead them out of the dining room and into the lobby. There was a small sofa large enough for two, and Vera walked to it. As she sat, she patted the seat for Roy to sit next to her. There was at least a foot of air space between them, but this was as intimate as Roy had been with a girl.

They sat in peace for a minute, both planning and waiting for the other to make a move.

"Your world changed today. You may never have a day such as this again. I know you loved Mr. Hanson as if he was your father, and he loved you as well, Roy." Vera touched Roy's arm and continued. "In a way, you may have more feelings for Mike than if he really had been your father because he chose you. You're a good man. A very hand-some, honest, and kind man. Here is a card with my address. Please write to me. I would very much like to see you again."

Roy looked at the card and mumbled that he would write. He took a breath and spoke. "I want to see ye, Vera. I want to see ye every day. If I didn't ha to see Mike back home, I'd find work here just to be around ye, but I cannot stay."

"Of course you must go. You will have a very emotional time ahead of you, and I will pray for you to find comfort. I am not certain what will happen with the both of us in the future, but I like you. More than I have ever cared for or enjoyed keeping company with anyone. Please write to me, and I will write to you." Vera reached for her coat and purse. She stood motionless, not wanting to leave.

"I promise to write ye. I'll tell ye what the news is with the ranch. Seven months ago, I was in Scotland, and now I work on a ranch in Montana. All thanks to Mike. He saved me life. And now I'm standing here lookin' at you, and my chest is aching." Roy was as honest as he could be with her.

He looked at her and boldly said, "I can no ask ye to wait fer me, but...I ask ye to not marry another man for a bit and give me time to come back for ye." Roy had no idea how he had mustered up the courage to say what he said.

Vera needed to be calm, but she was hoping Roy would say something meaningful. This was more than she expected to hear. Was this a proposal or simply an overheated young man talking nonsense on the most emotional day of his life? She alternated between feeling flattered and then mildly irritated by the request for her to pause her personal life. Was she a train to be shifted to a sidetrack while other locomotives steamed by, destined for beautiful and rich locations?

But then, no boy had ever looked at her the way Roy did. No one seemed to care about her like Roy. They had known one another for a few hours, but when the saddle fits and feels secure, cinch it tight. That was a feeling she had hoped to discover. How could she be upset when a handsome, kind, and generous young man had just told her he wanted her?

This was a lot to pack into a single day.

"Well, let us see what the future holds, Roy Douglas." Vera wanted to keep things alive and growing without making promises that could not be kept. "I am very busy at the hospital, and I have no beau." She looked up and smiled. "I will read your letters, and I, in turn, will write to you. You are a fine man, Roy, and I enjoy being in your company. We shall discover together what sweetness the future holds for us and what plans the Lord holds for us."

"That is a fair deal." Roy felt that his prospects could only worsen if he continued to talk. "I thank ye for bein' a help ta me today. You be a kind woman, Vera Daggett. Kind and beautiful ye are."

Vera felt herself weaken as she looked at Roy's face. She doubted anyone would ever say anything as simply and honest to her.

I WILL wait for him, she told herself, *but he will need to put in the effort.*

"I must be off. I'm very tired as I normally sleep during the day, and I have missed my rest, but I do not work tomorrow, so I will rest then." Vera waited for Roy to help her with her coat and then she gathered her things.

Roy touched her arm as he had one more thing on his mind. "Bein' honest will never ruin us. If you and me are ta be together, being truthful ain't the thing that will keep us apart. I won't lie to ye bout anythin'. I be a terrible liar…that's the truth." He winked and smiled. She pursed her lips and winked back.

Vera stood. She believed every word he said.

Roy walked out to the street and waved at a carriage for hire down the street. He opened the door for Vera, and she walked to the curb and climbed into the enclosed carriage.

"Please be strong and safe travels to you. I will be thinking and praying for you and your family. I hope we see each other again very soon." Vera sat back, told the driver the address, and looked straight ahead, knowing she would become emotional if she looked at Roy any longer.

Roy closed the door, turned the handle, and patted the side of the carriage. Away she went. There was no embrace goodbye, no classic kiss full of regretful farewells.

The single goal in Roy's life was clear to him. Marry Vera and build a life for them both. Being with and caring for her was all he wanted.

CHAPTER 25

The early morning walk to the mortician's was cold and sunny. Roy had his bag and Mike's bag, holding the few things they had packed. Mike's bag also held the doll that Roy had bought for Grace, carefully and symbolically wrapped and protected by Mike's clothes.

Roy arrived after a ten-minute walk and looked to the side of the building. He saw a black hearse with a team of matched black horses backed up to a door. He peaked inside and saw the wooden box that held Mike's body. He walked in, and a younger man approached him.

"I am Earl, the son. You are Mr. Hanson?"

Again, Roy played the role of kinsman to keep confusion at bay and replied, "Yep. Me name is Roy. Thank ye for the ride to the depot. It be a long walk on a cold day."

"Our pleasure, Roy. I am sorry for the sudden and early departure of your father. A trying time for all." The "Son" in Dickerson and Son was well practiced in the business of condolences and comforting words and was cut from the same black cloth as his father. "If you could lend a hand, we will be on our way."

The coffin was on a fancy table with wheels, and the son pushed the table directly to the back of the hearse. With Roy on one side and

Earl on the other, they very easily pushed the box into the back of the hearse using the rollers. Earl lashed a small rope over the coffin and tied it down. Roy was not expecting to be transported in this much style and thought they would be traveling in an open wagon.

"There is no room inside, so please take a place on the seat. Allow me to place your bags inside with Mr. Hanson." Earl set the two satchels in and closed the back door of the hearse.

After a light touch of a buggy whip, the solemn solo parade began. As they passed down the street, men would stop, remove their hats, and stand still until the hearse had passed. Roy was stirred by these simple displays of respect to a stranger. He tipped his hat to one man on his side of the wagon. He wished he could jump down and shake the man's hand in thanks.

The 20-minute ride to the Helena depot was smooth and soothing in a strange way. Roy realized that he would be Mike's guardian and protector for the next few days, and he felt honored to watch over him.

"If you care to go inside, ask for Mr. Keane. He is the shipping agent and will arrange to have Mr. Hanson properly handled. I will wait here for instructions." It was certain that Earl had transported bodies on the train in the past, and he would ensure a proper transfer.

After 10 minutes, Roy returned followed by Agent Keane who greeted Earl and told him to drive to the mail car directly behind the two passenger cars. Keane and three railway workers, under Earl's direction, rolled the coffin out, placed it on their shoulders, and slid it into the side door of the car. It was a luggage and mail car that was clean and much warmer than the boxcars that had delivered Roy to Montana. Keane secured the box to iron rings on the wall, gave a tug on the ropes, and left satisfied the special cargo was safe.

"Now, son, I know there's a part in ya that wants to ride in there and be a watchman, but I suggest ya don't." The agent spoke to Roy with experience and kindness. "It's cold in there, it don't ride so good, and you'd get weary of the chore in 10 minutes. I seen it before. Nobody expects that from you. Ride up in the passenger car."

Roy shook the agent's hand. He then walked over to Earl and shook his hand before taking the two bags and walking on the platform and into the car. He took a window seat and watched as the shiny black hearse headed back to Helena. He was familiar with Great Falls and the Hotel Arvon and that offered some comfort. He would sit for the next hours reading his book and spend time remembering his friend and fallen leader.

The Missouri River had steam rising and laid out the twisting route of the waterway. Roy was now a traveler on another level. He began to notice minor details along the way and saw more color now. Things came at him like a charging bull in the past and offered little time to analyze and reflect. Now, he had time to look deeper.

The train slowed and stopped at the depot near the river. Between the book, the study of landscape, and fatigue, the trip to Great Falls was calming and easy. The peaceful period passed much to fast.

After the train stopped at the Great Falls depot, Roy found the ticket agent's window where he explained his needs and plans to catch the train tomorrow to Stanford. He was unsure of the procedure for the handling and care of Mike's body, but the agent seemed to be well practiced in this process and assured Roy all would be well. They would keep the coffin in a secure room next to the Head Agent's office, and they would assume responsibility and deliver respectful handling of Mike's remains as well as the loading tomorrow on the Stanford train.

Roy bought his ticket for the next day's passage and for Mike's final train ride. The train would leave at 10:20 in the morning, allowing Roy time to ready himself for the final leg of this horrible expedition. He stayed long enough to see the coffin properly set in the room, tipped his hat to the man, and walked out.

He found the Western Union office three blocks away. He thought he'd send a telegram to the Lewistown office and ask if his previous message had been delivered Will Fix and to Elmer at the ranch. It would cost a dollar and would be worth the expense. At the wrought iron constructed clerk's window, Roy explained what he wanted and let the man decide how to word the message. He added that he would wait for the reply.

'CAN YOU CONFIRM MESSAGE OF YESTERDAY DELIVERED TO HANSON RANCH ON BEAVER CREEK? STOP'

Less than a minute passed, and the clicking of the telegram began. The operator quickly wrote down the answers to the magic tapping and handed it to Roy.

'MESSAGE DELIVERY CONFIRMED STOP ENTIRE TOWN KNOWS AND SEND REGRETS AND SAD REGARDS FOR HANSON FAMILY STOP'

"Sounds like your Hanson fella there had a lot of friends down in Lewistown," the clerk said.

Roy looked up, handed a silver dollar to the man, and said, "People liked him fer sure in Lewistown, but they loved him anywhere he was."

Knowing that the news about Mike was already out and that Elmer would be in Stanford to meet them was a relief. He needed any small victories available.

———

Roy knew the route to the Hotel Arvon well. The hotel had already become his second home away from the ranch. This was the one element of today he would allow himself to enjoy.

Opening the door of the hotel, Roy hoped he would see Mr. Perkins. He also wanted to avoid delivering the news about Mike, as he knew Perkins would certainly want as much of the story as possible.

"Good afternoon, Mr. Hanson," Perkins greeted him in an unusually tempered tone of voice.

"Good day, Mr. Perkins." Roy kept walking to the front desk and set both bags down on the floor. "Would ye have a room open for this evening?"

"I do, sir." Perkins paused and cleared his throat. "Please allow me to say my sorrows to you and any family that you may have. The news spread rapidly that it was Mr. Hanson's mortal remains that had returned to us on the train. He was a gentleman, and all shall miss him in this world."

Perkins' words sounded like a song. Roy reached over the desk and shook Perkins' hand. "Very kind words and well accepted by me and his family. Many thanks." Roy knew Perkins had genuine emotion in his words, and he felt as if Lowell Perkins would be a man he would count as a friend beginning today. He was an east coast dandy, but he was solid and smart. A bonny lad.

"I am afraid that the only room we have available is the same room Mr. Hanson, the senior, occupied on his visits with us. If that is discomforting, I would attempt to ask and cajole one of the younger male guests to exchange accommodations." *This fella can sure use up a full bucket of words*, Roy thought.

"No need. I find it an honor to be in his room." Roy took the key and the bags and walked slowly up the stairs. Opening the familiar door, he told himself not to fall into a dark hole of remembering. He knew all of that would come due tomorrow. He needed food and then sleep. He would read until his eyes ached and hope for a dreamless sleep.

The next day started with Roy waking to the sound of boots and spurs. He liked the sound of them but not their purpose. Mike had offered a pair of spurs to him the first day on the ranch, but he had refused. He wanted the horse to enjoy the memory of the ride, not the occasional pain of the spur poking his flank. of course, the first sound of the day was a memory of Mike.

Once dressed, he sat on the bed and allowed a minute of remembrance of the first time he, Mike, and the sheep all spent the night in Great Falls. Little things came forward that made him smile and laugh softly.

He recalled a few things: the 'get a load of this character' look on Mike's face when they first meet Lowell Perkins…how he turned confrontation into friendship…and how Mike splashed in the fancy tub like a toddler.

The more he recollected, the greater the loss was felt. He would need to work on balancing that problem out in the days ahead, or it would hobble him.

He closed the door with a final glance to the bed and visualized Mike lying there waving.

A final tip of the hat to Perkins and a handshake was all either man needed this morning. It was 7:00 a.m., and Roy would fill up on breakfast and then get to the depot early. He had a sensation that Mike was waiting for him. He knew better, but oddly, he liked the feeling.

His hat blew off his head as he left the café and landed on a small snowbank. He brushed it off, saw no damage, and pulled it down hard on his head. The dark gray hat was a part of him now. A hot summer had put a permanent sweat ring around the base of the crown. Two small blood stains, now turned to dark smudges, recorded the day his bloody hand reached up and removed his hat. By accident, a dimpled crease was sloped down to the front after he had dropped the hat, and a horse promptly, and with precision, had stepped on the front of the crown. He had punched it back out, but the slight dent had stayed, so he had chosen to push it in a bit, dunk the top of the hat in a water trough, and let the sun bake the crease into the hat. It had worked, and he would occasionally have someone remark that they liked how he personalized his Stetson. The Boss of the Plains model was an extremely popular and common hat, and many Westerners invented various creases to distinguish themselves and their hats.

After a hot and filling breakfast, Roy walked into the depot around 8:00 a.m. He walked up to the clerk and asked if he could look in on Mike. He also told the clerk that he would need to pay all fees. The clerk told him he could go sit in the room if he pleased and that all costs had already been paid in Helena except for Roy's ticket to Stanford.

The door squeaked and was loud as the station was empty and still chilly. A squint in the room showed no changes regarding the coffin, but Roy thought he'd go sit by the large wood burning stove in the waiting area. He would absorb as much heat as possible as he would endure all the cold he could handle on the wagon ride from Stanford back to the ranch.

———

Roy felt a hand shake his shoulder and heard someone say, "Stanford train is loading soon, son." He had napped for a short 10 minutes, but it was equal to the best rest he had had in days.

Roy walked to the storeroom and watched as four men carefully and respectfully placed the coffin on a wheeled cart and pushed it to the platform next to the enclosed railcar. They knocked, and a man inside slid the door open. The man could see Roy watching, added things up, and gave a nod to him to let him know that Mike was now in his care.

Roy found a seat close to the small pot belly stove in the passenger car, pulled out his book, and readied himself for the hardest part of this expedition. He would read his book and try to enjoy the scenery on this sunny cold day, January 2, 1892. He realized that he had missed New Year's Day.

This was the first time he missed Scotland. New Year's Eve and New Year's Day were a time of big celebrations back home. He hadn't had time or was aware of the date, and this would be the first Hogmanay in his life he had missed. No steak pies nor ceilidh to drink at, dance with the cute girls, and tell tall tales. Auld Lange Syne was sung at midnight. He promised himself that Hogmanay would be celebrated regardless of where he was in the future.

The sun was extra bright this morning as four inches of fresh snow had fallen, boosting the sunlight to a near blinding degree.

CHAPTER 26

This should have been a recognizable trip. Places, landmarks, and hills all should have been identifiable, but nothing looked familiar. Roy may as well have been traveling to Stanford from Great Falls in the dead of night. The sun was bouncing in all directions off the snow and made the scenery nearly invisible. Roy saw it, but it entered his head undeveloped. Mike and all goings-on filled his brain.

He knew that Grace, Elmer, Anna, and all of Fergus County had heard the news, but he was the only eyewitness to this upheaval, and he knew his role would be to fill in the blanks and stare at sad faces painted with pain. He would be called on to retell the saga for weeks and months ahead, with no concern for his anguish in narrating the first-hand details. He knew this was his water to haul, and he would face it the same way Mike would have behaved.

The train shook and lurched as it reached Stanford Depot. Like a metal hiccup, the train gave a sharp and sudden movement until the loud screech of steel wheels sliding over iron rails ended abruptly. Roy wished he could silently tell himself he was home, but he was hours away from that thought.

He looked out the frosted window and saw Elmer standing with his right foot slightly ahead of the left, bundled up against the cold wind and the reality that had recently reached him. Roy looked at him and tried to make eye contact, but Elmer never looked up and held that position. Roy gathered both bags and walked off the car and up to Elmer.

He wasn't sure what Elmer would say or how he would act as Roy approached. He knew that if he were there to meet him that the basic news of Mike's death was known and would not require an opening statement.

"In the last car?" Elmer asked and pointed at the freight car.

"Yep."

Just then, Leonard, the Stanford Depot Manager, came out to the platform with two other men.

"Terrible, dastardly thing this is. Mike, I mean." Leonard offered his hand to Roy. "Mr. Hanson was as likable as a red spring colt he was. He was good to them that didn't have much good in them. He offered more than most had earned. Damn fine man." Leonard stopped shaking Roy's hand and looked away as his voice trailed off. "Us fellas here will load Mike, or the box...damn it, whatever is the polite thing to say. What the hell do I know? I hate this bag of nails."

Elmer had the wagon backed up to the other side of the platform, and it took the three men and Elmer 30 seconds to off load and put the wooden box with Big Mike's body in the wagon. Elmer shook hands with the men, slid the gate in the back of the wagon closed and waved to Roy to load as well.

"You tell all your people how mad we are about this. Every soul around here knew Mike and his kindnesses." Leonard gave a quick wave to Roy and turned to go inside but then added, "Don't let ol' Elmer there get too crusty and mean. Him and Mike growed up together. Elmer ain't the most lovable bull in the barn anyhow."

Roy walked to the wagon, set the bags on some loose hay, and climbed up next to Elmer. A slight lift and drop of the reins on the Belgian's rumps moved the wagon and Mike towards home.

The sky was getting cloudy, and the men shared the elk robe over their legs. It was 20 degrees above zero and cloudy, but a small wind made it a warm winter day in Montana. After 30 minutes of no talking, Roy spoke. "Do ye want to know anything or have questions?"

"Nope. Not now." Elmer's answer closed the door to communications and any emotions he might hold.

Roy was surprised by the lack of curiosity but not shocked. He wasn't looking forward to a nearly six-hour ride sitting next to a breathing stump, with no conversation or evidence of life except the cloud of steam escaping from its mouth and nose.

"Mike had a lawyer fella in Helena write some things down telling how he wanted to see the ranch run." Roy thought that nugget of information might bait Elmer into conversation or a question.

"I reckon you seen them papers?" Elmer held his forward stare.

"Aye, I did. Had a wee squint, but it be things a schooled man might know all its meanin's. I reckon that Grace gets the ranch." Roy knew Elmer couldn't ignore that statement.

After a solid minute of silence, Elmer cracked. "So?"

"That's all I know. Not sure what to do with that." Roy hoped Elmer could throw some light on how this new arrangement would work.

"Huh. I reckon you be right." Elmer gave a typical unemotional, short reaction.

"A lawyer fella came up to the hospital and talked with Mike the day before he..." Roy still didn't want to say or hear the word.

Elmer stared straight ahead. "He known he was fixin' to die. You got them papers?"

"Aye. I got a few pages. The Helena man said he was sending all the papers to a lawyer in Lewistown." Roy took a breath. "Mike said you was like a brother to him. He wanted me ta tell ye that." Roy was unsure if he would get a response or if he wanted to hear what Elmer would say.

Elmer said nothing for a minute. "The lawyer is William Fix. He's a good fella but always jokin' around. Him and Mike was buddies. Lawyerin' ain't a funny line of work, so I reckon he needs it. I'm sure he'll be around in short order to let us know what to do."

The sound of crunching snow under wagon wheels and the shaking of lumber and iron was all the sound to be heard. There was no more talk between the two men for nearly three hours. Elmer could go three weeks without speaking. Roy thought he was a quiet man himself, but he was as noisy as a woodpecker on a tin roof compared to Elmer. Neither man had answers for the coming days, and the wise route was to not speak of the unknown.

Roy wanted to talk, ask questions, and start to get a jump on what the future might look like, but Elmer was not a man for small talk or big words. He had gotten used to Mike's conversations and teaching moments and would miss his style of manliness. He knew Elmer held his cards tight, but he was now seeing that Elmer was, well, dull.

Not dull as in being dumb or uninformed but dull as in he didn't give a damn about 90 percent of the world around him. Elmer knew what he knew, and that is all he was interested in knowing. This was unsettling to Roy as he was now going to be working with Elmer. It was then that Roy felt his future possibly would not be lived out on Beaver Creek in Fergus County, Montana. Elmer was not a man he would pattern himself after as he would Mike.

The shaking and rolling hours in the wagon passed slowly with only an occasional glance back to the box in the wagon. Roy was smart and clever, despite not having much formal education, and he was playing out the scenarios in his head.

Was Elmer grieving or was he showing his true nature? Was he merely pretending in the past to like Roy because Mike did? Now with the insulation of Mike's presence gone, was Roy's value and role to the ranch about to dissolve? The questions in his head were falling like a hailstorm.

Roy's instincts and experiences showed him the selfish and ignorant side of people, mainly through his aunt Helen. He was slowly seeing Elmer as a potential adversary and no longer a friend. Was Elmer ever a friend or had he been tolerant of Roy because of Mike? Roy had just lost the best friend he had ever had and now the other significant person in his world may soon work against him.

Roy was nervous and felt on edge. He would be relived to be at the ranch and bring an end to this miserable journey. Then he would see Grace and deal with the emotions of her father coming home in a pine box. His stomach was churning, and he found himself in the middle of an unsavory situation. Two weeks ago, his life was simple and good.

Now, he doubted his future, his ability to stay in America, and his place in the world.

———

The ranch was in sight. Roy watched the front door and porch for movement but saw none. Would Grace run outside and toward the wagon or would she hide?

"We got a table set up in the front room to set the box on. Don't know what to do past that, but we need to think on what's next." Elmer pulled back on the reins, set the handbrake, and took a deep breath. He tossed his bag on the ground before climbing off the wagon. Roy walked to the back and lifted the two bags over the tail boards. He was careful with Mike's bag as it held Grace's doll. He chose to take both bags to his bunk and decide later when to give her father's final gift to her.

Lon and Anders walked out of the barn, and the four men slid the simple pine box out of the wagon, placed two ropes under it, and carried Mike into the only real home he had ever known.

Anna was holding the door open and was empty of emotion. Her eyes were down, and her face was pale and blank. Roy thought she might look at him as the men carried the pine box into the house, but she held her attitude.

The long box was carefully set on the table. All four seemed to step back in unison, then stare in disbelief that their leader had fallen and what remained was a few feet in front of them. No one moved or had any notion of what to do next.

Elmer was the first to break away and headed back out to unhitch the team. He looked at Anders and Lon, and they followed. This was a convenient excuse for Elmer to disengage, and Roy did not expect him to return any time soon. Anna leaned against the kitchen wall as she finally released a small portion of feelings and dabbed at her eye with her apron. After a minute, she busied herself and returned to preparing a late supper for the fractured ranch family.

Roy stood next to Mike and felt it was his duty to stay and not abandon his mentor. He set his hat on a chair and took off his heavy coat.

He looked up and saw Grace peering around the corner of the hallway. They locked eyes. All Roy could hear in his head was Mike's voice asking him to watch over her. He moved slowly towards her and at the same instant, she walked slowly towards him. He stopped halfway and held out his arms. Grace ran to him and allowed Roy to swallow her up in his embrace. She tucked her face between his neck and jaw and softly cried. He had never hugged Grace before, but he knew she had lost her sentry and protector. The hug was as comforting to Roy as it was for Grace. Neither wanted to release and face reality.

Roy slowly raised up with Grace's arms still draped around his neck, just the way she had held on to her father a thousand times. He carried her to the pine box, turned to face it, and placed his hand on top. Grace looked at Roy, he gave a slight nod, and she reached out to place her tiny hand next to his. She felt the rough wood for a minute and then lifted and set her hand on top of Roy's. That was enough. The transfer of love and protection was quietly passed from her devoted father to his chosen son.

"Can I see papa?" Grace whispered into Roy's ear.

"Aye, ye can wee one, when the time be right. Maybe tomorrow. But I make ye a promise you'll be seein' him. He looks grand he does." Roy wasn't sure if the plans included a viewing, but he would guarantee Grace's request was granted.

Roy caught Anna glaring at him from the kitchen. She shot him a look of minor disgust that he didn't understand or expect. It was not a look of fondness or compassion. He was increasingly unsure of how he fit in or if he still belonged. More questions. Fewer answers.

Roy carried Grace outside to the front porch. He needed to separate himself and Grace from the atmosphere of Anna and her increasing resentment. He had grabbed a blanket from Mike's chair on the way out and wrapped Grace in her father's warmth.

"Did you watch papa die, Roy?" Grace had questions, and she was owed answers.

"No, Gracie. He passed early in the morning before I got back to the hospital. I sat with him the night before, but he was bad sick, he was." Roy decided to be honest and not hide any facts from her because she was a child.

"Was he in a bed or did they make him sleep on the floor?"

"He had a bed, a nice bed in a nice warm room. Why would ye ask that lass?" Roy was startled by Grace's question and wanted to assure her that her father had been well cared for.

"'Cause when we went to Billings once, we stayed in a room in a house that only had one bed, so he made me sleep in the bed, and he slept on the floor." Grace's constant memories of Mike were how caring and unselfish he was.

"Lassie, he had a big soft bed and had kind nurses watchin' over him."

"What were their names?" Grace continued with logical questions that seemed to have little importance to an adult's mind.

"There was one nurse that helped care for your pa." Roy would be careful not to release too much information and turn the story into his saga of love and adventure. "Her name is Vera. She was very kind and gave care to your pa more than the others."

"What color was her hair? Was she pretty?" The questions seemed out of place, but Grace's mind had its own reasons.

Roy would tread lightly here. "Aye, she was bonny. Just a wee thin' girl, but strong. Her hair was dark like a chestnut colt, and her smile was full of gentle."

"Good. Papa probably liked her, didn't he?"

"Aye, he did Grace. She was grand." Roy had more to say about Vera, but he'd store it away for another conversation.

"Roy, why are you leaving?" Grace didn't raise her head from his shoulder while asking this odd question.

"I'll not be going anywhere, Gracie. Where did ye get such a notion?"

"At breakfast, Anna and Elmer said it would be best if you left the ranch. I heard them. I don't want you to go, Roy. Why would you want to go?"

This day was taking a dark turn. Roy now needed to deal with betrayal and sabotage as well as mourning Mike.

Roy held her close and whispered into her ear. "Gracie, ye need to know this. Yer pa told me to watch over you and to protect you the way he did. I can't be your new pa, but I promised him. I can't do that if I go now, can I?"

Grace said nothing but clung to Roy the way she did with her father. This child, this new orphan, needed Roy. The reality of that firmly hit him.

His dreams of being a student of a professor named Big Mike Hanson were gone. While crossing the ocean and riding the train across America, Roy had been jammed full of excitement and dreams. He had planned to learn how to run a ranch, ride like a cowboy, and be an American, just like Mike.

Now, his future had no father figure, no mentor. In less than a year's time, he went from sleeping in a barn in Scotland with a handful of life experiences to planting roots in a new world with fresh burdens. He had, in effect, become a father to a young girl when he himself was still a boy. The transition from young man to adult had been painfully accelerated. He was now his own responsibility. His dreams had been changed to new and harsh realities.

"Anna will be havin' supper soon." Roy opened the door and set Grace down. "I'll be takin' the bags to me bunk. Go help Anna, sweet girl." Grace slowly walked to the kitchen while Roy picked up both bags and headed to the bunkhouse.

He paused outside halfway between the main house and the bunkhouse and looked at the clear, star filled sky. He had never prayed before and was unsure of the procedure to talk to The Almighty, but he was out of options and needed help. He wasn't sure if he believed in God or any celestial powers as he'd witnessed no benefits or advantages for faith holders over skeptics. He knew that Vera had faith and believed in God. Maybe he would explore her religion. It seemed to make her happy. But without influence and direction, he doubted any man would conclude that God was real and was all-knowing. And if God were the Creator, would he take credit for the destruction of a life as fine and valuable as Mike Hanson's as well as for the blooming bluebells in the spring pasture?

Reaching his bunk, Roy slid Mike's bag with the doll under his bunk and unloaded his own.

———

Back inside at the supper table, no one said a word. No questions, chatter about sheep, or the weather. And nothing regarding a service for Mike or details of a burial.

He felt like a stranger. He sensed that he and Grace were now outsiders and trespassers. Anna was cold and controlling toward Grace now. No love, no warmth. This was more than grief. This was her own fear for the future. Elmer now had complete control over her in every way. Roy was again shown that Elmer and Anna were not to be trusted, and both were working against Mike's wishes.

Roy felt a surge of power and purpose. It would be easier to deal with Elmer as a foe and not as an ally. He had tried to like Elmer and his cold and distant personality. He had respected his position and rank on the ranch, but now, he was done.

Roy was younger, smarter, and much stronger than Elmer, and he was finished being dominated by this wee unhappy man. He would have willingly worked with Elmer to continue Mike's vision and plans for The Hanson Ranch, but it was clear that Elmer had other plans. Selfish plans that would exclude all others, even Grace.

Roy owed everything to Mike. At that moment, he dedicated himself to live, work, and be the man Mike would want him to be.

Grace didn't eat much. She walked over to Roy and gave him a hug, just as she would have done with Mike, and then went to her room. Roy finished his supper, pushed away from the table, and stood behind his chair.

"I'll be riding into Lewistown tomorrow morn to visit with the lawyer, William Fix. He has all the details of what to do next. Mike told me on his last day to see the lawyer and have Mr. Fix help figure things out."

Mike had not instructed Roy to see the lawyer, but he felt this was the only way to wrestle control away from Elmer.

"I'll go. You stay here." Elmer muttered without looking up from the table.

"Mike said for me to go." Roy stood firm and would not be bullied. "If you be needin' to come, that be fine, but Mike ordered me to see the lawyer and that be what I do. I'll not be going against Mike's wishes. No one will. The law will be in control of this, and that's what Mike told me." Roy was done being controlled.

Elmer was knocked back a bit. He wasn't easily neutralized. People with no access to emotions are often unmovable. Elmer had few positive sensations about life, and he worked through each day with resentment. He could tell that Roy was willing to take a stand, and he would save his powder for the coming battles.

"Go then. Do what Mike told ya to do." Elmer continued to chew on a piece of bread and didn't look up.

Roy had one more issue that needed to be handled. "What about Mike? Do ye have a plan?"

"Well, we can't put him in the ground until Spring, Maybe April or as late as May." Elmer pushed back from the table. "We can put him in the root cellar for the winter. Is he…what is it…bombed?"

"Aye, he is, but I don't think that's what ye call it, but he's all fixed up. I made sure they did all that in Helena." Roy was in charge, at least for a few minutes. "I'll ask the lawyer fella what Mike wrote down and how things are ta be. All the decisions are in the papers, and that's what will happen. I'll go after sunrise tomorrow morning. I'll be stayin' over in Lewistown for the night."

Roy pushed his chair in and confidently walked out. He felt as if he was in control for the first time ever. He wondered how long this feeling would last.

CHAPTER 27

The view from the top of the hill west of Lewistown was like a postcard. It was cold with a stiff wind. The clear morning air was full of floating ice crystals. Early January was not the best time to travel in Montana, but this trip had to be made. It was just before 9:00 a.m., and Roy was cold and hungry. The Sapphire Café had a buggy and three horses tied up in front. He was reminded of a phrase Mike had told him: *Buy from a busy store, and live where it's peaceful.*

He found a table against the wall and placed his hat and coat on a chair opposite. A round faced, smiling woman walked up with a blue tin pot of coffee and began to pour without asking. Roy nodded and said a soft thanks. The woman instantly recognized him.

"You're from the Mike Hanson ranch are ya?"

He snapped up straight at being known by a stranger. "Yes, ma'am, I am. Roy Douglas is the name."

The waitress smiled. "Thought it was you. The whole town's been waiting to see someone from Mike's ranch. We all thought Mike was a fine man. Us girls in the back, we all cried when we heard the news of him passin'. We knew him since we was kids. Warren and Wayne they was real friends with Mike since they all was crawlin'." She pointed the coffee pot to the two men sitting by the wood stove drinking coffee. "Boys, this be Roy from Mike's ranch."

The men rose and came to Roy's table. Roy stood to greet them.

"Roy, I'm Warren Austin, and this be my brother Wayne. We couldn't a felt lower when we heard Mike had passed on. We knowed him our whole lives. He was like a brother, but dang near every man in Fergus County would say that." Warren dropped his eyes to the floor. His pain was obvious and genuine.

Roy knew that Mike lived his life amongst these people. He would discover that his admiration and respect for Mike was widely shared.

"Thank ye, sir, for the kind words." Roy shook each man's hand.

"Come sit with us if you'd like. We'll let you eat, but we'd like to ask a question or two." Wayne walked back and set another chair at the table. Roy gathered his hat and coat.

Warren got right to it. "You be the fella, I mean the man, Mike hired in Scotland ain't ya?"

"Yep, I am," Roy said in his best American voice. The 'Ayes' and the 'Bonnys' would slip out on occasion, but he wanted and needed to sound like a Montanan.

"So, you was the one that took Mike over to Helena and was with him at the end?" Wayne followed up.

"Yes, sir, I am and was with him. Brought him back on the train and met Elmer in Stanford. He's home now. I mean that Mike is home, at the ranch."

Both men had a reaction to hearing Elmer's name. Warren said, "Don't want to show no disrespect, but we never could understand why Mike put up with Elmer. You need to watch him, Roy."

Wayne gave Roy a nod to back up his brother's words.

"Why is that, if you could say?" Roy wasn't looking for dirt, but he felt reassured in his faltering opinion of Elmer.

"Well, Mike liked or could tolerate most anyone, and his paw had saddled him with Elmer since they was kids on the ranch. Mike was bigger and smarter, so Elmer fell into line with Mike, but he's got no friends anywhere. He got no smile in him at all. Like a fella with no music in his voice. He's...just there." Warren was toning down his dislike for Elmer out of respect for Mike. "We run the transfer and freight office in town here. You come see us if you have any problems. Anything. We all owe Mike and would be proud to help you and see after that girl of his."

The food was delivered, and Roy dug in. The brothers began a string of small tales about Mike. They would shake their heads and laugh often. Roy just ate and listened. These men were mourning and missing Mike just as he was, especially since they had been friends since boyhood. He would find the Austin brothers were just two of hundreds who liked and loved Mike.

The waitress picked up the plate and told Roy that there was no charge and that breakfast was on the house. Roy said nothing but shook the waitress's hand and smiled. The Austin brothers grabbed hats and coats and walked Roy out.

"You let us know when you need help, and if we find out you needed something and didn't call on us, well, we'll hunt ya down and throw you a beatin'." Warren winked but let Roy know he was serious about the assistance. "Why don't you come to our house for supper tonight, and we can talk more? We got a room and a bed for ya too. Be pleased if you'd stay with us tonight. Mike used to stay with us from time to time."

Roy thought it would be rude to turn down the offer; truth be told, he'd rather eat supper with friends tonight and not lay wake in a strange hotel room. "That would be bonn...good. That be good, Mr. Austin."

"Come to the freight office in the late afternoon or when you're done with your business. It's down by Central Feed on the Big Spring." Warren patted Roy on the shoulder, and Wayne tipped his hat. "See you, Roy."

Roy felt Mike was watching over him. He had made a connection with men that would now be his friends. Mike would be with him past death in a real way, not just in memories. He was starting to believe that now, he would be okay.

CHAPTER 28

R oy rode back west on Main Street. He turned right onto 7th Avenue and noticed the ground had been leveled and worked with a few pallets of red bricks. Fergus County had been created in 1886, and Lewistown was growing fast.

He took a left on Washington Street. He saw a small sign hanging near the door of a light brown stone house that read, Wm Fix, Esq. Roy had no idea what the Wm or the Esq. meant, but he knew the Fix part was what he was searching for. He tied up his horse, took the papers the Helena lawyer had given him from his saddlebags, walked to the door, and knocked. A young-looking man, tall and with some chin whiskers, answered.

"You're Roy I'll bet." The man stood with a wide smile and motioned Roy to come in out of the morning cold.

Roy walked in, befuddled that a stranger would know who he was. "Yes, sir, I am. Roy Douglas. You be Mr. Fix the lawyer?"

Lawyer Fix grabbed Roy's hand and shook it as if he was covered in snow and was vibrating his arm to release the flakes. "Yes, yes. I am him. Micheal described you to me and rambled on about how lucky he was to have found you in Scotland. He had nothing but high praise for you, Roy. Very good to finally meet you; wishing it were for reasons of enjoyment rather than grief."

Roy enjoyed being around smart men, and he could tell that Will Fix was many levels above the average man. He had a different manner but was not superior or aloof. It was rewarding to be in the company of a man who was wise and learned but not big-headed.

"Come sit down in here. I have a previous appointment due here in ten minutes' time, but if you can return in an hour, we will have more time then to go over the reasons you are here this morning." Mr. Fix patted the back of a plush chair for Roy, and he sat in a smaller chair he pulled up. Roy noticed he didn't sit behind his desk covered in papers but next to him as a friend would.

Roy handed over the small packet of papers that Lawyer Swindell had given him. "The fella in Helena give me these to read, but I cannot make out what they mean. I can read, but it be things a normal man can no recognize."

Fix grinned and looked at the papers. "We men of the law are not normal indeed. It's a secret code created to keep wise men in other professions confused and in need of our services. It's a silly occupation, but a greedy and sinful society needs to be watched over. I am unsure if we will ever succeed, but the effort is needed to save the Republic."

Roy nodded as though he absorbed the meaning of Will's short speech, but he was stumped by at least one quarter of the words and their true meanings.

Mr. Fix licked his finger and flipped through the papers. "I grew up on a sheep ranch myself near Dornix. They call it Big Timber now. Guess Big Timber is a prettier name. My father and Mike's father knew one another through the Montana Wool Growers Association, and I've known Mike my entire life. I'd say he was my best friend. Broke me when I heard the news." He dropped his head and cleared his throat.

"Well, let's get to the task, Roy." Will moved to his desk chair and held up a thick stack of papers. "This is all of Mike's legal papers including his Last Will and Testament. I received the papers from Mr. Swindell yesterday. I haven't had the time to look them over, but Mike had his affairs in order."

"I have no idea what to do Mr. Fix. Can ye tell me what be happenin' next?" Roy was searching for answers. If told, he would do what was asked of him.

"Would it be possible for you to come back in one hour, Roy? I need to read the additional papers and see what has been added. I am certain the papers you gave me are identical to what I have already in my possession, but I must confirm they are the same. This may take some time to sort out. Mike did well and has many assets and property."

Will walked back around the desk and sat down next to Roy. "I'm going to help you get through this. Mike made it clear to me this summer that he wanted to change some things and that you were important to him. All I can say now is that it will be interesting and will take time to resolve. Can you return shortly?"

"Aye, I can, sir. I'll be staying in town tonight with the Austin brothers, and I'll do what be needed." Roy stood and felt a wave of relief rush over him.

"Warren and Wayne are good men. They knew Mike for a very long while. Come back at 1:00 p.m., and I will spend the afternoon with you. And Roy, I'd be pleased if you call me Will. I thank you for the respect, but our destiny calls for us to be friends for many years ahead. I will call you Roy, and you need to call me Will."

"Thank you. I'll be back at 1:00, Will." Roy walked to the front door and out to his horse. The livery stable was a few blocks away, and he wanted to get Big Paint unsaddled and tended to. He would walk through town and give his horse a short holiday of fresh hay, oats, and a warm stall inside the livery for the night.

———

The gold rush in the Judith and Moccasin Mountains a few years back had helped the village grow. After the gold ran out, many miners and settlers came to Lewistown for steady work. Big Spring ran through the settlement and offered clean pure water to the entire area. Nothing lived or survived in the west for long without water, and this huge natural spring was an oasis for a growing region.

The sounds of hammers hitting stone was heard even in the cold of winter. While timber was available, the land in Fergus County was primarily open and covered with beautiful grass and rich soil in the bottoms. Sandstone was abundant, and a few European stone masons had been hired from Great Falls to build and begin a new business district. Lewistown had a population near 1,000 people and was not big by any measure. However, the Homesteading Act of 1862 had widely affected Montana. Growth started slowly at first as lands farther south and east were settled first. The often-brutal climate and severe environment drew the Nordic and Germanic immigrants. As settlers built and tilled, farmers and ranchers needed goods and supplies to live and grow. Towns and villages sprang up near logical trading routes. The more settlers, the more town folk appeared, and the natural cycle of commerce built the west.

Compared to Great Falls and Helena, Lewistown would not grow as fast or to be as important, but it had a critical role to play in the center of this new and enormous state. The future would see livestock and grain crops create wealth and generational stability. Montana, effectively, had a half dozen smaller states within its borders, and many had a favorite or preferred location or region. Fergus County was a blend of all things beautiful, strong, and wild. Wide grasslands, rolling hills, and the surrounding fortress-like mountains were beautiful and perfect for people that craved variety in their lands. A land that feeds cowboys, visionaries, and miners alike is near perfection.

————

Roy decided to have a lunch back at the Sapphire Café where he felt welcome and was assured of a solid meal. As he walked in, the same waitress greeted him and smiled. The day's fare was written on a blackboard on the wall, and she waited for his order.

"Is a pork chop a good meal?" Roy looked up with genuine boyish curiosity.

"Yes, it is; very good." The waitress was charmed by his honest question. "I'll bring you a plate, and you judge."

"And, ma'am, I be pleased if I could pay fer the food this time."

The waitress smiled and winked at him. *Just like Mike*, she thought.

Roy thought he should be writing down questions for the lawyer as he would never be able to recall the information that he would hear. His main concern was Grace. Once the lawyer explained her future to him, he would be able to think about his own prospects. He was a grown man and would be able to fend for himself and start anew if needed. There was no time now for selfish thoughts.

Roy was introduced to three more men and a young couple at the café, as it seemed that he was known by half of Lewistown. Each greeting began with a smile and was followed by a sad reflection on Mike's passing. Roy wanted to be thought of and remembered in this way. If he could harvest half of the friendships in his life that Mike had, he would feel complete.

————

Snow was starting, and the air was chilled by gusts. He reached the front door of the Fix home and office and knocked. Will ushered him into his small office in the front corner of the home and took his coat.

"We have a lot of things to discuss, Roy, so let's start straight away." Mr. Fix stood behind his desk, organizing four piles of paper. "Now, I read and reviewed the additional papers that Mr. Swindell sent directly to me. It was an addendum to Mike's Will. Addendums simply add things for the most part, and this one did make some big changes. Please ask me to explain things if you have a question. I don't expect you to understand all the legal wording, but I know you are able and I want you to grasp the meaning and intent of Mike's final wishes."

Roy had already heard two or three words he had never heard before and felt this was going to be a long hard ride. But if Mike had faith in Mr. Fix, so would he. "I'll do me best, sir. I just want to know how I can tend to Grace the way Mike wanted."

"We will get to that, Roy. I know that is your top concern to care for Grace. I see why Mike placed his trust in you." Will looked straight at

Roy, leaning his hands on the desk. He raised up and moved to the first paper pile. "I'll explain this as best I can, but there is a lot to deal with."

Will began with Mike's original last Will and Testament.

"The original papers gave Grace 100 percent of the ranch land and livestock, which would be held in a Trust with me, William Fix as Trustee in control until Grace was 18 years of age. At that time, she would have the freedom to do as she saw fit and sell or stay at the ranch. As Grace was Mike's only living blood relative, she was sole heir."

Roy thought for a minute as to how well planned and wise this was. Will Fix was raised on a sheep ranch and knew the legal world as well as the challenges of running a ranch. He was the perfect man for the job. Added to the fact that he was Mike's best friend, this was an excellent arrangement.

"I think Mike thought about this a long while fer sure. Sounds grand. I'm happy to hear that Grace will be safe." Roy spoke softly with the image of the wee girl on her father's lap in his head.

Will moved to the last mountain of papers to his right. "Yes he did, Roy. His only lasting concern was for Grace to be protected. But his addendum, from the Helena lawyer, changed things a great deal. This is where things get interesting for you and for everyone."

Roy had no notion of what was next or whether it was good news or bad. He sat up ready to hear how his life would now be lived.

"Mike made some big changes, and you are the main benefactor of these changes." Will could see Roy was already confused. "Benefactor means you get the most or benefit the most by these additions, Roy."

Will adjusted his position in his chair, paused, and looked straight at Roy.

"Roy…life will never be the same for you after I read this to you."

"Do I need to go back to Scotland?" Roy's voice was full of worry and fresh fear.

"No. Quite the opposite." Will let out a light laugh, took a deep breath , stared at Roy and smiled.

"Mike gave you half of the ranch. You will take over the ranch and run it for and with Grace. You will now be in charge and run The Hanson Ranch."

Roy gave no reaction. It was if he had heard nothing that Will had said.

Will paused and then read some more. "You, Roy Douglas, will get 50 percent of the ranch, Grace Hanson gets 50 percent, and Elmer Barney gets paid five thousand dollars to leave the ranch. Elmer will take the money and go because I, as Grace's trustee, will tell him he has no job and no claim to anything. Five thousand dollars is a lot of money, and Mike wanted to be fair, but he clearly wanted Elmer to be gone." Will waited for Roy to react.

Roy sat stunned at the news. He would be the foreman AND the owner. Mike had given him half of a Montana ranch? Why was he feeling sad and not elated? Why did this news weaken him? The only reason this was happening was that Mike had died. Roy was still a not a long way from getting past losing his leader.

"It's a great amount for anyone to understand." Will pulled a sealed letter out of the last folder of Mike's papers and handed it to Roy. "Mike wrote this letter and gave it to me last October. It's written to you. I'll get us some coffee or would you rather have tea? Read this, and I'll be back shortly."

William handed him the letter and left for the kitchen to allow Roy a private moment. The letter was sealed and had *For Roy Douglas to read if I dead* handwritten on the outside.

Roy took out the knife from the sheath on his belt and opened the letter. The writing on the envelope was Mike's handwriting, but the letter was typed. It read...

"Roy,

I hope you don't have to read this, because if you do, it means I'm dead and gone. But I know my friend Will is taking care of Grace, the ranch, and you. He's a fine man that I have known of since we was boys. I want you to trust in what he tells you to do and what I want to get done. He is the only man I trust, and he will be in charge of things until you can take the reins.

Will wrote things down for me a couple of years back when my sweet Clara passed, but I made some changes to those papers. I want Will to see a judge and make things legal after I die. Elmer won't like it, but that is how I want it to be. It took me a while to see that Elmer is not fit to be the boss. I told him a while back that he would take over the ranch if something happened to me, but now I don't want that.

Will has all the papers, and he can explain what I want. I hope you want it. If you don't, you can ride off and find your own way, but I hope you stay on.

Will is putting down the words and is making it pretty. He is using his fancy machine so it can be seen clearly and it is clear what I want done.

I hope I find the courage to tell you to your face what I'm writing in this letter before I croak, but I'm a weak man and probably won't talk to you the way I will in this letter.

I always wanted a son. I had dreams about having a boy to ride with and work beside. I love my Gracie, and she fills me with love, but a man wants a son. Somewhere on the train between Great Falls and Stanford, I felt like you was/were my son, and I wanted to say that to you.

I know that you will watch over Grace for me. Nothing means more than her being safe, and I know she loves you since you are her big brother now.

Wish I was around to watch Gracie and you grow to be old. I hope I grow old, and we can sit and drink whisky on the porch together, but if you are reading this, it didn't work out for me.

Be an honest man, Roy. Be kind to everyone, not just to them that can give you what you want. It makes a man feel good to do the right things. Don't fight unless you got no way out of it. If you do have to fight, finish the other fella so he knows you don't got any quit in you.

If you find a good woman, be gentle to her. Love her if you feel she is worth it. You can learn to feel strongly about a good woman, but if she's pretty and sweet and you can start out feeling that way, it will be better for both. Be a good man, and she will be a good woman.

I can't write down all the things I want to say if I was your pa and had 20 years to teach you. Think things through before you move. Be brave and treat the world with square dealing. It won't be fair or be good back to you, so don't bother keeping count.

I hope you think about me a few times and remember the things I taught you. I want you to think of me as your pa, and I hope you can talk kindly about me when I am gone from this world.

Mike"

The last words hit Roy hard. He dropped the paper, grabbed his head, and cried. He felt himself shaking, and he couldn't stop. He was releasing days of hurt and loss that had been boxed up. His pain was awful, but he had to meet it head-on. He had cried like this when he held his dog, Ned, in his arms as he died. That was sadness; this was massive grief. He had not seen or been touched by anything like this before.

He felt a hand set on his shoulder. Will had watched from the doorway and permitted Roy to privately release the hurt, but he sensed that after a minute, Roy needed to re-connect to the world.

"Quite a letter, huh? Mike wrote it out, and I typed it on my type writer thing over there. Few men talk like that, but Mike was, well, he was a one-off."

Roy gave a deep final sniff, wiped his eyes on his shirt sleeves, and looked up. "Sorry for the leakin' eyes Will."

"I'd think you to not be a human man if you did not, Roy. That should be the last of the apologizes from you." A light hand on Roy's back from Will put an amen to the moment.

"Mike added a few more things. Mainly…he wants you to go marry the Helena nurse. It says here her name is Vera?"

Roy let out a snort of surprise and amazement. "What now? What's that ye say?"

Will looked at the papers and read aloud. "Have Roy marry that pretty nurse Vera. Please give Roy two hundred dollars for the wedding and for him to buy her something nice." Will smiled and looked up. "She made quite an impression on him and you. It says you have six months to get married or no wedding money. He was a pisser, wasn't he?" Will laughed and smiled, imagining Mike, laying in a hospital bed, sick as a wet dog under the porch, dictating the conditions of matrimony to the lawyer.

"I have to marry Vera?"

"No, just that if you do, he wants to pay for the wedding and all the doin's. He seemed to think you took a hankerin' to her. Did you? Asking as a friend, not as your legal agent."

"Sure, sure I did. She's a bonny lass, full of kindness. She's a pretty…" Roy caught himself in mid-sentence before he rambled.

"Seems Mike was right about her and you. Smart man, he was. He must have seen a spark." Will winked at Roy like a big brother would. "One more big thing in here. And this is good."

Roy stayed still, ready to receive the final blow.

"Mike wants to adopt you. You will legally be the son of Mike Hanson." Will stopped to allow Roy to absorb this news. "Wants to name you as his son and heir. You and Grace would have equal rights and shares of the ranch and all holding of the ranch. Would you agree to this? You can keep Douglas as your last name."

Again, Roy dropped his head in disbelief. He slowly raised his head and looked at Will. "I be proud to be called the son of Mike Hanson." Roy said quietly, fighting back another wave of emotions.

"I knew you would. I told Mike you wouldn't buck at the notion. The adoption is a simple thing. We don't need to do much. Mostly folks just say they adopt a youngster and that's that, but we'll file a paper that Mike signed just so it's on the record. There's lots of money and land about to be given to you, and you'll be glad to have a judge signing a paper saying it's so. That will make things simpler in the future for all."

Legal adoption was a simple affair as families integrated orphans of kin or friends often in 1890's America. Death was a constant, and children of family, friends, or neighbors were sometimes abandoned. More often, these underlings found new homes as farms and ranches needed workers. Love and affection were not automatically included in these arrangements, and many orphans carried a sense of loss and detachment for life.

"I will get those papers filed this week." Will's tone shifted as he leaned forward. "Now comes the sorry part, Roy. I'll need time to get all these things in order. I have a feeling that Elmer will not go easy and will fight. He doesn't have any legal claims or rights, but he can be a nasty, mean son-of-bitch. I never liked him, and Mike inherited him from his father. Not sure about the story of why Elmer came up from Missouri with them. Mike could get along with pert'near anyone, and Elmer knew Mike could whip any man in Fergus County, except maybe Eugene Meier, so he fell in line."

"What would ye be needin' me to do?" Roy agreed with the assessment of Elmer's temperament and was more than glad to have Will take control for the coming campaign.

"I think the best thing is for you to leave for a short while. Maybe three weeks or a month. I'm not certain how long I will need to smooth the road. It will need to be long enough until I get all the knots out of the rope. Let me get Elmer settled and out of the road and then you can come back home. You don't want to be around him while this is going on. Heck fire, I may get ol' Gene Meier to come out to the ranch with me and throw a whoopin' on Elmer just for fun."

Roy remembered a promise he had made to Mike. "I'll do what you think be best, but I made a promise to Mike to stay at the ranch through the lambing season, and I not be breakin' me word."

"I know what that promise means to you." Will looked to the ceiling in thought and then offered a solution. "Let me look around and hire a man, maybe two, to help those Basco brothers through the lambing if you don't be back in time. Would that be acceptable?"

Roy thought for a second. "Sure, but that be costin' money. Don't want to spend money just on my account."

Will grinned. "That will not be a problem Roy. Let me explain." He stood up and walked around the desk and sat next to Roy.

"No one knows this besides a banker in Billings and me, but Mike is, well was, a man of great holdings. Meaning his estate is fairly large. He has thousands of acres of land and owns a large amount of railroad stock. His father began to buy up land all over the middle part of the state, and Mike continued that practice, buying a little land each year or when a deal presented itself. He was very smart with money and bought railroad shares early. Between the land and the stockholdings, Grace and you are wealthy young people. Good thing, or he would not have had the funds to travel to Scotland and buy those sheep. That kinda worked out for you I reckon." Will sat back to take in Roy's reaction to the news.

"But why do I get it? It should all be Grace's."

Will was again taken by Roy's unselfish position and response. "Grace does get all the railroad stock, and that alone will allow her abundant independence, but as an heir of the ranch, the land holdings will be shared. We are talking about a lot of money. Mike never wanted folks to know how much land he owned. Most is prime land with a few parcels of lesser value and use. He thought people would treat him poorly and keep their distance. He never wanted to be thought of in that way. He didn't trust bankers, gamblers, or politicians. He often said, 'bankers keep what's yours, gamblers steal what's yours, and politicians tell you what's yours is really theirs.'"

Still in a daze, Roy quietly asked, "How much land?" He was trying to get an idea of what he would soon control.

"Eleven sections of land, Roy. 640 acres to each section. It's in four different holdings, but all together it is…". William did the math on paper with a pencil. "Seven thousand and forty acres, not including the ranch on Beaver Creek which is four sections. That's another 2560 acres. All total, you and Grace will own just under ten thousand acres of good Montana grazing grass and some land suitable for grain crops. There are much bigger ranches around and men that own tens of thousands of acres, but you will control more than most men will ever own. Mike lived small and only bought what he needed. He paid cash when he bought the land. At roughly ten dollars an acre, you will soon be an very lucky man, Roy. Take into account that the land is not cash money. The ranch also has a good sum of money in the bank that will allow us to operate the ranch. My advice is, live like Mike did. It's 1892, and things look rosy now, but you never know when things will turn bad."

Roy sat motionless, staring at the floor. He didn't feel lucky. He felt saddled. Most would think positively of the money that had just fallen from the sky, but Roy would have chosen to have Mike alive and in control. He knew how to work and follow instructions from experienced and wise men. He suspected he was not prepared to be a leader. He was about to turn nineteen, was not married, and hadn't been in

Montana and the USA for a full year. He wasn't a U.S. citizen yet. He was smart enough to be scared.

"You will not do this alone." Will could tell that Roy was full of uncertainty and was trying to process the developments. "Mike would not have done this if he questioned your abilities and strengths. I will oversee the Trust for the next few years and will be in charge of the money and big decisions. I'll be with you as you learn. I grew up on a sheep ranch, and I am very familiar with ranching."

Roy sat up and realized he was appearing to be young and weak. "Aye, I'll do what you tell me ta do, Will, and I be grateful for the help. Just come from a wee village with nothing ta me name last year. And now…this."

"If you trust me, I will trust you, and we will make the Hanson-Douglas Ranch a success. That is what Micheal Grant Hanson would expect from us."

"Wouldn't be right to put me name on the ranch. I done nothin' to earn that." Roy leaked out a smile grin. "His full name had a Grant in there?"

Roy pulled his head back and raised his eyebrows at hearing Mike's full name.

"You never knew that? His mother was a Grant. Full Scot I believe. He was Norwegian and Scottish. The Hanson name is usually Swedish, but he was Norwegian. Some government fella wrote it with an o and not an e. Grace's mother was German."

Will added a bit of his own history. "Now my family came from Tennessee, and my paw always said we were half rascal and half polecat. My family is Scottish, English, and a little Chickasaw Indians, but we don't talk much about that." William clapped his hands and got back to business. "Sorry, Roy. I guess I did a little lawyer ramblin' there."

Roy enjoyed the side story. Mike never told him of his Scottish roots. Things started to make sense a bit more. He thought of the history and wisdom that Mike would have shared with him if only he had been afforded the years.

Will switched back to the Elmer issue. "Let me be honest. Elmer does not care for me, and I don't like him. I think he's a mean little man. I doubt he has a friend in the county. Not one soul will miss him when he's gone." Will looked at Roy and raised one eyebrow to emphasize how poorly Elmer was thought of by the locals.

Roy didn't like the idea of leaving his home and leaving Grace in the hands of the rivals. "Is this the only way to get this done?"

"It is not the single answer, Roy, but I think it is best for you and for us to get past the potential ugliness." Will walked to the corner of his desk and sat, intending to drive home his concern.

"You're a young man and full of trust whereas Elmer is an angry bitter man. When Mike's father passed, Elmer thought he was owed part of the ranch, and he got nothing. He cornered Mike in the barn a few weeks later and hit him with a pair of sheep shears. Damn near killed Mike, knocked him cold. He came to, got up, found Elmer and went to pounding on Elmer until he cried for him to stop. Mike told him to leave, but Elmer begged to stay, saying he had no place to go. Mike let him stay, but he never trusted Elmer after that. Wouldn't let him in the house for two weeks. He ate his supper in the barn. I'd a made him eat in the outhouse."

"I know him ta be quiet and surly, but I ha' no heard that story." Roy thought of how Mike had protected him from that side of Elmer.

"I fear that when Elmer is told that you get a sizable portion of the ranch, he may react poorly. He can be a real bastard, Roy. Let me and some of Mike's friends deal with that sawed-off runt. Warren and Wayne Austin would pay cash money to be first in line to put a bustin' on him. They know about Elmer jumping Mike in the barn. I need you to stay clear from trouble while this is going on." Will's voice got higher, and it was clear he was expecting a fight with Elmer.

"I got no family or friends anywhere...except in Helena. What do I do 'til ye get things smooth?"

"I'm giving you enough cash of your own money now, and you can travel around and see Montana. Go see Billings, Bozeman, and Butte, although Billings isn't all that pretty, and Butte is a hellhole." Will shook his head, obviously not found of the mining town. "We got Yellowstone Park, and the prettiest country God ever made up here. It is still winter, so you can't visit the park now, maybe someday soon. Go court and spark that nurse of yours in Helena for a spell. Send me a telegram each week or when you get to a town that has a Western Union office. Stay there until I answer you. I'll update you on things here."

Will knew Roy needed to hear the plan in some detail. He forgot for a moment that Roy was still new to America and to Montana. "Firstly, you will have all the money you need, Roy. Need I remind you that you will soon be in control of a large ranch and the sums of cash needed to operate. Let's tell people that you are the son of a rancher in Fergus County, looking for horses, cattle, and farming equipment. That is all true and will allow you to see and learn at the same time. Don't go buying any livestock yet, but you should look. Can you play the role, Roy?"

Roy had already been acting as Mike's son, and he enjoyed the part. "Yep, I can do that."

"I am certain you can and will, Roy. You need to get it in your mind that you are a young rancher of means, and we need you to be that man. 'Cause by God, that's what you are now."

Roy heard Will's instructions and for a moment felt happy. He was instantly the man he had hoped to be, and he would publicly be the son of a fine man. His joy was from being a son much more than a fresh man of means. "I know I be askin' many questions, but…"

"No worries, Roy, I know this is all new to you. You and I will be partnered in this enterprise, and I hope we are able to consider one another fine friends in the coming years."

Roy again felt flush with relief. It wouldn't last for long, but it was a pleasant change. "I know that you be lookin' to me best interests, and I trust ye, Will."

"Let us work to honor Mike's name. Now, let's deal with the coming days. I would recommend that you and I ride out to the ranch tomorrow. I will give Elmer the news and tell him how things are to play out. You will gather all your belongings and return to town with me, leaving your horse at the ranch. I will tell him that two hands will be hired to help with lambing as you will not be available to work. How does that sound to you?"

"That be a fine plan." Roy paused and then asked his most important question. "What is to become of Grace? I'll fret about her when I'm gone, and I think she'll worry about me."

"Mike's wishes were for Grace to come live with my wife Becky and me until you can get settled back at the ranch. And I mean settled with a wife. Then, when the time is right, Grace will return to live with you and your wife." Will was wearing a sly grin.

"I'll do me best." Roy understood the instructions and wanted to move past that issue. "Can we be holdin' services fer Big Mike before I leave? I'm not sure how to do that."

"You betcha, Roy." Will answered apologetically and was displeased with himself for not addressing the issue sooner. "Some of us in town have begun to organize a service for Mike. He cared not for preachers or politicians, but we thought a service of memorial in town would be appropriate. We have set a date and time at the Methodist church in three days. Would you agree to that?"

"That would be bonny as long as I no hav' ta say words."

"We have it all arranged, Roy. Just a time for his friends to say farewell." Will followed up, "May I ask where is Mike's body?"

"Elmer put the box down in the root cellar and covered it with a canvas."

"I am thinking of that big man in a box, and it knocks me down. Can't recall feeling this sad." Will looked down and cleared his throat. Neither man said a word, and both felt the same loss. "Elmer did the right thing there. Let's wait to bury Mike in the spring. Can't dig in frozen ground. You'll be back by then, and we will put him next to Clara."

During the entire conversion with Will, Mike's burial had been on Roy's mind and now he had an answer. He was bone-tired from dealing with endless questions, but each answer took a rock of burden out of his poke.

Roy stood up hoping Will was done. "I be stayin' with the Austin brothers tonight and doin' supper as well. They sure was good friends with Mike."

"He was the best of us. He lived an unselfish life. He kept his pain to himself and showed the world kindness. You are living proof of that. He lost his way for a time after Clara passed on, but he fought it.

Told me once he thought grief was like whisky: a little can help, but a barrel full can kill you. He still had Grace, and she became his world. And now, well, it's on your shoulders." Will felt he should stop as the future months would be trying for Roy. "Come back at 9:00 tomorrow morning, and we will ride out to the ranch together. We'll stay the night, and you, Grace, and I will return to Lewistown the following day."

Roy shook Will's hand and shuffled to the front door. All he wanted was a peaceful supper and sleep.

CHAPTER 29

I t was 4:00 p.m. The walk down to the Austin brothers' freight office took 10 minutes, and Roy took a deep breath before opening the door, expecting another round of well-meaning but exhausting conversation.

Warren waved him into the back office. "Bet you got a belly full of talking with ol' Will. Them lawyers are paid to talk, and you get your dollars' worth from Will. Us boys, we talk all day for free!" Warren snickered at his own joke, which he was famous for doing. "Him and Mike was tight as a wet knot, and he's an honest man. When Wayne and me come to the area, those two was the first to give us a welcome and offer help. The four of us sort a gathered up and stayed pals. We'll head home soon, have supper, and leave you to a good night's sleep."

Wayne came in a few minutes later, and the brothers put on coats and hats and then walked Roy up Big Spring to Warren's house a few blocks away. Supper was just being set on the big table as the brothers' wives delivered steaming platters of food, and five children all found places on a bench. The brothers shared the big house, and Roy welcomed the chance to hide in the large group.

Wayne's wife set a bowl of mashed potatoes in front of Roy and told him to start the meal off. No questions about Mike or digging for information, just time for a meal to be shared with friends.

The children finished, and the two girls went to the kitchen to help the women clean up while the boys went outside to haul firewood into the house for the night. Roy missed the contentment of routine and admired how even a busy house could be calm. Thoughts of Vera and a home the two could build were flying around in his head. The future was exciting, but the labor to get there seemed straight uphill.

The men moved to the parlor, and Warren tended the stove. "I'd offer you some whisky, but we don't drink liquor, so we ain't got none. You bein' a Scotsman, I reckon you like tea. We like coffee, but the wives can get you a tea." Wayne stood to go give the orders to the women.

"Coffee is grand. Never had much tea back in Scotland, and I come to like the coffee now." Roy wanted to be as American as possible, and coffee seemed to be a social passport.

The Austin ladies carried in a fine-looking coffee pot and cups. Warren's wife spoke. "We know you must be weary of talking about Mike, so we will not add to your burdens, Roy. Allow us a moment. We would like to organize a service for Mike, and we ask for your blessing to hold a memorial for our dear Micheal."

Roy had never been asked for permission by anyone in the past. He thought of how to properly answer. "That is a bonny notion, Mrs. Austin. We are busy with many other matters, Mr. Fix and me. I'm sure that little Grace would be pleased." He wanted to sound strong yet grateful.

Mrs. Austin offered a sweet smile and tilted her head. "We are pleased to hear you feel that way, Roy. You and Grace are Mike's family, and we want to follow your wishes. We would like to have a service soon. We have already talked to many people in town, and we will spread the word now. We will all be pleased to do this."

Warren wanted to change the mood and the conversation. "Whereabouts are you from, Roy? We heard that you come from Scotland with Mike, you worked hard, and Mike was thinking of you like a son. Tell us about you."

He told them about meeting Mike, the sea journey, the train ride with the sheep, and his first impressions of Montana. The 'hand burger' story got a laugh, and that broke the seal on a series of stories and memories from the brothers. Laughs were followed by throat clearing and small sniffles. After an hour of sharing tales about the life of Micheal Hanson, the room fell quiet, and the loss of their friend was deeply felt.

"You are surely exhausted from the day." Wayne's wife stood and brought Roy his satchel. "We have a bed made up for you in with the older boys. There is a wash basin in the hall, and the privy is out the kitchen door. Why don't you get to bed before these two old wobble jaws keep you yapping 'til dawn."

The brothers played along at being offended, and Warren pretended to shed a mischievous tear. Hands were shaken, thanks offered and accepted, and breakfast plans were fixed. Roy couldn't fill Mike's boots, but he now hoped to inherit the role of friend.

————

The next morning, the house was busy with boys bringing in wood and water, and girls setting plates, forks, and knives. Breakfast was hot and filling. The brothers told Roy to ask for any help in the coming days and said goodbye as they left for work. Roy told the ladies he had just had the first enjoyable meal and quiet rest in weeks. He tipped his hat as he left for Will's office.

The walk was cold, and the northwest wind was gusting as Roy got to the livery stable to get Big Paint. He didn't care for the idea of leaving his favorite horse at the ranch while Will played out the cards in The Hanson Ranch game, but his options were limited.

Roy tied his mount in front of Will's house next to a two-seat buggy with a gray mare, loosened the girth strap on the saddle a bit, removed the bridle, and tied up with the halter rope before untying the saddle-bags. Will greeted him at the door and pointed to his office. Coffee was waiting. Will was dressed in riding gear, not his usual legal costume.

"I need to go over a few details before we head out." Will was putting a handful of papers in an expensive-looking leather case.

Will realized he had told Roy what to do but not how to get the job done. "The two of us will sit down when we return, look at a map, and plan your journey. I think that time away will teach and entertain you. You've had a rough road lately. You need to be young, feel young, and not be burdened as you have been. Get a new suit or two and some snappy new traveling clothes. You need to look like a rancher of high means and wearing handsome suits will tell the world you hold some rank."

"I got some of Mike's clothes."

"Those don't fit you, and they're not the new style, Roy. You need your own clothes. You'll also need at least three suits, some new fancy boots, and a nice clean hat. We're going to get you looking like a copper baron. A man with no power needs to look like he has power. Only a strong man has the luxury to look weak." Will picked up his leather case and a small bag for his overnight visit at the ranch. He opened a desk drawer and pulled out a large, nickel-plated revolver and shoved it in the bag. He saw Roy watching.

Will got closer and lowered his voice. "I never leave town without my gun, and I would tell you to do the same. I'm not sure how our friend Elmer will take the news."

"Oh, I got me a gun. Have it on now. Mike told me ta wear it everywhere, even to the outhouse." Roy gave a small pat to his belt and grinned.

"Good to know, Roy. When we get to the ranch, we'll all gather up, I'll read the Will and explain the legals. You and I will talk to Grace alone and explain why she needs to come live with Becky and me for a spell. She likes my wife, and Clara was a friend. We've known Grace since she was born, but she will only hear you."

Both men knew that dozens of questions were still unanswered. Those would be dealt with soon enough, but now it was time to face Elmer and the future.

The men walked out to the buggy. Roy tied Big Paint to the back of the rig. The late morning was sunny and cold but windless. That seemed to define a January day in Montana as either cold or pretty decent. Roy took notice of the fields covered in sparkling snow and the beautiful yet hostile mountains. Winter was the time for man and livestock to find valleys, lowlands and shelter in Montana.

He had heard the stories about the winter of 1886. Many called it The Great Die-Up. Most in Montana had little interest in remembering the winter that nearly ended the livestock economy in the territory. The summer of 1886 was dry, with little to no rain. Fires swept across the grasslands, destroying thousands of acres on the prairies. What good grass survived began to wither and die in July. Streams, creeks, and water holes dried up. Cattle were moved to areas along the Missouri River that offered some fresh grass, but this tactic left these animals in open, unprotected country that would prove to be deadly in the coming winter. The mild winters in the past years created no urgency for ranchers to cut large supplies of hay and grass to ride out a long winter. Even if the desire to store up feed was there, the drought that summer made it impossible to stockpile hay.

The cruel cold began in mid-November. Wild animals and birds moved south early, and horses grew coats heavier than usual, all signs that nature was anticipating harsh conditions. Strong, howling winds drove icy snow sideways, and hard crusted snowbanks formed instead of the more common powdery snow. Days on end of blizzard conditions followed, and people prayed for a Chinook, the warming South-westerly wind that customarily made winters in this harsh country tolerable. Sadly, no Chinooks arrived, and the snow and negative temperatures increased.

Death was unavoidable. Cattle and the men that cared for them both suffered and died. The country was wiped clean of most living things, and many told stories of family and neighbors that never made it home, devoured by the vicious winter. The carnage continued through the end of March when Chinooks finally arrived, delivering some tardy relief.

Gruesome stories were told of how animals froze to death, standing in the snow like statues. Rivers were covered in carcasses from cattle falling through ice. Others got tangled in barbed wire, were trapped, and waited to die. The roundups began in May. That spring, cowboys were stopped in countless areas, as the stench of rotting beef was so strong in sheltered draws and coulees that they could not ride in to inspect. The Montana Stockgrowers Association that spring claimed that 50 percent, possibly up to 60 percent, of cattle in the Montana territory were lost, with over 350,000 cattle lost. The average value of cattle before the killing winter of 1886 was twenty dollars a head. James Fergus, for whom Fergus County was named, sold 1,500 hides from dead stock for slightly over one dollar a hide. Fortunes were lost, and pioneer families were forced to head back to the places they had left. Hopes and dreams were crushed as settlers left defeated.

Roy thought of the settlers and early pioneers and how they endured. He felt slightly embarrassed the he should be given so much with no requirement to pay his dues to be a Montanan. He was certain that he would face future trials and hardships, but he would remember the sagas of legendary men and women who had created and built a territory and a state. Living up to the benchmarks laid out by Mike Hanson and these pioneers would never leave his thoughts.

"Gotta unload some brown gargle from breakfast." Will climbed out and used the buggy as a wind break. Roy joined the relief party. "I love this part of the county, Roy. These wide-open benches are rich grass lands, and the drainages and coulees are rich in black dirt. You have some of the best land in America right here. Surviving rough winters is the trade we make for this beautiful soil."

Roy could only nod. At some point, Roy hoped he would be known as his own man with his own accomplishments. Until then, he would constantly, but proudly, travel in Mike's shadow.

"Three miles to go. Be there in an hour," Will informed Roy.

———

Big Paint let out a snort and a whinny as they dropped off the flat bench above the ranch. The other horses in the barn and corral heard him and answered back, causing both horses to throw their heads up and down and quicken their pace. The entire ranch went on alert knowing visitors were approaching, and Roy could see Anders and Lon walk out of the barn followed by their dogs.

"Don't see Elmer yet," Roy said.

"Let me talk, Roy. If I anger Elmer, that's a good thing for you. I'll be the villain in this." Will knew this would not be an easy time for Grace and Roy, but he would not backing down from a fight. He had the aire of a confident prize fighter about to rise from his stool ready to swing.

Anders met the men at the hitching post and smiled at Roy. He had not formed a strong bond with the Bosco Boys, but he respected their skills and friendly nature. He wondered how Anders and Lon would fit into this new arrangement and had hopes that they would stay on. Anders pointed to Big Paint and then to the barn and moved his head back and forth, silently asking if he should take the horse to the barn. Roy muttered a 'Yep' that Anders understood.

The men walked to the back seat of the buggy. Roy grabbed his bag; Will grabbed his satchel and the leather case full of papers. Lon took the lead rope and walked the mare and buggy to the barn. Roy could see Grace in the window, smiling widely and waving. He grinned back. He was pleased to see his sweet ward happy to see him.

Roy opened the door, and Grace jumped into his arms and hugged him around the neck, just like she had done to Mike hundreds of times. He wrapped her up and held her tight. Neither one of them had any desire to release the embrace. They shared an emptiness that would last them both until their final days.

"Don't leave me again. I miss you. I miss you and papa," Grace whispered in Roy's ear and hugged him harder.

"You won't be alone again. Mr. Will is going to make things better for both of us. Trust me, wee one?"

"I do, Roy. I'm scared that Elmer will be my new papa. I don't want that. I don't like him. He's got no happy in him." Grace was blunt and honest as usual.

Roy set her down and looked at her. "He won't be yer pa, Gracie. Nobody ceptin' your papa can do that. But I be your brother. Your pa told me to watch you, and that's what I'm doin." She smiled and kissed him on the cheek.

Will spotted Elmer in the kitchen, walked over to him, and offered his hand. Elmer looked down and kept his hand in his pocket. Will was not surprised by the adolescent move. He hoped that Elmer would stick to this tactic as things moved forward. If he stayed vengeful and angry, he would be predictable and could more easily be controlled.

"We came to stay for the night. In the morning, we all sit and talk about all the events and changes. If Anna could cook us all supper, we can rest and talk first time in the morning." Will laid out the plan. He expected no resistance, and none was given. "Roy and I will go to the bunkhouse and settle."

The supper was simple and quiet. Grace sat next to Roy, just as she did with Mike. Will commented on the soup and how filling it was, but that was the limit of the small talk. Will and Roy finished and headed out to the bunkhouse but not before Grace scurried over and gave Roy a hug around the waist. He assured Grace that he would see her at breakfast and told her to sleep well. The tension-filled evening was ending, but the angst would only increase by morning. Will held the joker in this poker game and he would play it in the morning.

———

It was just after 6 A.M. Roy woke to see Will sitting at the table in the bunkhouse with Anders and Lon explaining how their futures would be affected. Will spoke passable Spanish, and the boys where obviously pleased to be understood and considered important enough for him to speak with them. They nodded their heads in a constant rhythm, only once saying a quiet 'no', and then back to small smiles and affirming nods. Will looked in Roy's direction, said a few words, and the boys both smiled as Anders gave the okay sign with his hand and nodded. Will smiled, stood, and gave each man a reassuring pat on the shoulder. He then pointed to the door and received a "Si, Mr. Will."

Roy had his boots on and followed Will to the door. Anders and Lon both stood to shake Roy's hand and smile. Roy grinned back and shook hands.

"What was it you was tellin' the boys, Will?"

"I told them you would be the new boss man. That we wanted them to stay, and I would control things for a few months until you returned. I also asked them if they knew men looking for work that could help during lambing." Will walked slowly as the two walked between the bunkhouse and main house. "Their faces lit up when I told them Elmer would be leaving. Guessing they won't be crying about that news. Also told them I knew of Mike's agreement for partial pay in lambs. Lots of Basque sheepmen do that to start up their own herd. I told them we needed them and were happy to have them here. They seemed to respond well to that. They said they liked you and you worked hard, but you needed to learn a little Spanish."

Roy looked at Will and saw a sly grin. He felt good that the boys liked him. The remark about the Spanish was taken in jest, but Roy also recognized that it was a small suggestion from Will.

———

Inside the house, Will and Roy took their seats. Anders and Lon filed in a minute later as Grace came bounding into the kitchen with a smile and hugs for everyone...except Elmer. The Basco boys smiled widely as she hugged them, automatically declaring them to be her family by the gesture. Roy felt thankful that she showed this small amount of affection and healing.

Anna delivered plates to the table and breakfast began.

Will took one bite and then began. "I came out here to read Mike's Last Will and Testament to everyone affected by his passing. We have much to talk about." He reached down into his leather bag and set the papers out. "This will affect you Elmer, as well as Roy and of course Grace, but we will speak with Grace later."

Grace continued to eat her eggs, content to be in the presence of friends, hearing but not listening. The Basco boys finished and headed out for morning chores. Grace went to her room while Roy, Elmer, and Will sat. Anna poured coffee and left for her room. The meeting that would change the lives of Mike's family and friends was about to begin.

CHAPTER 30

Will took a sip of coffee, leaned forward, and looked at Elmer. "Everything is written down and are the final legal wishes of Micheal Grant Hanson. It is recorded as a legal document with the Fergus County Court. The wishes and instruction in this Will are legal and are to be enforced by the Sheriff of Fergus County if needed." Elmer sat still and stared but it was obvious that he was the reason for mentioning the County Sheriff.

Will began to read aloud the requirements and conditions contained in Mike's Will. When he got to the section regarding the payment to Elmer and he would be required to leave, Elmer finally reacted.

"Did I hear this right? This...BOY gets the ranch, and I get some money and kicked out? After 25 years of working for this damn land, some stupid kid from Ireland gets this ranch? Well, damn me to hell." Elmer fell back in his chair and looked at the floor.

Will was steady but forceful. "Mike was very clear in his wishes. I think he was very generous with the offer of $5,000 dollars. That is a very tidy sum, Elmer, and is more than enough to buy your own ranch. I would hope that we can do this without wrath or anger."

The money was clearly not the problem. Elmer expected, at the very least, the chance to buy his way into the ranch, but there would be no offer, no partnership, nothing but a bag of money and a kick out the door. His loyalty and work were equal to a small bag of money. He felt that his twenty plus years of work for his family didn't matter to Mike and that a dirty greenhorn boy from another country mattered more.

"I'm surprised to hear that you thought you were entitled to a portion of the ranch." Will looked at Elmer across the big table much like a lawyer in a courtroom would cross-examine a hostile witness. "Mike passed along to me that he had never, nor would he ever, promise to sell you any part of the ranch. He said you were a good hand and that you had earned and would deserve a substantial settlement if needed. Do you realize how generous it is to have Mike give you $5,000 dollars? Most ranch land in Montana can be purchased for $10 dollars an acre. A man could buy a very large operation with half of that amount."

Elmer spoke quietly and firmly. "THIS is my home. Been here for over 25 years. THIS land is MY land. Not lookin' at going to another place." A long pause was followed with a sour look on his face as he looked up at Roy. "More my land than this...this KIDS land!"

Will shifted in his chair and assumed another courtroom-style position. "No one is telling you, nor are you being asked to leave the county or Montana. You have free will and can apply your skills anywhere you see fit. Just not here. Not on The Hanson Ranch. I might add that it is an odd tactic for a man to not save money or look to invest in land or a business over 25 years, and then expect to be given assets simply for showing up for work. I find that to be a curious plan." Will held his stare straight at Elmer, knowing he had delivered an honest blow.

Anna was eavesdropping from around the corner and dropped a spoon. She behaved as if nothing had happened and came in to offer more coffee. Will pushed his cup toward her, and she filled it but did not offer a refill to Roy. By doing so, it was clear that Anna declared she was on Team Elmer. Roy was not shocked. She returned to her spy chair around the corner.

"I think I got some reason to go to town and ask another lawyer if this be all fair and square. I ain't leavin' 'til I get some answers." Elmer tried to sound defiant and strong, but his voice carried doubt and defeat.

"Mike believed that you could react this way. We will allow you time to respond and then to make arraignments to leave. Once the court makes the Will official in two days, I will assume all control of all ranch business and financial powers of The Hanson Ranch as Mike requested. I will have a check for $5,000 dollars for you. You can exchange that for cash at the Bank of Fergus County after you sign an agreement stating you will leave the ranch and have no further contact with the people or agents of The Hanson Ranch. It's up to you when you leave. It is the second week of January, and lambing will begin in a few weeks. I will take control of that and hire hands to help. I will speak with the Bosco boys and determine what they will do. Mike made an agreement to exchange some lambs for their pay, and I will work that out."

"I ain't goin' nowhere 'til I figure out if I'm getting' jammed up or not. I'll head into town tomorrow to get my own answers." Elmer pushed away from the table. He had heard enough. He behaved more as a man being robbed and not one who had just been given a small fortune.

"Please do, Elmer. We can all travel together if you would like. Roy and I are returning to town within the hour with Grace." Will could hear Anna gasp from the hall at this news. "Grace will come to stay with my wife and me in town until all affairs are settled. This is by request of Mike, and this is all written down. Roy and I will speak with Gracie now."

All three men stood. "A few more items to mention, Elmer." Will was clearly in control and left no doubt as to his authority. "Roy will be leaving the county for a brief time. It is no business of yours as to when and how Grace or Roy conducts themselves or when they return to this ranch. You will have no contact with either of them. If it is found out that you have talked to Roy in any manner, legal steps will be taken. I am the one in control, and I will follow Mike's instructions and wishes. He was my oldest friend, and I will not be discouraged by you or anyone in this matter. I hope that I have properly expressed my resolve to you, Elmer."

Everyone stood silent, waiting for the final declaration.

"It is January, the ground is frozen. We will wait until the earth thaws, then we will lay Mike to rest next to his dear wife, likely in April or May. I will make all decisions and arrangements when the time arrives."

Will looked at Roy and then Elmer, looking for a reaction and confirmation that Mike's burial plan was understood.

Elmer did not answer, but he had received the message. He grabbed his coat and hat and walked out. Anna hurried into the kitchen and behaved differently without Elmer present.

"Iz the little Gracie going from here? I love her much but dat iz the gut for her." Anna's voice was quick and nervous. She appeared relieved but sad.

"Mr. Will and his wife will care for her for a spell and then I..."

Will interrupted Roy, not wanting him to lay out the plans to Anna. "Anna, she will come to live with us in Lewistown for a short time until things are settled. You are welcome to stay here at the ranch for as long as you like. You are not being asked to leave. You have a home here."

Anna looked confused and was trying to give an answer that would make everyone happy. "Thank you, Mr. Vill. I vill stay but miss the Gracie very much." Her affection for Grace was honest. She would find herself in the crossfire of this battle. Roy liked Anna and understood that she was Elmer's girl and her loyalty was with him.

Roy and Will walked to Grace's room and knocked. She sat on Roy's lap, obviously feeling safe in his presence as Will explained to her what her father's wishes were. She seemed happy to hear she would be with Becky and Will as she had spent time at their home before. Will told her she would have her own room, and Becky would be with her constantly.

"What about Roy? Is he coming too?" Grace went straight to the thing she wanted most.

"Yes, Grace, I be comin' wee ye." Roy dropped back to sounding like a Scottish lad fresh off the boat. "Sure, sure I be there. But I need to go to some places and... look for some things fer the ranch ye know. Ah, like some horses and machines for growin' wheat and the like."

He was making things up on the fly but also revealed ideas in his head for the future.

Will jumped in. "Roy is going to stay with us in a room next to yours, but he must do some work for me and the ranch, things your father was going to do. Now Roy will do it. We don't want to let your pa down."

"But you come back, Roy, okay?"

"Yea, yea, Gracie. I have to come back and stay. You are me sister now."

Grace looked surprised. She looked at Roy then Will.

"That is correct, Grace. Your pa gave me papers to make Roy your real brother. It was a special surprise for you." Will raised his eyebrow at Roy, telling him it was fine to let the cat out of the bag a bit early.

"Does that mean I can tell people he's my brother and that I love him?"

Roy leaned back to see Grace's eyes. "Aye it does wee one. And I want people ta know that I love ye right back." His voice choked a bit as he pulled Grace in close again for a hug.

The two of them stayed connected for a time, wanting to let each other know that they were all the family they each had in the world.

"Let's have Anna come in and gather up some clothes and other things for you to bring along. We need to head back to town soon. Just you, me, and Roy." Will stood up to go speak with Anna and get things moving. No one wanted to stay any longer than needed.

Will walked to the kitchen and found Anna at the stove. He asked for her help to organize Gracie's things.

Anna wiped her hands on her apron. "Ya, Mr. Vill, I do dat now. I vill miss dat sveet girl. I knowed dis iz vat happens ven da papa dies. Make me sad to go."

"You can stay on here at the ranch, Anna. I hope you don't leave. We need you here." Will waited for her answer.

"I tink I go vith Elmer. He tells me vants a vife and dat he gets married to me. He get mad at me if I don't stay vith him." Anna reluctantly explained her limited life options and how her future may play out.

"Very good then. But if you should change your mind, you have a place here." Will stepped closer to whisper in her ear. "I don't want anyone else to hear this, but Mike gave you $300 dollars as a gift. He said to give you $100 dollars in paper money and then to put the other $200 in the bank in Lewistown in your name, and you can get that money in one year. He wanted to care for you now and in the future."

Anna broke down. There was too much going on. The sadness of Grace leaving, her fractured future, and now the lingering kindness of Mike all landed on her hard. She sat in a chair and sobbed. Will thought to touch her shoulder but thought it inappropriate for a married man to do so and pulled back.

Grace heard Anna crying and rushed out of her room and hugged her. "Don't cry, Anna. Maybe you can come with us to Lewistown." Her innocence produced a loving and logical solution in her mind.

Anna stopped crying and hugged Grace back. "Oh, little von, dat not a gut idea. I stay here. I stay vit Elmer."

"Will you visit me in town? You can see me when you come to town to get supplies." Grace tried one more time to stay attached to Anna.

"Gracie, you need to go, and I vill stay. Ve vill see us together again soon. I know vee vill sveet girl." Anna stood and held Grace's hand. "Now vee go back and get you some clothes for you trip, ya." Grace pulled Anna's hand, and the two walked slowly, knowing that daily life was less than an hour away from permanent change.

Lon was standing next to the mare at the hitching rail, after brushing and harnessing her to Will's rig. Roy had collected his things and placed them in the back of Will's buggy, along with two large sacks of Grace's clothing, toys, and belongings. He had taken Mike's elk robe, the one he used on his final cold ride, and would use it to keep Grace warm. He would quietly claim ownership of the robe and would always treasure this piece of Mike. Snow flurries started as Grace had Roy lift her into the back seat and close the black oil-cloth door.

Will had a quick word with Anna at the door. She stood on the porch, wrapped in a shawl, waved to Grace, and went inside. Lon held the halter rope while Will sat in the front and Roy climbed in the back next to Grace. The buggy turned north and away from The Hanson

Ranch. The new brother and sister stared at their home with heads full of questions and memories.

"I miss papa." Grace looked at Roy and put her head on his arm. He said nothing and patted her head.

Roy looked back through the small oval glass window and saw Elmer saddling up.

"Looks like Elmer will be trailing us into town."

Will looked at the mirror on the side but couldn't see anything. "He's a squirrelly fella for sure. He'll talk to old Winston, but he won't know what to do. Then maybe Frank Smith, but he's busy being the County Attorney. He'll head back to the ranch by the afternoon."

Grace looked out the window for nearly fifteen minutes before sitting back in the seat. It had been a few months since she had traveled anywhere, and she was enjoying the ride and the break in the sadness. A strong gust of wind pushed the buggy sideways. Grace looked at Roy with wide eyes and said, "I may not want to live on the ranch all my life, Roy. I think I want to marry a man in town and walk to the mercantile anytime I want. It's too cold out here."

Roy was slightly surprised by her comment but understood her desires for the future. "The ranch is a good spot wee one, but I do like Lewistown."

Grace sat back up and looked out the opposite side and over the front seat through the front glass over Will's shoulder. Will remained quiet, allowing Grace and Roy time to reconnect. Then all three riders got comfortable and silently took in the rest of the ride.

Lewistown was in sight as the buggy began down the west hill. Grace grabbed Roy's arm. "Remember when we sat here with papa and watched the fireworks?" Her smile was genuine and happy, and Roy gave nod. He would always remember his first and last July 4th celebration with Mike.

Roy turned and looked to see if he could see Elmer. There was no sign of him, but he was sure he was there. Elmer didn't scare him; he just made him uncomfortable. No one could predict what Elmer's next move would be.

Will's house was in sight. He turned down the alley and to his carriage house where they all unloaded belongings and went in the back door. Roy helped Will unharness the mare, push the buggy in, and put the mare in her stall. She would stay there for the day before going back to the livery where she was boarded for the winter.

Becky greeted Grace with a big hug and a sweet welcome. Grace knew her and had known Becky was her mother's friend, so the trust had already been established. Hot cocoa was ready for everyone, and this sweet treat helped Grace get content and relaxed.

Becky stood and fussed in the kitchen. She said, "When you two are done, I will show you your rooms. I have some of my old dolls in your room, Grace!"

Roy was impressed with the new two-story brick house. It was different than the main house at the ranch. The ranch house was made of logs. It had shorter ceilings and was cozy. This house had large windows, a wide staircase, and was the next generation in western living. He saw a couple of fireplaces downstairs, but they were not in use.

"How do ye heat this big house, ma'am? I see no fire."

"We have a coal furnace. Much warmer and easier than wood stoves, Roy. It's the modern age. Please call me Becky if you would. You two are family now." She had a strong, sweet way about her that made her easy to be around.

Becky led the visitors up the stairs. "Your room is here, and Grace, dear, this is your room. Even after you and Roy go back to your ranch, this will be your room." Will and Becky had no children after being married for over 10 years. Becky's first friend in Fergus County was Clara Hanson. Grace had been a baby when the Fix's came to Lewistown, and the bond between the families was long and strong.

———

The four had an early supper. Grace helped Becky clean up, and Roy followed Will into his office to plan for the next few weeks. As usual,

Will was prepared and had ideas written down that were well thought through.

"If there is any part of this that you do not agree with or find to be unsavory, let me know. I want you to be amenable to this strategy, Roy." Will was talking while thumbing through papers.

"I know ye only ha' me and Grace's interest in mind. Mike trusted ye and so do I." Roy cleared his throat. "But what is amean-somethin'? I do it, but that word is new ta me."

"Sorry, Roy. Means both of us approve of the idea. You and I will be working together for years, I hope, and I don't want to bully you. We need to be partners and friends."

Roy smiled. "Will, next ta Mike, you and Becky ha' given more kindness than I ever got. You both are bonny."

"I think you are a fine young man, Roy. When we are old men, I hope we can recall many shared adventures. Let's see how to navigate the coming weeks first." Will jotted down a word or two and then began.

Will laid out a plan that would be educational and fun as well as giving him time to file the legal papers on Grace and Roy's behalf. He told Roy to plan on being away for two to three weeks, maybe into March if needed. He would be home in time for most of the lambing and would allow time for Elmer to vacate the ranch. He suggested that Roy travel to Billings, Bozeman, and make a stop in Livingston. That would expose him to parts of Montana he had yet to see, and he would educate himself on topics important to a young rancher.

"Travel over to Butte, then up to Boulder and Helena. Do not spend any more time in Butte than necessary unless you care to part with some of your teeth and most of your money."

Roy was expecting a small laugh, but Will was serious.

"Butte is a dirty, rough town full of coarse men. There are only a handful of rich men but train loads of men fighting for their next supper. Pass through quickly if possible and stay clear of the Irish. The Finns are decent folk, but the Irish in Butte, well..." Will shook his head in disgust.

"I know a few Irish lads, and they was good ta me. Little fellas but very durable they was." Roy was attempting to defend his fellow Caledonian cousins.

"These boys ain't farmers like you knew, Roy. These are the men that got kicked out or pushed out of Ireland. Mean fightin' men looking for a donnybrook. Hell, Roy, my family is Irish and German, and we steer away from Butte. The smell and the air will drive you away soon enough."

Roy heard the warnings and would remember Will's advice. But now, he had to see Butte for himself.

"Take your time, explore, and be sure to spend some time in Helena."

Roy grinned. "I know me way around there a bit. Pretty place with a big future I reckon."

"Someone special there you'd like to see?" William gave a short, teasing laugh.

"Yep, I'll be seein' a nurse there fer sure."

"Best wishes to you there, my friend. Be cautious and decide wisely. Choosing a wife is the most dangerous thing a man can do. Like handling dynamite. It either will prove to be a great success or will destroy a man." This unexpected blunt counsel revealed a side of Will yet seen.

"A filly can be fun, but a mare often turns mean." Roy repeated a phrase he had heard Mike say once.

William smiled. "That sounds like Mike. Wise man, he was."

"Your Becky is a fine lass. You be a lucky man, Will." Roy attempted to show kindness but at the same time remain manly.

"She's a gem, but she has her spells as we all do. However, I prefer spirit over dreary." Will gave a wink.

Roy knew he was out of his depth and could not carry on a conversation about life with women. "So, I plan to be back by early February I hope. March be too long away. Anything else I should be doing while I'm gone?"

"I suggest you buy some new clothes. Get two, maybe three fine suits, new shiny boots for city walking, and some more winter gear. You have money now, Roy. I will give you plenty to begin, and you can send a telegram asking for more if necessary. I would suggest looking for a ring to give to Vera if she is your choice."

"So, me job is to play, not work, and spend money?" Roy asked, not pleased and slightly irritated.

"Not forever, Roy. Just a few weeks and then the ranch will be there to throw you a beating when you return. This may be the only time you get to have some fun. Unless you get married and have one of those, what do they call it, a...a honeymoons." Will gave Roy a sly grin, a gentle reminder of Mike's request for Roy to bring a wife back to the ranch.

"When should I leave?"

"In a day or two, after the service for Mike."

Roy yawned and stretched. "Will ye help me pick out a suit? Don't want to look like a fool or a Chicago dandy."

Will laughed. He promised he'd help outfit Roy and ready him to take his step up in the world as a gentleman rancher.

It was time for sleep after a full day. Roy took comfort in knowing that Grace was in the room next to his, safe and cared for. He could now face the world with friends and a plan for the future.

CHAPTER 31

Roy heard a knock on his door. He let out a grunt, and the door flew open. Grace ran in and jumped on the foot of the bed yelling a good morning to Roy.

"Morning, wee one! How was your sleep?" Roy cleared his throat of the morning gravel. He noticed how warm the room felt and thought how a coal furnace in a house was almost magical.

"What are we going to do today, Roy? Can we go to the Power Mercantile and look for a dress and some candy?" Grace loved coming to town as most young girls would, and all she could think of was walking through the rows of fancy fabric and shiny new goods.

Roy had been waiting until to the best time to give the German-made doll to Grace. The moment seemed to be right.

"Gracie, I got somethin' ta give ye. Yer pa bought this fer ye in Great Falls. He loved ye, he did." Roy kicked his legs from under the quilt and checked the back flap on his long johns was up and buttoned. He walked over to his cases, pulled out the cloth bag, and handed it to Grace. She pulled the cloth down and saw the beautiful blonde-haired doll. She laid it on the bed. She stepped back and stared a while before picking it back up and then hugged it hard. Roy said nothing. Grace said nothing. She set it back on the bed and touched the doll's face, hair, and dress.

"Is this what mama looked like?" The question took Roy by surprise. He was reminded how complex Grace's mind worked and to not anticipate her thoughts.

Roy thought quickly. "I think that's why yer pa bought her. Fer him and her ta be with ye all the time."

"She's perfect. I'll teach her to ride and to cook." Grace was obviously and instantly in love with her new companion. "I'm going to go show Becky."

Grace came over to Roy with her doll and with her free arm hugged him around the neck and then kissed his cheek. "I have a mama and a papa. Happy that now I have a brother."

Grace went out the door and down the steps to the kitchen where a soft cry of delight was heard from Becky. The doll would seldom leave Grace's arms in the coming weeks.

———

After breakfast, the new clan all gathered in the front hall, put on heavy clothing, and headed downtown. It was a small town, but all signs pointed to a healthy future for Lewistown and for Montana. Grace was controlled but antsy and ready to shop with Becky. Her youth didn't require constant mourning or displays of public grief. Roy was pleased, slightly jealous, that she could start a day feeling happy and unburdened.

Becky gave both Will and Roy black armbands to wear. She was dressed in black as well, and this display of public mourning and respect was important to her. She tied a black silk scarf around Grace's neck as well, and the team of four took off.

Once on Main Street, nearly each man that passed stopped to shake Will's hand and was then introduced to Roy. Condolences were offered, and hats were tipped at Becky and Grace. This scene was repeated eight times before they reached The Power Mercantile building. Roy was again witness to how Mike Hanson was held in high regard by the locals.

The female brigade had their own missions and disappeared into the forest of home and fabric goods. Roy required a suit, and the men headed to the far wall to fill that need. An older woman who knew Will was told of the need for new clothes and sprang into action. Roy tried on a jacket. The woman measured and then moved down to measure his waist and the length of his legs. Roy jumped as she reached around his waist, but Will winked his approval for Roy to relax and allow the exploration.

"You are a strapper are you not, young man!" She commented that Roy would require more material than the average man. Roy had grown and added muscle to his already strong frame in the past year. Hard work, bountiful food, and natural growth had built an impressive young man out of an underfed young sheepherder. He now stood just over six feet tall and weighed a brawny two hundred plus pounds. In 1892 Montana, he ranked as a large and powerful human.

She wrote down the measurements and returned with a small pile of cloth sample. "A size forty-four jacket. Biggest I've seen in quite some time." She smiled an approving smile and set out five samples to select from.

Roy picked a medium gray with thin strips and a light black fabric.

"We will have these ready for you tomorrow afternoon after 3:00. Should we look at shirts?" The outfitting continued as William wandered back to wrangle the womenfolk before serious damage was done.

Grace had found a green sweater that she believed to hold mystical powers and would urgently need. She discovered some lemon drop hard candies that she and Becky both found necessary. The clothing orders were placed, and a return visit tomorrow was planned. Polite farewells were given, and the four walked to the street.

Becky and Grace wanted to stop at the grocer and order a few supplies and items for the men to pick up after their other business in town was completed. Grace waved and grabbed Becky's hand, contently walking down Main Street with no residue of recent drama or grief.

"I want to take you into the bank and meet Misters Hobson and Moe. They want to meet you, and it will be a benefit for you to become acquainted. Good men but remember that they will protect the bank before they help you. That's not bad, just an honest thing."

The meeting with the bankers was pleasant and necessary. Sympathies were given and accepted as well as hopes for continued business and banking service. The bankers treated Roy well and with respect knowing that Will was effectively the ranch boss for now. He would remember being dealt with properly and stay with the Bank of Fergus County for years to come.

Next stop was the Austin Brothers Freight office. Will pointed east and said, "Need to stop here and talk with the boys about Mike's service."

Wayne was behind a desk, and Warren walked in from the back dock after hearing the bell on the door. Both smiled and shook hands with Roy first and then Will. Roy felt as if he was visiting family more than new acquaintances. Will spoke up first. "Came to see about the service for Mike."

"Day after tomorrow at 10:00 in the morning is what the women have worked up. Hope that pleases you fellas." Warren paused and added, "At the Methodist church."

Will turned to Roy and out of courtesy asked him if that sounded good to him. Roy shrugged his shoulders, offering no changes or suggestions as the planning was mercifully out of his hands.

"I reckon my Becky has been working on this with both of your Missus, so we should have it all cinched down." Will sat in a chair by the wood stove and took off his hat. He was reluctant to leave the company of men that felt Mike's loss as much as he did.

Roy leaned against the wall as the three other men all sat next to the stove, sharing Mike Hanson stories. Laughs would usually follow after a variety of tales. There was a story of an elk hunt with Mike and a banker from Billings that ended with both men taking a cold bath in the Yellowstone River when the horses got spooked. Another story about Mike rolling off a flatbed railroad car after a rowdy ram butted him got a solid chuckle from the men. Then a long silence filled the room as the friends all knew there would never be another new 'Mike did something crazy' story again. Mike was only one man, but he was an army of a man, full of life and friendship.

"Roy, we don't want to be late for supper and get Becky riled up. Better head out, gents." Will buttoned his coat and told the brothers they would see them at the church in two days.

A quiet and reminiscing walk gave each man the opportunity to protect their private pain.

The next day was quiet. The day rolled by slowly as each person in the Fix house recharged, relaxed and reminisced.

Each day teased the promise of his new beginning, but everything he had and would soon hold was a gift. He could not pretend to be in control or wield any power. He felt he had not earned anything. At least not yet.

CHAPTER 32

The Methodist church was circled with buggies and wagons. A constant line of men and women in heavy dark clothing moved slowing through the cold, clear morning and walked up the steps through the double doors. People were gathering to share sadness and compare grief.

Death was not unusual in 1892 America. Short, hard lives were lived in the West. A man in Montana could expect to not live far past his 45th year. One in five children would not live past their fifth birthday. It was rare for anyone, young or old, to go untouched by death. Grief was controlled by most through unfortunate practice and was expressed privately and softly. Reserved sorrow was the expected behavior. Loud and excessive anguish was seldom exhibited. Strong emotions were kept for private moments. Life was hard, sometimes brutal, and the extreme environment of Montana increased the harshness.

Grace was an orphan now. This was not an unusual occurrence. In the eastern U.S., children would often be sent to live with family or to an orphanage, but it was very common in the American West for an orphaned child to be placed with relatives, friends, and even neighbors. The bright spot for Grace was she would be cared for by people who loved her, and she would grow up in a world of plenty. Even so, the loss would be a part of her forever.

Space was reserved for four in the front pew. Roy held Grace's hand as they walked slowly to the front of the church, followed by Becky then Will. Without looking up, he felt a hundred eyes glancing, grading, and measuring. Roy sat near the aisle next to Grace, then Becky and Will.

Next to the pulpit was a chair draped in Mike's elk robe with a single white rose set on top. On the floor was a pair of Mike's boots that Will had quietly secured while at the ranch. The sight of the boots and robe hit Roy hard. He knew it was early, and all eyes were on him as he fought to stop the initial wave of grief.

Words of praise and sorrow were used to eloquently describe the life of Big Mike Hanson. The preacher spent a few minutes on the promise of an afterlife, filled with happy reunions with the departed and using phrases like no more sorrow, no more strife.

Roy got uncomfortable for a moment when he and Grace were referred to as Mike's children, but most of the assembled didn't know the true story, and it would legally be true in a few days, so who cared? He did appreciate that the minister did not pretend to know Mike or proclaim him to be a righteous or God-fearing man. The pastor had only been in Lewistown for five months and had never met him.

The preacher stepped to the side of the pulpit and leaned on his right forearm, a move by most public speakers that was meant to convey informal honesty, but it was also seen as a brash display by a few of the elders in attendance, triggering small coughs from two of the ancient and professional mourners in bonnets.

The preacher reacted and paused, then lifted his head.

"I have spoken with many of you in the previous days, and all have shared stories and yarns about Mister Micheal Hanson who moved here with his family when he was but a young boy. Each tale began with a smile, then a head shake of amusement, then a sad, crestfallen ending. I cannot relay each anecdote as that would keep us here past suppertime. I tell you, all of you, his friends and family, that as a newcomer, I dearly regret not meeting this fellow. As a man, I would pray that one day a similar assembly of my familiars would also be stricken with anguish and sorrow in a like fashion as I see in the faces before me today. I did not know Mike nor was I fortunate to number him as a friend. I share with you that I hope that God will assist me in being a man as loved and filled with purpose as Micheal Hanson." The minister turned and sat, his head bowed, and absorbing the collective sadness of the gathering.

Roy heard, felt, and agreed with the minister's words and felt tears filling his eyes. He heard sniffing and a single masculine say a reserved 'Amen' from the back. The assembled were given a moment of silence to work through their own sorrow and realities of abbreviated lives.

As he reached up to dab at his eyes, Roy felt Grace press against him and squeeze his hand. She whispered, "I asked Jesus, and he told me that you won't die, Roy."

He had managed to rope in his emotions to this point, but Grace's declaration broke him. He let out a single short sob and quickly halted his response, but not before causing a chain reaction of audible pain from several mourners. Roy was not alone in his failure to beat down his grief, and the church body seemed thankful that he had broken the seal. It was not an embarrassing outburst, but one that told the gathering that he was indeed, a son who had lost his father.

Roy put his arm around Grace and pulled her tight as a Deacon stood to lead the congregation in a final hymn. Thin dark books were opened as the Deacon said, "Number 147, please." The organist placed both hands on the white wood before her and pressed down hard. The Deacon raised one hand and made a short movement downward.

"Blessed assurance, Jesus is mine" The men sang loud as to clear their throats of emotion in an acceptable manner in public.

"Oh, what a foretaste of glory divine.

Heir of salvation, purchase of God

Born of his spirit, washed in his blood."

Spirit? Blood? Again, everything was new to Roy.

He had never been in a church, listened to a preacher talk, or been surrounded by a singing crowd. Some parts he felt were confusing; bits went against his common sense, and some moments were oddly comforting. He liked the song at the end. The 'washed in his blood' line was bewildering and, he felt, impractical, but he would explore its meaning later. Vera would know what it all meant. He would add this to a growing list of topics he would use as reasons to spend time with her.

The preacher stood, said another short and skillful prayer, and dismissed the crowd. Will picked up the elk robe, handed the rose to Grace, and the four turned to walk out as the grievers stood and respectfully allowed them to pass.

The Austin family assumed the task of greeting the assembled as they left, allowing Grace and Roy to avoid any awkward interactions.

The walk back to the Fix's house was quiet and full of relief. One more task crossed off the catalog of chores from the catastrophe of Mike's death. There was more to do, but this was a major event to get past. The sky had cleared, the air had warmed, and feelings of a burden lifted were greatly welcomed.

A stop at the Power Mercantile building took a short five minutes as Roy picked up the two tailored suits ordered two days earlier. He had forgotten to stop by and retrieve the tailored clothing, but felt not rush. The ladies offered to check the fit, but he expressed confidence in their initial fitting and asked for the suits to be wrapped. A somber and quiet walk home was peppered with the sounds of crunching snow underfoot and the brown wrapping paper.

A pleasant and calming supper followed filled with talk about anything except the ranch or Mike. This was nearly a normal evening, and Roy enjoyed feeling young again. He and Grace played Chinese checkers while eating popped corn, a first time treat for Roy. Feeling happy again was overdue.

Becky came over, put her hand on Grace's head, and told her that her bed awaited after a trying day. Grace offered little reaction to the memorial service and passed through the day with ease. Understanding often walks with confusion. She took shallow breaths of understanding that kept her from sinking into deeper heartache. Youth offers many gifts. Protection from harsh reality is one of the kindest.

Roy started to bed after a long day, a day that he feared would be painful, yet had unfurled itself to be healing and therapeutic. He told Will goodnight and headed to the staircase.

Will gave a small wave and told Roy they would discuss his trip in the morning. The expedition. The holiday. The teaching journey. Whatever it was called, Roy was eager to begin and then return to the ranch. He was a simple young man with ordinary desires dropped into a complex and unpredictable world.

CHAPTER 33

"The Postmaster just delivered a letter for you, Roy." Becky walked back into the kitchen after answering a knock on the door during breakfast.

He had never received a letter before and had no idea why he got one nor who had sent one now.

It was addressed to:

Roy Douglas, Scotsman

The Ranch of Micheal Hanson

The Fergus County Montannaa America

On the back was scribbled:

From Angus Muir

Farmer at Kyle of Lochalsh

Ross & Cromarty Scotland

Angus Muir was the man who had introduced Roy to Mike at the county festival. Mike had bought the sheep from him and then he had called Roy over to meet Mike. He thought of how this singular act had put him at this very table. He hoped one day to repay Muir in some small way for his life-changing kindness.

Grace continued eating her eggs and toast, but Will and Becky paused and watched as Roy opened the mystery post. Will sipped coffee and said, "Maybe you've inherited a farm in Scotland and a wee box of money, Roy." He took another sip and looked at Roy with a sly grin and a wink.

"Would ye be knowin' a good legal man that could help cash me out then?"

Will let out a short snort at the easy joke and shook his head. "Is it written in English or Scottish as they are not the same language?" Will was feeling relaxed this morning.

"Well, since I be the only person here that can read both, I be lettin' ye know, me friend." Roy was pitching it back as fast as he was catching the barbs.

"Didn't know you could speak Scottish, or what's it called... Gaelic?"

Roy was pulling out the letter from the envelope and said, "Nah, no I cannot. Can barely speak English enough to be understood by you Yankees."

Becky laughed at that last line and playfully slapped Roy on the shoulder. It was clear that the Fixs' enjoyed being around Roy and he them.

Roy took a second before reading the letter out loud. He scanned ahead quickly to insure there were no words or phrases that would fall harshly on Grace's young ears. Seeing no obvious profane sentences, he began.

"To Roy Douglas in Montannaa America.

This be Angus Muir who be from home. Hoping that ye and that Mr. Hanson found yer way to his ranch just fine. Me son Rory is writing this, but they be my words.

Yer ma's sister Helen died. They say she fell in the barn and died in July after ye left for America. She owed rent to Mr. McShay who sold the furniture in the cottage to pay for what's owed. Weren't enough, but he squared the account. She be buried in the churchyard if ever ye come back."

I wouldn't visit her grave if it were on the way to the outhouse, Roy thought.

He continued reading.

"The James Burns boy ye knowed as a boy sent a letter to his kin and tells that he found miner's work in Montanna. Elkhorn be the place. Sure he be glad for a visit.

Send word back when ye have news of fortune and yerself.

A. Muir"

Roy stared at the short letter with little emotion. "Jimmy Burns is in Montana. Huh."

"Sorry news regarding your aunt. Come into my office when you finish would you?" Will took a final sip of coffee, pushed in his chair, and walked to his office.

Roy gave Grace a kiss on the head, and she giggled. Roy then followed Will. He felt calm and hoped customary mornings at the ranch would feel like this.

"Need to get things rolling and get you on your way, Roy." Will sat, grabbed some papers, and read through his notes.

"Aye, I reckon you're right. Must be sayin', I like living like a normal man agin."

Will smiled and looked up at Roy. "Must say, you have comported yourself well these past days, and people have taken notice. A few folks in town questioned Mike's action to put the ranch in your hands, but I sense that chatter will soon settle, and they now see you as a fitting and able successor of Mike's legacy."

Roy squirmed a bit at the kind words. "Them be generous words, Will, even if I don't know what a few of them mean."

Will snickered, "You are a much funnier man than most would discover, my friend. I will remember that and enjoy watching others underestimate you in the future."

Will had come to realize that Roy Douglas was a very smart young man. The quiet Scottish boy wearing borrowed clothes had disappeared and had been replaced by a confident, solid, and well-tailored ranching heir. Like a tomato on the vine that originated as green and unready, Roy had filled out and matured quickly. Even his ruddy complexion, splatter of freckles, and strawberry blond hair made the ripening tomato comparison all the more accurate.

Will walked around the desk and handed Roy two papers. One had dates and places on it, and the other had names of towns and cities at the top of each paragraph. Listed were suggestions for places to visit and names of important people to meet if possible.

"I've put a few things down for you to take along. Just ideas. It's your journey, and it will be on your shoulders to see and learn." Will sat on the corner of his desk while Roy glanced at the papers. "I admit to you that I'm a bit envious of your adventure, Roy. The chance to travel and with no schedule to obey…that is a stroke of great luck. The reason this is happening is as bitter as burrow's milk, and we both hate the why, but let's make this a bonny time for you." Will hesitated, "Listen to me would you! Bonny I said. You're rubbing off on me, laddy buck."

They both gave a laugh at the barb. It was clear that Roy was the one mopping up mentoring and tutoring from Will. Both were satisfied with the current arrangement and were each banking on great returns on this investment.

"Tell me when to go and where to head to first."

Will handed him a leather pouch with tickets, four bank checks, and a map. "All you will need is in this; keep it with you, on your body, always. Sleep with it." He opened a desk drawer and handed him a bundle of bank notes. It was $500, a small fortune.

"This be more than a full year of pay." Roy flipped through more cash than he had ever touched.

"It should be plenty for you to travel with and buy more suits, boots, and guns." Will could sense Roy would need a little encouragement. "You need to spend some on additional and better clothes. You need to look and feel like a man in control. You will come up against men with much more money and dark hearts. Few men are as honest and strong as Mike was. Don't expect to be treated like an equal or dealt with like a man by anyone, Roy. The world has very few men such as Mike."

The advice was blunt but expected. It was easy for Roy to hold his emotions and trust close. He'd never had any real friends as a boy back in Scotland. Being cautious and keeping a small circle of friends was familiar and would be easy. As long as Will and the Austin brothers remained in his world, he reckoned he'd be fine.

"The Weisenhorn Stage leaves at 8:00 tomorrow morning for Billings." William was giving a final briefing and travel plan. "It will head east and then they turn south a few miles north of the Roundup station. Lots of cattle there and little else. I am looking forward to the day when the railroad reaches Lewistown. Then get to Billings and see what is available to see. More cattle, and the railroad is there, so you can ride the train from then on. That stage ride will be cold and will toss you around like a mouse in an alley cat's mouth."

Roy understood as much as he could or needed in order to begin his holiday of exile. Both he and Will knew he could manage himself and fend off any card sharks, soiled doves, or bandits he would encounter on the road.

"I like ta take Grace to town fer a wee walk later. Try to explain the goin's on before I go. I know that ye and Miss Becky will school her on the happenin's better than me; I just want to say some things in me own way."

"Splendid idea. You spend as much of the day with her as you are able, and we will enlighten her to the strategy of the coming days." Will spoke in a solid tone of agreement to put Roy's concerns to rest. He sprang from his chair, remembering one last item, and reached into a box on top of his bookcase. "I want you to take this. Better to have and not need, than to need and not have."

It was a finely polished revolver in an odd holster. Roy had become familiar with guns by now. He had a .45 Colt single action Army revolver that Mike had given him to use, but this one was smaller and new. "Ye want me to take this to someone fer ye?"

"Alas, no." Will was mildly amused by Roy's innocence; a condition he was trusting would disappear soon. "I want you to carry this and then return it to me. It is a fine weapon for a gentleman to carry for his protection. Don't seek out a conflict but always be steadfast in preparation. For each kind soul you encounter, there is a man full of devilment with intent to do you injury."

"Thank ye fer this, Will. I will bring it back unused I hope. What is this contraption?" Roy fumbled with the leather straps and buckles like a toddler with a ball of string.

"That is a gentlemen's holster. It goes over your shoulders, and you carry the pistol on the side of your chest, not the belt. This is a Smith & Wesson .45 Schofield. It is gentle to hold and fierce to fire. Keep it on you constantly, even in a bathhouse." Will motioned for Roy to stand and put the holster on.

"I like this, but it not be very cowboy now is it?" Roy slipped his arm through a leather loop and gave a pull on each leather strap over his shoulders. Leather and polished steel rapidly doubles a man's force and falsely stiffens his backbone.

Will stood back and looked for any possible adjustment in the rigging. "Not meant to turn a cowpoke into a cow boss. There's working guns, fun guns, and survival guns. This is a gun to protect a man of land and livestock. That is who you have become. That is who you need to protect."

Roy heard the decree and would follow the advice of his wise friend. He would be leaving a world of protection, of nurturing, and would feel the rough world alone, with his own hands.

"When you travel to Bozeman, I suggest you stop at Walter Cooper's Gun Shop and supply yourself with a pistol of your own. See if they have a nice rifle as well." Will was nearly ready to send his protégé out into the world. "Send me telegrams every week or when you are able. I will answer you each time you send a wire, and I will tell you when it is a good time to return to the ranch. We'll get Elmer out and then life can go on for you and Grace."

Both men were talked out and weary of planning.

It was time to ride.

CHAPTER 34

"Come back to me. Please." Grace looked at Roy unsure and pleading.

Roy dropped on one knee and held gently onto Grace's arms. "Girl, I only be gone fer a short while. I told ye that now, lass. I go to visit some men about sheep, cows, and horses. Then I be back, and we both be back to the ranch soon. I promise ye."

"Papa promised me he'd come home too." Grace didn't look up.

Roy took a breath. He doubted that Mike would have said those exact words to Grace as he raised her honestly and with no trickeries. Regardless, whatever may have been said, that is what Grace heard. "Crazy and wild things happen in a lifetime. Yer pa had other plans than what happened. What we say doesn't always work out, but that be what's in our heads. If I tell ye that I be back to see ye, then that be my plan." Roy looked at her with intensity, to double-down his message.

Grace stepped forward, wrapped her arms around his neck, and kissed his cheek. He returned the embrace and kissed her cheek. They were brother and sister, and they were all each other had. Grace could feel how deeply Roy missed Mike, and she was relieved to share the loss.

Becky leaned up and gave Roy a kiss on the cheek, took Grace's hand, and headed back to the kitchen. Farewells in Montana occurred often, and excess emotion was costly and painful. Will shook his hand, patted him on the arm and, with a hint of emotion, bid Roy a safe journey. Roy headed out the door as the stagecoach would leave in 30 minutes.

Roy pulled his ticket out of a small wallet, one purposed for public display. His primary leather pouch, secured next to the holster and pistol, held the cash and nothing else. He walked up and handed the ticket to the driver. The driver took his leather satchel and handed it to another man to place in the back of the Concord coach. There was one other passenger, an older man with a large fur hat and thick gray beard. He looked tired and unwell. Roy would allow the man to choose the level of conversation during the trip, as he appeared to be content cozied-up in his corner to the side of the coach. Roy tipped his hat, said nothing, and sat facing forward. It was a cold morning, and the coach had heavy oil cloth curtains, but he would look out occasionally to get his bearings and to see new but similar country.

The land opened up and flattened out east of Lewistown. It looked like fine grazing country but not very livable and was meant only for determined and durable people.

The ride to Billings would take nearly three days with overnight stops on the route. Cold, boring, and rough. The constant shaking of the coach made Roy long for the gentle rhythm of a railcar, and he would work hard to avoid taking a stagecoach again. The romance of the ride was no match for the discomfort.

The first overnight stop was a lonesome short cabin with sparse belongings. Four bunks offered travelers a horizontal, motionless respite and little else. The food was hot and tasteless but plentiful. Roy's fellow traveler appeared to enjoy the gruel that was served, asking for another helping and cleaning his plate. Roy felt sad that this man's past must have been difficult and lacking in luxury. It was obvious that he had seldom enjoyed a plate of quality food. Roy stored this image and, if the chance arose, he would buy the man a fine meal in Billings.

Two and one half days of often miserable conditions, of shaking and cold were ending as the stagecoach pulled into the Billings depot. The old man left the coach and then vanished. Roy would not have the chance to offer charity to the man, and he was disappointed that he could not show compassion or use his new wealth to help others. He didn't want to show off; he just wanted to practice the part of a man that was given more than his share and who wanted to help.

The Grand Hotel was a few blocks away, and the walk was welcomed after days of constant vibration.

Billings was not much bigger than Lewistown. It had a leg-up on growth and commerce as the Northern Pacific Railway reached Billings in 1882 and the Yellowstone River was south of the town. The river did not have a reliable deep channel and would not support steady travel. Many steamboat operators of the day would boast and brag about the shallow water abilities of their vessels, one claiming it could travel on 'a heavy morning dew', but the future in Montana was unlimited, and its primary tool for growth was the railroads.

The town was surrounded on the south by the river and an ancient, eroded bank the locals called Rimrocks. Billings sat in a bowl, carved out by wind and water over millions of years. The Rimrocks to the north covered miles. The Beartooth Mountains could be seen on a clear day to the west and south, but they offered no immediate color or beauty to this spot.

After checking in and dusting off his suit, hat, and long coat, Roy found the Cattleman's Café around the corner. Thinking this would be a place to meet and talk with his fellow ranchers, he found four teamsters, a mother with two young children, and two railroad workers, all engaged in their evening meal. His disappointment in the lack of peers was erased by a large and well-prepared beefsteak with boiled potatoes.

A slice of custard pie finished the meal. Roy was becoming a disciple of custard pies and puddings, as eggs and milk were available year round, and the taste was subtle and satisfying.

He thought to mention this treat to Anna but then recalled she would be gone when he returned. He liked Anna. He saw a change in her from his first days at the ranch. He was greeted by a friendly, slightly naïve girl full contentment, but her farewell was delivered by a cold and seasoned woman. He hoped to one day find the pleasant, kind Anna he had once known.

———

Roy spent the next day walking around Billings and talking with a couple of cowhands moving cattle in the stockyard by the rail station. They told him they would go back to Miles City when it warmed up in the spring. A buddy of theirs had lined up this job in town for the winter, and they were very happy to not be spending the winter in lonely Eastern Montana.

The town of Billings would soon be a city thanks to the railroad and cattle shipping to destinations back east. The growth would be sudden and dramatic. Some would say even magical.

———

The following day, the train pulled out shortly after 7:00 a.m. Roy found a seat close enough to the wood stove to chase away the chills but not overheat. He liked the cold in an odd way and could handle its effects. Age may reverse that skill, but in his youth, he welcomed the challenge of enduring conditions most men work hard to avoid. Many Montanans quietly enjoyed being viewed as a bit crazy and illogical when it came to the harsh climate. They quietly reveled in knowing this was a place few were hard enough or strong enough to endure.

The rail line didn't need to follow the Yellowstone River as the land west of Billings was fairly level and no large mountain ranges blocked the path. Small painted signs of future towns and developed areas passed by. A short stop at a depot in Laurel was the first delay. One man climbed aboard, and mail bags were exchanged by a rail worker in a boxcar and a man with a small black hat on the ground. The train rolled again, and the view improved as The Crazy Woman Mountains were seen ahead and the massive Beartooth Mountains were off to the left.

The rocky snowcapped peaks were bright white with shades of pale blue that appeared to change colors every mile. He had once traveled to Fort William back in Scotland and had seen Ben Nevis, the largest mountain in Scotland, and had been impressed. However, these mountains equaled a dozen or more peaks like Ben Nevis. The size of his Montana was once again on display, and he felt proud, though he had nothing to do with its creation.

The Crazy Woman Mountains, or The Crazies as the locals called them, seemed to lift straight up out of the prairie. It appeared as if a man could drive a wagon completely around the base of this range and never strain the team due to elevation. These mountains were much bigger than they appeared to be, and Roy thought these may be the prettiest that he'd ever seen.

"Ya know why they call 'em the Crazies?" A man sitting two rows behind noticed that Roy was locked in on the view.

"No, sir."

"Seems there was or still is a woman up there that come down insane after all her family got killed by the Crows. Found her on their homestead alone and talkin' gibberish. The Crow Indians think the mountains there have magic in 'em. They been going up in those mountains for a long while to dance and whatnot." The man sat back, satisfied that his lecture had helped.

"They be somethin' they are." Roy never broke his stare as the morning sun was hitting the southern slopes and igniting the peaks with light.

The tracks began to slip down next to the Yellowstone and began to follow the flow as the flat land changed into rolling hills. The train stopped for water. The sign over the depot said, BIG TIMBER, and Roy smiled knowing this was the area that Will Fix was from. He thought how it was a pretty place that looked like grand land for sheep and cattle. He would try to come back some day and see how green the land was after the snow left.

Miles down the track, the mountains grew and looked massive out the left side of the train. Roy asked the conductor what those mountains were called.

"Thems the Beartooth's. Granite Peak is the tallest, but it's pushed back deep there, and you can't see it from down here. Livingstone is the next stop."

Roy would stop and spend the night in Livingston. It was a beautiful place built up on the banks of the Yellowstone, and he looked forward to spending a day there to explore.

The train stopped. Roy picked up his leather bag and climbed down onto the platform. A gust of wind nearly took his hat, and he instinctively pulled up the collar of his coat. The gust settled down into a steady irritating wind, and he walked quickly out of the depot.

"First time in Livingston?" a voice from behind the counter asked.

Roy looked up and saw no one but answered, "Aye," just the same.

A man appeared from under the counter. "Wind never stops blowing here. Been here since '88, and the wind laid down about 10 days since then. Need a stampede string on your hat in these parts, young man."

Roy tipped and held on to his hat as he walked out to the town. He saw a simple sign with the word ROOMS hanging a block away. He thought he would find the closest lodging available that would get him out of the wind. Livingston was like a very pretty girl, but a girl missing a front tooth. Roy wasn't sure he could get past the tooth.

———

Roy woke to the sound of wind slapping a loose window shutter.

The wind. Good lord. What a mighty wind.

The gateway to Yellowstone National Park was growing, but it was slow in the winter. Livingston had more than 2,000 people, about half the number of Great Falls but more than double the population of Billings. The creation of Yellowstone National Park in 1872 gave a boost to the area. Some could see a bright future while others downplayed the potential. By 1892, the park had proven to be a draw for city dwellers, dudes, and dandy's from back east.

Roy's travels through Montana had shown him a variety of

economic opportunities. The Territory was built on mining, earning the nickname of The Treasure State. Outside investors took notice and felt the security of statehood in 1889. Statehood opened Montana to more ranchers, farmers, and tourists. The mining would come and go and create booms and busts, but the nation needed the agricultural products that the state could grow.

Livingston showed Roy how an economy is stitched together by multiple businesses and occupations. The railroad allowed any town or village to grow, and this area was learning how to expand.

A block away, Roy found a Western Union office. He decided he would update William on his trip.

TO WILLIAM FIX, ESQ., LEWISTOWN, MONTANA

IN LIVINGSTON STOP WINDY STOP BOZEMAN NEXT STOP SEND UPDATES ON RANCH STOP LODGING AT HUDSON BOARDING HOUSE STOP ROY D STOP

Roy had done his part and would wait to hear from Will before leaving town.

There was a saddle and boot maker in town. He thought he'd practice spending money on higher quality things. A new custom-fit saddle with his initials carved into fenders would separate him from the working hands. And new boots, well that would just feel good. He looked but didn't buy. He'd look in Bozeman and Helena for better deals. A good custom saddle was $1,200, and that price shocked him. Even if he had that much cash in his pocket, the Scotsman in him created doubts as to the value of such an extravagance.

A restaurant in the middle of town offered fresh fish as the Yellowstone River was a short distance away. Roy ordered the fish, not sure what it was. It was well prepared and tasty, but it was not as good as the Atlantic Salmon caught in the waters around The Isle of Skye in Scotland.

As Roy walked into the boarding house, the landlady handed him a telegram. It was from Will.

ELMER LEAVING SOON GONE IN 7 DAYS STOP COURT PAPERS FILED STOP ALL GOOD STOP WAIT 2 MORE WEEKS BEFORE YOU COME BACK STOP WILL STOP

His exile from the ranch would be shorter than expected. Roy would begin to head home tomorrow. He still had many days of travel and discovery ahead, but he took comfort in knowing he was headed in the right direction.

CHAPTER 35

The train began to slow and climb up Bozeman Pass. Leaving Livingston, Roy noticed a second train engine was connected to the back of the eight cars. This helper or pusher engine would give the train enough power to make it over the pass and then wait on the other side to push the next eastbound train back to Livingston. The Northern Pacific Railway was an amazing feat of engineering, allowing Montana and the entire United States to develop at a rapid rate. No railroad…no growth. And this state was one of the richest places on earth. Harsh, beautiful, and full of future.

"What parts are you headed to, young man?" A smartly dressed gentleman in his forties sitting across the aisle asked.

Roy thought about how to answer. Too much truth would be confusing and boring. "Butte, Helena, Great Falls then back home to Fergus County. Business." That sounded plausible and direct.

"And what business would that be…Mister…?" The man thrust out a hand.

"Ranching. I have a sheep ranch back home. Name is Roy Douglas." He returned the handshake and that made him feel older than he was.

"I see you are sporting an excellent new suit. Very handsome indeed. Am I hearing a bit of Old Scotland from you?" The man was not interested in sitting quietly. "Name is Bommel, Timothy Bommel. Like pommel. From Missouri."

Roy was looking forward to a ride observing the new terrain, but this Bommel chap had a friendly demeanor. He was certain that Mr. Bommel was a salesman, and Roy was sure he was successful as his manner was genuine.

"Aye. Scotsman I am but American now." Much more information would cause an avalanche of conversation. "What work ye be in yerself?"

"Haberdashery and Millinery. Men's clothing and hats as well as hats for well-to-do ladies. Headed to Butte. It's a very rugged town full of ruffians. But much like the ground, it has pockets of great wealth." Bommel seemed to know his business and people. "What is the name of your ranch?"

"The Hanson Ranch on Beaver Creek near Lewistown."

Bommel's face lit up. "I know Lewistown well. Lovely place. Perhaps we shall meet again."

Roy nodded and told the man to inquire about him when in Lewistown. He liked this Bommel fella and hoped to meet up with him again. Roy returned to being a tourist. The train had reached the apex of the pass and began to gently descend towards Bozeman.

Bozeman was a small town, half the size of Livingston and roughly the same number of citizens as Billings. It was sitting in a beautiful place surrounded by mountains. The valley stretched far off to the west. It offered an open and rich valley suited for crops and livestock. It just hadn't caught on yet as a place to settle and homestead. Roy thought that would change in the coming years.

The Hotel Bozeman was new and huge. A four-story brown brick building stood out against the mountains that surrounded Bozeman. Roy checked into a room with fancy furniture and, best of all, steam heat. January in Montana needs steam heat. He made an instant decision to spend at least two days here. He would sleep well tonight.

———

Roy slept late, past 7:00 a.m. Feeling a bit guilty for his morning of lazy luxury, he went downstairs for breakfast. After getting some information about the town, he sat and enjoyed a third cup of coffee. He was rehearsing having money and enjoying life.

He might have enjoyed the travel more if not for the constant thought of getting back home as soon as he could. The message from Will was great news.

This would be a time to rest. The day was cloudy and cold, and he told himself to relax a bit. He had no experience with not working. He never knew that slack time was an option. Even though there would be no work for a couple of weeks, he did have a giant task ahead. Vera. The mission was Vera.

He found Walter Cooper's Gun Shop two doors down from a boot maker's shop. Today, he felt like handling steel. The foot leather could wait.

The shop smelled of oil and metal. Roy thought if he found a church that smelled like this shop, he'd become a deacon.

The back wall was full of long rifles lined up in wooden racks. The counter was a glass case and had double rows of handguns. He knew he had found the right place. He would be spending some money today.

A man set four pistols on a cloth in front of him. He decided he would buy a small gun to carry when he was wearing his dude suits. He would choose another one to wear while working and riding in the mountains.

A beautiful, polished rifle stood out from the rest. "The third one from the left, please." Roy accepted the gun with both hands as if being handed explosives.

The gunsmith leaned on the glass counter. "The new Winchester Model 1892 lever action in .44-40. Don't have a nickel plated one yet, but most fellas want the barrel blued. Better for hunting. Don't reflect the sun when you see that big bull. Replaces the Model 1873. From the mind and hands of Mr. John Moses Browning. A genius."

Roy brought the rifle up to his shoulder and cheek. The balance was perfect, and he felt that he could hold the gun in this position all day.

The man selected another pistol from under the glass and showed it to Roy. "If you like that Winchester, and what man would not, this Remington Model 1890 is chambered so as to use the same rounds in both arms. Not a lot of these were made, but I got two. One shiny, one dull. Shiny one is two dollars more."

Roy was fascinated by these guns. He wondered how a man could make such a thing, with small springs, tiny pins, and such. The metal felt cold and flawless. He wouldn't leave this store without a few pounds of steel and brass.

Roy made his decision in less than a minute. "I'll be havin' this Winchester and the Remington revolver, sir. I also am needin' a smaller gun to carry here." He patted his chest. The man needed no more information.

"Many gentlemen enjoy this fine piece. Always good to have when traveling, in particular if you should be passing through Butte." A small wooden box was set out. Inside was a Colt Single Action Army or SAA with a short barrel. "Some call this the 'Gunfighter.' I call it the 'Civilian.' You can refer to it with any name you choose, my friend."

This gun would be on and with me for most hours of every day, he thought. The metal was blued but had a luster to it. The handle was like nothing he'd seen. "The handle, what the devil?"

"That is a special one, isn't it? Made from Mother-of-Pearl it's called. Made from oysters of something. Not for certain, but it is mighty sharp." Roy noted that if the man who sold guns all day was impressed, this was a weapon he must have.

"All three if you please, sir. And I be needin' some leather to carry these."

"I would suggest you walk two doors over to the boot maker and have him work you up the required holsters and such. Mr. Devlin has a fine eye and talented hands with leather." The clerk gathered up the three firearms and put them in the box in which each had come from the factories. "The Winchester is $15, the Remington is $16, and the Colt is $24. I have ammunition for each if you would like. Two boxes of each for a fair price. Total of $60."

Roy handed over six, ten-dollar notes. He'd never been this happy spending money, but there was still a totty of discomfort parting with a large sum. Scotsman's disease.

Next stop was the boot maker and leather works. Mr. Devlin was sitting at a bench taping and hammering on the beginning of something hidden in the leather. Roy laid out the new weaponry and made the request for holsters and cases to fit each.

Devlin pulled out a two-piece dark leather long rifle case with a strap and buckle that fit the Winchester perfectly. He then laid out three waist holsters suitable for the Remington. Roy picked one that was basic and suitable.

"I be needin' one for the Colt to wear under me jacket like this one. Just borrowing this one." He opened his jacket to show the shoulder holster.

"I have a couple I can make to fit you with little trouble. I can have it ready for you before close of business today." Devlin took two holsters off the wall and pulled out a cloth measuring tape.

Roy removed his jacket. Devlin took three measurements, wrote the details down, and told Roy to return later. Roy considered ordering some boots but thought he'd wait to get boots in Helena. He was looking for reasons to prolong his visit in Helena and extend time with Vera.

A corner restaurant had an interesting sign in the window advertising a 'Businessman's Plate Special.' Roy had no idea what that meant, but at least he may walk out with a dinner plate. The Special was roasted pork with onions and a baked potato. He left with no extra dinnerware.

A walk around town wasted enough time to give Mr. Devlin time to finish the leatherwork. He tried on the new holster and slid his new Colt in its new cradle.

Roy walked down the wooden sidewalk with the new leather scabbard full of Winchester's best, a burlap bag with Will's borrowed gun, his new Remington, ammo, and leather. He would take the train to Butte tomorrow and discover firsthand the beauty and hospitality of the most famous mining town in America.

CHAPTER 36

The Butte Short Line left Bozeman and would climb Homestake Pass in under three hours' time. The grade up heading west was difficult and required additional helper engines to make the grade. A rail yard in Logan, east of Homestake, was the location the trains would prepare for the trip over the pass. The number of helpers was based on the size of the train. A large number of railcars would add up to fifteen engines, with three to five in the lead and the same number in the middle and at the rear. The real peril was heading down into Butte. Trains needed assistance in braking as the steep grade was challenging to westbound descending trains with the danger of a train running free. Eastbound engines struggled mightily to climb, often so slow that children would walk next to the trains and chat with the engineers while underway.

Butte was twice the size of Helena but lacked the clean and pleasant atmosphere of its neighbor to the north. The differences were staggering.

Large timber towers, called headframes, peppered the hills to the north and up the mountain. These monster structures, standing from 100 to 200 feet tall, looked as if they were sliced in half down the middle as the side that held the giant cables straight up and down was exposed. The huge steam powered spindles that held the cable was set back, and leverage was used to lift ore and men up and down into the horrible holes that created wealth.

Roy was curious as to how mining operations worked but had no desire to ever work in any dark and dangerous mine shaft. He admired the grit of the men that did and was grateful that fate had not placed him in such a place. Mining towns had their own looks, smells, and sorrows.

Roy asked a rail clerk to recommend a hotel. The clerk said the Thornton Hotel was as safe a place as any, and the recommendation quickly turned into a warning. "Hold them bags and that gun close and don't venture out at night if you value your hide, young man."

On a pole next to the platform was a yellow sign with black letters.

NOTICE WORKERS! STAY AWAY FROM
BUTTE, MONTANA! OVERCROWDED NOW.

Welcome to Butte.

This was the biggest city in Montana in 1892. City fathers estimated the number of souls to be around 11,000, not quite double the size of Helena. It was also the hub of power and money in the state. Roy watched as small gangs of dirty men looked his way and tracked his movement. It wasn't unusual to see men carry rifles or shotguns on the street. Roy stood out with his new suit, polished scabbard, and leather travel satchel as a man with cash in his pocket. He looked like six-months' pay to the small and desperate men he passed. Fortunately, his size and youth, as well as his obvious gun ownership, stifled any casual attempt to rob the new explorer.

A fight spilled onto the street from the doors of the M&M Bar. One of countless bars in Butte, it was on Main Street and was generally a safe place for most. There were Irish bars in Dublin Gulch. There were Swedes, Chinese, Serbians, Cornish, and Italian bars in Butte. They all may have learned how to survive together, but they never learned to like each other.

Butte felt like a horrible place. It was a place for work and money. It offered better pay than most jobs available anywhere in Montana. The

Butte Miners Union fought for and won a daily wage of $3.50 for their members. It was good pay in exchange for terrible working conditions. The air was black with smelter smoke. It had a terrible stink that never left your clothes or your nose. Black soot was everywhere. The beauty of fresh snow usually lasted an hour or less as it was absorbed into the charcoal tinted snow on the ground. And from October to May, it snowed a lot. A lot. The town was built on the side of a mountain, so nothing was flat or level, except at the bottom of the mountain along Silver Bow Creek.

This was above ground Butte. The hell of climbing the hill to work on a negative 20-degree cold February morning, to then climb in a big bucket or elevator shaft to be lowered underground, possibly as deep as one mile, was quite unappealing to Roy.

The tunnels and shafts of Butte had their own stories and tales of pain that Roy would learn in the future and at a distance. The story of Butte is worthy of Biblical treatment, but there is no Butte Book of Revelations to read. The entire town faces south and that may be the nicest thing that could be said about Butte. There were lots of poems about Butte because the fantasy is better than reality. Roy felt he was surrounded by sad and desperate people. It's a good place...to be from.

Around the corner was the Thornton Hotel. Roy thought that a hotel with an Irish name and run by an Irishman might serve up a little more hospitality for a Scotsman. There was a wee man behind the front desk in a jacket two sizes too big for him who said nothing and stared at Roy.

"I be needin' a room for a night, maybe two if ye ha' one." Roy set his bag on the floor and the rifle case on the counter.

"Just you?" The man was short on manners as well as vertical inches.

"Aye, I mean yep." Roy was finally tiring of being polite to people who had done nothing to earned his respect.

"Just me, just one night. Please. Sir." *Sir?* He couldn't help himself.

The little fella passed a key to him and pointed to the elevator. Roy was grateful he didn't need to play nicely for long. He went up to a second-floor room to stow his belongings. He ate supper across the

street and watched each person going in and out of The Thornton. He
thought it to be a safe place, but he felt he was being watched, even
targeted. It was the way people looked at him that rang an internal
alarm. There would not be any sightseeing or curious walks in Butte.
Roy would leave Butte the next day, in the daylight.

————————

The next morning, a friendly younger man was at the desk. He asked if
Roy had spent a comfortable night and told him to please visit again.
Roy did not sleep well, as he was too concerned for his safety and
belongings. But as he was walking out, he saw a tall man outside the
front door, with a huge mustache, wearing two pistols outside of his
coat and cradling a double barrel shotgun. The hotel was guarded, and
Roy had missed out on a solid night's sleep for no good reason. The
man tipped his hat. Roy thought he had misjudged The Thornton and
would consider returning someday to redeem his fearful opinions.

His opinion of Butte, though, was unchanged. It was 7:00 a.m., and
the streets were covered in dirty snow. It was good that the ground
was frozen, or mud would have multiplied the misery. Drunken men
leaned against walls on the main street. Wagons full of liquor or
mining equipment seemed to roll down the streets of Butte day and
night. The mines kept a constant rotation of work and drink as bars
would empty then refill at odd hours.

Roy knew he could never work the mines. Dark, wet, cold, then
hot. He felt sympathy for the men who came here to work. Many were
his countrymen or from other oppressive places with no chance to
move up in life. Once here, these men and their families found a land
of dreams, but those visions were often delayed in jobs that only paid
for a roof and a plate of food. There was little opportunity in the dark
holes of Butte unless you owned a business. He would use his memories of Butte to adjust his emotions in times of struggle or pain.

He saw the hard side of new beginnings and realized that his immigration path was lined with gold in comparison to these men and
women. His disgust was slowing dissolving into respect with pity.
These people were enduring a world that he doubted he could survive.

He told himself that these may be the toughest, most durable people he'd seen. His initial feelings of harsh judgement and superior position made him regretful and humble. He was much closer to these men that he wanted to believe.

Roy told himself that a difficult day on the ranch was heaven when compared to the life of a Butte miner.

CHAPTER 37

At the Butte train depot, Roy told the man he needed a ticket to Elkhorn. The clerk said to take the Montana Central line through Basin then a stop in Boulder. Elkhorn was at the end of the line and was a spur line to the south. "You don't look like no miner fella. What business do you have in Elkhorn?"

"An old chum from back in Scotland lives there."

The clerk huffed and said, "He must owe you money for ya to go up there." He then handed Roy a ticket and muttered, "next" to the man in line behind Roy.

Roy could see the mountains to the north and east of Butte and saw smoke from another train climb up out of Butte through a sliver of canyon. He doubted that this would be a fast journey.

The train had three engines at the head, one in the middle, and three more at the end. The grades would be long, steep, and slow. A fellow traveler, a mining supervisor, told him this train had two passenger cars and twenty-five cars hauling copper ore to Great Falls. The ore belonged to the Anaconda Copper Company, owned by one of the Montana Copper Kings, Marcus Daly.

Marcus Daily and William Clark, the other Copper King, owned and ran Butte as well as much of Montana. Each was running campaigns to choose the permanent State Capital for Montana later this year. Daly wanted Anaconda, a city he owned and built from nothing. Clark was pushing for Helena, the acting and current Capital, to remain the seat of government.

Great Falls, Helena, Anaconda, Butte, Deer Lodge, Bozeman, and even tiny Boulder, north of Butte and south of Helena, would all be on a statewide ballot later this year. Daly called Helena a 'City of Snobs' and called Anaconda 'The Home of Plain People', referring to the population of mainly working-class citizens.

Clark countered that Helena was 'Everyman's Town-Anaconda is One Man's Town', referring to Daly's dominance and ownership of that area.

1892 was an election year, and Roy thought of becoming a U.S. citizen this year but had discovered it would take five years and numerous steps to become a citizen of the USA. He would have to wait until 1898 to vote, but he already showed a keen interest in American politics and how governments functioned. He believed that government was generally a thorn in the side of business and looked for ways to say no instead of trying to help the average citizen. 'A healthy caution' was the saying Mike had told him once about life in general, and he adopted that philosophy for most things in life. Mike had also said that weak men create a world that needs and wants more government. Mike believed in people but despited government and both party's.

The canyons were deep north of Butte. Passing through Elk Park, Roy could almost see the windows freeze up before his eyes as the temperature seemed to drop ten degrees in ten minutes. Heavy lodgepole pine forests covered the slopes from Elk Park to Basin, another mining town. The train stopped to take on water and to allow passengers to release their stored-up liquids. A woman in the small depot sold cake donuts and hot coffee for a nickel, and Roy went back for a refill and a second treat.

The train snaked its way through the canyons following the Boulder River. Trestles and short tunnels seemed to comprise half of the route, and the progress was slow, but it was a beautiful place despite the cold and desolation.

The train stopped in Boulder, where he would catch a train down to Elkhorn. Roy made it a habit to take a few steps from the train, stop, and make a complete rotation to absorb each new location. His scan of Boulder laid out a beautiful valley engulfed by tall mountains to the south and east with more round-topped mountains to the north towards Helena. He then saw a grand building with turrets and a tower near the center of town. It was the Jefferson County Courthouse, completed in 1889. He thought that this building was as grand and beautiful as any he'd seen. He would make a point to see this impressive brick and stone monument to Montana's future.

The train to Elkhorn would leave around noon, as it was winter with only two trains traveling up and down per day. The first train would leave Elkhorn early in the morning loaded with ore and stop in Boulder on its way to Great Falls, and an empty train would return to Elkhorn each afternoon.

Roy had no way to contact Jimmy Burns and alert him to his visit. Both knew that the other was somewhere in Montana and that was all that was known. He was hoping to seeing a face from his boyhood and a chap he considered to be a friend.

James, Jimmy Burns, was a fun and happy lad with a full and hearty laugh. He was a year older than Roy, but the two had known each other since their school days and had built a bond. Roy had always been the biggest boy for his age in the village, but Jimmy had been the one chap he knew never to challenge. There had been no need to, as neither had an angry bones in them and they trusted each other. Roy was realizing that Jimmy Burns was the best friend he had in life, next to Mike Hanson. He hoped Jimmy was prospering and happy.

The wait for the Elkhorn train was short as the ride from Butte to Boulder took up the entire morning. Roy had a quick lunch at the Windsor Café a block away and hurried back to the depot as he heard the southbound train's whistle in the distance.

This train had one passenger car and fifteen empty ore cars. There were only two other men traveling, both looked like miners. The back of the car was loaded with food sacks and barrels to resupply the town. Roy asked the men if they knew Jimmy. One shrugged and said, "No Englés," while the other thought he might and described him to

Roy. The description sounded familiar. The man said there were few Scotsmen in the town, so Jimmy would be easy to find. He suggested that Roy go to the mine office to help find him.

———

The train moved fast along the Boulder River as it wound its way to the southeast before making a sweeping lefthand turn, then pointing north and climbing. The valley was open then suddenly closed in and became full of timber. Roy could see patches where any and all trees had been cut and taken to Elkhorn for smelting use and firewood for houses.

The train slowed but kept a constant pace. An hour later, Roy could see the town in a bowl to the left and well below the tracks. Elkhorn was a boomtown. It had nearly as many people as Bozeman had but was jammed into a much smaller area closely surrounded by mountains at high elevation.

The depot was above the town. A large red wooden water tower was farther past the depot as trains climbing to Elkhorn used enormous amounts of water. Roy took his bags and slung the rifle scabbard over his shoulder. He asked for directions to the mining office.

The short walk was at the top of the valley, and the view to the south was vast and scenic. Roy looked left to see miles of trees and mountains. Turning back to the right was the mine and piles of tailings from the mine shaft. He thought that ranching was beautiful and how mining was often ugly. He again felt fortunate to work above ground.

A sign said OFFICE above a dirty door.

"Looking for work?" A man walked up behind him and reached for the doorknob.

"No, sir, I'm lookin' fer a man here in town. Name of Burns. James Burns. Do ye know of him?"

The man looked Roy over. "Are you a lawman? If you are, we have our own town marshal to which you should talk."

"No, sir, just an old mate from home in Scotland. Jimmy and me, we grow up together. I live in Fergus County now and got a letter sayin' he be here."

The man seemed convinced of the story. "Come inside, and I'll get you a house number. He works here. Good worker."

Roy took a piece of paper with, 'Burns J, 14 Holter St' written on it. He was surprised at how little trouble he had in finding Jimmy. He was minutes away from seeing a familiar face.

The town was busy with mule and horse carts hauling wood up the hill and men covered in dirt making their way down from the mine. The curious thing he noticed was children. The town seemed to be full of children with mothers walking behind. This was not a normal mining town; it had the feel of a family neighborhood more than a typical mining camp. But there was a stillness and somber air that was undeniable. Roy would soon discover the reason.

The shacks were narrow, long, and packed tight to each other. Numbers were hand painted next to the doors. Number 14 was a faded whitewashed house with two wooden stools on the small porch. Roy knocked.

A woman in her thirties wearing a scarf and looking tired answered.

"Me name is Roy Douglas, and I be lookin' fer Jim Burns. We was boys together back in Scotland."

The woman looked relieved and returned a small smile. "I was thinking you was from the mine company with bad news about my Albert." She reached for the door frame to steady herself. "Jim stays with us in a back room. I'm Mrs. Bennetts, Pearl. I'd ask you in but…" She gave an apologetic pause.

Roy set down his gear, held up a hand, and said, "Oh no, ma'am. I wait out here if that pleases ye."

"The men should be home within the hour. They have been working up on the north slope today." Pearl relaxed. "Can I fetch you some water? It's cold out, but a man still needs refreshment."

"I would much appreciate that, ma'am," Roy replied as he tipped his hat to her.

Pearl returned with a tin cup full of water. "I am sorry to have you sit out here."

"Would not appear suitable in any other way. Pleased to be

welcomed to ye door." Roy understood the proprieties and was happy to have found his friend at last.

Thirty minutes later, Pearl opened the door and tapped Roy on the shoulder. "There they are." She pointed up the street to two men walking.

Roy stood and walked down the steps. Ten feet away, Jimmy recognized Roy and stumbled a bit, then walked quickly to shake his hand. Roy took his hand then wrapped his arm around Jimmy's shoulder.

"HOOTS, MON! Jings it's grand ta see ye, laddy buck!" Jimmy grinned wide and laughed. "What are ye, how did ye…" He shook his head in amusement.

"Angus Muir sent a letter to me in Fergus County. He sold sheep to Mr. Hanson, the fella I come here with. Told me where ye was in the letter." Roy knew there was a year's worth of news to cover, and he preferred to be inside and warm.

"Roy, this be me mate Albert. Him and me, we cut wood fer the mine and for firewood to sell."

Albert stepped up and shook hands. "You're welcome to stay in Jim's room if you can find space."

Roy quickly replied. "I'm getting' a room at the Elkhorn Hotel, but I thank ye fer yer kind offer."

Albert seemed relieved to not have another body stay in the already small house. "It's two blocks over. Why don't you fellas go inside and talk for a spell, and I'll go walk over and tell Mr. White you'll need a room. Tell Pearl I'll be home shortly."

Jimmy waved at Albert as he walked away and told Roy, "He be stopping at The Silver Cup for a drink or two. Albert likes the jar. Likes it more since he buried two baby children." The smile left his face for a second. "Come in, lad."

Jimmy went first. He had left Kyle of Lochalsh six months before Roy. He had spent time in St. Louis with a cousin who worked for Anheuser-Busch as a teamster delivering beer. His cousin had found work for Jimmy in the company stables. The heat and humidity in south St. Louis had brought him to his knees the first summer he was there. He met an Irishman at work who was heading west to work the mines in Butte, so Jim had tagged along. He thought any place would be more comfortable that St. Louis in the summer. He told Roy he had seen a man stabbed to death the first hour he was in town.

He didn't want to go in the holes, so Jimmy had taken work cutting wood. He didn't find Butte to be a welcoming place. He had heard about work in Elkhorn cutting wood and wanted out of Butte. He'd been in Elkhorn for a week when he had met Albert out in the woods. They had become work partners and then friends. Jimmy had moved into the Bennetts' house a few days later to help with the rent.

Roy took double the time to tell his tale. The old chums sat in chairs facing each other. Jimmy sat listening, staring in disbelief for one minute, laughing the next.

After twenty minutes, Roy scooted to the edge of his chair and leaned in. Jimmy did the same. "Mike gave me and his wee girl the ranch. He gave me half of a real American ranch. A real belter aye?"

Jimmy's eyes opened wide, and his jaw dropped. "So ye be rich now?"

"Aye, I reckon I be richer than I was before. Got plenty a money. Will, the lawyer, has been telling me to buy clothes and guns. I'll buy you somethin' pal. A gun or boots?"

Jimmy stared off for a second. "Aye, that be bonny, Roy. There be no fancy stores in town. Maybe when I come to visit ye later." The volume of information that Roy had shared was overwhelming. Jimmy felt a small amount of jealousy, but he mostly was pleased that Roy had been lucky and was doing well. He thought, *if you can't be lucky, find a lucky friend.*

The small, narrow house was chilly but not cold. Few belonging of any sort were visible. There were three modest chairs with worn fabric attempting to fill the tiny space. One well-worn wooden table with a dirty oil lamp was in-between two chairs. The bleakness wasn't surprising, but it felt sad. This basic, clap wood structure was simple protection from the elements and nothing more.

Albert walked in smelling of whisky. He was quiet and sat at the table waiting for Pearl to set his supper down. She set a plate down, put her hand on his shoulder, and walked back to the stove.

Roy stood up. "I thought Jimmy and me would get some supper in town. I need to get me room fer the night." Jimmy nodded approval at the instant new plan.

Albert finished chewing. "You got a room waitin' at the hotel."

"Thank ye, Mr. Bennetts. I'll steal Jimmy for a wee bit tonight. Thank ye fer the kindness of lettin' me into yer home, Mrs. Bennetts."

Pearl walked over to Roy and clasped his hand in hers. "Come back anytime, Roy. How long will you be in town?"

"Just a day maybe two, ma'am. I ha' business in Helena that needs tendin' to."

Just then, Roy heard a young boy cough loudly. The coughing and hacking didn't stop. Pearl spun around and rushed to the back room. The child's coughing finally slowed, then stopped.

Jimmy nodded towards the door telling Roy they needed to leave. Roy, with gear in hand, walked out with Jimmy to the street.

As the two walked, Jimmy told Roy about the struggles and pain the Bennetts had endured while in Elkhorn. "The diphtheria come through Elkhorn a few years back like a banshee, taking most of the babies in town. Albert and Pearl buried two of theirs. A wee lad not yet two back in '89 and a baby girl last year."

Roy stopped walking and looked at Jimmy. "I have not the imagination to feel that much pain. Sweet lord."

"And now they got a wee one four years in age who's being sick. Ye hear the lad coughin' and wheezin' in the back? He be sickly for two weeks now. Pearl be in a terrible fuss thinkin' she be losin' another."

The two friends reached the hotel. Roy checked in, dropped his bags in his room and returned to the lobby. They walked over to the Silver Cup for a drink. Roy had tried American Whisky with Mike one night and was not impressed. He had been raised drinking fine Scots Whisky and peatreek or moonshine as it's called here.

Jimmy had acquired, or more aptly built up, a tolerance for the brown water in the bottles labeled whiskey. Roy ordered a bottle of beer.

"How do ye fancy the work up here, mate?" Roy gambled the answer would be short and not so sweet.

"Don't hate it, but it's terrible damn cold up here. Long as ye keep cuttin' and choppin', it be possible to stay warm. It's outside work, but

I rather be with the horses and such, like back home, eh?" Jimmy took a sip and squeezed his eyes shut as the harsh fluid hit his tongue.

"Fergus County is a bonny place, it is. Good grass for the sheep, beautiful mountains, and a clean creek runnin' through the ranch." Roy took a sip of the beer.

Jimmy had the look of a man hoping to hear good news and grinned when the news was delivered. He looked at Roy and winked. They had been mates since school days. "Albert has been kind to me and has helped me more than me own kin would ha'. Pearl and him is good folk. Feel like I owe them some help now that the lad is sick. Been a bad week. Both go mad if they lose another child they could."

Roy sat up a bit. "Could the lad be gone soon?"

"He's not well, and I think he be comin' round, but the two of them, they be thinkin' to dig another hole." Jimmy shook his head and took another sip of his whisky.

Roy had come at a bad time. He was unsure if he should stay. "I don't want to be the cause of the morbs fer Mrs. Bennetts. She has a pot full of sorrows and don't be needin' anymore."

"Ye just got off the train, mate! Stay a spell." Jimmy stood and put his hand on Roy's shoulder. "Yer the first face from home I seen in close on two year now. No work tomorrow. Stay 'til past then, Roy. We got days a talkin' to do, lad."

One more round, and they went their separate ways. Jimmy shuffled back to the Bennetts and Roy over to the hotel. The reunion was comforting and unsettling all at once. Both had been through a decade of change in less than two years. Neither man knew what the future would offer.

CHAPTER 38

Jimmy met Roy at 7. A breakfast of venison steak, potatoes, and an egg started the day. It was snowing hard, and the initial plan of renting a wagon and seeing the country was scrapped. Consequently, the morning was mostly spent drinking coffee in the café by the two chums.

When two boyhood chums reunite, most of the talk covers the past and the good times shared. The time and locations of memorable events are agreed upon, but the actions and results are often in dispute. That's what makes conversation and reminiscing a prized possession for content people.

Truths and lies were shared, disputed, and laughed about. A seemingly endless reserve of memories of their homeland took the men through the morning until the waitress asked them if they wanted to order lunch. Roy quickly paid the bill and tipped the girl an entire dollar, which was unexpected but welcomed.

"So ye went and fell into a tun full of money did ye now, Roy?" Jimmy slapped Roy's back as they walked to the hotel.

"Aye, I did. Just terrible bad luck followed by a wee bit of good. I'd give it all back if it would bring back ta life Big Mike. Never have I been looked after and been learned to like Mike did." Roy didn't want to get in the weeds and dredge up the pain and thoughts of Mike's passing right now. He'd share that with Jimmy later and over time.

The men walked into Roy's room. Jimmy wanted to see the fine guns Roy had obtained. Jimmy was not familiar with firearms of any kind. Guns were an American thing, but he quickly discovered they were necessary for free men to live independently. He carried a six-inch blade, but it was no match for the protection and utility of a reliable firearm.

"Albert carries a shotgun in the woods, but the mine boss don't like the men to have guns. There be a constable in town, and Elkhorn is a good safe place. Lots of families here. I like that, but this place has lost more children than it should." Jimmy was referring to the diphtheria that had hit the town from 1884 through 1889. "One fella told me that a man he knew buried six of his children and then the mother. Don't know how a man can stand up to that."

Elkhorn was a peaceful place, high up in the mountains, over 6,000 high, with good air. But there was a cloud of death that covered the place. People were pleasant, but sorrow was like cold water flowing beneath a thin layer of ice. The townspeople knew not to wander onto the frozen pain.

Roy had one issue he wanted to cover. "I don't know how things at the ranch will be handled when I get back, but I'll have work fer ye and a place you can land if need be, Jimmy." He knew Jimmy was not an experienced ranch hand, but he was honest, strong, and had a kind delivery. "I know ye ta be a good hand with stock. I buy ye a new gun as a bonus. I'm talkin' true, lad." Another Scotsman on the place could only improve the situation. He wanted Jimmy to know he had a place, just like Mike had offered to him.

"I'll not say yes, and I won't say no, but I feel like Albert and Pearl need me, and I can't leave them just yet. The boy being sick has them spinnin'."

Roy gave a quick nod of understanding. Jimmy was a loyal chap with a tender heart. That's why they were chums in their youth and why Roy wanted him to come with him to Fergus County. "Ye know how to reach me now. The offer is open to ye 'til ye get grey hair."

Jimmy shook his head, not looking up, and pretended to inspect the

Winchester while he wrestled back his emotions. Two days ago, he had no knowledge of Roy's location or situation, and now he was with his old friend and receiving a life-altering offer. Hard work was necessary in life, but luck was often the joker in the deck.

Roy told Jimmy to go and tell the Bennetts that he wanted to buy them supper and return the kindness. Jimmy returned an hour later with a counteroffer of dinner at the home. The boy was not well enough, and a sickly child was expected to remain quarantined.

A pleasant dinner was had with light conversation. Most talk was about a young Jimmy in Scotland and what a rascal he was then and remains to this day. It was very apparent that the Bennetts cared about Jim, and he was more than a boarder.

"Please come to breakfast in the morning and then you can ride with us up to visit the children." Pearl made an offer that would have been rude to not accept. Jimmy shot a look of, 'I'll explain later' to Roy as he left for the hotel. His time in Elkhorn would be stretched one more day.

——————

Roy knocked on the Bennetts' front door, and Jimmy let him in from the cold, dark morning. Breakfast was eaten, and a basket full of bread and cheese was put on the table. Jimmy corralled Roy in a corner and explained.

"They go up to see the graves every week since the girl died last November. Baby Lillian. Not two months old she was. Snow or cold don't stop Pearl. She don't say a word up there, and Albert just tends to the ground." Jimmy had been a faithful companion on the family trip these past weeks.

A diphtheria epidemic had come to Elkhorn sometime in 1884 and lasted for 5 years. The Bennetts lost a son, Richard, in 1890. He was almost two, and then their infant girl Lillian, died a week before Thanksgiving. There were no holidays celebrated last year.

The cemetery sat high above the town. Albert, Pearl, Jimmy, and Roy all rode up the snow packed wagon road. Tucked in the trees, graves were scattered over the slope in random. The location was nearly a mile from the town and had been chosen to keep the bodies full of diphtheria far from the town.

Roy walked slowly, reading the headstones. The ground was full of babies. He imagined mothers falling to their knees full of grief and brittle from aching loss. He watched as Pearl brushed the snow off the white stone marker. There was a lamb carved in stone laying on top. The mine owner had donated funds for the markers set for small children. Pearl laid her hand on top of the lamb's head and gently stroked the stone. She then took off her wool mitten, kissed her fingertips, and then pressed them against the names chiseled on the face of the marker. She lowered her head in what appeared to be in prayer, but Roy could see she was scanning the ground covering her children's bodies. He wondered what she was thinking while she looked at the snow. Was she visualizing her babies napping or was she watching for a sign of life she knew could not exist? Grief for the dead could destroy the living. Roy hoped that Pearl and Albert could weather the storm of heartbreak and find fragments of joy again. Pearl turned away and walked down to the wagon where Albert took her hand and helped her up to the seat.

As the wagon made its way back down to town, Roy felt the sorrow that draped the graveyard and the daily lives of the Bennetts. He hoped to never understand their level of pain, as the only way to share the agony was to experience the death of your own child. He knew that Mike's death was anguish, but that nothing could surpass the misery of watching your child leave the earth. Elkhorn was a beautiful place coated in sorrow.

The party returned to town around 1:00 p.m., and the two Scots needed a walk to talk and to allow some recovery from the sadness. Jimmy held most of the chatter with questions about the ranch, possibly working for Roy, and as much Vera information as was proper. Roy felt that he would not see the last of Jimmy Burns. His side trip had accomplished more than he had expected.

Supper was prepared and eaten quietly, and Roy thanked the Bennetts, wished them well, and said goodbye. He would leave tomorrow for Helena. Jimmy walked with him to town for a final whisky. The two friends sat in silence for a time before Roy spoke.

"How do they wake up and face the day them two? Watchin' yer own babies die is an awful time."

"I wasn't here when the boy passed, but I got to town before little Lillian was born and then watched her die in Pearl's arms. Hard to stay believin' in any Almighty God after seeing that. And now that oldest boy is laying there coughin'. Pearl told Albert she wants to leave Elkhorn. Can't bear to lose another baby here."

"Where would they go? Would you stay here?" Roy asked.

"They go back ta Butte, I reckon. Plenty of work there, but sweet Jazus it's a dirty, awful place. I'd go along ta help. Can't leave 'em yet. They both be on the edge of breakin'." Jimmy took a long pull on the glass jar.

Roy had been working up a plan in his head all day. "I want to give ye some money. Some for you and some for them. I give it to you and then you tell them you been savin' up and you want them ta have it. I give you $50 dollars. You keep half and give them the rest. Then you use that money to travel and come over to Fergus County and live at the ranch when you be ready. If no, use it to get yerself to where ye need to be."

The offer had Jimmy in a state of mild shock. "Why ye do that, Roy? No need. We have food and a roof."

Roy took a sip of beer and looked down at the table while he talked. "It not be charity; it be friendship. I have money in me pocket now, more than I need, and I want ta help people that are feelin' weak or are needin'. Help them get through this time. And after you get done helpin' them, I want ye to come and be me right-hand-man at the ranch and have coffee wi' your old friend each morning. You'll find Fergus County to yer likin', ye would."

Roy slid a fifty-dollar bank notes across the table under his hat to hide the cash from other men in the saloon. "Take it, or we be goin' outside for a scrap. This money be for if ye come to the ranch or no. I know ye not want to cut wood for the rest of ye days."

Jimmy sat for a minute, not sure how to respond. He looked at the hat, then at Roy with a confused grin. "Takin' money I ain't earned feels bad, Roy. Nobody give me anything in life before."

Roy leaned in and spoke low. "How does ye think I feel, lad? I work for Mike for not a full year and then I get half he had. Still rattlin' in me head. But America is where these sorts of things happen. We have the chance to be real men here."

Jimmy looked Roy in the eye and said, "I can no promise ye, but I'll figure out how to get to the ranch. I owe the Bennetts. Can no desert them now. But I thank ye, Roy. Two days ago, I wasn't sure you be alive and now you be here offerin' me a small bag of gold. If I wasn't lookin' at ye sittin' here in front of me, I be feelin' like a drunk."

Roy felt the offer was understood and he wouldn't press any further. "Ye know how ta get me and where the ranch be."

The two friends walked out. They shook hands, and Jimmy gave Roy a pat on the shoulder. Plans were offered and interest was expressed, but neither man could be certain if they would see each other again. Roy headed to the hotel, and Jimmy headed back to the small shack.

Jimmy stopped after a few feet, turned to Roy, and said, "Ye remember sittin' in the shore back home lookin' over at the Isle of Skye on a foggy morn, not able to see anathin' Roy?"

Roy looked up, smiled, and nodded yes.

"Well, I ha' that same feelin' now. I know the future be out there, and I can no see it clearly. Wait a wee bit for the fog ta lift, mate. Maybe I see ye soon." Jimmy gave a small wave and walked into the dark.

CHAPTER 39

The long grade down to Boulder had the train heading south before a long sweeping curve in the valley had it going to the northwest. Roy stayed on the train during the short stop as this train would head north to Helena. Four engines were added in the front for the pull up Boulder Hill as the train was pulling loaded cars full of ore north. Two more pusher engines at the end completed the upgrade in power.

Roy glanced out of the windows a few times, but his mind was focused on his final and most important task: tracking down Vera. He thought of what to say, how to move, and how widely to smile when she unexpectedly saw him walking down the hall. How would the conversation start? Would he shake her hand? A hug wouldn't be proper. What if she didn't seem happy to see him? *Wait. That could happen*, he thought. He had little experience in talking to girls. Would she brush him aside and tell him she was busy? Or would the wheels of his world come flying off if she said she had a new beau?

He leaned back in the seat, rubbed his head, and felt a bit dizzy. How could just thinking about seeing and talking to a girl make him this wobbly?

He wasn't thinking about 'A girl'…he was planning to see THE girl. Vera.

The train finally reached the top of Boulder Hill and began down slowly, twisting toward Jefferson City. A short stop found a beautiful little bowl next to Prickly Pear Creek that had a spur line to the south up to the mining town of Wickes. Wickes was famous for not having a saloon, as the mine manager forbid drinking and would not tolerate drunken miners. Jefferson City was a pretty spot. Roy thought that one day, this sweet valley would draw wild dreamers who would someday settle here, build homes on top of mountains, and find their own dreams.

Three more cars were added for the trip into Clancy through Montana City and then to Helena. Coming into Helena from the south was more dramatic and sudden than from the north.

"See those mountains to the north and a little to the right?" An older woman holding a basket in her lap tapped Roy on the shoulder and pointed.

"I do, ma'am, but what am I lookin' for?" Roy studied the range out of the window on the right side of the car.

"It's the Sleeping Giant! He's layin on his back looking up to the heavens. His bald head is to the right, then his big bulb of a nose, and then you see his big belly. Looks like a man who enjoys beer to me." The woman waited for Roy's reaction.

"Blazes, I see him! Ain't that a wonderment?" Roy turned back with a big grin as the woman gave a wink of agreement. She was pleased to have been the one to help a young person discover this local landmark.

As the train slowed and stopped at the Helena depot, Roy saw more details in the mountains where the Sleeping Giant napped. He hoped to one day point out this curious feature to his own son and daughter.

Being familiar with Helena would save Roy time and money. His time here would be spent pursuing and acquiring two things: New boots…and Vera.

He found a carriage and told the driver to take him to The Hotel Helena. The recognizable surroundings helped him feel confident and more mature. He also was returning with fine tailored clothes that told the world around him he was capable and qualified.

The clerk asked if Roy would prefer to put his new Winchester in the gun room in the hotel. He was told it was a locked and secure room available to guests for any oversized valuables. Roy agreed and asked if he could put his other guns in as well, to which the clerk told him yes.

He was given a room on the fifth floor. Roy tried to remember if he had ever been this high in the air on a man-made device but quickly realized the ship he and Mike had steamed back to America in was considerably taller. He enjoyed the view and could see Mount Helena clearly from his room.

He sat on the bed, formed a plan in his head, brushed off his overcoat and hat, and left for the hospital. The familiar path up the hill to the hospital was covered in packed snow. Roy feared rejection from Vera more than any icy fall.

It was 4:30 in the afternoon, and the sun was already disappearing. Roy walked up to the main door of St. Peter's Hospital hoping to find Vera quickly. Any delay would be as painful as a rotting tooth.

A woman was behind the sliding glass window to the left. Roy waited to be recognized before speaking. "Good day, ma'am. I'd be pleased if ye could tell me if Nurse Vera Daggett is on duty?"

The woman spoke without looking up. "Do you have business with Nurse Daggett?"

"Yes, ma'am, I do. Important news about her future in Montana." Roy surprised himself with the phony but accurate statement.

"Let me check the roster." After a quick review of a paper on a clipboard, she told Roy she was not working.

He began to walk away slightly dejected. The woman tapped the desk to get Roy's attention. "I said she is not working now, but she is scheduled to work this evening beginning at 5:00."

His luck was holding. Things were looking up.

He thought he would wait outside by the front door and catch her before she entered. The wind had died down and the bench near the entrance offered a wide view of Mount Helena in the twilight. He looked down the street like a soldier on guard duty.

5:00 came and passed. Roy worried she might be reprimanded by her boss for being late. Each body that approached the hospital proved to not be Vera.

Minutes passed. A firm and delicate voice from behind was heard. "Do you have plans to sit out in the cold all night?"

It was Vera poking her head out of the door. She had entered the hospital through a side entrance.

Roy turned and felt his face stretch with an uncontrollable smile. He saw Vera's face and felt like a mule had kicked him. All his planning and practiced lines evaporated in his head and all he could do was smile and say, "Ye look bonny ye do."

That honest comment was all he could produce, and it was all Vera needed to hear. She smiled, her eyes sparkled, and she waved him inside.

"Get inside, Mr. Douglas. You're no use to me frozen." As Roy walked inside, she brushed some snow off of his shoulder, and he felt a vibration in his chest from her touch. He stood in front of her within arms-length and looked at her sweet and beautiful face. She reached up to flick off a few lingering snowflakes and then moved her hand back to his face and softly touched his cheek. That touch would stay with Roy for a lifetime.

They walked inside and up the stairs. "When did you arrive in town? Do you have business to attend to? What are you doing here?" Vera asked with a coy, playful tone, hopeful she knew the true reason.

Roy was cold and nervous. He had no experience with wooing or intimate conversation. Mike had talked about many things but never how to court and spark. However, Roy had a firm grasp on honesty, and that was the only skill he held in this moment.

Reaching the chairs at the top of the staircase, he replied, "I'm here ta see you." Roy took a breath. "Lots has happened to me since I seen ye last, Vera. Life's flyin' around me head like a cyclone." He told himself to breathe deeply and say what he felt but do it slowly and calmly.

Vera again primed the pump and demurely asked Roy for a declaration. "What has changed? Did you come here for advice? Did you have a question you wanted to ask me?" She was ready if THE question was asked.

He had felt like this once before. Mike had told him to jump on a spring colt, grab a hold of the rope, and wait for an epic ride. "I come here to see if it would work out ta see if ye would think about bein' a wife ta me. I mean being me wife." Roy exhaled, felt his knee buckle, and released the burden.

Vera tried to suppress her smile, but she grinned and asked, "Was that supposed to be a proposal of marriage, Roy Douglas? Was it your intent to ask me if I'd marry you?" She pretended to be a bit put out by the awkward invitation and put her hands on her hips.

"If that's what ye hear, that's what I meant." Roy was eagerly waiting for an answer, but Vera seemed to be toying with him a bit, and he wanted to stop the game. "I did; I do. Land sakes, girl...will ye get married to me?"

She tilted her head in an irresistible way and looked at this Scottish man/boy with wet eyes. "Yes. I think I will agree to be married to you." She let out a gentle cry, threw her arms around his neck, pulled herself up, and kissed her future husband. Square on the lips she did. And for more than two seconds.

Roy didn't let go of her and whispered in her ear. "Good. That's a grand thing." He pulled her back in, and she let out a sigh as he pulled the wind out of her.

"I need to breathe, Roy! You are twice my size and could break me." Vera laughed at the moment of pain and was hopeful for a lifetime of breathtaking embraces.

"And now you are saying good and not bonny? You're all Montana now." She smiled and reluctantly pushed back. "Now, I must return to work, or your future wife will be with a fortune. May we talk in the morning after my work is completed?"

"I be...I am at the Hotel Helena again. Should we have breakfast when you be done?" Roy was in a fog. He was enjoying each second of being with this kind girl.

Vera began to walk away slowly, needing to return to the ward. "Yes, I will be there at 7:00 in the morning, and we can talk more and speak about details." She put her hand to her mouth and blew him a small kiss. The entire chat and proposal took slightly more than five minutes.

Roy knew he needed more of her. A lot more. Of everything about her. He had waited weeks to see her again, and now she was suddenly floating away.

"Vera, one more thing I forgot…Mike gave me half the ranch. Half of all the land. I…we have a ranch to run."

Vera stood still as the news hit. Her eyes widened, and she grinned. "You own the ranch?"

"No. WE own the ranch. The Douglas family will own the ranch." Roy doubted he would ever feel this happy and complete again in his life. "Wanted to see if you would marry a poor ranch hand first." He gave her a smug head tilt that held both jest and truth.

Vera reached up and dabbed her eyes that were filling with tears, gave a smiling glance to Roy, and walked around the corner.

Roy had no religion in him. He wasn't raised in it. He was a practical man. Nevertheless, he felt that a divine hand was at work in his life.

Nothing that had happened to him in the past year was logical at all.

CHAPTER 40

Roy laid in bed, arms straight at his side, looking at the ceiling for hours. He woke up but had no idea how long he had slept. He sat up and looked at his pocket watch.

4:48.

He thought he may as well get up and go for a walk and then drink coffee until Vera came for breakfast. He double checked how he looked in his suit and headed downstairs.

It was just before 5:30 in the morning, and the lobby was already busy. Men exchanged courteous nods as they passed one another. An elegant lady gave a slight but well-mannered dip as she passed Roy, who returned the gesture with a small nod. Roy had come to enjoy the pleasantries and welcomed the polished manners of others. He liked being a member of polite society and the kindness it offered to strangers. He would soon be a married man and would refine his public demeanor so as not to embarrass his new wife.

He had time to waste, and a brisk walk would burn off some excess time and energy. Roy stepped outside with happy intentions, but the reality of a dark January morning in Montana changed his plan and chased him back inside. Too cold. He would be content drinking coffee in the dining room.

What would they talk about? What would Vera need to say? All the thinking he'd done about a life with Vera brought him to a tactical solution. He would let Vera do most of the thinking, and he would do the doing.

Vera walked through the door, briskly and full of purpose. She kicked off a bit of snow from her boots at the door, untied her scarf, and quickly found Roy staring at her. She smiled, tucked her scarf into a pocket, and walked over to him.

They stood, face to face, absorbing each other's affection. Roy tried to find the one thing, physical or invisible, that made Vera so attractive to him. He loved it all, from the dimple in her chin to her square jaw line. But her eyes, good lord, those eyes. She could speak through her eyes. She could look very serious and intimidating at times. People often thought she was angry or perturbed. She was simply concentrating and people would often avoid her when she looked this way. It was a miraculous combination of determination, concentration, and intelligence.

The same woman could then break out a smile that could melt snow and show the world the kindness inside of her. Roy had seen all of this the first minutes he had met her in the hospital. He saw how kindhearted she was with Mike and knew this gentleness was real.

She was one year older than he was, and she was wise, confident, and strong; she was all the things he wanted to be. He would use Vera as his guidepost for the remainder of his days. He knew she would make him a better man.

"May we sit?" Vera knew he would stand there for an hour if she didn't take control.

"Aye...yep."

Vera unbuttoned her coat. "I've noticed that you are speaking more like an American. I like that but don't lose the Scotsman in you. I like that fella, you know." She smiled and winked, acknowledging his social progress but warning against false behavior.

"I'll always be a Scot, just want to be taken serious by them around me. I'll ramble on like a bampot in front of you, my darlin'." He heard the last word spill out.

Vera heard it too. She reached over and put her hand on top of his.

"I suppose you can call me that now that we are to be wed." A smile and short head bob added sweetness to her reply.

She would be his Darling from now on. It was still sinking in.

They walked into the dining room that had just opened, took a corner table, and ordered food.

"What do we do now?" Roy got straight to it, as was his manner. "I mean, please tell me what you want, and I'll do it." He would not pretend to know how to make any of this wedding work. He would gladly allow Vera to captain this ship, and he would swab the decks.

"This is all new material for me as well, my dearest. I have a sister that got married, but I was engaged in my nursing studies and was away. We will figure all this out together." Vera reached over and touched his arm.

Roy was bursting. "I love ye, Vera. Wouldn't think of ye as being a wife if I was not holdin' love fer ye. You be the most handsome little gal I ever seen. But if you wasn't a beauty, I still love ye." He felt it was safe to say these things at this point.

Vera blushed a little, looked at Roy, and replied. "I am in love with you as well, Roy Douglas. No one has ever looked at me as you do. I feel that. We have not known each other for long, but I saw the man you are in the hospital with Mr. Hanson. I see an honest, tender man who has no guile in him."

Roy had never heard words like these. He worried that his emotions would run down stream, flowing one way, but Vera was swimming upstream to meet him. This crazy notion of working and loving every day might just work for them. Clearly, Vera was smitten with Roy and had spent long hours thinking about him as well.

The plates of food were heading their way as Vera placed the linen napkin on her lap and looked firmly at Roy's face. "And if our sons are one half as handsome as their father, they will be fortunate lads indeed."

Roy smiled. His future bride thought he was handsome!

He reached up, brushed his hair across his forehead and sat up straight. He decided he would always try to be tidy and neat in appearance to hold her opinion of his looks.

"Now that hair though, Roy, it is a mop. We can comb that out a bit if you'd allow me too." She cut into the sausage patty and shot a playful side glance at him.

Roy would allow her to take sheep shears to his head if she wanted.

Courtship and marriage in the Victorian age was a formal and well-structured affair. Families often made arrangements that benefited both clans and would set up the couple for future success. Marriages could be more of a contractual agreement based on money and practicality. However, even in Victorian America, love had become a stronger factor in these unions. Romance was becoming fashionable, and Roy and Vera were a part of the new wave of emotional unions.

"Do I need to ask yer pa if I be allowed to marry you, Vera?" This was the number one question Roy had about this entire procedure.

Vera threw back her head and laughed softly. "My lands, Roy, my mother and father gave up on controlling me many years ago. I'm the middle daughter and well-schooled. My father called me a stubborn filly. I love my parents, and they love me, but no, you will not be called upon to ask for my hand."

Every day and each hour seemed to unburden Roy. This new life he was creating came at a cost, but the payments to satisfy these debts were smaller than expected. The road to marriage just became a bit smoother.

"I will send a telegram to my family and tell them of our engagement. My older sister will be shocked as she told me I was an old maid when I turned twenty years of age last month. I hope she finds comfort in my news." Vera smirked as she thought of her sister's reaction. "I would suggest you send your family a message as well, as not to give them a start when you return home."

They agreed to send telegrams to announce and warn. Then they quietly enjoyed a warm breakfast and each other's company. Roy watched Vera's every move. He chewed and watched. He cut some ham, then watched some more. He was looking at his future, and he loved what he saw.

The talk turned to the wedding. It was obvious Vera had been thinking and quietly planning for this event well before Roy reappeared. She pulled out a small notebook and a pencil. It was full of notes and even drawings. This was one very organized, thorough woman.

Vera suggested they marry in late May back in Minnesota at her brother's farm near Windom. Her parents were selling the farm she was raised on near Sibley, Iowa, and they planned to move to Windom to be near him.

Her oldest brother had bought a farm in Cottonwood County three years back, and it was proving to be a wise purchase. The ground was rich and fertile and demonstrating to be excellent row crop land. They had built a fine two-story home on the farm, and it was surrounded by a thick grove of cottonwood and walnut trees.

Roy had no objection to any of this. He was pleased he wasn't consulted or asked to do any thinking on the matter. He gave an approving smile and nodded for Vera to keep the session moving.

She suggested they travel separately to Windom and then honeymoon on Lake Minnetonka near Minneapolis. A friend of hers had stayed at the Hotel Lafayette, and it was highly recommended.

"What on earth is a hineymoons?" Roy had never heard of such a thing. Since she mentioned a lake, he wondered if it was a type of boat or fishing reel of some sort.

"HONEYMOON." Vera spoke it out slowly and giggled. "It is a short holiday for newlyweds after their wedding. It's become very popular."

Roy mumbled, "Popular for the women I'd bet." He quickly realized he had said that bit out loud and looked up to Vera.

She pretended to be irritated by his unguarded response, but she giggled and shook her head. This would not be the last time she would be amused by his subdued wit.

"What about the date? Have to have the lambin' done with before I can go anywhere." This was as forceful as Roy would be, and he felt manly in making such a declaration.

Vera flipped through her notes to a small calendar. "How does May 28th sound? You will be free of lambing by then, won't you?"

Roy thought about it and then agreed. Lambing would be over sometime in April, and that would allow time for travel and a short break. He felt that Lon and Anders could handle the chores while he was gone.

Roy would give Vera total control over the planning and events. He would simply show up and marry this beautiful but rugged girl.

Vera put her hand out to seal the deal. He took her hand and didn't let go. He looked around the dining room. The room was empty. He made his move.

Without releasing her hand, he stood up, pulled Vera to her feet, and pulled her in for a strong embrace. He then took her face in both hands and kissed her. Deeply. He felt weakened and a bit dizzy. She gave no resistance and yielded to his actions. She was much smaller than he was, and she fell limp in his big arms. The kiss was overdue and exciting. Roy wrapped her up and pulled her close as she laid her head on his broad shoulder. They heard a dish rattle in the kitchen and broke the embrace.

Roy knew he might never feel better than he did at this moment.

A plan was made for the next two days. Roy would wander and rest while Vera slept and then worked. They would meet briefly before she began work tonight and then again for breakfast each day. Roy wanted to get new boots, and that would require a day to complete. He also wanted to find a small gift for Vera before he left as they would not see each other before the wedding.

With breakfast done, Roy asked the doorman to hail a carriage. He would ride with Vera back to her house and then continue his day.

The carriage was warm. The two of them sat in the back together as close as possible, holding hands. As the carriage turned the corner and headed back to the north, he saw a familiar sign.

JAMES P. BALL AND SON...PHOTOGRAPHER

The idea popped quickly as he told the driver to pull over in front of the storefront.

"Let's take a photograph, Vera."

"Now? I look a fright, Roy. Not now. Please." Vera wasn't complaining, but she made a valid point.

Roy thought fast on his feet. "Would this afternoon before you work be better? I'll bring you here and then deliver you to the hospital."

Vera knew it was a fine plan, and she also wanted a photo of the two of them.

"If you must, I will agree to that."

Roy told the driver to wait as he jumped out. The door was locked. He knocked on the glass loudly hoping for an answer. After the fourth rap on the window, the curtain to the back opened, and Mrs. Ball walked out.

"We are closed until 9:00, could you..." Her voice stopped as she recognized Roy.

"Mr. Hanson! Please allow me to find the key!"

She opened the door and gave Roy a motherly hug out of reflex. "So very good to see you, young man. So many questions, but how may I assist you?"

Roy smiled and explained how he had just asked the pretty nurse that she had met a few weeks ago to marry him, and he wanted a photograph. He asked if it would be possible to return around 4:00 p.m.

"We would be very pleased to photograph you and your fiancé this afternoon." Mrs. Ball began to write the appointment down.

"I look forward to seeing you both a bit later." *I like this innocent young man*, she thought.

Before he left, Mrs. Ball pulled him aside and spoke softly. Roy looked puzzled and shook his head no and asked, "Is that what men do and the women need?"

"It has become an accepted tradition, and it is a loving gesture." Mrs. Ball handed a note to Roy and said, "Stop at this shop. Ask for Mrs. Woodcock. Show her this note." She smiled, patted Roy on the back, and directed him to the door.

Back in the carriage, Roy told the driver to take his time and give them a tour of the city. He wanted to spend as much time with his sweetheart as possible.

The ten-minute ride turned into thirty and cost Roy an fifty cents. He would have paid ten dollars if needed. Roy didn't move once the carriage stopped. Vera looked at him, but he stayed frozen. She tilted her head to let him know that he should open the door. He reluctantly left her side, opened the door, and helped her step out.

"It is much too cold for a long goodbye, my sweet." Vera kissed Roy's cheek and walked toward the house steps. "Will you return at 3:30?"

Roy gave a wave to confirm. He watched her walk up the steps until she disappeared inside.

Once again, he had multiple stops to make in a short time. Boots. Gunsmith. And this particular shop Mrs. Ball had encouraged him to visit.

First, he headed back to the hotel. Roy stepped down and arranged for the carriage driver to meet him at 3:00 p.m. in front of the hotel. He thought how easy it was to get around in towns and cities and to find desired goods. He enjoyed visiting but knew he could never live amongst this many people or tolerate the noise.

A short walk found him in front of a giant painted boot hanging over a door. Frederick Gamer's shop had been in Helena for many years before statehood and came highly recommended. Roy had been wanting a fine pair of boots with high shafts that came just under the knee.

He was greeted by a man sporting a fine waxed mustache. He told the man what style of boot he desired. He then thought how he might need a new pair of boots for the wedding as well.

Measurements were taken. A price of $8 dollars for each pair was given and agreed to. Roy asked if it would be possible to pick the boots up by tomorrow afternoon and was told it would be fine for an additional charge, which he gladly paid.

Roy remembered that he needed to send a telegram to Will with an update. Walking into the Western Union office, he wrote down the message, and the clerk read it back to him.

"'To be wed end of May to Vera the nurse stop Be in Lewistown in 3-4 days stop All is well stop Roy stop No reply needed stop.' Is that all, mister?" The clerk wrote out a receipt.

Roy nodded, handed the clerk $1.10, and wondered if that was enough information. He took the receipt and left.

It was now time for more gifts. This would be an honest gesture of appreciation for loyalty and untroubled work. Roy crossed the street to a storefront with a hand painted sign on the door:

Chas. Morrell, Gunsmith

Roy loved the smell of a gun shop. The aroma of oils, freshly shaved metals, and a pepper-like fragrance from the gunpowder hit him like a fresh baked pie. He thought it odd to enjoy these manufactured smells as none of them existed in nature. These were very American perfumes.

Roy knew what he wanted. A purchase was made. He requested that the items be boxed up for shipping as he was leaving on the train the next day. He knew these gifts would be unexpected and greatly welcomed. He wanted to show his gratitude to two men. He would share his good fortune with others in his world when possible. Mike would have done the same.

Roy spent the next hours in the hotel lobby reading Mark Twain. He was learning how to read his books, but many phrases and words were not familiar, and he had a loose grip of their meaning. He wanted to learn more and add to his storehouse of words. He understood humor, but Twain opened his mind to clever thinking and the art of disguised insults.

The doorman walked up to Roy and told him a carriage was waiting for him out front. It was time for his final and most important gift acquisition for the day.

The carriage delivered him to Vera's house. The front door opened and out she came. He thought of how elegantly she walked, how her posture was upright and strong. She was tiny but tough.

Roy stepped out and waited for her. He fought the urge to grab and kiss her the instant she reached him. He would maintain the accepted social rules and would not embarrass her with any rascal-like behavior.

"Did you have a good day, Mr. Douglas?" she asked as she settled into the seat and adjusted her hat.

"Yes, I did, me darlin'." Roy thought that if physical affection was out of the question, then sweet verbal butter would have to do.

She patted his leg and smiled as they contently rode together back to the downtown business district.

The first stop was the Ball Photography Studio. Roy paid the driver and tipped his hat.

Mrs. Ball greeted them as they entered, took their overcoats, and directed them to sit.

"Mr. Ball is setting up the portrait in the back. Do you have a certain pose or style of photograph in mind?" Mrs. Ball set out a large album of photos as examples from which to select.

Roy shrugged and looked for Vera to take the lead. "A simple engagement remembrance would be most perfect. If you can offer us your suggestions, we would be most grateful." Vera knew what to say and what to do. "And if I may, do you have a frock or shawl that I may use to cover my uniform?"

Roy quickly responded. "I like you wearin' the uniform, Vera. It be the first thing I see ye in, and I fell fer ye like this. Ye look bonny, ye do."

Mrs. Ball clasped her hands and tilted her head with a smile. The romance that was playing out in front of her was delicate and honest. "I would agree with your betrothed, Miss Daggett. It is a very striking presentation."

Vera was happily outnumbered and agreed quickly. She was proud of her career, and the nurses' uniform was bright and unique. The dark cape with white lining pulled over one shoulder was an elegant accent that turned the workwear into fashion. "If you both agree, then I will not protest."

"I hope that one day my son will find a similar young woman of quality and beauty as you have, Roy. Well done." Mrs. Ball held her right hand over her heart as she spoke. She could not be prouder or more impressed with this couple if they were her own blood.

Mr. Ball poked his head out of the curtain, introduced himself, and asked them all to come to the back room. There were two lights aimed at the chair in front of a gray cloth hanging on the wall. He sat Vera in the plush velvet chair. He positioned Roy in back of her, slightly to one side, and had him put his hand on her shoulder. He then had Vera reach across her chest and place her hand on top of Roy's.

Mr. Ball crawled under the black fabric behind the camera and said, "Hold, please." A few seconds later, he pulled a large flat plate from the camera and replaced it with a similar plate. "Hold again once more, please, just for insurance of a successful exposure. I will use the best."

Mr. Ball stood up, thanked the couple for their patience and cooperation, and disappeared into an adjoining room behind a dark curtain. Mrs. Ball quickly stepped up and took control. She possessed the social skills to conduct business. Her husband was a technician and more comfortable with contraptions than with people.

Mrs. Ball sat at her small desk writing while she spoke. "We will have these available tomorrow morning. Now, how many reproductions would you care to purchase?"

"Ten. I like ta have ten if ye please, Mrs. Ball." Roy was putting on his coat while answering.

"Ten? My gracious sakes! Ten is quite a large number, Roy. And at one dollar per photo, well…" A flustered Mrs. Ball took a breath.

"That be ten dollars by my reckoning." Roy confidently pulled the cash from Mike's old wallet that was now his. "I need photos of Vera, lots of them. I plan to give her some fer her kin." He recognized a once-in-a-lifetime moment.

A beaming Mrs. Ball answered, "Then ten it shall be my young man. Please stop around tomorrow no sooner than 11:00 a.m."

As they were leaving, Roy pulled Mrs. Ball to the side. "We be going back to Minnesota to be married in May. I know it's far from here and we not be kin, but I want ye to know that you be invited. Wanted ye to know that, ma'am."

Mrs. Ball gave Roy a motherly hug and wiped away a tear. "My boy, that is precious of you, and I thank you. That is a great distance to travel, but I will be there in spirit with you both on that wonderful day."

Roy had found his American mother in Mrs. Ball. He would not lose touch with her.

The young couple walked back to the street. "Have one more stop, Vera."

"I don't have a great deal of time before I must be at the hospital, Roy."

"Shakes of a lambs tail it will take, my darlin'."

There was that 'darling' again. Vera tried to hide how much she enjoyed hearing him call her by that endearment, but she tingled at the sound of it.

They walked half a block and went into the store. Roy pulled out the note from Mrs. Ball, read it, and opened the door for Vera. He asked for Mrs. Woodcock. A refined woman in her fifties stood up from behind a desk.

Roy handed her the note from Mrs. Ball. She read it, looked at the couple, and smiled. "I am very proud that you selected Charles H. Pratt Jewelers for this special moment."

Vera gave Roy a puzzled look.

"Ye should have a proper ring. Mrs. Ball called it a betrothal ring. Needs a diamond she said." Roy was simply repeating what he had been told.

"I don't need anything that expensive. I'm not highfalutin." Vera spoke in a modest tone and was protesting with little enthusiasm.

"I'll not boss ye, but I be the man and yer husband soon. I'll buy ye a ring that can make ye proud. A wife of mine will be respected." Roy winked at her and held her hand. "Throw it in the outhouse after, but you be startin' out with a proper jewel."

"You are a very handsome couple. Do you have a wedding date?" Mrs. Woodcock asked while lifting a tray of shiny gold and sparkling stones.

"The end of May at my home in Minnesota." Vera looked at Roy, waiting for any hint of disagreement but saw none.

Mrs. Woodcock laid out the rings. They twinkled in the late afternoon sunlight. "We can very quickly size most of these while you wait, so please let us focus on the beauty and clarity of the stones."

"I want ye to have the one ye love. It only costs money once in life. Pick out the best. Please, Vera." Roy looked at her with love and determination. She smiled and covered her lips with her hand. A small head nod told him she would obey his loving command.

Roy watched with genuine pleasure as Vera leaned over the trays, smiling and asking Mrs. Woodcock for details about a diamond.

Vera slipped on a beautiful gold ring with a medium sized stone and held out her hand to admire and dream. "This one is very elegant. Do you have any thoughts, Roy?"

"I think if it makes ye happy, then it be bang up to the elephant." Roy smiled and reached for his wallet.

"I don't know what that means. Is that a good thing?" Vera was amused by Roy's comfort with humorous slang.

"Aye. It means perfect, darlin'. Perfect." Roy turned to face Vera. "Will ye give me the ring?"

Vera wiggled the ring off and put it in Roy's palm. He cleared his throat. "I read about this part in a magazine." He took the ring in his right hand, took Vera's left hand in his, and tried to put the ring on her middle finger.

"Roy, honey, it goes on this finger." She pointed to her ring finger and giggled.

He laughed while placing the ring on her finger and kissing her cheek. "Never said I finished readin' the magazine."

The three ladies in the shop all clapped politely at the spectacle. Roy smiled at the audience, turned to Vera, and kissed her hand. This visit to the jewelry store had gone better than he had hoped.

Mrs. Woodcock took the ring to the back to quickly size it as it was a bit tight. Roy moved to the large brass cash register to pay. A woman handed him the bill. It was $45 dollars. Vera stood next to him and saw the amount.

"Roy, no! This is not necessary. This is not sensible. I will be fine without a ring." Vera was from a farming family that worked hard and lived practically.

"I know ye don't need it, Vera, but I need for ye to have it. You'll not be telling me no now, will ye? Can ye wait 'til we been married fer a month before ye sass me?" Roy cracked a smile and continued counting out his cash without looking up.

Vera touched him on the shoulder softly and said, "No, Roy. No sass today."

Mrs. Woodcock returned with the ring and handed it to Roy to repeat his prior performance. Vera lifted her left hand, and Roy gently slid the ring on the correct finger.

They bid the ladies goodbye and left to get Vera to work on time. Roy tried to walk slowly, but Vera pushed the pace.

"May we have breakfast in the morning again, or are you heading home?" Vera walked inside, and Roy helped with her overcoat.

"Yes, we may. Of course." Roy was waiting to see Vera's reaction to his American speaking style. "I need to stay one more day. Boots won't be ready 'til tomorrow afternoon. I want to spend every bit of time I have with ye, Vera."

"Keep that Scotsman in you, Roy. I love that fella. See you in the morning at the hotel around 7:00?" She offered a quick kiss and turned.

Roy watched her walk up the stairs, trying to memorize how she moved. She reached the top, turned back, and held up her left hand to show Roy the ring. She pursed her lips together and sent a kiss his way.

These two were quite fond of each other.

CHAPTER 41

Roy had a solid night's sleep as the stress of gift buying, boot fittings, and marriage proposal had been removed. His pocket watch read 6:20, and he panicked for a moment before he remembered Vera was coming to him.

He still hustled to get dressed and presentable and made it to the lobby by 6:40. He hated to be late.

Vera walked in a few minutes early, looking tired but pleasant. "Last day in Helena, Mr. Douglas? I hope you enjoyed your time here." She knew he had and took pleasure in prodding Roy into an obvious answer.

He liked being called by his formal name, at least by Vera. It did not matter what moniker she used, as long as she was the one speaking. "Yep. Start back tomorrow. Train leaves at 6:00 in the morn. I'll find me a pool hall to spend the day in. Sure, be a bonny way to relax today." He matched her wise remark with his own.

"Then when you are done in the billiards parlor, we shall use as much of this day as possible to keep company with one another, and we will discuss wedding plans and the such." Vera winked, then yawned. "I must tell you, Roy, that these have been the best two days of my life."

Roy sat his coffee cup down, stared at Vera and, without hesitation, said, "I love ye, Vera. Not sure I said that out loud, but I do. I love ye somethin' fierce I do." He didn't move or change expression. He just gazed at her and smiled.

"I love you my sweet man. I cover my feelings, but I am learning to feel and allow your affection for me. No one has spoken to me with respect as you do. It is very new and peculiar to me." Vera reached over to touch his arm. "When you left Helena after Mike's passing, I felt alone and confused by how I felt. It bothered me greatly. I prayed each night for your return. I missed you. And when you reappeared, well, it was an answer to my prayers."

Vera looked at Roy with tear-filled eyes. She did not wipe away tears or disguise her emotions. She wanted him to see what she felt. A tear fell on her cloth napkin, and Roy reached over, took it, and stuffed it into his coat pocket. "I need to save that."

The next hour was full of small talk. Information was shared of family and friends, preferences in food, and preferred color of horses. All of the tiny details that people who care for each other are in need of knowing.

"You don't care for beets? Why, Roy, that is mighty curious. I love beets." Vera was shocked at Roy's hatred of beets, and she discovered he would not surrender on this topic. "Well, as long as that is the only item you will not eat, I will adjust to your fussy tastes."

"Horseradish too. Bitter as a homely widow, it is." Roy felt these two items were critical knowledge his soon-to-be bride should know.

Vera laughed and knew there would be a longer list of likes and dislikes, as this seemingly shy boy was actually a man of strong opinions.

After breakfast there was a long carriage ride around Helena. Sightseeing and handholding were the objectives. Both goals were achieved before a weary Vera asked to be taken home. She needed sleep. She would see Roy a final time in the late afternoon before returning to work.

This time, he kissed her after she climbed out of the carriage. It was a brash but much appreciated maneuver, as Vera held on to the kiss longer than Roy expected. More of this. Please.

Roy felt contentedly sad watching Vera walk up those stairs. *So, love was more than wanting to kiss a girl*, he thought. *Huh. Whatya know?*

The carriage ride back to town felt colder although the sun was shining and it was a warm day. No Vera. Roy stopped at the Frederick Gamer's Bootery to pick up his new boots. He tried on both pairs and found them to fit perfectly. He asked to have the wedding boots wrapped and boxed as he would not wear those until the wedding.

He held the carriage driver this morning as he would have boots and guns to take back to the hotel. The stop at the gun shop was quick as two men carried the long, thin, wooden crate out to the carriage.

The driver helped carry Roy's bounty inside the hotel, and a bellman took over in the lobby. The guns were taken to the hotel's gun room as Roy carried the boots up to his room.

Once there, he took off his coat and boots and fell back on the bed. The boot fitting would wait. A long nap would recharge him for his final hour with Vera.

————

He woke up two hours later and called down to the front desk asking for laundry service. He was told the clothing would be returned before suppertime, and a four-bit tip was given and happily accepted.

It was time for a walk to the bath at the end of the hall. He hadn't shaved for a week since his beard was not a fully functioning object at his age. He hoped once he turned nineteen next month, the beard would bloom like spring clover in a pasture. Conversely, his hair, well, was always growing. His wavy/curly light brown hair had reached his shoulders since last August when Mike had taken the sheep shears to his mop. Vera had mentioned that she liked his curly hair and had even touched it once. He was sure that she would prefer it to be a little shorter for the wedding.

The bath and shave felt revitalizing. An hour later, his suit and laundry were returned early. He wanted to look his best for his last visit. It was now time to hail a carriage, collect the photos from earlier in the day, and then pick up Vera.

"What would you like to do in the time we have?" Vera snuggled up to him in the carriage, closer than she had before. Roy put his arm around her, and she laid her head on his shoulder. The contentment of the moment was short-lived as Roy began to think about the misery he would feel in an hour when they would part.

Roy opened up a large paper bag and slid out one of the photos he had picked up an hour before. He held it up for Vera to see.

"Oh, Roy! My, oh goodness, this is…" Vera was overwhelmed as she looked at the image. Roy had already exhausted his emotion but was affected a second time by Vera's reaction. She sniffed and touched his cheek with her hand.

"I'll give ye all ye want of these, but can I take three?"

"Roy, honey, you take as many as you need. I'll take what you don't use. This is your notion, and you have paid."

Roy thought for second. "I only be needin' three. One for meself, one for Grace, and one for Will and Becky. You take the rest. I want ye to have all you want. Any left-over, we can hang in the house after."

"After the wedding do you mean? I shall take six, and you will take four. And thank you for thinking of this for us. I will send my mother one of these to show her my handsome rancher husband." Vera made sure to emphasize the word handsome.

Roy was jolted for a second. He would have a mother-in-law soon and a new father and sisters. An automatic family. He hoped they would accept him and know that he loved Vera. If not, he had Vera, and that was enough love for him.

They pulled up to St. Peter's. The couple walked arm-in-arm to the door.

"I will write you each week and hope you will send me a note when you are able." Vera turned to face Roy and held his hand. "It's nearly February now, and I don't expect to see you before our wedding in May. Will you please write to me and let me know any news regarding the ranch and you?"

"I will, darlin'. I can write, but I don't know how to write like I be talkin' to ye."

"You are a smarter man than you present yourself to be to the world, Roy Douglas. Just tell me what you did, what you plan to do, and how you are feeling. As if we were sitting at the breakfast table talking over coffee. That will be all I ask for." Vera was speaking low, knowing they were moments away from a bittersweet goodbye.

Vera shared her initial plans for the wedding. The date and location were already agreed upon. Roy would travel with Grace, Becky, and Will. Full accommodations needed to be made. The minister, food, and all other required or desired details would be handled by Vera and her family.

Roy was pleased to learn that all he needed to do was show up. He was happy to be a follower when he had no experience in the matter. He knew his abilities and understood that limitations were not the same as weaknesses.

Vera suggested that they travel separately to Minnesota. She had an aunt in Cheyenne who would meet her in Billings and probably chaperone her back to Minnesota. She suggested that Roy and company would travel the Hi-Line through North Dakota and then down through Minneapolis and St. Paul. They could get a train from there to Windom.

Roy gave a smile of admiration and approval. He had no doubts regarding any plans Vera would make. She was the smartest person he had ever met. Smarter than Mike she was.

With the wedding plans discussed, the final issue was Roy leaving for home early in the morning.

"I don't want to leave ye, darlin'. Reckon that be a good thing fer how I feel about ye." Roy pulled her close. "I'm gonna be kissin' ye now. Not just a wee kiss. A fine proper one, lassie."

The young couple held each other as tight as possible while still allowing necessary breathing. The embrace lasted twice as long as any previous kiss and lasted until they heard the front door creak and open. Roy brushed Vera's hair over her ear and gave her one more peck on the cheek. She, in turn, put both of her hands on his cheeks and returned one final kiss.

Vera took a handkerchief and dabbed at her lips. "Let us say our farewells now and not prolong the parting, my dear man. I will say goodbye and dream of the moment I see you next."

She took two steps, turned back, and looked at Roy with a tear rolling down her cheek. "I love you, Roy Douglas. I am very pleased that you will be my husband and I your wife." She wiped her eyes, took two more steps, and turned back again. "I was thinking about the wedding vows. Must we include the word OBEY in the ceremony?" She grinned, half in jest and half in sincerity.

Roy ran the question through his mind and answered before allowing deep thought to take hold. "Will it work if we don't use that word? I mean the marryin'. Will it work without that?"

Vera laughed and then feigned a frown. "Mr. Douglas, you are from the old world are you not? I am sure my mother will insist it be in there."

"I love you my beautiful girl." Roy took a final look up, turned, and opened the door. The walk down the hill to the hotel felt cold and lonesome. He thought he needed to feel excited, but he hurt knowing it would be months before he would see Vera again.

He would feel her absence, but he would never feel lonely again.

CHAPTER 42

Roy had accumulated more packages, crates, and bags on this adventure. There was no longer just a single satchel to secure as in his past travels. He thought back to the dirty burlap bag that held all he owned when he had first come to America. Very large steps in a very short time had been made. He now needed claim tickets for the bags and the crate. Tipping the baggage handlers was also required, but Roy was happy and eager to do so.

His way home would take him from Helena with a short stop in Great Falls and then to Fort Benton. As no tracks had been laid to Lewistown yet, the best route home was the stagecoach from Fort Benton. First settled in 1846, the river town was a vital port for the westward expansion of America. As the railroad grew and reached the town in 1887, steamboat traffic shrunk.

It was now February, and the long cold ride home would take one and half days, with stops to change horses but no overnight stops and would cost $16 dollars. The lonely train pulled into Fort Benton. The stagecoach office was one door down from a Western Union office, so Roy decided to send a short telegram to update Will on his progress. He had hoped to never ride in a stagecoach again, but it was better than walking. The gun crate and both satchels were loaded. Three other men boarded, all destined for Lewistown.

Time passed slowly. As before, the coach rocked and bounced. Roy marveled how thousands of people had tolerated traveling in these rattle boxes for decades. He appreciated the service, but each mile increased his love for trains.

The four men all preferred to sit in silence and pass the hours with little conversation. Roy was in full agreement with the pact as he had a head full of thoughts and the notion of talking to strangers for over 30 hours was as painful as a splinter in a finger.

The next day in early afternoon, the coach came up from the bottom of the coulee and reached the northern edge of Lewistown. Minutes later, the stage stopped in front of the new Lehman Brother's Store on Main Street.

Roy climbed out last and saw Will standing on the sidewalk.

"Welcome home, pal. Tired?" Will asked him. It was obvious that Roy was exhausted and was relieved to be home and not in motion. "How much gear you have now? Any of that cash left?"

Roy laughed and pointed at the wooden crate. "Six dollars and some pearl buttons are all I got left. The box is full of silver bars from Butte."

Will picked up one end of the case and gave out a fake groan. "Feels like white cake and not gold bars. You were robbed, brother."

Will was a quick wit, and Roy thought of how he would have enjoyed being around Will and Mike listening to the two men spar. That would have been a fun rodeo to see.

The baggage and crate were loaded and the men climbed aboard for the short ride to Will's house. "Just so you know, Elmer took the money and left town two days ago. He was not pleased." Will shook his head with disgust. "He didn't so much as grin when the bank teller laid out the cash in front of him. He's a loon for sure. But he's gone. For now."

Roy felt good until that last line from Will…for now?

———

Grace came running out the back door of Will and Becky's house as they stopped the buggy. Roy jumped out and scooped her up. They hugged each other hard. "Told ye wee one that I be back. How ye be little sister?" He lifted her higher and kissed her cheek.

"Are you going to leave again Roy?" Her little voice was cautious and uncertain. "'Cause I really don't want you to leave again."

One more hard squeeze. "Not going nowhere, sister. Just you and me." Roy wanted to tell her about Vera, but that could wait for a few more hours.

Becky poured another cup of coffee for the men as Roy set the matching brush and comb sets on the table for the girls. Both showed genuine appreciation, and Grace followed that with a quick hug and Becky with a soft hand on his shoulder.

Will finished his coffee and told Roy to come to his office when he was finished yakking with the womenfolk.

Roy walked in and placed the tissue paper-wrapped letter opener in front of William.

Will grinned and opened it. "First-rate, my friend! You even had my initials carved in it. Most grateful. I will think of you each time I open a letter full of bad news." Will flipped the gold-plated blade over a few times. "May need this handy tool in our dealings with Elmer." Will handed Roy an old folded and faded letter. "Read this."

Will had a sour expression. He rolled his eyes as he watched Roy open the old, yellowed letter. "Get ready my friend."

The letter was in poor condition and had ink blots that covered some letters. Roy pulled out the letter. It had writing on the front and back and was not well composed. He looked at it and tried to read it but could only make out the first sentence. "I thought I was a reader, but I reckon I cannot see what it may say."

Will reached for the letter. "It is a mess. Indeed, it's a challenge to understand. I'll read it to you the best I am able." He grabbed a large round-looking glass and hovered over the faded words.

Will began, "It says it's from Olie Hanson to his son Mike. No address was written on the outside."

"Where did this letter come from, Will?"

"Well now, that is what makes this letter such a surprise." Will lifted a small wooden box from the floor to his desktop. "I went out to the ranch to gather up any of Mike's personal and legal papers that may have lingered in his bedroom. This here little letter was stuck in a book called *Book of Common Prayers* along with a few letters from Clara to Mike. The book had the year 1851 next to the name Grace Hanson written on the first page. That was Mike's mother. Now we know who our little Gracie is named after."

Will showed the first page to Roy, and he grinned. He continued, "Here is the odd thing. This letter was firmly stuck in this prayer book, and I have my doubts that Mike even knew it was there. He was not a reliable reader of prayer books. I was never a witness to such activity. The letter was sealed, and I believe was never opened and read."

Roy was following so far. "You judge that Mike never laid eyes on this letter?"

"I do suppose that he had never opened the book past the first page and thus would have not seen nor known of the letter." Will cleared his throat. "Now here comes the curious part. Listen to this."

"My son Mike. I might should have told you this when you was a boy. I ashamed to tell this news. You are my son, and I leave you all I own. You been a golly good boy. Never a minute that I not proud to be your paw.

I been a rascal with poor intent before I married your maw. Liked her fine, and she was pretty. A year before we was hitched, I got drunk a night in Rocheport. A woman was there. She had red hair and she had a baby boy a year after. She said I was the paw, but she moved down river to Jefferson City, and I never laid eyes on her after."

Will looked up at Roy. "Wait, this tale is far from over. Grab the horn Roy."

"A month before you and me left Rocheport for Fort Benton, a priest come to town with a small boy asking for me. He said the woman I knew here had died in Jefferson City and she ask the priest to bring the boy to me and told me to watch over him. Told the priest I was his paw. Boys name was Elmer Barney."

Roy let out a hoot and a muffled curse word. "I be go to Jericho. That be howlin' fer sure. I let you read more before I ask anything."

Will nodded his head in agreement. "Just a bit more. Then we each need a whisky."

"Me and you and Elmer all come up here on the riverboat in 1861. I never tell him I was his paw. Told him his paw was kilt in the war, and his ma fell from a riverboat and drown in the river. He never asked me more.

You are a smart boy, and I have it written that you own the ranch and all lands. Take care of Elmer if you see fit. He don't say much and has not much happy in him. But he work hard.

Sorry I wasn't a better paw to both you.

Olie Hanson"

Willam walked over to the bookshelf, pulled a bottle of whisky from behind a book, and set two glasses on his desk. "Reckon we could both use this."

Roy sat in silence. More ground shaking news. He was not a drinking man, but the whisky seemed like a grand idea. He sipped while Will tipped the entire glass back, wiped his mouth with his fingers, and released a small laugh.

Roy spoke quietly. "Do this mean that Elmer gets part of the ranch if he be Mike's brother?"

Will poured himself another shot. "Noooo! That jackass ain't getting a thing more except for the cash Mike gave him."

Roy had no notion of how to feel. He felt anger rising up in him. He had had enough change and drama over the last couple of months. "I tell ye, Will, I'm wore smooth from all this."

"I recognize the strain all this has put on your young shoulders, Roy, but it will fade. Very soon, things will even out, but then there will be something new to deal with no doubt." Will took another sip and leaned forward. "There is no possible outcome that would have Elmer getting any more than has been laid out in Mike's will. Don't matter if he is a brother, half-brother, or a monkey's uncle. He ain't getting nothing more. Do not be concerned, my friend."

Roy shifted in his chair. "But don't he deserve a part? Him and Mike had the same pa, and I ha' no blood connection or rights to anything." Roy was struggling with this even as Will was steadfast in his legal opinion.

"That runt doesn't deserve a thing! Get that out of your head, Roy. Even if Mike knew, I doubt he'd have given him more. He gave him a bucket of money to go away. He needs to be happy he got that. He'll never gets a dime more than he's been given." Will was combative and resolute. He did not try to hide his borderline hatred for Elmer.

"I know what ye be sayin', but it don't feel right ta me." Roy looked to floor in obvious distress.

Will walked around the desk, grabbed Roy by the shoulders, and spoke sternly. "Get that horseshit out of you head right now, Roy. Mike wanted you and Grace to have the ranch and all the land, and that's how it's gonna work. Elmer is not being cheated or slighted on any way. He is getting more than he deserves."

Roy looked up and gave an obedient nod. This was not an issue to challenge. Will gave Roy a pat on the shoulder, lowering the heat and to reaffirm their friendship. Message received.

"Okay, my friend, you mentioned you had some big news in your last telegram. I did not say a word to Becky." Will wanted to hear it from Roy in his own voice.

"Aye, I do. Can we have Grace and Becky listen? I'd like to share the news with them. If you call them in, I'll fetch something from me room."

Will walked into the kitchen., Roy went up the stairs and came back down quickly. All four assembled in the kitchen. Roy took out a large paper bundle wrapped up with string and untied it.

"Got news. And since you be my family, I want ye to know first." Roy took a breath as Grace sat on her knees on the chair next to him, waiting for the burst of excitement.

"I be gettin' married. This May in Minnesota. It be the nurse, Vera. And she be as bonny a lass as I ever seen. I want all of us to go. Will, I need a man to stand with me." Roy was nervous and fumbled with the paper bundle.

Will stood up quickly, walked to Roy, and shook his hand hard. With a wide smile, he nodded yes and looked to be fighting back strong emotion. Becky rushed over, gave Roy a hug around the neck, and wiped her eyes. Grace was frozen in her chair. No response at all.

"Does this mean you will live at the ranch with her and not me?" Again, Grace's mind was processing events well into the future.

Roy stood up, grabbed her up from the chair, and hugged her. "Wee one, why would ye think that? NO! It means you and me AND Vera will all live together at the ranch. I need you there, lass."

Grace hugged Roy and would not release her hold on his neck. Her little head lay on Roy's shoulder with relief. "Good," was all she said.

Roy lifted Grace back into the chair and sat back down. "I need ye to stay here over the winter with Miss Becky and Will until we get back from the wedding this spring. Then you, Vera, and me will all go and live at the ranch. Understand?"

Grace smiled and nodded. She loved being around Becky, and the house in town was much warmer than the ranch house.

"Got some photographs to show ye." Roy flipped over a photo of Vera with him and showed it to the women folk.

Becky teared up again. "Oh, Roy, she is lovely! What a fine couple the two of you make!"

Grace piped up. "Will she be my new mother?"

The question knocked Roy back a bit. "She will be me wife and if you want her to be your ma or ye sister, she be happy both ways."

Grace seemed satisfied with the answer and went back to studying the photo.

Roy had one more surprise for Grace. He allowed her to finish soaking in the photograph of her new family before showing her the next picture.

"I got two more for ye, Gracie. I want you to have this." Roy handed her the photo of Mike in the hospital bed.

She stared and said nothing. After a minute, she raised the photo and kissed it. "Thank you, Roy," was all she could say. Becky was wiping away a tear and even Will had moist eyes.

Roy replayed that day in his head and needed a moment to steady himself. "I wanted one of yer pa and me." He showed the others the photo of him leaning over to get close to Mike. The matching bolo ties were obvious as the large Ms where on display. "Mike said the M meant Montana, but it means Mike ta me."

Everyone smiled but said nothing.

"May I have that photo too, Roy?" Grace asked softly.

"Aye, ye may. I had two made knowin' you would want both, lassie."

All four sat at the table looking at the photos, thinking about Mike, Vera, and how all the events of the past months had moved their world. Everyone exchanged a quick glance, with Grace and Roy locking eyes with happy faces.

The end of the nightmare was in sight for Roy and Grace.

Or so they thought.

CHAPTER 43

The next morning, Will and Roy knew it was time to face the cold and get out to the ranch. "I see you the next visit I make to town, wee one. Have fun with Miss Becky, 'cause when ye come back home after the wedding, I be puttin' ye to work shearin' sheep!" Roy winked at Gracie and gave her a hug. Grace kissed his cheek.

"You tell big fibs just like Papa did. Next time you see me, I want you to tell me all about Vera. Do you think she'll like me, Roy?" Grace asked wanting an honest answer.

"No. Don't think she be likin' ye...she be lovin' ya, girl. I told her about my Gracie, and she worries that ye won't like her. But both me girls are bonny." Roy patted Grace's head, waved to Becky, picked up his last bag, and walked to the back alley where Will had the buggy ready.

Will would stay an extra day if needed to help get Roy and the Basco boys settled in. Play time had come to an end for Roy. He was anxious to get back to a familiar routine and the place he knew as his home.

It was early February now. The snow had drifted up to four feet deep across the road in many places while in other spots bare earth could be seen. The wind was a demon in wintertime. A clear, cold day below zero could be comfortable, but a windy day in the 20's could prove to be unbearable. Today was cold, clear, and windless. It was as good a day as February could offer.

The ride went by quickly as the two friends talked the entire way. They were steadily evolving into a big brother-little brother world. Roy told Will about his adventures, and Will followed with stories of his own about each locale. Then the talk finally swirled around to Elmer and how to handle him in the future if necessary.

Will laid out the tactics. "We need to be prepared if that little weasel returns. I talked to him at the bank two weeks ago when we gave him his money. I gave him one week to leave. I told him he could take one of the older buckboard wagons and one horse, but the Belgians stayed at the ranch. He'll be gone when we get there. I told Lon and Anders to cook for themselves the best they could as Anna was going with Elmer." Will paused, "I don't understand that at all."

Roy agreed. "She be a sweet girl and a fine cook. Wish she would find a better fella."

The mare started to trot as she saw the ranch and could hear the horses in the barn whiny and snort. Will kept a tight rein on the mare and pulled hard to bring her under control in front of the house. The Basco boys walked out waving and smiling as they tied up to the hitching rail.

"Hello, Roy! You are home amigo!" The boys each shook Roy's hand firmly and each had a big smile, clearly happy to see him. "Elmer he go!" Both men clapped and raised their arms in the air, glad to be rid of the menace.

"Just you and me now, fellas. We work hard and smile, just like when Mike was here." Roy liked Anders and Lon. With all the recent changes in his life, Roy was glad to have the boys stick around.

Anders and Lon picked up Roy's bags and the wooden crate and headed for the bunkhouse. They stopped and turned back towards the main house.

Roy held up his hands and pointed to the bunkhouse. "Not yet, boys; I still want to stay in there." Anders smiled and gave a nod. Roy would make Mike's room his room, but he'd wait until he was a married man.

Roy hollered to Will to come to the bunkhouse where all his gear and the wooden crate had been taken.

Roy stood and motioned for both men to open the crate. He handed Anders a flat metal bar to pry off the top. With the top off, Lon reached in and pulled out one of the Winchesters. He handed it to Anders then reached in for the second rifle. They both stood looking at the guns and then at Roy as Anders gave a shrug and said, "Good gun for you, boss."

Roy smiled and pointed at each man. "Not for me...for you. Thank you for taking care of the ranch, fellas."

The boys looked at each other and stood frozen for a second before breaking out in huge smiles and laughing. They each set the new rifles on their bunks and came up to Roy and gave him a hug. It was not customary for men, not even family, in Montana to hug, but this was a unique moment, and the bonus appreciation was honest.

Roy pulled his Winchester out of the new leather scabbard, and all three men stood at attention and smiled. The Hanson Ranch Army had now been formed and was ready for varmints and villains. Roy handed the boys two boxes of cartridges each, and the gifting was complete.

"Anders and Lon got new rifles, and I got a letter opener. What do ya know!" Will jokingly put out his empty hands and faked a frown. All laughed. Roy reached into one of his bags, and handed Will the .45 Schofield revolver and shoulder holster that he had loaned him.

Will gave a short snort and said, "You could be a government man, Roy. Giving me something that is already mine!" Will took it, looked it over, and handed it back to Roy. "You may need this for a few months. Keep it in case you get an unwelcome visitor."

"No need, Will; I got me own now." Roy pulled out the two new guns he had bought in Bozeman. "This be the Remington 1890; it uses the same round as the Winchesters. Got this for wearing for work and in the mountains." He pulled the Remington out of the new hip holster and handed it to Anders, who checked to see if it was loaded and then handed it to Lon for a look.

Next, Roy unboxed the finely tooled shoulder holster along with the Colt SAA and handed them to Will. "This be me town and train barker. One fella called it a Smoke Wagon. Don't care fer that. It be a Colt ta me."

Will admired it, gave it back, and said, "Fine pieces, Roy. You will hand these down to your sons and grandsons someday. Well done."

Will had given the extra money to Roy hoping he would spend it wisely and purchase quality items. He was pleased that Roy had invested wisely.

The four men agreed to have supper in a few hours at 6:00. Will would stay in the main house and sleep in Mike's room. They all agreed that there should be at least one man in the house to keep guard.

Roy unpacked, hung his two new suits on wooden hangers, and changed back into his everyday gear. He liked the fancy costumes but felt honest in the work clothes Mike bought for him. He brought the photo of Mike back into the house and set it on the fireplace mantle.

A plain dinner was tossed together by Anders that fulfilled the need for nutrition but lacked much style. Anna was already missed, and no solution to the vacancy was available. Will had mentioned to Roy that he would search for a new cook and ask around in Lewistown for a widow or a woman with matronly qualities.

Anders and Lon finished the kitchen duties and went back to bunkhouse. Roy was sure that they both wanted to look at and handle their new rifles before bed. The fireplace was stoked, and a strong fire soaked the log house with warmth once again. Will yawned. Roy stood, said goodnight, and headed to the bunkhouse. The long day was closing, and sleep was a welcome necessity.

Roy lay in his bed unable to shut down his brain. His head was clogged with thoughts of Vera mostly, but other kernels of worry filled in the voids and kept his mind churning. He thought of tomorrow's work with Lon and Anders filling the wagon with hay and feeding the flock and how badly he had missed the pleasure of simple labor.

He finally felt his eyes close and his body relaxed, welcoming a night of sleep and honest rest. He took a deep breath and slowly let it go.

Suddenly, the dogs jumped up started barking loud and with intensity. They slept between Anders and Lon on the floor and never barked while in the bunkhouse.

Something was going on outside. All three men knew there was trouble. Roy quickly dressed and grabbed his new holster and Remington pistol. He threw on his old work coat and walked to the door. He told the boys to stay where they were and try to keep the dogs quiet.

Roy heard a voice near the front of the house. It was not Will's. He walked through the dark and to the front porch. He peaked around the corner of the house and saw Will standing in his red long johns with a blanket wrapped around his shoulders. Will looked to his right and saw Roy in the dark peering around the corner, then he turned back to the front.

That's when Roy saw the trouble standing twenty feet from the front door.

It was Elmer.

He was drunk, angry, and leaning against the big cottonwood tree in the front yard, boiling with revenge. He was half-hidden in the shadows. Roy heard a horse pawing the ground, looked up and saw Anna sitting in the seat of the buckboard, wrapped in a quilt. She was staring at the ground and looked uneasy.

"What do you want Elmer? You have no business here. And you are drunk you bastard." Will spoke loudly to take command of the moment.

Roy slowly walked up next to Will and made sure to stand next to him and not behind. He wanted to show Elmer he would not hide behind Will and was ready to go toe-to-toe with any threat.

Elmer stepped closer into the light of the kerosene lantern Will was holding. "There's the boy king! Did you send him to school to learn how to speak like an American or does he still sound like the stupid immigrant he is?"

Elmer felt free to say what he had thought for months. Whisky is often a reliable truth serum.

Will leaned forward and held up the lantern to get a better look at Elmer. "Sounds like a five-dollar Stetson covering a five-cent brain.

You want to keep going or should we find your equals out in the barn digging in the hay?"

"'Bout had my gullet full of your big mouth, lawyer man. You be the reason I got kicked out to make room for this stinkin' little England boy." A drunken Elmer walked closer to Will, pulled out a pistol from his coat pocket and held it down at his side.

Will didn't flinch. He stood his ground as Elmer advanced with gun drawn. He lowered his voice and spoke slowly to Elmer. "Take your money and leave town, Elmer. You got a bag full of cash that will let you go anywhere you want to go."

Elmer said nothing. He was breathing heavily, looking for a reason to unleash his hate.

Roy took a step forward. "I know ye don't care fer me. I dunno why Mike did what he did, but Will did nothin' that Mike didn't want done." Roy walked slowly while talking to Elmer until he was standing in front of Will. "This man got a wife and don't deserve no shootin'. I give ye the ranch and I take $100 and go away, but that ain't what Mike wanted. He asked me to watch over Grace, and that what I be doin'. I don't care nothin' 'bout the money, but I do fret about Grace. I be willin' to fight and die to keep Gracie safe."

"I'll fight ya, boy! I'll fight ya for this land!" Elmer was getting hotter and more worked up by the minute. "I worked this land and lived on this land more than half my life. You drag your foreigner ass here and a year later you got MY ranch? This is MY land!"

Elmer was screaming while he raised the gun and pointed it at Roy. "Tell me it's my land, boy! TELL ME!"

Roy closed his eyes and softly answered. "This be Grace's land." He opened his eyes and stared at Elmer. He was bracing and waited to feel the force if Elmer pulled the trigger.

Elmer pointed the gun at Roy with a shaking hand and legs giving out. "I should..."

The sound of two lever-action rifles cocking broke through the still, cold night air. Then the sound of boots crunching through snow made Elmer look back over his shoulder. The end of a gun barrel was close enough for him to smell fresh gun oil.

"You should probably drop the gun...jackass," Will said firmly.

Anders aimed at Elmer's ear, ready to fire without hesitation. "I shoot you, you son gun."

Elmer spun his head around and saw Lon slowly moving to the opposite side, shiny new rifle at the ready.

Elmer dropped his gun, turned to face Anders, and said, "All these years and now you boys turned on me. I was good to you fellas. Damn boys." He put the gun back in his coat and crossed his arms in disgust.

"You no good to me. Only good to Elmer." Anders used enough English to deliver the honest message. "You bad man. I shoot you and no cry."

"Go to hell, every man of ya, go straight to hell!" Elmer staggered back to the wagon. He tried twice to climb up to the buckboard seat before falling onto the wagon seat on the third attempt. He reached down for the reins, pulled them up, and then noticed something was missing.

Anna. She was gone.

He looked toward the lantern light and saw her standing on the porch next to Will, holding her carpet bag full of all she owned.

"What the hell, Anna? Get up here. We're headed out." Elmer got louder and the Basco boys stepped closer, rifles still shouldered and aimed in his direction.

"Shut your mouth, Elmer. Stay still for a minute." Will was tired of Elmer's bullying.

Elmer got quiet and softly asked, "Anna, what are you doing, girl? Why'd you get down off the wagon?"

Anna pulled the dark red scarf off of her head and exposed her left eye, black and swollen, as well as a large bruise on her right cheek. "He hit me. I felled down and den he kick me. I tink he beat me more now. Please. Bitte. I stay here. My home. This my home, ja?" She didn't cry, but her voice trembled with fear. Her nerves were frayed, and she was cold. She was hoping for pity and a small dose of compassion.

Will looked at Roy and shrugged his shoulders. Roy walked up for a closer look at her injuries. "Anna, I be getting' married in three months and then I'll bring me wife back to the ranch. I want ye ta stay here, but I can no promise for ye to stay here after the wedding. Do ye understand? Me wife will run the house, aye?"

Anna reached up and grabbed Roy's jacket and started to cry. "JA, JA, I stay 'til de new vife come. I do dat. I stay and cook and clean for you yust like you vas Mister Mike. Danke Roy. Danke. You gut boy yust like Mike say. He say you good fella. You been gut to Anna. Danke."

Will picked up Anna's bag, opened the front door, and led her inside.

Roy walked towards Elmer and the wagon. "I be inside in a moment," he called back to Will.

Will did not like Roy's tone. He closed the door and called out. "Roy. Come back."

Roy walked quickly. Anders and Lon held their positions on either side of the wagon but lowered their new rifles.

"Get down, Elmer." Elmer sat still and spit on the ground towards Roy. Roy put a foot up on the wheel, reached up, and pulled Elmer down by the collar onto the snow-covered ground.

"I been fair to ye, but I can no abide when a man is cruel to dog nor beast or puts hands on a woman or child." Roy pulled his right hand back and delivered a brutal blow to Elmer's left eye. He then let him drop and roll before picking him up and waiting for an opening to punch him in the ribs. "That's two. Ye earned more, but I seen where ye beat Anna in two spots. If I find out that ye hit her a third, I beat ye with an axe handle. You be a hateful man with a black heart. Come back here, and I'll find a hole fer ye up in the mountains."

Anders and Lon wanted to join in but felt that Elmer understood the message. Instead, they helped him back into the wagon. Elmer stared at Roy with drunken hate, took the reins, and headed into the dark. The three men stood outside listening until they couldn't hear the wagon or horse.

The boys said nothing. They raised their rifles in a small salute to Roy and walked to the bunkhouse. Roy gave them a small wave of thanks for standing up for them.

Anna was already unpacked and busy in the kitchen making a fresh pot of coffee and cleaning up. Will was sitting at the table rubbing his head, processing the skirmish and all that had happened.

"Reckon I don't want to tangle with you, Roy. Good that we are pals." Will grinned, recognizing that Roy was a powerful young man with a gentle nature. He also had little back-down in him. "I'm hittin' the hay. See you at breakfast."

Roy walked up to Will and hugged him, finishing with two pats on the back. "We be more than pals, Will. You be like a big brother ta me. I be lost wi' out ye."

Will nodded, gave Roy a small jab to his arm, and walked down the hall.

Roy thought about going to the bunkhouse, but he knew he would not sleep tonight. He threw three more logs on the fire, took down Mike's old rifle from over the hearth, leaned it up against the wall, and sat in the big leather chair.

Anna walked in with a cup of fresh coffee, handed it to Roy, and touched his shoulder. She said nothing, but she looked at him as a tear fell down her cheek and then went back to her kitchen. He was her protector now.

His life was complicated, but he felt a sense of duty now. He would be married soon and hoped to be a father someday. He would run a ranch and be a part of building a handsome new state. He would work towards becoming a naturalized citizen of the United States of America.

Mainly, he felt appreciated. He couldn't understand why a stranger, a man from Montana gave him a new and exciting life or why a bright and beautiful woman considered him worthy of love.

Roy then thought of that mighty man, at perfect rest in a wooden box in the root cellar. He would go out tomorrow and check on him and spend a few minutes alone with his mentor and father. Spring would bring the tender task of placing him next to Clara. He hoped that time would dilute his strong emotions when that job came around.

Mark Twain could write the story of his life and tell this fantastical tale, but most would not believe it to be true.

Understanding is not required to live a happy life, but love is, and he had more than he felt he deserved.

Roy took a long drink of coffee, pulled the old elk robe over his legs, and opened his copy of Mark Twain's *Roughing It*.

Looking around the room, he felt safe and at peace.

A rush of calmness cover him. He felt like a man ten feet under water, breaking the surface of the ocean, filling his lungs with air, knowing he would stay alive.

He opened his eyes and looked up at the mantle and the photograph of Big Mike Hanson.

He was home.

ABOUT THE AUTHOR

Born into a farming family in SW Minnesota, his life was filled with close family, the hard work of farming and learning the history of his pioneer roots. His grandparents first home was a sod house with packed dirt floors. Growing up on the original family homestead surrounded him with family history and curiosity never left him.

As a radio talk show host in the days before podcasts, Barry learned how to interview, listen and learn.

Barry first came to Montana from St. Louis in 1981 on a Greyhound bus. He went through the FWL Outfitters School near Hamilton, worked as a hunting guide south of Ennis. He lived in an old line shack for months while herding and working cattle on the West Fork of the Madison River.

He returned to Montana in 1990 with his young family and lived near Lewistown in Fergus County and spent time on KXLO radio.

Before moving back to Montana, Barry was a motorcycle tour guide, taking Americans to Europe and riding through the Alps and through Scotland. He would also lead Europeans through the American West, showing them the beauty of America.

He lives on a mountain south of Helena off-grid, in a house he built from scratch with his nearly perfect wife Sheila.